STORM OF STEEL

THE BERNICIA CHRONICLES: VI

MATTHEW HARFFY

HEAD
of ZEUS

First published in 2019 by Aria, an imprint of Head of Zeus Ltd
This paperback edition first published in 2020 by Head of Zeus Ltd

9 7 5 3 1 2 4 6 8

A CIP catalogue record for this book is available from the British Library.

Author Photo © Stephen Weatherly

ISBN (PB): 9781786696335
ISBN: (E): 9781786696380

Printed and bound in Great Britain by
CPI Group (UK) Ltd, Croydon CR0 4YY

Head of Zeus Ltd
First Floor East
5–8 Hardwick Street
London ECIR 4RG

WWW.HEADOFZEUS.COM

Storm of Steel is for Simon Blunsdon.
Legend.

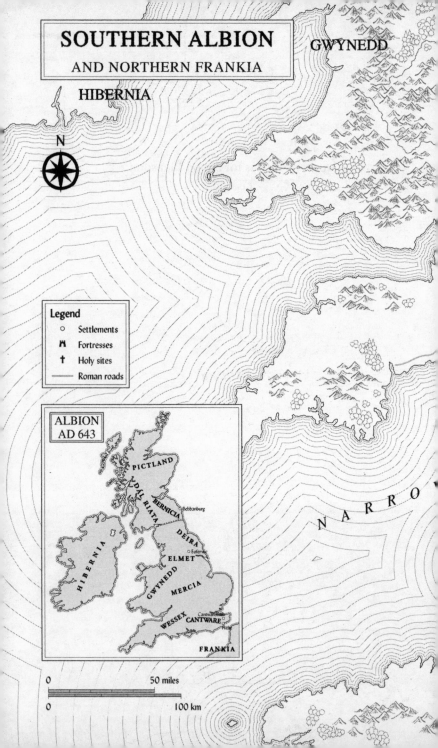

SOUTHERN ALBION
AND NORTHERN FRANKIA

HIBERNIA

GWYNEDD

N

Legend
- ○ Settlements
- ⋔ Fortresses
- † Holy sites
- —— Roman roads

N A R R O

**ALBION
AD 643**

PICTLAND

DÁL RIATA

BERNICIA

Bebbanburg

DEIRA

ELMET

Eoferwic

HIBERNIA

GWYNEDD

MERCIA

WESSEX

Cantwaraburg

CANTWARE

Rithir

FRANKIA

0 ——————— 50 miles

0 ——————— 100 km

Place Names

Place names in Dark Ages Britain vary according to time, language, dialect and the scribe who was writing. I have not followed a strict convention when choosing what spelling to use for a given place. In most cases, I have chosen the name I believe to be the closest to that used in the early seventh century, but like the scribes of all those centuries ago, I have taken artistic licence at times, and merely selected the one I liked most.

Addelam	Deal, Kent
Æscendene	Ashington, Northumberland
Afen	River Avon
Albion	Great Britain
Baetica	Southern region of the Iberian peninsula, loosely corresponding to modern-day Andalusia.
Bebbanburg	Bamburgh
Beodericsworth	Bury St Edmunds
Berewic	Berwick-upon-Tweed
Bernicia	Northern kingdom of Northumbria, running approximately from the Tyne to the Firth of Forth
Bristelmestune	Brighton

Caer Luel	Carlisle
Cabilonen	Chalon-sur-Saône
Cair Chaladain	Kirkcaldy, Fife
Cantware	Kent
Cantwareburh	Canterbury
Carrec Dún	Carrock Fell, Cumbria
Dál Riata	Gaelic overkingdom, roughly encompassing modern-day Argyll and Bute and Lochaber in Scotland and also County Antrim in Northern Ireland
Deira	Southern kingdom of Northumbria, running approximately from the Humber to the Tyne
Din Eidyn	Edinburgh
Dommoc	Dunwich, Suffolk
Dor	Dore, Yorkshire
Dorcic	Dorchester on Thames
Dun	River Don
Dyvene	River Devon
Elmet	Native Briton kingdom, approximately equal to the West Riding of Yorkshire
Engelmynster	Fictional location in Deira
Eoferwic	York
Frankia	France
Gefrin	Yeavering
Gernemwa	Great Yarmouth, Norfolk
Gipeswic	Ipswich
Gwynedd	Gwynedd, North Wales
Hastingas	Hastings
Hefenfelth	Heavenfield
Hibernia	Ireland
Hii	Iona
Hithe	Hythe, Kent

Inhrypum	Ripon, North Yorkshire
Liger	Loire River
Liminge	Lyminge, Kent
Lindesege	Lindsey
Lindisfarena	Lindisfarne
Loidis	Leeds
Maerse	Mersey
Mercia	Kingdom centred on the valley of the River Trent and its tributaries, in the modern-day English Midlands.
Muile	Mull
Neustria	Frankish kingdom in the north of present-day France, encompassing the land approximately between the Loire and the Silva Carbonaria.
Northumbria	Modern-day Yorkshire, Northumberland and south-east Scotland
Pocel's Hall	Pocklington
Rendlæsham	Rendlesham, Suffolk
Rodomo	Rouen, France
Sandwic	Sandwich, Kent
Scheth	River Sheaf (border of Mercia and Deira)
Secoana	River Seine
Seoles	Selsey, Sussex
Snodengaham	Nottingham
Soluente	Solent
Stanfordham	Stamfordham, Northumberland
Tatecastre	Tadcaster
Temes	River Thames
Tenet Waraden	Tenterden, Kent
Tuidi	River Tweed
Ubbanford	Norham, Northumberland
Wihtwara	Wight (Isle of)

Anno Domini Nostri Iesu Christi
In the Year of Our Lord Jesus Christ
643

PART ONE
LOW TIDES AND ILL TIDINGS

Ne mæg werig mod wyrde wiðstondan
The weary spirit cannot withstand wyrd

'The Wanderer', author unknown – *The Exeter Book*

Chapter 1

Beobrand had never known such terror and misery before that foul night.

His stomach clenched and heaved, but all he could manage to bring up was a thin string of spittle and bile. He hawked and spat into the leaden, opaque waves that caused the ship to list and roll.

The storm had caught *Háligsteorra*'s master ill-prepared and too far from the shelter and safety of land and they had been buffeted and blown far out into the North Sea. They had lost sight of their escort as the sky had grown bruised and full of anger. Sharp flickers of lightning had lit the white-fretted waves and the terrified faces of the men who clung to the fragile timbers of the ship as the furious sea crashed over its wales and thwarts. The winds had made the taut ropes thrum and the mast bend, despite the sail having been furled and secured.

To start with, Beobrand had looked to the master, an old, leathery-faced man who exuded confidence and experience, and had believed such a veteran seaman must surely know how to deal with the squall. But, as the wind-lashed, wave-soaking night had dragged on and after one hapless sailor, a young lad that had reminded Beobrand of Tondberct, had been washed overboard, to disappear into the dark ocean without so much as a scream to be heard over the roaring ire of the storm, Beobrand's faith in the captain had waned. The ship had begun to rapidly fill with water and all of them had bailed out as quickly as they were able. More than once, Beobrand had puked into the hold as he had scooped the chill water out and flung it over the side.

Utta and the other Christ priests and monks lent their own energies to the task of trying to keep the vessel afloat. Utta even led them in prayer to their nailed god. Before he became overcome with sickness, Utta produced a flask of oil that he said had been given to him by Abbot Aidan of Lindisfarena.

"Our Father of the Holy Isle foretold this storm," Utta said, his face white and his voice tremulous. "He told me to pour this oil upon the troubled waves and all would become calm."

Everyone paused to watch as he trickled the holy oil over *Háligsteorra*'s side. But nothing happened. The wind continued to rock the ship terribly and the cold waters still sluiced over the sides.

Coenred smiled at Beobrand, perhaps trying to show he wasn't scared. But his pallid skin and pinched features told the truth of it. He was fearful for his life and Beobrand thought no less of the monk for it. He had stood in the gut-spilt, stench-filled clamour of shieldwalls and had faced great swordsmen in deadly combat, but he was terrified, sure that this wind-tossed sea would send them all to their doom.

The Christ neither listened to the monks' supplications nor paid heed to the magical oil. The storm did not abate and they were tossed about on the surface of the sea like a twig thrown into a rushing stream. The skipper wrestled with the steerboard until it came adrift from the frame that attached it to the side of the ship, leaving them adrift, at the mercy of the elements and the gods.

Beobrand pulled a large chunk of hacksilver from his pouch and threw it far out into the darkness. It winked as a flash of distant lightning caught it and then it vanished. He hoped that was a good sign and that the gods of the ocean had accepted his offering. Muttering the words so that none could hear over the raging torment of the night, he offered the gods the silver and the life of the boy who had looked like Tondberct. The boy was already dead, but perhaps his could be a sacrifice that would save his shipmates.

Whether it was Woden and his children, or the Christ god who responded to their desperate pleas, Beobrand knew not, but as the dawn painted the horizon like an iron sword blade, the storm's vehemence fled. The waves began to lessen in their ferocity and Beobrand believed, for the first time since dusk, that they might actually survive.

"Sails ahoy!" shouted a voice and Beobrand pushed himself up from where he had been leaning over the side of the ship.

Peering into the early morning gloom, Beobrand at first saw nothing but endless foam-flecked waves. But then, as the ship rolled down once more into a gully between two peaks of water, he saw three dark-sailed ships cutting through the water towards them. The sail of the foremost ship was a dark blood red. These were not the vessels that had been escorting them southward.

"Those ships mean us no goodwill," said the skipper. "They be raiders, or I'm a Waelisc man! The gods alone know how they have ridden out that storm." He spat over the side. He scanned the horizon in all directions and Beobrand followed his gaze. There was no sign of their escort or land.

Beobrand pushed himself up. Bassus reached out his one arm, his right, and hauled Beobrand to his feet. Bassus looked old, his beard and hair rimed with white, as if salt from the sea had dried there. His face was the colour of week-old hearth ash.

"I hate sailing," the giant warrior growled, "always have. The sea and the sickness is bad enough, now there are pirates too. Why couldn't we have ridden? You know where you are with a horse."

"Yes," replied Beobrand, pausing to spit once more to clear his mouth of the sour taste of vomit, "for we never get attacked when we are on land, do we, old man?"

Bassus grunted.

"At least on land we can run away."

Beobrand raised an eyebrow.

"But we never do, do we?"

Bassus appraised him for a moment, before offering him a thin grin.

"True, but if we get knocked down on land, we don't sink and drown."

"Then we must do our best not to get knocked down."

Around them a few of the sailors were pulling weapons from chests. They produced knives, seaxes and short axes. Despite their toughness and resilience, these were not fighting men and Beobrand wondered whether they would even put up any resistance to those who came sliding towards them in the sleek-prowed ships atop the surf. He glanced about them once more, in the opposite direction of the rising sun, but the horizon was still empty of land and any other vessels.

By Woden and all the gods, where were the escorts? Most of the fighting men were there. Wynhelm and his men rode in one ship, and that fat bastard Fordraed and his gesithas in the other. What few warriors Beobrand had been permitted to bring were in this ship, along with Utta, Coenred and the other monks. But Oswiu was concerned about his power and so had forbade him and Bassus having more than half a dozen men accompany them south. The raiders were closing fast. If all three pirate crews attacked at once, they would surely be overrun.

"Captain," snapped Beobrand. "Do you mean to leave us here wallowing like pigs in shit awaiting our wyrd?"

For an instant Beobrand wondered whether the grizzled mariner had heard him, and then, as if awoken from a deep sleep with a splash of cold water, the skipper shook his head and began shouting orders.

His crew was experienced and the men knew what they were about. In a few heartbeats they were rushing over the ship, repairing rigging and preparing to outrun their attackers. The captain called to one of the older sailors who quickly ran over, his bare feet steady on the heaving deck.

"Fix the steerboard."

The old man nodded and set to his task.

"Well," said Beobrand in a hushed voice, "will we be able to escape them?"

The captain gauged the speed of the incoming vessels and looked up at the clouds above them.

"I doubt it," he said, in a voice meant only for Beobrand, "but we'll give it a good try. We are not travelling heavy, so we might yet give them a run they won't forget. But if they catch us, there will be nothing for it. They'll board us and take what they want. We'll be lucky if they leave us with our lives. To fight them when we are so few would be folly."

Beobrand glowered at him, his expression as dark and brooding as the sky.

"Do I seem like a man to surrender without a fight?"

The sailor looked up to meet Beobrand's icy gaze, taking in the scar beneath the huge thegn's left eye, the thick neck and broad shoulders. After a moment he swallowed and dropped his gaze.

"Come on, you whoresons," he bellowed. "Get that sail aloft and get the oars in the tholes. Or do you want to be buggered by those bastards?"

Beobrand looked over to where Cynan was struggling into his byrnie. The Waelisc warrior was jumping up and down with his arms upstretched. Beside him, grim-faced Dreogan had strapped on his sword belt and hefted his black shield, but he had not donned his own metal shirt.

"I may die from a sword thrust or the barb of a spear," he said, his tattooed cheeks pulling into a grimace, "but I will not be dragged into the depths of the ocean by the weight of an iron-knit shirt." He placed his helm onto his bald head.

Beobrand nodded.

"Dreogan speaks sense, Cynan," he said. "If you fall in, you'll be drowned in an instant."

Cynan had finished wrestling his armour into place, cinching his belt tightly around his waist to take some of the weight of the byrnie.

"Then I had better not fall in!" he laughed.

Beobrand looked over to where his four remaining warriors stood. Attor, Bearn and Fraomar all looked ready, poised and alert, as if they had not just suffered through a storm of nightmare. Fraomar and Garr, he saw, had also both eschewed their war harness and Attor, as ever wore his light leather jack.

The last of his gesith on board was Bearn. The warrior looked even more haggard than Beobrand felt. He leaned heavily on the ship's wale, pale and trembling.

"Will you be able to fight?" Beobrand asked. He didn't wish to shame the man, but he needed to know he could count on him when the time came. By way of response Bearn raised his sword in the air and nodded. He did not open his mouth, as if he feared he would puke again if he did. Beobrand gave him a long, hard stare and then nodded. Bearn was a good man, who had stood by his side countless times in battle. If he said he was up to the task, Beobrand believed him.

"Fetch me my shield, my helm and Hrunting," Beobrand said to the youngest of his men. Fraomar nodded and quickly did his lord's bidding.

A wave hit the side of the ship, causing it to lurch and creak. Beobrand staggered, reaching out his left, half-hand to clutch Bassus' shoulder.

"By Tiw's cock, Beobrand," said Bassus in his booming voice, "you are as pale as lamb's wool and you look about as strong."

Beobrand squared his shoulders. Maybe he looked as bad as Bearn, he thought. He reached down for a leather flask of water that lay near his feet. It had been tossed there along with other unsecured contents of the ship during the storm. He shook the flask, unstoppered it and took a swig. After swilling the water around his mouth he spat it over the side of the ship, finally washing away some of the bitter taste of acid from his throat. He took a long draught and forced himself to swallow, despite his stomach clenching at the thought. He offered the skin to Bassus, who took it after a moment's hesitation.

"I'm sick to the stomach, old man," Beobrand said. "I cannot recall ever having felt worse." For a fleeting moment he recalled the terrible fever that had racked his body after the battle of Gefrin's ford. He had lost two of his fingers from his left hand and had become elf-shot. The wound rot had almost killed him then, but that was long ago, ten years in the past, and seemed like a distant dream. "I may still be weak from all that puking, but by Woden, I can still kill me a few mangy sailors."

The old man who was working on the steerboard looked askance at Beobrand, as did a couple of the closer seamen. Beobrand scowled back at them as he took his belt and scabbard from Fraomar. He fumbled briefly with the buckle, but he had long since ceased to struggle with the mutilated left hand, and the belt was quickly fastened. The sailors watched as he placed his great helm upon his head and rested his infamous black shield against the ship's strakes. Their eyes quickly flicked over his arm rings and the bone-handled seax that hung from a finely tooled leather sheath at his belt and their gaze came to rest on the golden, intricately wrought hilt of his sword, Hrunting. Perhaps his words had angered them, but they swallowed whatever retorts they had in their mouths and turned back to their tasks. They might yet survive this day, but they were not sure they would live if they crossed the warlord who stood before them now.

Suddenly the ship lurched again, this time as the sail was hauled aloft and the brisk wind caught it with a snap. Beobrand staggered and his mouth filled with spit as he felt his gorge threatening to rise again. He spat and took a deep, open-mouthed breath. The foremost of the three approaching ships was almost upon them now. Its crimson sail was rounded and tight, gravid with the wind, propelling it through the waves as straight as a spear throw.

A sudden movement on the ship drew his attention and for an instant Beobrand thought he had seen a sea bird wheeling in the sky, but an instant later he understood what his eyes had noticed. An arrow flickered upwards from the raider's vessel and arced towards them.

"Arrow!" was all he had time to shout before the projectile reached them. Bassus had been grabbing for a shield, but the arrow thudded into the deck, two paces from his feet.

"I'm done catching arrows in my flesh," he said, kicking the shaft and snapping it from where it quivered. He had lost his left arm following an arrow wound from the bow of Torran mac Nathair. Beobrand had avenged his friend, and Coenred and the monks of Lindisfarena had saved Bassus' life. But nothing could save his arm. Such an injury might be the end of a lesser man, but Bassus had seemed to grow in confidence as the years went by. The giant warrior lifted the shield and held it before him.

"Protect the oarsmen," yelled Beobrand and his men raised their shields and made their way down the ship to hold them as cover for the men pulling on the oars. The sail was unfurled and the oars were in the water, but still the ship floundered.

"Come on, damn your eyes," roared the skipper at the old man who was frantically looping and tying rope in an attempt to fix the steerboard once more in place in its timber frame.

The lead ship loomed ever nearer. More arrows darted into the sky.

"Shields," screamed Beobrand, rushing clumsily along the deck to offer some protection to the man who yet worked at the steerboard. A handful of arrows sliced down into the ship. One clattered against Bassus' shield boss before skittering away. Beobrand surveyed the crew, the holy men and his gesithas. None were injured, but that would not last long if these arrows kept falling. The monks and the priests cowered low behind the ship's sheer strakes. As Beobrand watched, a white fletched arrow thumped into the oak boards of the deck a mere hand's breadth from young Dalston. The slender monk's eyes grew wide and he let out a whimpering sob.

The lead raider ship was less than a spear's throw away now. At the prow stood a huge figure, broad and strange. His great head was tusked and grey-skinned. What manner of creature was this? Beobrand's skin prickled. The raider ship ploughed into a wave, sending up a huge sheet of foam. The water splashed the creature at the prow of the oncoming ship and it reached up a hand to wipe its eyes. In that moment, the illusion was shattered. This was no creature, but a man, wearing the skull and hide of some beast the like of which Beobrand had never seen before.

Beobrand fixed the man with a glare and a sudden calm came over him. These were but men, who breathed and bled like any other. He was Beobrand, thegn of Bernicia, lord of Ubbanford, and with half a dozen of his black-shielded warriors by his side, he would wreak havoc on these pirates.

"Come on then," he bellowed over the waves. "Come and face us if you dare."

He thought he saw the beast-man leader grin from beneath his skull helm.

More arrows flashed through the wind-riven sky, but again, none struck flesh.

The slap of sudden footfalls on the deck made Beobrand turn. Garr, slender and almost willow-like in his grace, took a few quick steps forward and launched a short throwing spear into the air. Everyone watched the javelin as it flexed on its upward flight before plunging down towards their pursuers' ship. Garr was a fine spear-man and could throw further and more accurately than any man Beobrand knew, and it seemed that even when throwing from a rolling ship on uneven seas, his aim was unerring, for the spear lanced down and struck the pirate steersman in the shoulder. The man fell and immediately their attackers' ship veered away and began to lose speed.

At the same instant, the old man who had been furiously tying ropes and wrestling their damaged steerboard back into place, let out a cry. Beobrand did not understand the man's words, but it seemed clear to the master of the ship, who shouldered the old man out of the way. The grizzled captain grabbed the rudder in his meaty hands and yelled at the crew.

The men pulled at the oars with renewed vigour and the sail cracked and bellied, once more full of the brisk wind. The hull trembled beneath Beobrand like a stallion being given its head. As he watched, Beobrand could see that they were pulling away from the three ships that had descended upon them like wolves in the dawn.

Beobrand grinned at Garr. The tall spear-man nodded soberly in response.

The ship's master cast a glance over his shoulder.

"Looks like your man has killed one of them. They'll slay us all for certain, if they board us now." He was ashen-faced and sombre.

"Not if we kill them first," said Beobrand.

The prow sliced through a white-tipped wave, sending up a great wash of spray as the ship cleaved through the water, heading westward, away from the open sea and the rising sun.

"Besides, it seems the gods are smiling on us this morning," shouted Beobrand. "Keep this up and we will outrun them yet."

And with that, as if the gods themselves responded to his words with their displeasure, one of the ropes securing the sail snapped.

Chapter 2

The sail luffed and billowed like a battle banner. With the bottom corner unsecured, the wind was lost and the ship lost its speed instantly. A judder ran through its boards as a wave crashed against its beam, threatening to capsize her. With the sail gone, *Háligsteorra* floundered once more. The few sailors who were at the oars pulled valiantly, but it was instantly clear to Beobrand that they would never be able to produce enough power to escape their pursuers.

He watched as the lead pirate ship regained control. Another man took the rudder and once more the ship sliced through the waves towards them. The other two ships seemed content to allow their leader to attack alone, but there was no doubt now that the attack was coming. Beobrand staggered. The deck lurched beneath his feet as *Háligsteorra* wallowed, at the mercy of the waves. The pirate ship was bearing down on them quickly. In a matter of moments, it would be upon them.

"To me, my brave gesithas," Beobrand bellowed.

His warriors drew their weapons, raised their shields and moved into position beside their lord to form a small shieldwall at the stern of the ship, facing the oncoming attackers. It seemed the enemy ship would seek to close with them on the steerboard side and this is where Beobrand and his men waited.

"Get to the prow," Beobrand yelled at Utta and the priests who had been huddled in the rear of the ship. "Give us room to kill these whoresons."

The holy men scuttled towards the front of the ship. The captain too, seeing the pirate ship coming in fast towards them, leapt up from the steering oar and fled away from Beobrand and his warriors.

"Raise the oars," he screamed as he rushed down the ship, but his sailors did not understand the danger and were still attempting to heave the ship to safety. The long oars were yet in the water when the pirate ship smashed into the side of the ship and scraped along its length, splintering the oars like kindling. One man was thrown from his sea chest with a screech as his oar smacked into his ribs with terrible force.

The early morning air was filled with the crash and crack of the colliding hulls. The raiders added their roaring cries of doom to the cacophony. They held axes, seaxes and wicked knives and leaned over the edge of their ship, leering and eager to be upon their prey. They screamed words of hatred and horror in several tongues, most of which Beobrand could not comprehend. But their purpose was clear. These men came for death and plunder and with their screams they hoped to weaken their foe with fear. Beobrand scanned the ire-filled faces of the men. They snarled and spat and he knew that other men might be unmanned by their terrifying display. But Beobrand had stood in shieldwalls where the earth had turned to a quagmire with the blood of foemen and friend alike, where the ravens had been fed so well on the torn flesh of the corpses that they could no longer fly. He had seen the slaughter of friends and enemies and had witnessed the savage killing of lords and kings. Neither he nor his gesithas would be cowed by the ravings of these seafaring brigands.

The pirates might not be armoured hearth warriors and thegns bedecked in fine war harness, but there was no denying their mettle. Without pause, several of the pirates leapt from their ship onto the Northumbrian vessel. A few carried ropes which Beobrand assumed they would use to lash the two ships together. Blood fountained as the first of the oarsman was slain. Pinned by his shattered oar, he was unable to escape the first wild axe swings from the marauders.

More attackers swarmed over the side of the ship. The master, crew and holy men moved backwards towards the bow. All the focus of the attackers was on the midships and the prow. Beobrand realised he had positioned his men poorly. They had not been able to fend off the raiders. But now they would make them pay for boarding the *Háligsteorra*.

"Bassus," Beobrand snapped, "lead the men and kill those bastards."

Bassus grinned.

"What about you?" he asked.

"I'll join you shortly." He turned to Cynan. "Follow me, and," he glanced quickly at Cynan's iron-knit byrnie, "don't fall in."

Bassus, huge and shieldless, was surrounded by the black linden boards of Beobrand's gesithas. The giant warrior bellowed and raised his sword above his head.

"Death!" he shouted, and the small shieldwall stamped forward towards the invaders, who turned to meet the threat.

Beobrand did not wait to see the outcome of Bassus' attack, or whether Cynan would follow him. Gone was the sickness and fear of the storm. The night had been full of uncertainty and angry gods. Now, in the watery light of a new day Beobrand could see his enemies and he welcomed the certainty of death-dealing. He was born to the battle-play and he allowed the joy of bloodletting to flood through him like a spring tide, washing away his doubts and sadness. He had known so much death. So many of those close to him had died, it was as if death was ever in his shadow. He had discovered long ago that killing did not bring him happiness, but he had decided that if he was to always walk near to death, he would make it dance to his sword's song.

Beobrand stepped up onto the wale of the ship. The cold wind tugged at his sodden kirtle. For a moment, he teetered there. The two ships pulled away from each other, rising and falling on the choppy sea. The water between them was churned and dark. If he should fall, he would be crushed between the two hulls and drowned in the sea's bottomless depths. Suppressing a shudder at the thought, Beobrand fixed his gaze on the pirate ship. Taking a deep breath, he hesitated for a heartbeat, allowing the deck to rise towards him, and then he flung himself across the gap.

He landed hard, stumbling and cracking his shins against a thwart. But he remained on his feet. A moment later, something crashed into his back and he staggered.

"Sorry, lord," Cynan said, laughter in his voice. "I didn't want to fall in."

Beobrand grinned at the Waelisc warrior, but he did not speak. There was no need now for words. Now was the time for screams.

On the far side of the ship lay the injured steersman, Garr's spear yet jutting from his shoulder. The newly appointed helmsman stared wide-eyed at the two Northumbrian warriors. He released the rudder and tugged a long seax from his belt. Beobrand dashed across the deck. The sailor swung his seax wildly, but Beobrand caught the attack effortlessly on his shield and hacked Hrunting into the man's neck. Dark gore gushed in a great arc, painting the oak beams of the deck crimson.

The man that Garr's spear had pierced cried out from where he lay on the deck.

"Spare me!" he whimpered, blood bubbling on his lips.

Cynan plunged his sword into the prone figure, silencing his pleading.

Beobrand and Cynan turned, and side by side they strode quickly towards the amassed men who crowded amidships.

Sensing the approaching danger, some of the pirates turned to face them. Cynan and Beobrand did not hesitate. They threw themselves forward, easily deflecting the sailors' clumsy attacks on their black-painted shields. With practised efficacy, the two warriors lashed out with their blades and hot blood once again splashed the deck. These seamen were savage and brave, but they were no match for Beobrand and his finest gesith.

Beobrand and Cynan stepped forward on the slick boards, again hammering their blades into the soft, unarmoured flesh of their adversaries. The sailors were trying to run now, to break away from the two implacable killers who bore down on them from the stern of their own ship. But the belly of the boat was thronged with men, and there was no escape. Men stumbled and fell before the two Northumbrians, only to be sent to the afterlife where they lay with rapid downward thrusts of the warriors' blades.

From the Northumbrian ship came the sound of more screams. More death was being dealt there, and Beobrand's heart swelled. These were his men, and their exploits were sung of the length of Albion. Here, despite their small number, on the wind-tossed waves of the Whale Road, his gesithas were once again proving themselves worthy of song.

The sailors before them retreated, shying away from their gore-slick blades. Beobrand scanned the horizon. The two other pirate ships were close by, but did not seem to be doing anything to enter the fray. And what was that? There, in the west. Yes, there was no doubt. They were yet distant, but there, coming from landward, were the two ships that bore Wynhelm and Fordraed, and with them, many more seasoned fighting men.

"Death!" Beobrand bellowed in his battle-voice. "We will win this day, for behold, our countrymen have found us and sail to our aid."

Was that a ragged cheer from his men aboard *Háligsteorra*? He could not tell, but suddenly another voice rose above the chaos of the fighting, cutting through the tumult.

"Halt!" the oddly accented voice shouted. "Put up your weapons!"

Beobrand strained to see the owner of the voice. The men before him shuffled further out of Hrunting's reach. A few of them glanced towards the Northumbrian vessel and Beobrand followed their gaze. There, at *Háligsteorra*'s prow stood the huge pirate leader, the man Beobrand had seen standing at the bow of the raiders' bark. He was tall and broad and still wore the strange helm that seemed to be fashioned from the skull of some tusked creature from legend. Before him, held tightly in an iron grasp, was Dalston. The young monk's face was the colour of whey. The brigand leader pressed a vicious-looking seax to the monk's throat. In his slender hands, clamped to his slim chest, Dalston gripped the bejewelled casket that carried the precious gifts they were bearing to Cantware.

The sound of battle died away and all the men aboard both ships paused, staring towards the massive pirate captain and his hostage. The beast-helmeted man cast a glance over his shoulder. He tensed. He too had spotted the approach of the other Northumbrian ships. He raked his gaze across the blood-soaked decks, clearly weighing his chances against the handful of warriors on *Háligsteorra* and whether his men could hope to be done with them before the reinforcements arrived.

The hulls scraped and groaned where they had been lashed together. The ships rolled and pitched. Above them, a gull let out a shrieking cry. The leader fixed his gaze on Beobrand.

"Get off my ship or this boy dies," he said. It seemed he had decided to cut his losses and retreat. Beobrand gripped Hrunting so tightly that his knuckles cracked. His blood roared in his ears. He looked about him at the dead and the dying. His body screamed at him to continue, to drench this ship in the blood of these pirates who had dared attack them. He took a step forward, but the pirate leader shouted again.

"I will slice his throat like a pig for bleeding. Get off my ship now."

Dalston's eyes were white-rimmed with fear and he was trembling like the severed sheet that flicked and shook in the wind. The pirate pressed his wicked blade into the pliant flesh of Dalston's throat and the monk moaned.

"You will withdraw from our ship too," Beobrand said, his voice as cold as the slate-grey sea. "And sail your ships away."

The pirate met his hard gaze for a long moment, then nodded.

"Go, Cynan," Beobrand whispered.

Cynan stepped away from the sailors and scrambled over the side of the ship, back into *Háligsteorra*. Beobrand followed him and quickly joined Bassus and the others where they stood before a pile of bloody corpses.

The pirates clambered off the ship even more quickly than they had boarded. Their leader was last, and he shuffled towards the wale still clutching Dalston to him, with the sharp seax blade digging into the skin beneath the monk's chin.

When he reached the side, he stepped over, steadied by the welcoming hands of his men. He lifted Dalston bodily and carried him over with him.

"Take the treasure the boy carries," shouted Beobrand. "Send the boy back."

The dull thuds of axe blows signalled the ropes that had held the ships together being cut. Using their oars, the pirates shoved the two ships apart. The gap between the vessels widened quickly, soon it would be too far even for an unarmoured man to jump.

"Send the boy back!" yelled Beobrand again, but as he said the words, he tasted the bitterness of defeat and deceit in his throat.

Beneath the animal skull helm, the pirate's eyes gleamed and his mouth widened into a gap-toothed grin.

"Here," he said, "you can have him."

With one hand, he plucked the finely decorated casket from the monk's grasp and with the other hand, he sawed his blade across Dalston's pallid throat. Blood welled and then rushed from the wound in a torrent. The blood streamed down, splashing over the strakes of the pirate ship. Dalston's mouth opened and shut, as if he were trying to speak, but no words came. The pirate held him upright for several heartbeats as the ships drifted further apart. Dalston gurgled and blinked in terror.

As if from a distance, Beobrand heard Coenred let out a howl of anguish at seeing his friend's fate.

When the pirate at last tired of holding the monk, he shoved him forward and Dalston tumbled into the seething sea. He made no sound and there was only the briefest of splashes. For an instant, the foam was a blur of red, and then the monk vanished, swallowed into the darkness beneath the waves. It was as if Dalston had never been.

Chapter 3

Ardith knew that something was amiss the moment her father awoke early.

Had she had an inkling of what was to pass that morning beneath the ashen, autumnal sky, she would have leapt from her bed and sped off barefoot into the woods to the north of their hut.

She had planned to be up long before her father, to be far from the house by the time he roused himself. But here he was, filled with an urgent energy she did not recognise. The sight of him, face blotched and eyes shot through with red veins, terrified her. He was not one to rise in a good humour, and she had learnt to dress herself and to leave their home silently so as not to disturb him.

He had been out late the night before, his drunken stumblings around the farmhouse had awoken her in the deep of night. She had lain there, her body rigid and still with fear that he might be angry, as he so often was. She had pressed her eyes tightly shut, willing her breathing to be even and deep, feigning slumber in the hope that he would not come to her. She had prayed silently to the Blessed Virgin, for her mother told her there was no one more holy than the mother of Christ and that Maria would surely answer the prayers of womenfolk over the supplications of men.

There had been a crash and her father had cursed. Ardith had held her breath then, more intent on not being noticed than pretending to sleep. She had remained perfectly still while in her thought-cage the words of her prayers to the Virgin tumbled and churned like the frenetic paddling of a swan beneath the still surface of a pond. The mother of Christ must have heard her frantic silent pleading, for with a loud belch and a grunt, her father had collapsed onto the pallet, where he usually slept beside her mother, and within moments his snores had filled the room.

The house had settled and creaked around them, as if it too had been woken and now once again would return to its secret dreams. Outside, the breeze had picked up and whispered through the boughs of the hornbeams and oaks that grew close to the house. The wind had blown under the eaves and the timbers groaned and sighed.

The soft sounds of the night and the all-too-familiar sawing snores of her father had eventually ushered her back to sleep. In her dreams she had walked through fields of waving barley with her mother. They had laughed and talked of all manner of things and Ardith had been content.

Her father's rough voice had shattered her sleep and her happy dream. Fingers of grey dawn light found their way through the shutters and beneath the door. Her father's grizzled face stared down at her and for an instant Ardith was filled with horror. She recoiled, before forcing herself to appear at ease. She knew her father hated it when they showed any display of nervousness around him.

He seemed not to notice her reaction. Flinging open the shutters, he allowed more watery light to wash in.

"Come on, girl," he said. "Get up. No time to dawdle. Brush your hair and put on your best peplos. The green one that mother is always telling you not to make dirty." He grinned at her conspiratorially. His tone was jovial, yet brisk. Despite his drunkenness of the night before and the stench of sour ale that rolled from him like the fog that wafted over the fields before the sun climbed high, his body seemed to thrum with excitement.

Unease rippled through her. She wished her mother had not been called away to help tend to aunt Inga in her confinement. Or that she had allowed Ardith to travel with her. She had taken Tatwine, and he was only five. It wasn't fair.

"What is it, father?" she asked, keeping her voice even and calm, in spite of the anxiety that flapped its wings around her. "It is very early. Should I prepare food? There is some pottage left from last night. It won't take long to warm." Her words tumbled from her in a rush.

Her father shook his head and sat on his favourite stool. He glanced at the window, perhaps gauging the time from the light, and then began to quickly bind his legs.

"There is no time for that," he said. "Just do as I say."

Ardith climbed from her bed. She knew not to argue.

*

The sun had barely crept above the horizon when they walked down the main path between the buildings of Hithe. The settlement was waking from slumber, shaking off the shackles of sleep. From the houses off to the east came the wails of a child, followed by the harsh words of a woman, angry and tired.

Ardith's toes hurt. Father had ordered her to wear her finest shoes, made of supple calf's leather. They were soft and had been comfortable when her father had bought them for her from a merchant from Wessex. But that had been the year before and her feet had grown considerably since then. She had grown in height too, and the peplos, made of finely spun linen, green and vibrant as the grassy hilltops to the north of Hithe, was now too short. Like the shoes, the dress was tight and uncomfortable.

Her breasts had blossomed in the last few months and the fabric of the peplos pressed against them, accentuating her burgeoning feminine form.

"Must I wear this dress, father?" she had asked when she had seen how much she had outgrown the garment.

He had looked up from where he was fastening his leg bindings. His hooded gaze took her in, from her golden braided hair to the peplos that was stretched over the curves of her chest. He nodded appraisingly.

"Yes. That dress makes you look pretty."

In the distance, Ardith saw smoke rising from Byrhtísen's forge. As they walked past, Byrhtísen called a greeting. Her father grunted a reply. Ardith kept her eyes turned downward. She felt her face flush hot. She could feel the gaze of the smith's son, Brinin, upon her. She tugged the hem of her dress, trying in vain to make it longer, to cover more of her pale slender legs.

"Where are we going?" she said in a small voice. She had asked her father the same question several times already, but each time he'd given her no answer.

"You'll see soon enough," he said. "We're almost there."

Her unease grew as their destination became clear. They had passed the houses of the village, leaving the great hulk of Folca's hall looming on the hill in the distance behind them. All that was between them and the iron-grey expanse of the Narrow Sea was the strand of shingle. Three large ships had been pulled up onto the beach. Several men lounged in the wind-shadow of the canted keels. Smoke curled above the pebbles where the men had kindled driftwood fires. They were traders who had put ashore the previous afternoon. These were the men in whose company her father had spent the night drinking. Usually, travellers were welcomed in the great hall, where they paid for Folca's hospitality with news of the world, tidings of the comings and goings of kings.

But these men had not been welcomed to Folca's hall. No, the lord tolerated them, allowed them to land upon his beach and to trade with his people, but he did not invite them into his home, to warm themselves at his hearth. For these men were not men of honour. Not men to trust. They were a slovenly band from many remote places. Waelisc, Hibernians, Franks. One even had skin as dark as burnt oak. God alone knew which faraway land he came from. These were the roughest sort of men and Ardith prickled with disquiet as her father raised his hand in greeting and one of the men who lolled by the smoking fire heaved himself to his feet.

He was a hulking man, and for a sickening moment she thought him a creature from legend. A night-stalker, one of Cain's kin, a fell giant, broader than any man, but walking upon God's earth on two legs. She shivered as the figure approached, his massive booted feet crunching in the shingle.

"So, you came back," the night-stalker said, its voice thick with a strange accent. She saw then that what she had thought of as his head was in fact a strange helmet made of the skull and savage, dagger-like tusks of some terrible creature. Over his shoulders he wore a thick, wrinkled leather cape. The cape was topped with a hood that was pulled over the skull helm, making it seem as though his skin was the grey hide and the skull and vicious, hand-length teeth that framed his face jutted from his own jaws. But this was no beast, but a barrel-chested man who walked with the rolling gait of one who spends most of his life at sea. His face was wide and whiskered, his eyes deep-set and dark. He flashed an appraising look at her and she felt his stare roving over her body. Again she tugged at the hem of her peplos in a pathetic attempt to cover her bare thighs.

He smiled at her, the great slabs of fat of his jowls twisting and quivering. There were scant teeth in his fleshy maw and what few there were protruded, brown and pitted, at odd angles like ancient, canted grave markers. He moistened his lips with a fleshy tongue. Ardith shuddered, but could not look away. Her eyes were wide and glistening.

"I told you I would come," her father said. He spoke with a forced friendliness. "I kept my word."

Again the beast-man's eyes flicked in her direction.

"Yes," he nodded, once more licking his lips, "yes, you did."

"Wait there, child," her father said. His mouth stretched in a smile, but she could see the lack of love or mirth behind his eyes. He turned, leading the huge sailor back towards the fire and the ships.

The two men talked in hushed voices, more than once glancing in her direction. As she watched, her unease grew, as did her hatred for her father. All of the men on the beach were now aware of her presence and she stood uncomfortably, squirming her feet further into the pebbled beach, wishing that she could hide from the hungry eyes of the sailors. A chill breeze blew from the sea, tugging at her hair and her dress. The skin on her legs and arms pimpled like that of a plucked goose.

Her father and the leader of the seamen must have reached an agreement, for they spat into their palms and clasped each other's hands. Then the sailor handed over a large pouch to her father. He weighed it in his hands and pulled open the thong that fastened it. Peering inside, he nodded, apparently content.

Until then, she had not understood what it was that her father had planned for her, but watching the exchange, in a sickening instant, she knew. If she stayed in this place, rooted to the shingle like the sea campion that grew above the tide line, she would be lost. She must run. She should have fled as soon as her father woke early; the moment he had told her to put on the damned, too-short peplos. And yet, she had clung to a thin hope. He was her father. Surely he could mean her no harm. He sometimes had good days when he was happy, jubilant and exalting in the joys of life. His exuberance on such days was unnerving, and she had grown to know that they were always followed by bouts of drinking and darkness, sour moods and slaps or punches if she wandered too close. Still, when he was in such a buoyant mood, her father was generous, buying her gifts such as the fine shoes that even now pinched her toes. And yet this morning, when he had roused himself before the sun had risen, she had known this was something different. But how could she have imagined the horror of what he had agreed with these sailors?

Their business concluded, the leader of the sailors and her father turned back in her direction. Her father looked away from her. Was he ashamed? They trudged over the strand towards her. The beast-cloaked sailor stared at her and nodded as they approached, clearly pleased with his purchase. He clapped his meaty hands together in an expansive gesture of his contentment.

The sharp sound made her start and she awoke as if from a nightmare. She must flee. Now!

Spinning around, she made to rush back up the beach. But before she could take more than a couple of paces she was brought up short. Directly before her stood the black-skinned man. His eyes and teeth flashed a brilliant white in his dusky face. Ardith took a quick step to the left, but there was another of the sailors, a red-haired man with a plaited beard and a dark, scarred hollow where his left eye should have been. He reached out to stop her. His arms were long and muscled, as thick as her thighs. She darted back to the right, but another man blocked her path. The three sailors must have risen unnoticed from the campfires and positioned themselves behind her, clearly anticipating her actions. Behind her, she sensed that her father and the leader were close now.

With a sinking in her stomach, she knew that the moment for running had passed.

"She's a feisty one," said the leader in his heavy accent. "We'll need to keep an eye on her, lads." The red-bearded man grinned at her, opening his single eye wide. The scarred skin around the empty eye socket stretched sickeningly.

"They'll be no touching, Draca," the leader said. Raising his voice, he continued, "That goes for all of you. This treasure," he reached out gnarled, callused fingers to stroke her hair, "will fetch a lot of coin in Frankia. I know of men who would pay a fortune for such a sweet, golden-haired virgin."

She recoiled at his touch, pulling away and once again trying to run, hoping to catch the watching men unawares. But strong hands gripped her and she was pulled back. With a start, she realised the hands that had restrained her belonged to her father. He leaned in close to her.

"Do not fight them, Ardith," he said. "It will be better for you, if you go easily and don't cause trouble."

As suddenly as lightning flashes in a storm cloud her anger flared, burning away her fear. She spat a great gobbet of spittle into her father's face and tugged her arms free of his grasp.

"It would go easier for me if you had not sold me to pay for your next drink," she screamed, her fury giving vent to words she had longed to say. "You are no man. And you are no father to me. Do not speak to me. You have no right."

As quickly as her own ire had sparked, so did his. His face contorted into a mask of rage and his hand lashed out, striking her on the cheek. She did not see the slap coming and the force of it sent her reeling onto the pebbles.

Belying his bulk, the leader of the sailors sprang forward quickly and without pause smashed a fist into her father's face. Her father staggered and fell. Instantly, the sea captain was upon him. He punched her father again, making his head rock back, before dragging a wicked-looking seax from a sheath on his belt and holding it to her father's throat. The ship's captain grabbed a fistful of her father's hair and pulled him onto his knees. Blood welled from his split lips and he spat into the gravel of the beach.

"She is not yours to strike now, you drunken toad," the trader hissed.

Ardith pushed herself to her feet. Her cheek stung, as did her knees and hands where she had grazed them on the stones. Her father's face was white. Gone was his rage and he was once more the man she had tried to love. The drunk she despised. The blood from his mouth was bright against his pallid skin. For a heartbeat, Ardith hoped that the sailor would draw the blade of his seax across her father's throat. She would see him slain, like a pig at Blotmonath for what he had done to her.

The sailor yanked savagely on her father's hair, tugging him up onto his feet.

"Begone, before I gut you and take my silver back."

He gave him a rough shove and her father stumbled back up the beach, away from the ships. Away from Ardith.

She shuddered again. Her hands trembled, clenched into fists at her side. By the Virgin, so help her God, but if she had her own seax now, her father's blood would be drenching the beach. She glared at his retreating form as he hurried away, willing him to die. He hesitated a moment and for a fleeting instant she thought he might turn and come back, understanding the terrible thing he had done. As sudden as her ire and loathing had come, so it was replaced by a surge of hope and love. He could not bring himself to do this. Surely that was why he had paused. It was the devil in the drink that had made him behave so. Now, he would repent and take her back.

But he did not turn.

Pulling his cloak about his shoulders, he lowered his head and hurried on. He did not look back.

The burly leader of the traders began barking orders. The men snapped into action, kicking out their fires and bundling their bedding and supplies into the ships.

"I wouldn't be surprised if that maggot says we have stolen her," he said to Draca. "If we tarry here, Lord Folca's men will be down upon us soon enough, I would wager." Ardith scowled at his words. The man clearly had her father's measure.

In moments the crews had prepared the ships and were heaving them into the waves of the rising tide.

Ardith did not struggle when one of the men lifted her and placed her into the bow of the largest ship. The fight had fled from her with her father's utter betrayal. As the men grunted the words of a sea song, with each beat of the words pushing the keel further into the awaiting sea, she felt nothing. The ship righted itself as it reached water deep enough for it to float. The swaying, rolling of the deck made her stagger and she reached out a delicate hand to grasp the sheer strake.

With practised ease the sailors fell into position on the thwarts and their sea chests and began to pull the ships out into the Narrow Sea with great sweeps of the long oars. The ranks of oars rose and fell like slow beats of a great bird's wings. And despite the wind blowing landward, trying to push them back onto the beach, the ships flew forward.

She stared at the settlement she had known as home all her short life. There was the golden thatched roof of Folca's great hall. There the ash trees that led up to the steading and the small hut she shared with her mother and father. Smoke hazed the early morning air above the buildings. She could make out the shape of the low, sod-turfed roof of Byrhtísen's forge. She strained to hear the sound of the hammer striking the anvil, but the wind rushed in her ears and all she could hear was the splash of the oars and the chanting of the sailors who sang as they heaved to propel the ships forward. Everything on the land looked familiar and yet strange and different from out here on the Whale Road.

Her father had vanished from view. But she noticed another figure standing out on the edge of the beach they had just departed. A man stood there, hand shading his eyes as he seemed to stare directly at her. She could not make out his features, and wondered absently who it was, this last person she would ever see from Hithe.

She shivered. Her face was cold where, unnoticed, tears streamed down her cheeks and neck, staining the neckline of her best peplos until it resembled the dark green of the chill water that surrounded the ships that carried her ever further from home.

Chapter 4

Beobrand watched as Bassus strode back and forth like a caged bear. A soft breeze wafted in through the open shutters of the small room they had been allocated by King Eorcenberht's steward. The old man had served Eorcenberht's father, Eadbald, and recognised both Beobrand and Bassus from previous visits. He had welcomed them with genuine warmth the previous day when they had arrived. He had sent food to their chamber and had seen that the others from the Northumbrian delegation were given comfortable lodgings. Fordraed and Wynhelm had each been housed in a similar building, while all of their gesithas had been put up at one end of a large barn. They had been supplied with copious amounts of food and drink, so they were happy enough. From time to time sounds of laughter or shouting drifted to Beobrand. The warrior retinues of the Northumbrian thegns seemed to be enjoying their stay in Cantwareburh.

Bassus however, was not taking the waiting well. Beobrand understood his friend's annoyance. They had travelled far to visit the new king of Cantware, and neither of them had wished to make the journey. And, when compelled to travel by order of the king of Bernicia himself, they had even suffered the attack and loss of Dalston at the hands of pirates. Now they had been made to wait for more than a day.

Beobrand pushed himself up from the stool where he'd been sitting and joined Bassus by the window. He placed a hand on the huge warrior's shoulder, stilling his incessant pacing.

Outside, in the warm light of the lowering sun, a bondsman was burning a great mound of dry leaves. Thick smoke billowed from the fire, bringing with it the scent of autumn. The dying of things. Other smoke, from distant cooking fires, mingled with that of the leaves, adding the pungent smell of roasting meat. Beobrand stared at the flames that hungrily consumed the fallen leaves. For a moment, his vision blurred as his eyes brimmed with tears. He had seen too many fires eating away the last vestiges of lives cut short.

Unbidden came the vision of Reaghan's bone-fire. The wound she had received from the thrall, Sulis, had become elf-shot and there had been nothing anyone could do to save her. She had been dead when he had returned from the Great Wall after killing Halga and the Mercian raiding party there. Coenred had tried his best to keep her alive, working his healing magic and praying to his god, but the fever had never left her and she had slipped away the day before Beobrand had come back to Ubbanford. Coenred had begged Beobrand not to burn her, but she had been no follower of the Christ god. No, she had worshipped the all-mother, Danu, and whilst Beobrand did not know the rites she would have wanted spoken over her, he knew that she would wish her spirit to be sent on to the afterlife on the smoke of a pyre, and not mouldering in the dark, beneath worm-crawling loam.

He cuffed at his eyes, blinking away the tears that threatened to fall. Gods, he had done enough crying for a lifetime.

The man tending the garden outside brought another large load of leaves that he had raked from the paths around the royal enclosure. He lifted them and dumped the lot onto the fire, almost smothering it in the process. Dense smoke oozed from the pile, like the tendrils of smoke wafting from a charcoal mound.

Beobrand could have told him not to place so many leaves on at once. The fire needed space to breathe, just like any other living thing. With so many loved ones to burn, he had become skilled at lighting fires. He snorted, amused at his own dark thoughts.

"By Tiw's cock," boomed Bassus, "why does the king make us wait so? Perhaps we should just leave this place. If Eorcenberht is not interested in talking to us about his cousin, then perhaps we should forget the whole thing. The worst that would happen is that Oswiu would be left without his new peace-weaver. And I do not think she would be too upset by that prospect, poor girl."

Beobrand sighed. He harboured similar thoughts.

"Eorcenberht will see us soon, I am sure," he said. "He is young and does not have his father's certainty in his power. Kings like to wield power the way a warrior swings a sword." He thought back to another untried monarch. Ecgric of East Angeln had also made him wait. Then battle had been brewing and Ecgric was dead only days later, his host shattered and his kingdom ravaged. This visit was different. They were here to forge an alliance for peace; to unify the kingdoms of Bernicia and Deira by marriage. "Making us wait is just Eorcenberht flexing his muscles."

Bassus frowned, but nodded.

"You are probably right. Eorcenberht is young and needs to make such petty displays. But it does not sit well with me."

"Why do you think she asked for us?" asked Beobrand, changing the subject and returning to the question that had been preying on his mind.

"Well, she knew me as a child. I was her father's champion." Bassus gave him a sidelong glance. "The gods alone know why she wants to see you again."

Beobrand offered Bassus a thin smile.

He was as unsure as his friend as to why Eanflæd had demanded that he be among those who came to bring her back to Northumbria. He had only seen the girl twice before, once on the day he had arrived at Bebbanburg and then later, after fleeing the destruction of Ecgric's warhost in East Angeln. That had been some seven years ago and he remembered Eanflæd as a sombre, willow-like child, with hair of burnished gold and skin as pale as ewe's milk. Her father had believed in Beobrand, allowing him, as an unproven youth, to join his warband. That was when he had met Bassus and the path of his life had been that of a warrior ever since. Now, despite having served her father's enemies for many years, it seemed that Beobrand's wyrd was once more entwined with Eanflæd's life thread.

"Who knows why she asked for us," Beobrand said. "But I wish I had not come. There can be no good reason for us to be here. There is much to do yet in Ubbanford. We should be there."

Much of the settlement had been rebuilt following the savage raid by the Mercian, Halga, but there was still a lot of work to do. Beobrand was determined that the great hall would be even grander than before and he had used up much of his hoard of treasure paying craftsmen from Eoferwic and even further afield to help in its construction.

"Gram will oversee things well. You need not worry on that front. And besides," Bassus grinned, "Rowena will see to it that everything progresses faster than if the king himself was there ordering the men to build."

Beobrand smiled. It was true that Bassus' woman, the lady Rowena, would ensure that none of the thralls or craftsmen would waste a moment. Gram too, he knew, was loyal and a safe pair of hands, not to mention a strong warrior. Most of his warband remained at Ubbanford. Following the attack by Halga, he would never leave his people so poorly defended again.

"I just wish I had stayed in the north."

"It little matters what you wish," Bassus said, staring out of the window at the setting sun hazing in the smoky air. "We had no choice."

Beobrand clenched his hands into fists at his side. The muscles of his jaw bunched. Bassus had the right of it. Oswiu had summoned him to Bebbanburg, and he had run to do his lord's bidding. The thought of being oath-sworn to such a man filled him with dismay. But there was nothing for it. He had given his word that upon Oswald's death he would swear his allegiance to the king's brother, Oswiu, and so it had been.

"I had no choice," Beobrand said. "That is for sure."

As if the bond of his oath had not been enough, Oswiu had further ensured Beobrand's loyalty and service when he had called him to Bebbanburg. Beobrand had feared the worst when the messenger had ordered him to bring his son, Octa, with him to meet the king. He had promised himself he would never send his son away again. But he could not deny his king.

Bassus looked at him askance, sensing the shift in his lord's mood. Beobrand reached for the jug of good Frankish wine that a servant had brought for them some time before. He poured himself a cup and took a long draught. The liquid was deeply satisfying and rich. It warmed his throat.

"If only I had sent Octa with Cynethryth," he said.

"You were not to know what would happen," said Bassus. The impatient anger had gone from his voice now and was replaced by a tenderness that was at odds with his grizzled appearance.

"I should have seen that Oswiu would do this thing." Beobrand sighed. "Octa would have been safe on Hii."

Fearing that Penda of Mercia would seek to destroy anyone who could make a claim on his kingdom, Beobrand had sent Cynethryth, Penda's brother's widow, and her sons into the north-west, to the lands of Dál Riata, to the sacred isle of Hii. There he hoped her sons would find sanctuary from Penda, just as Æthelfrith's sons had been safe from King Edwin's reach when they had been exiled. He felt he owed it to his friend, Eowa, to protect his kin. He had failed to protect Eowa at Maserfelth and the burden of Penda's brother's death lay heavy upon Beobrand.

"Octa will be safe enough with Oswiu," Bassus said. "And remember what Rowena said. It is a great honour that the king himself offers to foster your child."

Beobrand snorted.

"An honour?" He shook his head and looked sidelong at Bassus. The giant warrior could not meet his gaze. "You know as well as I that this is no honour. Oswiu holds my son as hostage. He does not trust me."

"Oswiu must know you better than that. You have given him your oath."

It was true that Oswiu had his oath, as had his brother before him. Beobrand had sworn his pledge to Oswiu in Caer Luel. He was Oswiu's man now. He had given his word, first to Oswald, and then to Oswiu, and he did not give his word lightly. And yet, Beobrand knew that Oswiu was cunning to hold Octa. For any promise could be tested. His word was iron, but, even the best wrought iron could be broken. Just as a blade might bend or snap in combat, so an oath could shatter, if enough pressure were applied.

Beobrand watched the flames licking at the leaves. The ceorl was returning with yet more fuel for the fire. The wind shifted, blowing the smoke in a great cloud towards the bondsman, engulfing him. The man began to cough uncontrollably, a dry hacking bark that bent him double. For a moment Beobrand thought the man would drop his armful of leaves, but after a moment he spat, straightened himself and made his way through the fog of smoke to the fire, where once more he tossed a thick blanket of leaves onto the flames.

Again, the flames were smothered. But the fire was hot now, and would soon burn again. It would take more than leaves to extinguish it. Beobrand looked beyond the smoking bonfire at the buildings across the courtyard. They were well maintained, and several were still roofed with the red tiles favoured by the erstwhile rulers of Albion. The men of Roma had long left these shores, but the memories of them were everywhere to be seen. From these buildings in Cantware, to the paved roads of Earninga Stræt and Deira Stræt, to the Great Wall that divided the island from east to west across Bernicia. The buildings reminded him of those that remained in Eoferwic. Much of Deira's capital lingered intact from the days of those giants among men who had conquered this whole island many generations before. The city walls were crumbling in places now, but they were yet formidable.

"You have gone very quiet," said Bassus. "I worry when you become so still. It usually means you are thinking of killing someone."

Beobrand took another swig of wine and shook his head.

"I am not plotting anyone's death. But I do not doubt that Oswiu is." He filled the other cup that rested on the table and handed it to Bassus. The one-armed giant hesitated, before lifting the cup and taking a sip. He was looking at Beobrand inquisitively. "I was thinking of Eoferwic," said Beobrand, as if this was answer enough.

Bassus frowned, but nodded. He drank more wine.

"You think he would seek to slay Oswine?"

Beobrand smiled without mirth. He thought of what he knew of Oswiu. How he had sent men all the way to Frankia to slay children who might pose a threat to his brother's reign. But Oswine was no defenceless child. Beobrand recalled Oswiu's ire when he had summoned them to Bebbanburg. As Bassus and Beobrand had strode into the great hall of the fortress, Oswiu's voice had reached them from where he addressed his closest ealdormen and thegns. Unlike his brother, who had always talked with a quiet confidence, Oswiu's voice had been strident and full of rage.

Beobrand and Bassus had exchanged a glance and Beobrand had told Fraomar to keep Octa with him and the rest of the men. Leaving his gesithas and son to find refreshment, Beobrand and Bassus had continued the length of the hall, past the smouldering hearth fire, all the while feeling the eyes of the gathered warriors upon them.

As Oswiu caught sight of them, he had turned the full glare of his anger upon them.

"By all that is holy, what took you so long? I sent for you days ago."

Beobrand had swallowed the retort that had threatened to burst from his mouth.

"We came with all haste."

Oswiu had glared at him for a long while. Behind the king, most of the other men had glowered at Beobrand. Fordraed had scowled, his podgy face twisted with open hostility.

"What are you staring at?" Fordraed had asked, disdain dripping from his words.

"I was recalling what it felt like to punch your ugly face," Beobrand replied, unable to control his contempt for the man.

Fordraed had blinked. Bassus had chuckled, causing Fordraed's scowl to deepen.

"You paid handsomely for that if I recall," Fordraed had blustered, reaching up to caress the thick gold ring that he now wore squeezed over the flesh of his upper arm. Beobrand had given him the arm ring as weregild for striking him. It was much more than such a crime warranted.

"I have never regretted the cost," Beobrand had said. "And I have plenty more treasure still if the urge to strike you again becomes unbearable." Beobrand was certain that Fordraed had played a part in Halga's raid on Ubbanford. There was a tight web of plots and lies around the new king and the plump thegn was as tangled in them as anyone.

The only man at the table who had offered Beobrand a smile of welcome was Wynhelm. The older thegn had met his gaze and seemed to be trying to convey some message with his expression, but Beobrand had been unable to fathom his old friend's meaning.

"Enough of this," snapped Oswiu. "We have no time to waste. We have been awaiting your arrival."

Beobrand had turned his cool gaze back to Oswiu.

"As I said, we came with all haste once we had received your summons, lord."

"'Lord' is it?" sneered Oswiu. "Yes, I am your lord. And your king. Am I not?"

"Yes, lord king," Beobrand replied in a flat tone. "You have my oath and I am your man."

"It seems not all men are so keen to recall their pledges and oaths." For a moment, Beobrand had wondered what Oswiu was referring to, but the king did not wait long to explain his anger. "That ill-begotten whoreson Oswine has been declared king of Deira by the Witena Ġemōt. When I rode to Eoferwic, they welcomed us as guests. As neighbours. But they did not welcome me as their king!" In a moment of sudden rage, Oswiu had scooped up from the table one of the ornate glass beakers his brother had so loved and flung it against the wall. It had shattered and a thrall had scurried forward to clean up the mess. The shards of green glass had twinkled and shone like jewels as the slave had brushed them up.

And there it was. The reason for Oswiu's anger. Beobrand had stayed away from Bebbanburg and the royal steadings during the long summer months, not wishing to be reminded of the oath he had pledged to the new king. But he had heard tell of Oswiu's intentions to travel to Eoferwic and there to have the Witena Ġemōt of Deira declare him the ruler of that kingdom, as his brother, Oswald, had been, thus uniting both Bernicia and Deira once more into the powerful kingdom of Northumbria. But it seemed all of Oswiu's scheming and bribes had not had the desired effect and Oswine, son of Osric had been given the throne of Deira.

Beobrand had met Oswine several times over the years. He had always seemed to be a fine man, honest and brave in battle.

He was handsome and tall and carried himself with a noble bearing. Kingly even. Beobrand could well understand why the wise council of Deira would prefer him to rule over them. But their decision was a terrible blow to Oswiu's ambitions.

As he recalled his humiliation in Eoferwic, Oswiu's features had darkened. He signalled for more wine to be brought. A slim, dark-haired girl had rushed over and Beobrand had noted the shaking of the thrall's hand as she had poured fresh wine into an unbroken glass goblet. She had spilt a few drops on the cloth that covered the board. She had hesitated then, flinching, as if expecting a blow. Beobrand had tensed. He knew he could not intervene if the king should choose to chastise a slave, but he could not abide violence to women. After a heartbeat, the thrall had hurried away, without Oswiu seeming to notice her mistake. Evidently he was more interested in explaining why he had summoned them to Bebbanburg.

And so it was that Beobrand had learnt of Oswiu's plan to wed Oswine's cousin, Eanflæd. Her father, Edwin, had been the king of Deira and Bernicia before Oswald. With Oswine now on the throne of Deira, Beobrand could not see what was to be gained by this marriage. After all, Oswiu already had a wife, and children, and the rumours were rife of the many women he bedded. Why seek a new queen? But it was not Beobrand's place to understand the ways of royalty. He had listened quietly as Oswiu had given him his orders, all the while studying his features. The brotherly similarities with Oswald were clear. The same chestnut hair and intelligent eyes. Each had the same energy and presence, that made men turn to them whenever they entered a room. And yet Oswiu, stockier and more solid than his brother somehow, had none of the calm confidence of Oswald. He always seemed to be battling to keep his anger in check and his eyes, whilst the same shade of dark brown as Oswald's, darted and shifted, as if he saw threats in the very smoke and air of the hall.

When the king had finished laying out the plans, Beobrand had nodded. All he wished was to be away from Oswiu and these men who gathered around him the way flies cluster on a carcass.

He had turned, ready to return to his men, who were seated at the far end of the hall, but Oswiu's voice pulled him up short.

"There is one more thing," he had said.

Beobrand swung back to face Oswiu. His stomach twisted in anticipation of the words he knew the king would utter.

"Yes, lord?" His words were clipped, his throat tight.

"I see you have brought your son as requested."

Beobrand could not bring himself to answer, so merely inclined his head.

"Good," continued Oswiu, a smile tugging at his lips. "It is my pleasure that Octa be fostered in my household. It might do Alhfrith good to have a new playmate."

Beobrand had clenched his jaw, nodding once more.

"As you wish," he had said, at last. The ealdormen and thegns still glowered at him, their dislike of him washing off them like the stink from a midden. Wynhelm gave him a small smile of commiseration. Fordraed's eyes glowed with triumph. Perhaps he had been the one to suggest this to Oswiu.

"It is a great honour the king does you," Fordraed said, barely concealing the mirth that threatened to bubble out of his flaccid lips.

Beobrand had felt a terrible emptiness then. Octa was all he had left of his kin. To have him live in the household of one such as Oswiu was almost too much to bear. And yet there was nothing he could do. Oswiu had his oath, so he must obey. Octa would stay with the king and Beobrand would thus be more tightly bound to Oswiu than with any words, no matter how strong his oath might be.

Beobrand had fixed Fordraed with a withering glare. Fordraed had recoiled. Beobrand had held his gaze a moment longer and then stalked off down the hall towards his gesithas, and his son.

Bassus had not uttered a word, but Beobrand had been glad of his friend's calming presence at his side.

Now it was Bassus' voice that brought him back to the present. Beobrand noticed absently that the bonfire now burnt hot, with great gouts of flame spouting from the pile of leaves. The bondsman was nowhere to be seen.

"Well, do you?" Bassus asked.

Beobrand blinked.

"Do I what?" he snapped. The memory of the meeting at Bebbanburg had worsened his mood.

"Think that Oswiu will seek to kill Oswine?"

Beobrand sighed and drained the wine from his cup. He had been wondering the same thing since they had been sent south for Oswiu's new bride. Surely if Oswine were to die, Oswiu could reap the true value of a queen from the royal house of Deira.

A soft knocking on the door to the chamber interrupted his thoughts before he could answer.

The door swung open quietly, on well-greased hinges. In the doorway stood Coenred and, behind him, the priest, Utta.

"We have been summoned to King Eorcenberht's table," said Coenred. Beobrand noted that the colour had returned to the monk's cheeks, but his eyes were encircled by dark, blotchy skin. Their ordeal and Dalston's death had hit him hard.

Bassus emptied his cup of wine and slapped it down on the small table. He let out a great belch.

"About time too," he said, his booming voice filling the small room. "I feared we would be left to starve. I hope that meat I can smell cooking is from the feast Eorcenberht has had prepared."

Chapter 5

Sweat trickled down Beobrand's neck. The hall was warm, with its blazing hearth fire, dozens of guests sitting at the long benches arranged down its length, bustling thralls and servants and several hounds that snarled and growled, fighting over scraps of meat that fell or were tossed into the rushes strewn on the floor. But it was not the heat that caused Beobrand to perspire. It was the young woman who sat at his side.

He could scarcely believe this was the same girl he had first met in the darkness of the stable in Bebbanburg all those years before.

She was watching him closely and he felt his face grow hot. He reached for his horn of ale and took a long swig, hoping it would cool him. The sweat ran down his back under his kirtle and he squirmed uncomfortably beneath Eanflæd's gaze.

"You have changed," she said.

He let out a guffaw that was too loud. She smiled.

"Why do you laugh?" she asked.

He wiped his mouth with the back of his hand.

"I was just thinking you were a child when I saw you last."

She raised her eyebrows archly. Just as he had remembered it, her hair had the lustre of molten gold. Her skin was smooth, like polished stone, and he wished to reach out and touch her cheek.

Gripping his eating knife tightly, he skewered a sliver of roast boar. He had not been prepared for the change in her. Gods, she was no longer a child. When she had entered the hall, every man there had turned to watch her passing. Her flowing red linen dress and golden-clasped girdle accentuated the curves of her body, filling his mind with images of what she would look like without the finery covering her lithe legs, plump hips, ripe breasts.

She reminded him of Sunniva. She had that same effortless beauty that made her irresistible. And there was something else, beneath the soft womanly exterior, there was a strength to her. Sunniva had been strong, bending metal to her will as her father the smith had taught her. Eanflæd too had a strength about her. Beobrand recalled meeting her father, King Edwin. Watching Eanflæd's slender form glide down the hall towards the high table, Beobrand had recognised some of her father's warrior strength in her imperious gaze when she had glanced his way. He had been pierced by her look just as surely as he now stabbed roasted meat from the laden board before him.

Beobrand had been seated at the end of the high table, far from Eorcenberht and he had been ready to drink himself into a stupor whilst Utta discussed the affairs of the church and the kingdoms of Albion with the young king of Cantware. But Beobrand had not contended with being faced with Eanflæd. He rose as she passed, his mouth agape and she had smiled at him.

"Brave Beobrand, I am so pleased to see you came," she had said, her voice recognisable as the girl from the stable, but with a new huskiness that made his breath catch in his throat. He had bowed his head, but had said nothing. "Come," she'd continued, "you are a guest of honour and must not be so far from my cousin, the king. Or from me."

She had proceeded to rearrange the guests, so that when she sat in the finely carved chair that was reserved for her, Beobrand was to be seated on her left. He had done as he was told and moved to his new position at the table, but he was acutely aware of the gaze of everybody in the great hall upon him. Eanflæd forced a disgruntled Fordraed to move further from the king, relinquishing his place to Beobrand. The fat thegn had glared and Beobrand had been unable to contain a grin. Wynhelm had merely smiled quietly when he was asked to move, and offered a knowing nod to Beobrand. Bassus had raised himself to his full height and, before anyone knew what he was about, he had enveloped the princess in a huge one-armed embrace. She had let out a peal of girlish laughter and wrapped her arms around her father's erstwhile champion.

"Bassus," she had squealed breathlessly, "it has been too many years since last I saw you." She took in his missing arm. "I see you have not been looking after yourself." She had turned her attention to Beobrand then. "You really must take better care of your gesithas," she had said, laughter still ringing in her tone. Beobrand had frowned, reminded of all those brave men he had lost to the spear and sword. Shield-brothers. Friends.

If she had noticed the change in his humour, she did not mention it. She had lowered herself into her chair and patted the seat to her left.

"Here, Beobrand. You must sit beside me and tell me all of your tidings."

Despite himself, Beobrand felt her lightness of spirit and easy words driving away the solemnity that had threatened his mood.

And so he had done as he had been ordered by this daughter of Edwin. He had told her of the years since they had last met. He spoke at first of battles, victories he had won over the Picts or the Mercians, but she had quickly steered him on to other matters.

"I have heard the tales of your exploits in battle, Beobrand, as have all the folk of Albion," she had said. "I would hear of your life. Of the people who call you their lord. Of your son. Of your lovers." Her eyes had twinkled in the firelight and Beobrand had needed to moisten his dry throat with a great swallow of the strong ale Eorcenberht's steward had served. And yet, despite not usually being one to talk of himself, he had told her much. When they had reached the telling of Reaghan's death, Beobrand had been surprised to see Eanflæd's eyes brimming with tears.

"Did you catch the men who did it?" she'd asked.

"It was not a man who slew her. It was a thrall."

"But you said that men from Mercia had raided your lands."

"Yes. Halga, son of Grimbold, came upon Ubbanford in the dark of the early morning. His warband killed many of my people." Beobrand's mind had been filled with the darkest of memories. The charred, smouldering bones of buildings, the pallid, blood-streaked corpses.

"And the slave? The one who stabbed Reaghan?"

"She was from Mercia. She fled with Halga and his men."

"And you caught them?"

"Aye," Beobrand's voice was as hard and jagged as shards of granite, "we caught them by the Great Wall."

Eanflæd had stared at him for a long while then. The hall was filled with the hubbub of the feast, but the two of them were an island of hush and calm.

"What happened?" she asked in a small voice.

Beobrand swallowed. He did not wish to remember. Not here, next to this beautiful creature. She should not hear of his bloody deeds. He was no great warrior of legend, a hero for a princess to dream of. He was a butcher.

"Well," she pressed him.

"I slew them all," he said, his voice as harsh as a slap.

She flinched.

"And the thrall?"

Beobrand sighed and took another mouthful of ale.

"No, not her." He could still picture the madness in Sulis' eyes as she had launched herself at him. How close he had come to striking her down, to adding her death to his list of foes slain. "No," all the anger had drained from him, "I let her go."

47

After that they had been silent for a time.

Beobrand had taken a long drink of ale and watched as Utta spoke at length to Eorcenberht. But even as he looked to where the priest and the king conversed quietly, no doubt deciding the future of the young woman at his side, he could feel the pressure of Eanflæd's gaze upon him. And, from the edge of his vision he discerned the comely shape of her form beneath her fine clothing. Sweat traced a line down his back.

Perhaps content with the level of his discomfort, Eanflæd had finally broken their silence. She laughed easily, her humour infectious. Beobrand's sombre mood fled, as shadows are banished by the rising of the sun.

"So, how is it that you say I have changed?" he asked.

"When I first saw you, you were crying." She held his gaze in her lambent eyes. "Now it seems to me you are done with tears."

Beobrand sighed.

"I have wept more than my share," he said. "But you speak true. I cry no longer. Tears bring no relief from hurt."

From the head of the table, Eorcenberht's voice cut through the din of the hall.

"Cousin Eanflæd," he said, "come here. I would have you speak with Utta. He is the holy envoy of King Oswiu."

Beobrand noticed that, despite her outward appearance of calm, Eanflæd tensed; a slight rigidity in her shoulders and neck.

"Cousin Eorcenberht," she replied, her voice light and clear, "I will join you shortly. I am not yet done listening to Lord Beobrand's tales."

Eorcenberht's face clouded. The two cousins stared at each other for what seemed a long while, Eorcenberht scowling, Eanflæd responding with an innocent smile. For a moment Beobrand thought the king would repeat his request, perhaps raising his voice and making it an order. But there was something in the way that Eanflæd held her head, the set of her jaw, that told him she would not bend. At last, Eorcenberht waved a hand dismissively.

"As you wish, cousin," he said. "But do not tarry too long, Utta has travelled far and suffered much hardship to be here."

"And so has Lord Beobrand," she replied, with a mischievous glint in her eye. Turning away from the king once more, Eanflæd winked at Beobrand.

"Eorcenberht is such a bully," she whispered. "But he knows not to cross me."

Beobrand marvelled at the young woman. She was as bright as a flash of spring sunlight on the sea. He wondered if Oswiu realised what he was getting with this new alliance being brokered by Utta.

"What is he like?" she asked suddenly.

"Who?"

"Oswiu."

Beobrand's mind raced. What could he tell her of the king of Bernicia? That he was callous and power hungry? That he would stop at nothing to get that which he desired? That he had ordered the death of innocent children to protect the throne? That he had almost certainly sent the very enemies who had raided Ubbanford, killing many there and stealing Beobrand's wealth? But he did not wish to cause her harm. What good could be achieved by such words?

"He is not unhandsome," he said at last.

She laughed again, but the timbre was different, thinner and somewhat wistful. Bitter even.

"You truly think that is my main concern? Our fathers were sworn enemies. And now I am to be tied to this son of Æthelfrith to weave peace between Deira and Bernicia? And what of his wife? Is he not married to a daughter of Rheged? And do they not have children?"

Beobrand took another bite of meat, chewing slowly to give himself time to think. Looking down the hall at the lower benches, Fraomar spotted him and raised his cup with a grin. Beobrand lifted his drinking horn to his gesith in silent salute, then took another long, slow swallow of ale. Gods, he was not the one to talk of such things with this girl. It was Utta, the king's emissary, who had been given the task of discussing all the affairs of the union.

But when he set aside the horn, Beobrand found Eanflæd was staring at him. He could not avoid her gaze, or ignore her plea for answers. She deserved to know.

"Indeed," he said, "Oswiu was married to Rhieinmelth..."

"Was?" she interjected. "What has become of her?"

Beobrand swallowed.

"I heard tell she has been sent to a new minster, where she will pray with the Christ monks."

To his own ears the words sounded hollow.

Eanflæd looked aghast.

"And her children?"

Beobrand thought fleetingly of Octa. Was he being treated kindly? Did he play with Oswiu's son, Alhfrith?

"They remain with the king's household."

"So I am to be queen to my father's enemy and mother to another woman's children."

Now it was Eanflæd's turn to drink deeply from her cup. Did her hand shake?

Beobrand said nothing.

"And what is to stop Oswiu from treating me in the same way as he has dealt with Rhieinmelth?"

Beobrand stared at her, allowing his eyes to drink in her glowing beauty. Her shimmering, golden hair, the long smooth curve of her neck, the intelligent eyes and full, expressive lips. What man would spurn such beauty? And yet, was Rhieinmelth not also beautiful? If Oswiu tired of his new bride, or if he believed he could attain more power by casting her aside, Beobrand knew the king of Bernicia would not hesitate.

Eanflæd guffawed, a deep belly laugh, startling him. She laughed long and hard. He watched on, bemused at her sudden mirth. His skin prickled.

"By Christ's bones," she said when her laughter had subsided, "you are lucky that you are good with a sword, for I fear you will have no luck when it comes to tafl or riddling. You do not need to speak, your face gives away your thoughts as loudly as if you had shouted them."

She wiped tears from her cheeks, then smoothed her dress over her legs, composing herself.

"Do not fear, Beobrand," she said, "I will not make you answer my question. You do not need to say the words that would make you speak ill of your lord." Beobrand couldn't help smiling grimly at the thought. Eanflæd continued, seeming not to notice his expression. "But you and I both know that my prospects of happiness in Bernicia are as likely as my father's ghost approving my union with a son of Æthelfrith."

Beobrand didn't answer, instead he reached for the pitcher of ale and refilled both his horn and her cup. It seemed they would both benefit from a drink.

Chapter 6

For a time Beobrand and Eanflæd shied away from talk of her future. The mood in the hall was convivial and warm as the ale, wine and mead flowed, loosening tongues and relaxing tensions. The strong ale warmed Beobrand's body as he listened to Eanflæd speak of her memories of coming to Cantware when still a child. Bassus had sworn to Edwin that he would protect Eanflæd's mother, Ethelburga, and their children following the terrible defeat at Elmet. Beobrand's left, half-hand crept up to the scar under his left eye, a reminder of the battle in which he had first stood in a shieldwall and slain a man. He had killed countless men since, too many to remember, though their faces often haunted his dreams. But Beobrand would never forget that first foe-man, how his spear had skewered the Waelisc man through the eye, killing him instantly and becoming lodged in the gory socket. Bassus had been by his side then, watching over him, as he had later watched over Edwin's family when they fled south.

"For a long while I did not believe father was truly killed," she said, her voice becoming hollow with distant memories. "He was so strong. Nothing scared him and he never lost a battle."

Beobrand sipped at his ale and looked at the flames of the great hearth fire in the centre of the hall. He recalled how Edwin had seemed an unstoppable force to him when he had pledged his allegiance to him in the hall of Bebbanburg. Later he had served Scand, an old thegn who, with his grey beard and gruff confidence also seemed unbeatable. And then he saw in his mind's eye the horrific sight of King Oswald's head and limbs, skewered on waelstengs as sacrifice for Woden. Despite the ale and the hearth, Beobrand shivered.

"Everybody loses a battle in the end," he said, his tone flat.

"Yes," she said, "I suppose they do. Even you, brave Beobrand of Ubbanford?"

Beobrand snorted.

"Even me. I have suffered my share of defeats."

"And yet you live."

Beobrand frowned. That he still lived when others were but memories was a mystery to him. Often he wished it were not so. Would it not have been better for Acennan to have escaped Rheged and for him to have lost his life? He thought of Acennan's widow, Eadgyth, and their children in the great hall Acennan had built for them. Acennan had so much to live for, and he had given his life for what? For his lord and his friend to be able to rescue their king's remains. Lives sacrificed for a corpse. Beobrand's jaw clenched and he sensed his mood growing as dark as the autumn night outside the hall.

"I am sorry for turning the conversation to death," Eanflæd said. "Let us speak of more pleasant things."

Beobrand nodded, drained his horn once more and wiped his mouth with the back of his hand. He was not yet drunk, but he was well down that path he realised with a start. A quiet voice within told him it would not be wise to drink more. He was in the presence of royalty.

Ignoring the voice, he signalled to a thrall to bring him wine.

"You seem to have prospered here, amongst your mother's people."

"Yes. Eadbald King provided us with everything we needed. He was a great man. He treated me as one of his own children."

Beobrand glanced at Eorcenberht, who gazed in their direction with increasing frequency, clearly frustrated at his cousin's refusal to do his bidding. Beobrand could only imagine how the young king felt at having had to share his father's affections with the vivacious Eanflæd.

"And your mother? She is well?" Beobrand remembered Edwin's haughty, handsome queen. She had been every bit as formidable as her husband.

"My mother fares as well as can be expected for one of her years. She lives now in the minster of Liminge, where she spends most of her time in prayer." She chuckled. "Much like poor Rhieinmelth."

Beobrand fidgeted, uncomfortable to be straying back to talk of what lay in store for Eanflæd in the north. He sipped at the rich wine that had been placed before him. It was even better than the jug that had been brought to their quarters earlier in the day. It was sour and sweet and as dark as blood. It conjured up thoughts of berry-bejewelled bushes, bone-fires and the sacrifices of Blotmonath. He swilled the liquid around his mouth appreciatively.

"There is something I have pondered these past days," he said. "I understand why you would like to have Bassus at your side, for he has ever been a trusted friend of your kin. But why ask Oswiu to send me with the delegation?"

Eanflæd looked him in the eye, amusement tugging at her eyes and mouth.

"That is simple," she said. "I would be protected by the greatest warrior of Northumbria and a thegn of honour who is known to me. I would have the mighty Lord Beobrand as my protector."

Before he could answer, she rose fluidly to her feet.

"I must go and speak to my cousin and the priest now," she said. "They are getting anxious at my disobedience." Beobrand saw that both Utta and Eorcenberht were looking at the princess.

Eorcenberht's face was hard, his eyes narrowed, lips pressed together.

Eanflæd bent down, her face close to Beobrand's. Reaching forward with a slender hand, she tugged free the carved whale tooth hammer amulet that dangled from a thong around his neck.

"You do not worship Christ?" she asked.

"I keep to the old ways," Beobrand answered. "Though I am sure the gods merely watch our deeds on middle earth as we might watch ants or beetles. We are just playthings to them." For an instant his mind was full of thunder, blood and mud; gloom-laden memories of shieldwalls and death and ravens gorging on the broken corpses of valiant men.

Eanflæd leaned in close, so that her voice could not be overheard.

"You pagans have a saying, 'Wyrd bið ful aræd', do you not?" she asked, her breath like butterfly wings on his cheek. "Do you believe that? That one's wyrd is fixed and cannot be changed?"

He swallowed, acutely aware of her closeness and the eyes of the king and the priest boring into him.

"Wyrd goes ever as she will," he replied. "The Sisters weave the threads of our lives. We mortals must just live them as best we can."

She made the sign of the cross with her right hand, touching first her head then chest, then her left shoulder and finishing with her right. Perhaps she was dismayed at such open disregard for the teachings of Christ. But she quickly dispelled that thought with a wink and a mischievous smirk.

"Mayhap it has always been our wyrd to be together, Beobrand," she murmured, letting the amulet fall back against his chest. "I have known you ever since I was a little girl, and I always thought you would one day return."

He well remembered the gangly child he had first met in the stable at Bebbanburg. He took in the curves of her lithesome body beneath the red linen gown. He swallowed once more against the sudden lump in his throat.

"You are a little girl no longer," he said, his words halting and awkward.

She laughed, a rich ripple of giggles.

"Well, I am glad you noticed," she said.

And with that, she turned and swished away towards her cousin, the king, where he waited with the dour little priest from Lindisfarena to discuss the arrangements of her marriage to King Oswiu of Bernicia.

Chapter 7

"What will happen now?" asked Bassus, flinging the shutters open and taking a great deep breath of the cool, crisp air. Thin autumn sun shone through the window.

Beobrand groaned from his pallet.

"How should I know?" Beobrand mumbled, squeezing his eyes shut once more against the stabbing brightness of the chamber. Bassus had awoken him from a pleasant dream. He had been making love with a beautiful woman with hair the hue of gold. Sunniva, he thought, but then, in a flash of guilt and excitement he realised the woman who had come to him in his sleep was Eanflæd. He pulled his blanket over his face and tried to bring back the sensual warmth of the dream-Eanflæd. Already he could only half remember the dream, the memory of it scattering in the light of day like the early morning mist outside. In the darkness under his blanket, he frowned, feeling an acute pang of loss. He had been too long without a woman.

Bassus pulled the blanket away and handed Beobrand a cup.

"Well, it seemed to me that Eanflæd might have told you of her plans last night. You were whispering and giggling like old friends."

Beobrand sniffed the contents of the cup Bassus had given him. Wine. His stomach churned. He rose from his bed and set the cup aside.

"Nonsense," he said, without conviction.

"Nonsense?" Bassus smiled. "Next you will be telling me you did not drink too much last night."

"No, old friend," replied Beobrand, glad that the conversation had moved away from Eanflæd. "I will not make such a claim. The merest whiff of that wine has turned my stomach."

Bassus chortled.

"You never could hold your drink. Get up and we'll go and find some food for you. A full belly is what you need."

Beobrand's mouth filled with spittle at the thought of food, but he took a couple of calming breaths of the fresh morning air and began to dress. As he pulled on his kirtle and began to tie his leg bindings, Bassus paced about the room as he had done the previous day. Beobrand marvelled at the older man's energy. Bassus was already clothed, which Beobrand knew was no easy feat with only one arm. But Bassus was proud and would never accept any help, so Beobrand never offered any. Beobrand knew it was different with women. Bassus was keen to allow Rowena to fuss over him and he had never minded when Reaghan had helped him to fasten his cloak or wind his legs wraps. She had always been kind to Bassus, had loved him as a father. Beobrand could scarcely believe Reaghan had been gone a year now. Anew he felt the stab of guilt at his half-remembered dream.

"You must take care, Beobrand," Bassus said, surprising Beobrand with the intensity of his tone. Gone was his usual jesting, the casual hint of laughter behind his words.

"Care?" asked Beobrand, still fumbling with his bindings whilst fighting the urge to vomit. Looking up at Bassus, he saw the huge warrior was speaking in deadly earnest.

"She is not for you," Bassus said, his face sombre.

Beobrand did not ask Bassus who he was talking about. It seemed his friend was not done with the subject of Eanflæd quite yet.

Beobrand sighed.

"Can't this wait until after I have eaten, or puked? Or both?"

"I don't know. Can it? I know you are not one to listen to advice, but I saw you last night. Gods, everyone saw you. You must be careful. Ploughing another man's field will get you in trouble. Sowing your seed in a furrow owned by a king will get you killed."

Beobrand stood, anger flaring in him as suddenly as the flames had caught on the leaves of the bonfire the day before.

"I am no fool, Bassus. I do not deny that Eanflæd is comely. Any man would be proud to have such a woman at his side." He thought then of her breath on his cheek. The scent of her hair. "But she is not for any man and certainly not for me. She is promised to our lord king. And that is all there is."

He knew that all present at the feast had witnessed the unseemly closeness between the two of them. He could not deny Eanflæd was beautiful and beguiling, her wit as intoxicating as the ale and wine. But she was promised to Oswiu. It would do him no good to think of her. She was as distant a prize for him as if he had sought to pluck the sun from the sky.

As quickly as it had come, so his anger dissipated. Suddenly, surprisingly, Beobrand realised he was hungry.

"Come on," he said, "enough of this nonsense." Bassus raised an eyebrow at that word again. "Let's find some food. I'm famished."

Beobrand grabbed his cloak from where it was draped over one of the stools and strode from the room. Bassus stared after him, his lips pressed together into a thin line. After several heartbeats, he let out a long sigh and followed, shaking his head.

Chapter 8

Sweat plastered Beobrand's hair to his scalp. He skipped backward out of reach of the wooden practice sword Cynan had swung at his chest. It missed him by a finger's breadth. Too close. By Woden, the young Waelisc had grown in skill these past years. Grown in confidence too, from the beaten thrall who had fled Mercia and joined Beobrand's gesithas.

Some of the onlookers, those from Cantwareburh, gasped, sure that they were about to see the mighty Beobrand brought down. The watching Northumbrian warriors were not so quick to pass judgement. They had seen these two spar before, and they had watched both men slaughter countless foe-men before them in the heaving fury and horror of shieldwalls. Both men were tall, strong and as fast as thought. And as deadly as a pestilence.

Cynan could have pressed his attack, Beobrand expected him to, but the younger warrior held back. Beobrand frowned. Was Cynan going easy on him? Beobrand cuffed sweat from his eyes with his forearm and forced a laugh.

"What is the matter, Cynan? Scared I was ready for your next clumsy attack?"

In truth he was glad of the short respite. He had felt better after eating some pottage and taking a drink of water, but he had not expected to exert himself in this manner. But the men had been restless, their talk loud and jarring in the great store hall where they'd slept and had broken their fast. Beobrand understood them. They yet smarted over having allowed the pirates to escape, at losing Dalston. They knew their one task had been to protect Oswiu's emissaries and they had failed. Beobrand spat onto the grass at his feet, already churned and muddy after the opening blows of this bout with Cynan.

Beobrand understood well the anger that came from failure. He had all too often tasted the bitterness of his mistakes. Dalston's death was his fault.

Cynan seemed unencumbered by any sense of remorse or regret. He laughed and took several quick dancing steps, flourishing his wooden blade in an intricate display of prowess.

"I thought you might like a rest, lord," he said, his eyes glimmering in the late-morning sunshine. His breath steamed in the air. It was bright, but the chill of the winter to come was ever present.

Beobrand spat again. Damn the man. Had Cynan not drunk of the rich ale and heady wine in the hall the night before? Beobrand's head pounded and the sweat poured from him as if he had been running a long while. It had been his idea for the men to practice their sword-skill, but he had not thought to participate. But as they had left the stale air of the warriors' barracks behind, Cynan had called out to him in a loud voice. And Beobrand could not ignore the challenge.

"I thought you just wanted a few moments to prance about like a woman," he said. Some of the onlookers chortled.

Without waiting for Cynan to respond, Beobrand sprang forward, leading with his shield, then feinting with his sword at the Waelisc man's knee. At the last moment, when he was sure that Cynan had committed to parry his sword thrust, he darted to the right, flicking out the light practice blade and rapping it against Cynan's shoulder.

Cynan grunted; the smile did not leave his face but Beobrand knew the blow would have hurt. The blades were blunt and not heavy, but neither of the combatants wore any protection. They were stripped to the waist, and were only armed with a wooden sword and a shield apiece.

A cheer rose from the onlookers. Beobrand heard the hurried whispers of wagers being made.

Cynan seemed set to voice another retort, but Beobrand gave him no time. Leaping forward once more, he rained blows down on the Waelisc warrior's shield. Cynan staggered back.

More cheering from those watchers who had bet on the lord of Ubbanford. Beobrand noted there were some groans from the crowd, indicating that not a few had sided with his opponent.

Cynan recovered his balance and danced away, his feet treading lightly on the muddy grass. Beobrand did not chase him, knowing instinctively that to do so would be his undoing. He would be walking into a trap of Cynan's making. No, he would play out this combat for a while longer. He would not be defeated by a cheap trick. He had been bested by Cynan before in such practice bouts, but the man's arrogance rankled. Beobrand would trust him with his life, had done so many times, and he knew that Cynan loved him and was loyal. And yet, Beobrand recalled the moment when they had stood, both bloody and panting, screaming at each other over Sulis' fate. The slave had inflicted the wound that was to kill Reaghan and her life had been forfeit. Cynan had not allowed his lord to strike her down. Ever since then, something had changed between them. Beobrand still trusted Cynan, and Cynan was yet loyal, but there was a tension, an unease. And the two men seemed to often find themselves on the opposing sides of contests of skill or games of chance that were played during the long, dark winter months.

The crowd grew silent as they realised the fight would not be decided so quickly. The outcome was still very much in the balance. The two swordsmen circled each other, shields hefted before them, wooden blades raised and ready.

Cynan gave away his intentions with a barely perceptible tightening of his eyes, but it was enough for Beobrand to anticipate the flurry of savage blows that came. He took the sting from them on his linden board, quickly countering with a low swipe of his blade. Such was the speed of Beobrand's counterattack, coupled with the reach of his long sword arm, that Cynan was forced to retreat once more. His left foot slipped on the wet grass and he stumbled.

Seeing the sudden fear in Cynan's eyes, Beobrand seized the moment. He pushed forward, ready to batter aside the Waelisc man's defences. Victory would be his and he could rest, as he had intended all along. He grinned, sure that he had timed his attack perfectly to capitalise on his gesith's loss of footing.

The crowd were hushed, not breathing, sure this was the moment where the victor would be decided.

A sudden movement behind Cynan drew Beobrand's gaze. A flash of brilliant red and yellow, as bright as any summer flower.

"You see, my dear Godgyth," came a clear, ringing voice, "it is Lord Beobrand."

A ripple ran through the onlookers as they parted to allow the newcomer to view the fight. It was Eanflæd, beautiful and out of place surrounded by the grizzled warriors, with her golden hair, braided and resplendent, a cloak of the finest red-hued wool over a flowing yellow dress of soft linen. Beobrand had the briefest of glimpses of the lustre of her tresses, the bright colours of her clothes, before he hit the ground hard enough to rattle his teeth and to drive the air from his lungs.

For a moment, he lay there, dazed and blinking, the cold, damp of the grass and soil leeching into him. Noise erupted from the crowd and Beobrand understood they had their loser. A shadow fell over him and Cynan offered his hand.

Grimacing, Beobrand took the proffered hand and allowed himself to be hauled to his feet. His gaze met Cynan's. The younger man was no longer grinning. Beobrand's anger was legendary, and it was no small matter to tumble one's lord onto his backside, especially before so many witnesses. For several heartbeats, Beobrand clenched Cynan's hand in a crushing grip, their eyes locked. All around them, the men chattered about what they had seen. Someone whistled at the princess and her maidservant. Bassus' loud laughter broke the stillness that had fallen on the two fighters.

At last, Beobrand offered Cynan a rueful smile.

"You did well," he said. "I almost had you."

"It seems the Sisters of Wyrd smiled on me this day."

Beobrand dropped his shield with a clatter onto the wooden sword.

"It would seem so."

Cynan said, "Perhaps the Sisters are repaying me."

Beobrand frowned.

"How so?"

"Well, I once saved a woman from your sword, and now a lady saves me from your blade."

Anger flashed within Beobrand, hot and deadly. There was nothing to be compared in not taking the blood-price from a murderous, mad slave, and him being distracted by the arrival of a lady of noble birth.

Beobrand had to resist the urge to lash out, to scream at the Waelisc man. But this was Cynan's way. He meant nothing by it. And yet Beobrand felt his ire roil within him like a living thing. He clamped his jaw shut, his teeth grinding and turned away without a word.

Eanflæd stood before him. Her smiling eyes, glistening in the sunlight, made her appear even more delightful than she had at the feast.

"I was looking for you, Lord Beobrand," she said, the smile in her voice too. "I was prepared to wait until you finished your training, you did not have to let your adversary beat you quite so quickly."

Her laughter washed over him like a balm. Beobrand felt his ire melting away, like blood being scrubbed from battle harness.

"Well," he said, raising his voice for all those gathered to hear, "I would rather trade words with one of your beauty than have to deal with the clumsy blows of this Waelisc butcher who thinks himself skilled in battle-play." Laughter from the company. "Besides," he said, leading her away from the men, but allowing his voice to still carry to them, "I need a rest after all that wine you plied me with last night."

The sounds of laughter followed them.

Chapter 9

They had only taken a few paces when Beobrand shivered, his skin prickling with the sweat drying in the cool air.

Gods, he had stripped off his kirtle before crossing blades with Cynan! Without a word, he hurried back to retrieve the garment. Bassus, clearly waiting for him to realise his state of undress, was holding the kirtle out to him. Beobrand snatched it from his friend's grasp and tugged it over his sweat-drenched hair and wriggled his arms into the sleeves. Bassus shook his head.

"Be careful," he whispered. Beobrand met his gaze but said nothing.

The gathered men grinned at Beobrand. He growled at them to cover his embarrassment. Without a word, he jogged back to where Eanflæd waited patiently with her gemæcce. His face was hot now, gone the feeling of chill in the air.

Laughter followed him again, and he saw the princess bite her lip to avoid sniggering. Angrily, Beobrand strode off. After a moment Eanflæd caught up with him, matching his pace. Godgyth, her maid servant, did not rush, but followed several paces behind them, a disapproving expression on her face.

Beobrand and Eanflæd walked in silence for a while.

He felt foolish and diminished before his men. Cynan was ever testing his strength, his resolve, his leadership. To lead men was a lonely task. Success did not merely rely on oaths, but on reputation and respect. Each were built over years, but could be lost in an instant. This meant nothing to his gesithas, he told himself. They were the most loyal of men. He glanced at the slender beauty at his side. By Woden All-father, he had run to her like a puppy. The men would think him weak to be so easily controlled by a girl.

For a moment, he thought of Eowa, and how he had almost lost his life and plunged Albion into war over just such a girl. Eowa, gone now, but he would surely not be the last man to have his head turned by a pretty girl, or the last to act stupidly whilst in love's thrall.

What was he thinking? This was not love. He could never have Eanflæd. Beobrand shuddered.

To avoid the shade of the buildings, he led them towards a row of old box trees. Beobrand had noticed the lifelike marble statues that stood there, gazing blindly at a world their creators had long since departed. In the distance Beobrand could make out the huge vaulted walls of the amphitheatre. Crumbling and overgrown with weeds, it was seldom used now, and never for the purpose for which it was built.

Beobrand remembered coming to Cantwareburh with his uncle Selwyn. He winced at the memory. He had believed him to be his uncle then, now he knew the truth. The father he had wished for but had never had. He recalled Selwyn bringing him and his older brother, Octa, all the way to this place, a day's journey from their steading on the coast. On one such trip, the strangely semi-circular building he could now see rising above the walls of the courtyard had housed a slave market. He had begged Selwyn to take them, but his uncle had refused. "We have no money for slaves," he had said and had led them away from the huge building and the raucous shouts of the vendors hawking their wares.

Later, Selwyn had entered into a deep conversation with an old friend of his, a burly smith who had welcomed Selwyn like a lost brother. The two men had sat by the warmth of the banked forge talking of old times, better times as old men always believe. The smith had produced a flask of strong mead and they had not noticed when Octa and Beobrand had slipped away. The boys had run back through the streets of Cantwareburh, drawn towards the noise, smells and excitement of the slave market the way wasps are attracted to rotting apples. When they had arrived, their senses had been assaulted. The stench of shit mingled with that of ale and roasting meat. The slavers led their captive thralls onto the platform beneath the tiered ranks of seated prospective buyers. They screamed out the good qualities of the enslaved Waelisc they sought to sell.

Beobrand had not thought of that day for many years, but the sight of the amphitheatre brought it all tumbling back into his mind. The building had been a cacophony of noise, but it was the silence that had stayed with Beobrand. The stillness of the slaves. They would shuffle forward when their owners tugged their ropes, but they did not move unless forced to do so. They did not speak. Some of the thralls were tall, strong, muscled and scarred with the reminders of sharp blades and battles. Warriors, no doubt. Proud men. Men who had served a lord once, sworn oaths, riddled and laughed with their spear-brothers whilst basking in the heat of a great hall's hearth fire. And yet these men did not fight for their freedom now. All around them echoed jeering yells and shouts, the slave masters prodded their flesh, pulled open their mouths to show the strength of their teeth. And yet these once proud men had stood, shoulders slumped and heads down, as placid as kine. All of the slaves there had one thing that united them, a trait that made them seem to be of one kindred: their eyes. No tears, no defiance. The eyes had been empty; the people broken.

Beobrand did not know what he had expected to find there in that great, bustling edifice, but the shuffling, still, broken men, women and children had filled him with dismay. He had not mentioned how he'd felt to Octa, but they had not been there long when, as if by unspoken agreement, they had turned and left the noisome market behind them.

Looking up at one of the statues, a bearded, well-muscled man, Beobrand snorted. It reminded him of Selwyn. When Octa and he had returned to Selwyn at the forge, their uncle and the smith had still been talking, laughing and drinking, recounting tales of the old days, the better days when they had been young and had raided foreign lands. And made thralls of their defeated enemies. The brothers had settled down to wait for their uncle to finish. If Selwyn had known they had disobeyed him that day, he never spoke of it.

"You are deep in thought," said Eanflæd, her soft voice breaking his reverie. A light breeze whispered through the boughs of the trees above them.

"I was thinking of my brother," Beobrand said, his voice more gruff than he had intended.

"I often come here and look at the statues," she said.

They walked on. The next stone figure was of an older man, slimmer, with a sharp nose like a seax blade. Both the arms had been snapped from the statue, leaving nothing but rocky stumps. Beobrand thought of Bassus.

"I wonder about the people who made these images," she said. "The features of these men live for eternity, and yet we know not who they were. Did they have children? Were they honourable? How did they die? We will never know. But it saddens me that we have lost the skill to carve stone in this way." She reached out long, sensuous fingers and caressed the cold, unyielding cheek of the statue. "You and I have both lost many loved ones," she said and sighed wistfully. "I can barely remember what my brothers or my father looked like. I come here and I imagine them to resemble these long-forgotten men from far-off Roma."

She strode along the line of statues. It was Beobrand's turn to hurry after her. She halted at a bust of a bald, square-jawed patrician. It conjured up the impression of King Edwin's features; the same bold glare, strong forehead and broad, corded neck.

"I would like to have statues of those I have lost," she said, gazing up at the bust's face. "My memories are weak."

"Memories are all we have," said Beobrand. "A carved face would change nothing. Do these men yet live?"

"No," she whispered, subdued by his harsh tone. "But their faces can be seen. That is something, is it not?"

Beobrand looked at the unmoving, frozen faces, captured in stone by the skill of some long-dead craftsman. He searched the statues for features to remind him of Octa. Or Acennan. He saw none.

"Dead is dead," he intoned, the words like a curse. "No stone will change that."

She turned away from him. The maid servant glowered at him and Beobrand felt sorry for his words. The girl sought comfort and he gave her the hard truths of a warrior.

He was about to apologise when a commotion from the direction of the great hall caught his attention. A small group of people were rushing towards them. Beobrand's hand fell to his belt, fingers seeking out the reassuring hilt of Hrunting or the bone handle of his seax, but they were guests in Eorcenberht's hall, and none of the Northumbrians bore weapons within the grounds of the royal vill.

Some of the men who were hurrying across the grass carried long spears, the thin autumn light flickering from the sharp points. Unease scratched at his neck and he moved to stand before Eanflæd. She halted, looked to him quizzically. She had not seen the approaching figures. But Beobrand's gesithas, who had continued their weapon-play, were not so oblivious to the possible danger. The snap of Cynan's warning reached Beobrand and he watched as they ceased their practice and, armed only with the oaken practice blades and their black-daubed shields, his men sped to intercept the spear-men who came from the hall.

Cynan led the men at a run and met the approaching warriors a few dozen paces from Beobrand, Eanflæd and her gemæcce. Beobrand's pride in them swelled. Even unarmoured, they sought to protect their lord.

"Wait there," Beobrand snapped to Eanflæd and strode forward. Eanflæd followed close behind and he shot her an angry look. She ignored him, taking control.

"What is the meaning of this, Thurstan?" she asked, her voice steady and loud. Despite himself, Beobrand smiled. Who was he to order her? This was her cousin's land. She was the daughter of Edwin, Bretwalda of all Albion, and she would answer to no man.

"I am sorry, my lady," one of the three spear-bearing guards said. He was a thickset man, with a fighter's lithe gait and broad shoulders. His face was red and sweat beaded his forehead. "We told her she would need to wait," the man panted. "We said we would see to it that your guest received the message, but she was past us as quick as a stoat."

The red-faced man stepped forward then, and grabbed at the shoulder of a figure that Beobrand had failed to notice before. It was a woman, shoulders heaving from exertion, the hem of her dress mud-stained. Now she was trapped between the door wards and the ragged shieldwall formed by Beobrand's gesithas.

Thurstan pulled the woman back roughly, but she shook off his grip and wheeled on him, a desperate fury upon her.

"Unhand me," she yelled. Thurstan hesitated, then released her.

There was something in that voice, in that tone of contempt. Something familiar.

"Who are you?" Eanflæd asked, and as the woman swung to face the princess, Beobrand knew the answer.

Chapter 10

"**M**y name is Udela, wife of Scrydan of Hithe," the woman said.

Beobrand could make no sense of this. Udela was a childhood friend and he had not seen her in years. Their last encounter had been some six years before and it had not ended well. Beobrand had given her husband, Scrydan, the reeve of Hithe, a beating and left Udela tending to his wounds. He had not thought to see her again.

Gods, what was she doing here?

Eanflæd asked the question for him.

"What business do you have here?" she asked.

"Pardon, Lady Eanflæd," Udela said, her breath coming more easily now. "I am sorry for disturbing you, but I must speak with Beobrand."

"And what would you say to Lord Beobrand?" Eanflæd asked.

"I would speak with him of an urgent matter, lady."

Udela was much as Beobrand remembered her. Perhaps her face was a little less plump and her eyes bore a certain strained expression he could not place, but she was still the Udela he had known, comely, wide-hipped and heavy-breasted.

Eanflæd turned to Beobrand.

"You know this woman?"

"I do."

Eanflæd fixed him with a lingering gaze.

"I see."

Eanflæd assessed the situation and waved the guards away.
"This woman poses us no threat."

"Let her pass," Beobrand said to his men. They lowered their
black shields and Udela approached hesitantly. All the while she
stared at Beobrand as if she was searching for something in his
face. Though what she sought, Beobrand had no idea.

Beobrand's gesithas followed her passing with undisguised
interest, their gaze tracking the sway of her shapely hips and the
ample curve of her chest. Beobrand scowled at them.

"Away with you. Back to your sword practice."

The men grumbled, and trudged reluctantly back to the
expanse of grass they had been using for their bouts. Cynan
nodded and raised his wooden sword in salute to Beobrand.

"You did well," Beobrand said. Cynan grinned and jogged
after the rest of the men. The Waelisc warrior's confidence was
galling, but there was no doubt of his skill. Or of his loyalty.

The avenue of box trees and statues was once more peaceful,
a haven of scattered shadows, the languid whisper of wind in the
leaves, and the impassive gazes of men who passed no judgement
on the lives of those who walked beneath them.

Beobrand looked down at his hands. They were trembling.
Clenching his fists to halt their tremor, he spoke to Udela at last.
Eanflæd was looking on eagerly, expectantly awaiting to hear
what tidings could have brought this woman from Hithe in such
a hurried frenzy. Beobrand was just as keen to know, but he had
a sinking feeling that he would not like what news Udela had
brought with her.

"Well," he said, his voice sharp, "what brings you to
Cantwareburh?"

Udela did not react at his harsh tone. She smoothed her skirts
and returned his gaze.

"I heard you had come here, from the north," she replied. "When I learnt this I thought perhaps God had sent you to aid me." She spoke with a measured tone, as if she had long thought of this moment, but there was an urgency to her every word, her every movement. It seemed to Beobrand she was willing herself to speak slowly, to use each word carefully as one might pull stones from a dam, scared that with each new stone, the pressure would prove too much and the dam would burst, letting out a torrent.

Beobrand's sense of unease grew. Eanflæd said nothing, but her eyes were wide as she listened.

"And why would God send me? What has happened that you would rush here and risk being struck down by the wardens of Eorcenberht's hall to see me?"

"I knew not where else to turn. I thought that if anyone could help me, it would be the great Beobrand." Was there a tinge of sarcasm in her words? Beobrand recalled mistaking her for a would-be attacker and striking her face. He was certain of few things, but that he was not great was one of them.

"But help you with what? Is it Scrydan?" He searched her face for signs, bruises. Much can happen in six years.

"No, not Scrydan." Udela's words caught in her throat as she stifled a sob. "It is Ardith."

Ardith. Udela's daughter. Beobrand remembered the pretty, stern, fair-haired girl.

"What has happened to Ardith?" he asked.

"She is gone."

"Gone?"

"Taken." Again the sob.

"Speak clearly, woman," Beobrand said. "Who took her?"

Udela took a steadying breath, willing herself to be calm with obvious effort. Eanflæd shot Beobrand an angry glance. He ignored her. It seemed something terrible had happened. He would know what.

"I don't know who they were," Udela said. "They came in ships. Brought things to trade and were gone with the next tide. They took Ardith with them."

"You were there?"

"No, I was away at my sister, Inga's, at Tenet Waraden. Ardith was with her father."

"And yet you are here." Beobrand frowned. He felt nothing but disdain for his former friend, Scrydan.

Udela lowered her gaze. "He told me you would turn me away. Or not see me at all."

"What did he say happened on the beach?"

"That they took a liking to my girl and snatched her into their boats." Seeing the expression on Beobrand's face, Udela continued, "I know what you think of him. No man is without flaws, but Scrydan fought for her. His face was battered and bruised and he has wept ever since I have returned from Inga's."

"And he is now searching for your daughter? Has he set sail after these men?"

Again she looked to the ground.

"No," she said, her voice small.

"And you are here," he said. "To find a man who will search for her. For one who will bring her back to you?"

"Yes," she said, and met his gaze. Her eyes were red-rimmed and full of woe. "He told me I was a fool to come. That you would never see me, and certainly not agree to seek out Ardith. But I told him he was wrong."

"I am sorry that this thing has happened. I remember Ardith and I am sure she is a fine young woman now. But she might have been taken anywhere in Albion. Or even to Hibernia or the gods know where. I cannot go searching for every girl who gets taken by slavers." Even as he said the words, he regretted his harsh tone. But it was the truth and she must hear it. Better to be told the truth than to be given false hope. She stared at him now, her mouth working, but she uttered no words. Tears traced lines through the dirt of her face. "I am oath-sworn," he continued. "Even if I wished to do this thing you ask, I am bound by my oath to my lord."

"Scrydan said you would not help, but I told him he was wrong. Because," she said, rubbing the tears away roughly with the back of her hand, "I know something that he does not."

"What is that?" Eanflæd spoke for the first time.

Udela turned to the slender beauty. She made to speak, but no sound came.

"Do not be afraid," Eanflæd said in a gentle voice. "You can speak freely here, Udela, wife of Scrydan."

Udela gave her the slightest of nods and swallowed.

"Ardith is Beobrand's daughter," she said.

Chapter 11

Eanflæd took Udela under her wing; the youthful, slender princess caring for the older, dishevelled and distraught mother as if it were the most natural thing in the world. They shared few words after Udela's revelation. Beobrand's mind spun as if he had been struck a blow to the head, and Udela's veil of calm finally ripped apart. She began to weep, angry at herself as she cuffed the tears from her face, apologising all the while to Eanflæd and her gemæcce as they led her away. Eanflæd looked towards Beobrand then. He said nothing, but her expression pained him. She was disappointed in him.

Bassus approached him shortly after. Beobrand told him haltingly of the tidings Udela had brought.

"By Tiw's cock," Bassus said, "is it true, lad?"

Beobrand did not answer, a look was enough. He remembered the night he had lain with Udela. It was not an experience worth pondering, it had been over quickly, a momentary elation rapidly replaced by guilt and regret. But no man forgets his first woman.

Bassus cursed again and left him alone, only to return a short while later with a flask of the steward's good wine. Beobrand snatched the flask eagerly and took a long pull.

"You wish to talk?" Bassus asked.

Beobrand shook his head.

"No. I'll walk awhile."

"Someone should be with you."

"I am safe here. I would be alone."

Taking the flask of wine with him, he wandered along the path between the box trees and their carved guardians, the empty eyes of the statues mocking him. The crack and snap of the wooden practice blades and the grunts and shouts of the men receded as he drew further away from the sparring gesithas. He rounded a corner, taking him around the far side of the barn where the Northumbrian warriors were being housed. There he found a slab of masonry, a door lintel perhaps from a previous structure that no longer stood. Whether by chance or design it was placed in such a way as to capture the thin autumn sun as it sank into the west. He sat, gazing absently at the smoke drifting up in a haze from the buildings of Cantwareburh. He sipped the wine and shivered. The stone beneath him was cold, the sun not warm enough to heat it. The tranquil solitude of the place contrasted with the maelstrom of thoughts that flapped and fluttered in his thought-cage like so many ravens after a great battle.

A daughter! Could it truly be so? In his memory's eye he saw Ardith as she had been when last he had seen her. Fair hair bouncing as she ran, the serious expression and sombre determination in those piercing blue eyes. He took a swig of wine. His stomach threatened to rebel, a sudden queasiness gripping him. He was not sure if it was the drink that caused the feeling or his certain knowledge that he had another child. A girl. A half-sister to Octa.

If she yet lived.

Gods knew where she was. Beobrand shuddered again, this time not from the cold of the seat. By Woden and all the gods, he had abandoned his daughter. First, to a life with that miserable whoreson Scrydan, and now to a fate as a slave, taken from her home. Terrified. Abused. He thought of Reaghan and the sadness and fear that had always been a part of her, like a snaggle-toothed pike lurking expectantly beneath the still surface of a dark river ready to strike the instant a hand trailed in the water. Reaghan had been stolen from her family many years before. She could scarcely remember them, but such scars were never truly healed.

The thought of Ardith, his own kin, suffering at the hands of rough men, filled him with a terrible, impotent rage. Beobrand drank more wine, feeling it now blurring the jagged edges of his thoughts. He spat. Closing his eyes, he leant back and sighed. He'd thought he was done with Hithe forever, but it seemed his birthplace kept pulling him back with its secrets and his own blood.

A soft crunch of a footfall on the path's dry leaves alerted him to someone approaching. Opening his eyes he saw the familiar figure of Coenred. The young monk tentatively stepped closer and Beobrand sighed again.

"Shouldn't you be praying?" he asked.

Coenred sat beside Beobrand on the stone slab.

"Utta gave me permission to come and speak with you."

Beobrand closed his eyes once more. Perhaps Coenred would leave him be.

"I don't want to talk."

"Bassus thought you needed a friend to speak to."

"Did he indeed?" said Beobrand, his eyes snapping open. "I told him I wanted to be alone."

"He merely worries about you, Beo," Coenred said, his tone soft, soothing. They had known each other a long time and Beobrand could not maintain his anger at the monk for more than a short while.

He took another draught of wine.

"What did he tell you?" he asked.

"Nothing, save that you had received bad tidings. If you would like to unburden yourself, I would hear of what ails you. Gothfraidh always used to say 'A shared pain is halved, a shared joy is doubled.'"

Beobrand let out a long, ragged breath. Perhaps it would help to speak to Coenred. He was a good listener and Beobrand trusted him completely. They had been through so much together since they had first met all those years before in the small monastery of Engelmynster. The mention of old Gothfraidh, who had been slain during the attack on Ubbanford the year before, was a harsh reminder of how much Coenred had suffered through knowing him.

Taking a deep breath, Beobrand told his friend of what he had learnt from Udela. Coenred waited patiently until he was finished, face sombre, hands clasped in his lap. When Beobrand had concluded his tale Coenred, usually so eager to speak, sat silently. After a time he reached over with his slender hand and plucked the wine flask from Beobrand's grasp. The young monk took a deep swallow and then returned the vessel with a rueful smile.

"What are you going to do?"

"What can I do?" asked Beobrand, his voice desolate. "I have abandoned my daughter and now she is lost."

"Those words do not sound like those spoken by my friend, Beobrand of Ubbanford. No matter the obstacles placed before him, he has never shied away from doing what is right."

"I am no craven, Coenred, as well you know." Beobrand's voice took on the hard edge of steel. "I am not scared for myself. But I have failed my children. They are the only kin I have and I have failed them both."

Beobrand took another sip of the wine and then passed the flask back to Coenred. After the merest hesitation, Coenred took it and drank again.

"You cannot be blamed for what has happened to Ardith, Beobrand. You knew nothing of her blood ties to you. And you have not failed Octa."

"He is with Oswiu's household. He is not safe there."

Coenred pondered this for a moment, frowning.

"Surely Octa is safe enough with the king," he said. "No harm will befall him."

"My son will be safe for as long as I keep my oath to my lord." Beobrand took the flask from Coenred, lifted it to his lips and drained the last of its contents.

Coenred said, "All men know that your oath is like iron. You will not break it, so Octa is safe."

"But if I do that which Oswiu has ordered, I must turn my back on Udela. If I return to Bernicia with Eanflæd, who will search for Ardith? The man she thinks of as her father is a nithing. Scrydan will do nothing and with every passing moment her trail grows colder. It may already be too late to ever find her. I cannot bear the thought of merely walking away and leaving Ardith to her wyrd."

Coenred turned to face Beobrand, his face serious, eyes fervent.

"It seems to me that in everything God has a purpose," he said. "It was the Almighty that saw to it that you were here, in Cantwareburh, at the very time that your daughter was taken. I do not believe the Lord sent you here to know more torment and to do nothing. If I know how you will respond, so does our Heavenly Father who knows everything. He knows it is your nature to seek justice." Coenred took a deep breath and ran his slim fingers through the hair that grew long and lush at the back of his head. "You have never turned away from me when I have been in danger. I do not believe you are able to turn away from a friend whose life is at risk."

Beobrand frowned.

"I did not protect Dalston." For an instant he recalled the splash of red and the pallid, terrified face as the monk had disappeared beneath the slate-dark waves.

Coenred sighed. He took a deep breath and wiped a hand over his features.

"You are but a man, Beo. Even you cannot save everybody."

Coenred's words stabbed like a seax blade. Anger suddenly sparked within Beobrand. The faces of so many dead crowded his dreams.

"I do not need you to remind me of all those I have lost. Too often have I failed to protect those in my care. Those I love."

"And yet you have saved my life several times. And there are many alive today who would be dead if not for the strength of your shield, your skill with a sword. You are but a man, Beobrand. But one born to help others. I believe this is God's purpose for you. You wield a sword better than any other warrior I have witnessed, and without your sword many more lives would have been lost. You are God's instrument. The Lord's weapon on middle earth."

This talk of gods unnerved Beobrand. Oswald had said similar to him before.

A solitary crow flapped overhead. Beobrand recalled ravens croaking in delight at the bloodshed before the Great Wall. Blood that he had spilt in the name of Woden. He shivered.

"Even if it is as you say, and the gods know that I would follow Udela to Hithe to find out what has happened to our daughter, if I do so, I will have defied Oswiu. I cannot set myself on the path of saving a daughter I do not know whilst placing my only son into danger." He spat, his mouth sour now from the wine. "Oswiu is not a forgiving man."

Coenred's brow furrowed as he thought on the problem.

After a time he said, "Perhaps there is a way."

"I can see none."

"You must trust in the Lord."

Beobrand snorted. He thought that if the gods watched him, they would enjoy the chaos and confusion.

"I do not hold out much hope. I can see no clear way forward. And I do not think your god cares for the likes of me."

As if in answer to his comment, Eanflæd swept around the corner. Her face was flushed and her eyes twinkled.

"I have been thinking of your situation," she said, her voice breathless, as if she had been running, "and I believe I have a solution."

Coenred smirked at the princess's sudden arrival. The young monk raised an eyebrow and looked at Beobrand.

"You were saying?" he said.

Beobrand shook his head in disbelief. Above them, more crows flew overhead, their croaking calls like harsh chuckles of mirthless laughter.

"Well then, Eanflæd, daughter of Edwin," Beobrand said. "Let's hear this plan of yours."

Chapter 12

Ardith's face was dripping wet. Her cheeks stung from the chill wind as it cooled the tears and sea spray that mingled there. The prow of the ship lifted over a white-flecked wave and then plunged down the other side, sending up another great sheet of water. The sea splashed over Ardith in a torrent, drenching her. Her bedraggled hair was whipped about her face by the strength of the breeze, and yet she was unable to push the damp strands away, for to do so she would need to loosen her grip on the stay that she clung to, and she feared that if she did that, she would lose her hold on the ship and be flung from the pitching deck into the dark, frigid waters of the Narrow Sea. Like most of the people of Hithe, Ardith could swim, but she knew that she would never be able to remain afloat long enough for the ships to swing around to search for her. Even if she could swim for long enough, they would have a hard time finding her in this rough sea of foam-flecked waves. And, given how cold it was, with the promise of snow in the air, she thought she would surely die long before the pirates would be able to rescue her.

On the first day after she had been carried aboard, she had thought about throwing herself into the sea, to end her life before she should know more misery. And yet, although she cowered and shook and wept where she had lain, huddled in the stern of the ship all that long day, she had not acted to cut short her pain in the most final of ways. As that first day had grown dim with the setting of the sun through the watery clouds that lay low on the horizon, Grimr, the leader of the pirates, had brought her a bowl of thin stew that one of the sailors had cooked on a smoky fire that smouldered on the ballast rocks in the belly of the ship. The pirate captain had not spoken, merely passing the food to her with his gnarled hands, nodding when she had taken the bowl from him and had begun to spoon the pottage into her mouth. It had been watery, with stringy pieces of grey meat, the flesh of hapless gulls that the sailors caught with lines trailing from the ship. But Ardith had been ravenous and the stew was warm. As she'd swallowed the food, she had resolved that she would not succumb to the dark thoughts of death that had assailed her.

She would live. And she would return home.

The rope thrummed in her grasp and the boards of the ship groaned and grumbled from the sea's buffeting, as if it sought to engulf the vessel, to smash the puny timber bark and to scatter the pathetic men and one small girl who dared ride upon its ever-moving surface.

Ardith had been frightened the first time she had stood at the prow, allowing the water and wind to slap her skin, to drench her peplos. But in the days since she had been taken, she had grown to love standing with the ship behind her. Her feet, soaked by the spray, squelched in her shoes. They leaked terribly. She had not worn them for a long while before the morning her father had led her down to the strand in Hithe and the leather had not been properly coated in tallow. Many of the seamen were barefoot, their callused feet gripping the slick planks of the deck better than any shoe. Ardith's shoes pinched her feet as she made her way forward, past the hungry eyes of the men, but she refused to cast them aside. She had little to remind her of happier times, but she recalled her mother's smile when she had first spied the fine leather shoes.

Ardith planted her feet, holding the rope tightly in both hands, and watched the sea rolling towards them. She would remain there for as long as she could bear the chill. Until shivering overcame her and she would totter on legs stiff from cold, back through the whistling and laughing seamen to the relative warmth of the blanket Grimr had tossed to her on her first night aboard.

She had taken to sleeping wrapped in the coarse woollen cloth at the stern of the ship, on the opposite side to the helmsman. There she had the wooden wale of the ship's side at her back and beyond that, the endless sea. All the sailors were before her, where she could watch them and be warned if any approached. So far, none had done more than shout obscenities, but she was no fool, and knew well what men wanted. Grimr had told them to leave her be, and the men had obeyed their leader. And yet she felt the men's eyes roving over her, as they might a laden ceapscip, a trading vessel, that they hoped to plunder. She prayed to the Blessed Virgin that the pirate leader's hold on his men was strong, and she pushed the thoughts from her mind of what awaited her when they reached their destination and Grimr found the wealthy buyers he had spoken of. Men who would pay handsomely for a young, fair-haired girl.

It was easier to forget about the men, Grimr and what her wyrd would bring when she stood gazing out at the waves. In those moments she felt alone. Alone with the roar of the ocean, the snap of the sail, the rush of the wind and the creaking of the beams and thwarts. There was seldom any other sign of men on the vast expanse of the sea. The ship that carried her was called *Saeslaga*, and it was Grimr's ship. The other ships, *Waegmearh* and *Brimwulf*, always followed in *Saeslaga*'s wake.

Ignoring the ship behind her, she imagined herself to be alone and free. She watched white fulmars swooping over the waves, dark cormorants and bright gannets diving into the water like spears from the heavens, and brightly coloured puffins streaking low over the water, wings beating furiously as they flew to their rocky homes on the cliffs and rocks on the coast of Albion. Despite herself, she smiled at the sea birds, laughed for joy at their freedom and imagined herself to be one of them, speeding along close to the wave tops.

Without warning a sleek shape broke the surface of the water and flew through the air in front of the prow. Before it struck the water and darted beneath the waves, she made out the powerfully muscled body, the colour of cold iron, the fin that arched from its smooth back, the snout and the clever eyes that seemed to stare at her. Ardith's breath caught in her throat. She could still see the creature, powering its body through the water just beneath the surface, keeping itself just before *Saeslaga*'s bow wave. With a sudden burst of speed, the great fish leapt once more from the sea. For an instant it hung in the bitter air and appeared to smile at her.

Despite the cold and the misery that threatened to overwhelm her, Ardith let out a laugh. She did not mean to, but the animal was so full of joy at its own energy, seeming to relish the chance to show her its skill and agility.

Once more it slipped beneath the waves, and then, instantly leapt high before the ship. She laughed again, as the animal jumped and cavorted in the waves as if for her amusement. It easily kept ahead of the ship, but seemed to enjoy the company of the girl who stared down at its play from the prow of the sleek wooden wave-steed. Beyond the playful dolphin, Ardith spied several more. They too shot out of the surf, spinning in the air with abandon. But they did not approach so close to *Saeslaga*. Fleetingly, Ardith wondered what it was that made this one animal braver, or more curious, than the others of its family. What made some men brave, and some cowards? She thought of her father, and how his feet had crunched into the shingle of the beach as he had walked away from her. He had not turned around, despite her cries for help.

Another, sudden flash of movement caught her attention. Draca, the one-eyed, red-bearded sailor who had restrained her on the beach at Hithe, was at her side. He held something high above him, his arm outstretched. For a heartbeat Ardith could not make sense of what she saw, then the westering sun glinted from the wicked, barbed tip of the spear the pirate held poised, and she shuddered. Draca drew back his arm and grimaced with concentration, clearly anticipating the movements of the dolphin that sped along just beneath the sea's surface.

With the now-familiar surge of power from its tail, the animal once more sprang from the waves into the cold air.

"No!" Ardith cried out, whether in anger at Draca, or in warning to the dolphin, she was not sure. The single word was filled with all of her pent-up misery and anger and the sound of her own voice shocked her with its intensity. Did the dolphin falter in its headlong flight? Was it possible that it had heard her and attempted to make sense of her cry?

But even as she thought this, the glimmer of hope was snuffed out as Draca's arm lashed forward and his lance flew fast and true, trailing a slender line behind it. He let out a roaring bellow of triumph as the iron head of the harpoon buried itself deeply into the sea creature's flesh. Crimson billowed in the water and the dolphin, once so graceful and full of joy, tumbled clumsily in the waves. Its tail thrashed, churning pink-foamed surf around *Saeslaga*'s bow.

"No!" Ardith screamed again. She flung herself at Draca, beating upon his shoulder, left arm and chest with her small fists. The brawny sailor just laughed and began to play in the line, pulling it in and coiling it with expertly practised movements.

More laughter rolled across the deck, as the other sailors watched Ardith berating Draca.

All the while Ardith screamed and cried.

She sobbed, tasting the bitter tang of salt on her lips as her tears streamed down her cheeks. *Saeslaga* ploughed into another wave, sending a fresh wall of spray over both Ardith and Draca. The water tasted like her tears. Was that the metallic hint of blood on her tongue?

She scanned the waters around the ship. The dolphins had vanished. Draca cursed as the injured creature pulled itself beneath the hull, threatening to snag or tangle the line.

The terrible sorrow that had filled Ardith at seeing the joyful animal struck, fled as quickly as it had flooded through her. In its place was an all-encompassing rage. Gone was her fear of these men, or of losing her hold on the rigging and being lost overboard into the icy waters. All of her terror and sadness vanished in an instant, as if the wave had washed it away. She felt her skin grow hot, as though she had bathed in an ocean of fury, and she lunged forward.

This was no random flailing of weak fists against the huge sailor's bulky frame. No. Ardith fixed her gaze on the knife that hung at Draca's belt. It was of simple design, bone handled, with a blade not much longer than a man's finger, but it would suffice, she was sure. If it had a keen edge.

Without warning, she grasped the knife and slid it from its leather sheath. For a moment she thought about plunging it into Draca then, into his exposed neck. He was fully focused on reeling in the line, on capturing his prize. No, she must do something first, then she could stab the red-bearded bastard over and over. Her ire broiled and brimmed within her, as rough and huge as the sea.

Before Draca could react, she snatched the line and, thanking the Virgin that the man kept his blade sharp, she sawed through the hemp cord with two fast slicing cuts. It slithered over the side of the ship and disappeared into the darkness beneath the prow.

There was an instant when Draca continued to pull in the loose line, then his eye narrowed and he spun on Ardith.

She meant to slay him then. Her anger was a living thing within her and she had lost all control of it. But she was no trained killer. She was just a girl, with a tear-streaked face and sodden dress plastering her slender form, quivering with rage before a broad-shouldered sea-thief.

Ardith screamed and threw herself forward, swinging the wickedly sharp knife at Draca's face, hoping to take his other eye. The pirate swayed out of the reach of her clumsy attack and caught her wrist. He squeezed, his powerful hands grinding the fragile bones together. Ardith yelped and dropped the knife. Draca lashed out and caught her a thundering blow with the back of his left hand, which sent her staggering away. Her head filled with bright light and she fell to the wet deck, dazed.

A moment later, Grimr was there. He pushed Draca away from Ardith.

"Leave her, brother," he shouted. "It is like throwing gold over the side to strike her and damage what we mean to trade. She can give us back all we have lost!"

Draca allowed himself to be restrained. Grimr shoved him away and Draca shouted at Ardith as he stalked down the length of the ship.

"Stupid bitch. You know that fish will die. Better we should eat of its meat than have it go to waste."

Ardith pushed herself shakily to her feet. Again she tasted blood. She wiped her hand against her mouth. It came away smeared red. Her hand was trembling, and she realised her whole body shook. She did not answer Draca, but she wondered at his words. She did not know if the ocean creature was capable of thought, but she had seen its eyes, watched it playing and enjoying the connection it had made with her. The sorrow that had so briefly been swept away on a wave of ire, returned, trickling through her shaking body.

She prayed that the dolphin might live, unlikely as that might be. But if it were to die, she thought it would be better for it to die free, surrounded by its kin and kind.

Chapter 13

They left at first light on horses borrowed from Eorcenberht's stables. It was a crisp, chill morning and their mounts' breath smoked in the air. The courtyard was filled with the hubbub of riders and horses, hostlers and servants. Beobrand glanced at the horse he would ride, a fine chestnut-coloured mare that reminded him of Acennan's favourite steed. He sighed, his friend's loss still cutting keenly when memories surfaced unannounced and unexpected. Cynan led a tall, dappled stallion over to Garr. It trotted daintily on long, slender legs and Beobrand marvelled at the quality of horseflesh Cynan had convinced the steward of the hall to part with. Beobrand gave Cynan a nod but said nothing, not wishing to draw attention to the Waelisc horseman's keen haggling with the head hostler the previous night. It was not a long journey to Hithe, but Cynan was clearly concerned that the search for Beobrand's daughter might take them further and did not wish for them to be poorly horsed.

A powerful voice carried over the throng, making Beobrand turn.

Bassus strode towards him.

"May the gods guide you, Beobrand," he boomed. The giant clapped Beobrand on the shoulder and lowered his voice. "Do not take too long though. I know not how late Fordraed and

Utta will delay travelling north." He said no more on the subject. They both knew that Beobrand was risking Oswiu's wrath by diverting from his mission.

It was Eanflæd who had settled matters. She had laid out her plan in the gardens the previous afternoon.

"Do you doubt this woman, Udela?" she had asked him. "Do you believe she lies?"

Beobrand looked over now to where the stern, earnest Udela was climbing onto a stocky, gentle horse that Cynan had selected for her. His belief in Udela had not wavered.

"I do not doubt her," Beobrand had replied to Eanflæd, as the afternoon sun had dipped beyond the crumbling walls of Cantwareburh.

Eanflæd had nodded, as if she'd expected this reply.

"Then this girl child she speaks of is your daughter and there is nothing for it but that you seek her out."

"But what of Oswiu?"

Eanflæd had stared at him then, as if he were simple. He had felt foolish, a stupid child, not a renowned death-dealing thegn.

"I am to be a peace-weaver between two nations, Beobrand. I will be married to a man from a family that mine has hated for decades." This was true, but Beobrand did not understand how this served to unravel the tangled threads of his predicament.

"Oswiu is already married," Eanflæd had continued, "and has children."

Beobrand had squirmed uncomfortably at the thought of Rhieinmelth of Rheged.

"Yes, my lady. You know this, but he has put Rhieinmelth aside for his marriage to you to take place. Yours will be a powerful alliance."

"Indeed," she'd snapped. "But it seems to me that if Oswiu can so easily leave one wife, what might he do to me in the future? I am in no hurry to head north, Beobrand."

"And yet I am oath-sworn to Oswiu, lady," Beobrand had said; he could still see no way to be free of the obligation to his king.

Eanflæd had smiled, and it had been as if the sun had once again lit the small corner of the garden, bathing the stone bench in warmth.

"Ah, but Oswiu is not here," she'd said. "And he sent you south on my behest. I requested that you be part of the retinue to take me north. And it is now my wish that you do that which is noble and right in the eyes of the Lord."

And so it was that in the hall that evening, Eanflæd had told her cousin and the men of Northumbria that Beobrand was to ride in search of his lost kin and that until he returned, she would remain at Cantwareburh. Fordraed had spluttered and fumed, furious at the turn of events.

"By all that is holy," he had cried, spitting half-chewed gobbets of meat across the board, "you are to be brought forthwith to Bebbanburg, to Oswiu King. It has been agreed."

Eanflæd had stared at the portly thegn calmly, unmoved by his outburst.

"Is Oswiu a good follower of Christ?" she had asked.

Utta had intervened then, lowering his cup to the table and raising his hand.

"Oswiu is the most holy of kings. He is a true brother in Christ, giving joy to the Lord and adhering to all his sacred teachings."

Eanflæd smiled.

"Just so," she said. "And therefore I know that the lord Oswiu would agree with me, for surely Jesu would not have a man turn away from one of his flock that had been taken by wolves. If there was any chance of rescue, both Christ and my soon-to-be husband would seek to bring the stolen lamb back to the fold. And so Beobrand will seek out Udela's daughter. Not because he wishes to break his oath to his lord. He does not! His word is

94

iron and let no man say that Beobrand of Ubbanford would ever break faith with his sworn lord. No. Beobrand will do this thing because it is what I command, and what God and Oswiu, as a true follower of the one true Lord God would want."

Utta had opened his mouth to respond, but then, seemingly unable to find words, had closed it again.

Fordraed's face had clouded, thunderous and filled with rage.

Wynhelm had offered Beobrand a thin smile and a nod. He appeared to appreciate how smoothly the princess had cornered the Northumbrians.

The warmth of the hall seemed distant now, with the horses stamping and blowing all around. Bassus offered his hand and Beobrand grasped his forearm in the warrior grip.

"You sure you won't come?" Beobrand asked.

Bassus shook his head.

"I'd only slow you down. Besides, it is the lady Eanflæd's wish that I remain here." His mouth twisted in a sardonic smile. "It would seem she is the one who plays the tune now, and we merely dance."

Beobrand said nothing.

He took the reins of the chestnut mare from a bondsman and swung himself into the saddle, shifting his weight to get comfortable.

One of the horses whinnied and stamped angrily, unhappy with its rider. Someone cried out in dismay. Others laughed, the sound raucous in the early morning mist. The angry horse kicked a couple of times, its unlucky rider clinging to the saddle and the beast's mane. It was Coenred, his face flushed, his robes flapping about his pale, slim ankles. The monk had never been a natural rider and the brethren of Lindisfarena usually walked from place to place. But Beobrand could not hold his gesithas back to wait for Coenred, and so he was mounted like the rest of them.

Beobrand spurred forwards and caught Coenred's mount's reins. The horse, a small, hitherto docile-looking pony that

Cynan had said was sure to pose no problems, rolled its eyes at Beobrand, but it quietened with a final shake of its head and a snort. Beobrand handed the reins to Coenred.

"Are you sure about this?" Beobrand asked.

"It is the lady Eanflæd's wish, and bishop Utta's too." He patted the horse's neck nervously, and the animal flicked its ears. "I just pray that God will see that this beast is calm on the journey."

Beobrand smiled at his friend. Coenred often seemed timid, but Beobrand knew his worth. He met Coenred's gaze and saw the anxiety there. And yet there was something else. A flicker, a spark. Could it be excitement? Some of the men had grumbled at the monk accompanying them, but not those who knew him well. Eanflæd had suggested he travel with Beobrand, but at first Utta had refused. Once again, she had deftly convinced him to do her bidding. She had heard that Coenred was skilled in the arts of leechcraft, she'd said. It was possible that Ardith might need healing if she had been treated harshly, and, she had gone on, wouldn't the child be in need of spiritual guidance after her ordeal? Utta had been unconvinced until Eanflæd had pointed out that the description of the men who had taken Udela's daughter from Hithe seemed to match that of the men who had attacked *Háligsteorra*, killing Dalston and stealing the precious gift meant for her from her future husband. This had swayed Utta, who had taken Coenred to one side and whispered frantic instructions about what to do if they should find the casket.

Beobrand grinned at the memory. He was in awe of Eanflæd and the ease with which she had guided men of power to her bidding. He supposed that he too was in her thrall. For him to head off in search of Ardith played into her hands, delaying the dreaded journey north to a man she did not wish to marry.

Casting about him he saw that all his men and Coenred and Udela were mounted, awaiting his order. He was about to give the command to ride out, when a voice pulled him up short.

"Leaving without saying goodbye?"

Swinging his mount around, he spied Eanflæd, draped in a fur-lined cloak, standing beside Bassus' bulk.

Beobrand nudged his mare closer, so that he would not need to shout to be heard.

"There is not a moment to waste, but I thank you for seeing to it that I can go without being known as an oath-breaker."

"What friend would I be to prevent you from going in search of your kin?" Eanflæd said, her eyes glimmering.

Beobrand smiled, aware that the eyes of all those in the yard were upon them. Beside Eanflæd, Bassus grinned at him.

"So, we are friends, my lady?" Beobrand asked.

She stared at him for a long while. Once again he felt clumsy and simple before such grace and beauty.

"I have known you for longer than almost any person who yet lives," she said at last. The warmth of her breath clouded the air between them. "I think I should like to call you my friend."

Beobrand swallowed, his throat suddenly dry.

"If it pleases you."

Eanflæd raised an eyebrow.

"Does it please you?"

Beobrand thought for a moment.

"Aye, it pleases me."

She smiled, and her face was radiant.

"Then I bid you farewell and Godspeed, friend," she said.

Beobrand gave a nod to Eanflæd, wheeled his horse about and dug his heels into its flanks. The mare jumped forward into a canter.

"To Hithe," he yelled, and behind him, the rest of the riders followed.

Chapter 14

"By the bones of Christ, what is he doing here?" Scrydan lurched to his feet, toppling his carved chair with a clatter. It was dark in the house, the only light coming from the flames of the hearth fire. But even in the dimly lit room, Beobrand could see that Scrydan had aged beyond his years. His former friend had put on weight and his beard was unkempt and unruly. And the erstwhile reeve of Hithe had been drinking. If the slurring of his speech and his swaying stance had not been enough to show his drunken state, the stench of ale and strong mead oozed from him in a sour miasma that engulfed Beobrand and the others who had entered the building.

Beobrand recoiled from the man's stink. For an instant he was a child again, the smells of the hut bringing back the ghost of his father. Beobrand clutched Hrunting's pommel, its familiar solidity grounding him, banishing the dark memories from a past best forgotten. Grimgundi was long since gone to the afterlife.

Udela moved towards her husband, raising her hands placatingly.

"Beobrand has come to help," she said.

Scrydan ignored her and took a step towards Beobrand.

"What are you doing in my home?" Scrydan said. Droplets of spittle spattered Beobrand's face. But he did not flinch. Gods, this man had been his friend once. It saddened and angered him to see what he had become.

"It is as Udela says," Beobrand replied in a calm tone, "I have come to help find Ardith. Tell me what happened."

Scrydan's eyes narrowed.

"What are you accusing me of?" he snarled.

Beobrand frowned.

"I accuse you of nothing, Scrydan," he replied, forcing himself to remain calm in the face of Scrydan's drunken ire. He'd hoped that Scrydan could shed a brighter light on what had transpired than the scant flicker of illumination that Udela had provided.

They had ridden hard from Cantwareburh. There were few people abroad at this time of year as the ceorls readied themselves for the long winter months ahead. They'd passed through ploughed land and saw smoke rising in thin, pallid plumes from charcoalers' fires deep inside the gloom of a beech forest. Shortly after they had seen a swineherd in a clearing. The man's pigs rummaged and rooted for mast amongst the beech trees while he gazed on, seemingly in a daze. He had started as they had reined in their mounts, clearly terrified to be surrounded by such a group of armed men. No matter how many times Coenred had told the man they meant him no harm, he would not listen, or perhaps he feared it was a falsehood. He had refused to speak to them. He had whispered to himself and backed away, before turning and hurrying into the forest, leading his pigs by dropping beans before them and whistling a shrill tune.

As his whistles grew faint with distance, Cynan had turned to Beobrand.

"Simple, you think?" he'd said.

Beobrand had thought for a moment, imagining himself in the swineherd's position.

He'd shrugged.

"Not simple. Just cautious of men wearing swords." He'd scratched his head, listening to man and pigs crunching away under the canopy of the trees. "Perhaps he is wise to run. I cannot say I blame him."

The sun had set just before they reached Hithe, but Beobrand had not wished to tarry, instead, sending Bearn, Garr and Coenred to Folca's hall to announce their arrival, and heading with Udela and the rest of his gesithas straight to the lands that had once been his family's and were now owned by Scrydan. As when he had last returned, the shadowed shapes of the buildings and trees they passed were familiar and yet as distant as half-forgotten dreams. He had never thought to come back here. Now the memories of the place assailed his mind as if he had disturbed a cave filled with sleeping bats.

A log shifted in the fire, sending up a flurry of sparks, and in the sudden light Beobrand noted the blotched bruises on Scrydan's face. When he had last seen Scrydan his features had been battered and blood-smeared. Beobrand well remembered his knuckles splitting as he had pummelled Scrydan.

Scrydan could not hold Beobrand's gaze. He spun to face Udela, staggering slightly as he lost his balance. Reaching out, he clutched one of the timber pillars. Seeming to gain strength from the rough wood of his home, he straightened his shoulders and pulled himself up to his full height.

"Why did you bring him here?" he hissed. "And what of Tatwine?"

"Tatwine is well," Udela said in a soft voice. "He is at Inga's. My sister will have him for a while."

Scrydan balled his hand into a fist and shifted his bulk towards his wife.

"How dare you disobey me, woman?"

Udela flinched and then, as if remembering there were others in their home, she lowered her gaze.

"Scrydan!" snapped Beobrand, his voice cutting through the tension in the dark, smoke-heavy room. "Do you remember the last time we met? Do you recall my promise to you?"

Scrydan's eyes darted back to Beobrand and then to the warriors who crowded around the doorway. For several heartbeats Scrydan looked from one man to the next, perhaps weighing his options. Finally he nodded at Beobrand. Scrydan was drunk, but he was no fool. The threat of violence was in the air like bitter fumes billowing from the hearth.

"I remember," he said. He bent, clumsily reaching for the fallen chair. Scrydan missed it once before snagging one of the ornately carved legs. He righted the chair and slumped once more into it. Picking up a wooden cup, he drained its contents.

"Know this then, Scrydan, son of Scryda," said Beobrand. "I have not come here to cause you harm, but to help, if I can, to find your daughter," he hesitated almost imperceptibly at the words, but he thought he saw Scrydan's eyes narrow. Did he know the truth? Did Scrydan suspect that Beobrand was Ardith's father? He pushed the thoughts away. It was of no matter what Scrydan thought or knew, unless his knowledge could guide them to find the girl. "But my word is iron," Beobrand continued, "and I will make good on my promise, if I must."

Despite the fire, the room seemed to grow chill. Scrydan picked up a flask of mead and filled his cup. His hand shook. He did not offer the drink to the others.

"Enough of this," Beobrand said. "There is no time to waste and we must rest before we can pursue the men who took Ardith. Now, tell us what happened."

"I am sure Udela has told you all that I know," said Scrydan, his tone sour and scornful.

"I would hear the tale from the scop's mouth, not from his woman's."

"It is no tale," said Scrydan, angry again, "it is the truth."

Beobrand said nothing.

Scrydan took another deep draught from his cup. It seemed to Beobrand that the man's hand shook more than before.

"There is little to tell. There were three ships pulled up on the strand. Ardith and I went down to see whether the traders carried anything worth having."

"Traders, you say?" said Beobrand, his voice sharp. "Did they have a leader?"

Scrydan's hand flitted to his bruised face.

"Their leader was a great beast of a man."

"A beast?"

"A beast in action and in form."

"How so?"

"He wears the skin of a seal for a cloak and the skull of a sea monster for a helm." Behind Beobrand, his gesithas stiffened and muttered at the description. Scrydan shuddered at his own memories. "His name," said Scrydan, "is Grimr and when he laid eyes on Ardith he asked if he could have her for his wife. I refused, saying she was too young yet and besides, we have made a good match for her with Byrhtísen's son."

Scrydan drank again. Outside, one of the horses whinnied, another stamped. Cynan slipped out into the darkness to check on the mounts.

"What happened when you refused this Grimr?" Beobrand asked.

Scrydan put down his cup and refilled it again with his trembling hand. Some of the liquid splashed onto the board.

"He took her."

Udela let out a small sobbing cry. Scrydan ignored her.

"And what did you do?"

Scrydan swallowed more mead and then spat into the embers of the fire.

"I am not the great Beobrand of Ubbanford," he said. "But even you would not have been able to beat the crews of three ships. I was unarmed and alone, but even so I fought them. But they were too many." He drank deeply once more and sighed. "Grimr had them hold me while he beat me senseless."

Beobrand stared at him for a long while.

"You are lucky they did not slay you. Or take you also. I have seen thralls less healthy than you fetching a fine price."

"Lucky? You call this luck?" He waved his arm, sloshing mead. "Look at my face! Behold my face! I did not beat myself so."

Beobrand stared at him as he blustered and raged. At last Scrydan quietened.

"I do not believe you hit yourself about the face, Scrydan. But I recall the last time I saw you. Your face was a mess then and that was not because you had been defending the innocent." Scrydan looked away, withering beneath Beobrand's cold stare.

"Can you tell us anything else of value?" Beobrand asked. "Do you know where Grimr was heading?"

"I do not." Scrydan's voice was almost a whisper now. "I was senseless. I told you." He reached once more for the mead. He would be of no more use to them. Even if he had fought for Ardith, it seemed Scrydan had done nothing save drink since she had been snatched away.

Udela's face was pale in the dim firelight.

"Please find our daughter, Beobrand," she said. Tears streaked her cheeks, glittering red like garnets.

"I will do all I can, Udela. I give you my oath. If Ardith lives, I will bring her back to you."

And with that, he made to leave. Attor, Dreogan and Fraomar went before him into the night. He heard their whispered voices and the creak and jingle of harness as they mounted. He paused in the doorway, one hand resting lightly on the jamb.

"Remember, Scrydan," he said, "my word is iron and I will make good my promise if I must. Do not doubt it."

Outside, it was full dark, cold, still and clear after the closeness of the overcrowded farmstead. Beobrand swung up into the saddle of the chestnut mare that Cynan was holding for him.

"My lord?" said the Waelisc man.

"Cynan?"

They kicked their mounts into a trot back towards the settlement of Hithe and Folca's hall.

"What is the promise you made Scrydan?" Cynan asked.

Beobrand let out a long breath. It steamed in the moonlight.

"Scrydan had struck Udela. Ardith too perhaps. I told him that if I found out that he had ever raised a hand to either of them again, I would come back here and kill him."

Chapter 15

The gravel of the beach crunched beneath Beobrand's feet. The night was cold and still, scarcely a breath of wind blew from the sea. The chill light from the stars and moon gilded the waves that rolled up the shingle and then slid back into the Narrow Sea with a sigh. There might be no wind, but, like the thoughts tumbling in his head, the water was in constant motion. Beobrand felt as though his head were filled with crashing waves; memories tossed in a bitter storm.

The taste of the ale from Lord Folca's table was sour in his mouth. The drink he recalled from his youth had kindled ghosts of memories he would rather have left in the past. Where they belonged.

Scooping up a sea-smooth pebble, Beobrand flung it out into the darkness. It disappeared into the gloom and the sound of its landing was lost as another wave broke with a muffled grumble. The water caressed the strand, slipping its foamy fingers towards his feet. Beobrand watched as the water, bubbles glinting in the moonlight, halted its graceful progress and returned to the sea, tugging shells and stones with it.

He spat into the foam and watched as the dying wave carried the bitter taste of his memories away.

Casting a glance over his shoulder, Beobrand saw the shadowy form of Cynan, standing someway further up the beach. When

Beobrand had pushed himself up from the high table in Folca's hall, leaving a half-filled horn of ale and a barely touched trencher of fish, Cynan had followed him outside. Ever since they had returned from Maserfelth, Cynan had been his shadow. Beobrand looked back to the roiling dark of the sea with a thin smile. At first, he had told the Waelisc warrior to leave him be, but he had long ceased to order him away. It did no good. Whatever their differences, Cynan was a good man and as stubborn as Acennan had been. He had taken it upon himself to guard his lord, and he would not give up his role. Perhaps he thought he needed to replace Acennan at Beobrand's side. Beobrand spat again. Nobody could ever replace Acennan. Gods, how he missed his friend. The thought of him always brought with it a rush of anger; fury at himself for sending Acennan to his death.

He picked up another stone and threw it as far out into the darkness as he could. He grunted with the effort.

So many dead. So many ghosts.

Peering into the gloom, he pondered Ardith's plight. Was she staring out at the same sea? Was the moon glimmering on her golden hair? He barely knew the girl, but the weight of her situation was heavy upon him, like a physical thing hefted on his shoulders. He recalled the same feeling of desperation when Reaghan had been taken by Nathair's sons. The thought of what the men might be doing to her twisted and scratched at his mind. In his memory, Ardith was but a tiny child, smaller even than his son, Octa. The idea of rough seamen snatching her from her home filled him with dread and dismay. He could think of little else save finding her now that Udela and Eanflæd had set him on this course.

Eanflæd.

There was another quandary. He was not blind to the feelings she stirred within him. Her beauty and wit were an intoxicating brew. And yet she was to be his queen. She was promised to Oswiu. She had offered him her friendship. That would have to suffice.

He sighed. His breath smoked before him. He pulled his cloak about his shoulders.

Looking to his right, he stared out to the sea westward. If the men who had taken Ardith were those who had attacked the Northumbrian ships on the east coast of Albion, it seemed likely they would be heading west. Beobrand shook his head. What had happened here? Scrydan's tale did not ring true. He was lying about something, of that Beobrand was certain. The man was a drunk and a coward. Beobrand could scarcely believe that he had stood up to Grimr and his crews. But the bruises on Scrydan's face gave credence to his words.

"Friends of yours?" whispered a voice, close by.

Beobrand started, spinning around. He had been lost in the tangled forest of his thoughts, but now he was instantly alert again. His hand dropped to the seax sheathed at his belt, the familiar bone handle reassuring. He had left Hrunting with the door wards at Folca's hall and he suddenly felt naked without it.

The voice belonged to Cynan. Beobrand cursed himself for allowing his gesith to get so close without him noticing. He had grown accustomed to the Waelisc man's protection, relying on his eyes and ears. He would do well to keep his wits about him. It was not wise to put one's safety so completely in the hands of others.

Cynan pretended not to notice his lord's discomfort and nodded towards the shadowed buildings of Hithe. Beobrand followed his gaze. Four figures were approaching along the strand.

Beobrand did not move. He watched as the men drew closer. When they were still a spear's throw distant, he recognised three of them. They were the brawlers who had been in Scrydan's employ when last he had visited Hithe. Acennan and he had toppled them from their mounts and beaten them bloody and unconscious. The fourth man was tall and broad, younger than the others. The three trudged across the shingle, almost wading through the shifting stones. The younger man walked lightly on the balls of his feet. There was an eagerness about him that drew Beobrand's attention.

"They are no friends of mine," Beobrand said in a hushed voice. "If they come seeking a fight, we will have to give it to them. But let's try not to slay them. Killing Folca's people will not help us here."

Cynan did not reply.

Beobrand took a couple of steps towards the men, away from the surf rolling up the beach. No need to get his feet wet should it come to a fight. Cynan followed him, once more Beobrand's silent shadow.

Planting his feet in the gravel, Beobrand waited for the group to reach them. His arms hung loosely at his sides. His face was shadowed.

Beobrand could scarcely remember the fight with the three men outside Scrydan's house. It had been years before and there had been countless battles betwixt then and now. But he did recall that it ended with all three of them bloody and with more than one of them nursing broken bones. Was it a trick of the moonlight or did the shortest of the men walk with a limp? Beobrand had a fleeting memory of twisting the man's ankle until the tendons and bones ground and snapped.

A wave crashed behind him, a growl followed by a hissing sigh. Beobrand felt the anger building within him. Did these fools believe they could stand before Cynan and him? It would be easy enough to rush forward, to unleash the animal fury that always rattled at its fetters within him. It would be a welcome release, a few moments in which to forget about Ardith and Udela, Eanflæd and Oswiu. A brief respite from his grief over Acennan and Reaghan. The savage peace that he knew he would find in conflict and bloodletting. Beobrand breathed deeply of the cold night air, calming himself. The air tasted of salt.

Still several paces distant, the four men halted, standing in a line facing Cynan and Beobrand. The unspoken threat was clear in their stance, shoulders bunched and fists clenched. The youngest of them made to take a step forward. One of the others, a massive hulk of a man with a broad, twisted nose that had been broken many times, placed a hand on the young man's shoulder, pulling him back.

"Easy, son," he said.

His son. That explained who the keen fourth member of the band was.

Beobrand did not move. For a long while the men stood in silence. The young one, Broken-Nose's son, was almost dancing on the spot, such was his excitement. At long last, the man with the limp spoke.

"You are not welcome here, Beobrand, son of Grimgundi," he said, his tone gruff.

"I do not need your welcome, Morcaer," Beobrand said. He knew Morcaer from his childhood. The man had always been a brute and a bully. "These are Lord Folca's lands, not yours."

Morcaer blinked. Undeterred, he continued.

"We heard you went to Scrydan. Threatened him."

"It was no threat. I am a thegn of Bernicia. Lord of Ubbanford. I do not make empty threats. If he has harmed Udela or Ardith, I will seek him out, and I will kill him."

Morcaer swallowed.

"Scrydan may not be the reeve any longer, but we are still his friends."

Beobrand spat.

"I am sure he praises the Christ and all the gods for his good fortune."

"Leave here and leave Scrydan alone," Broken-Nose's son said, his voice strident and jagged in the night.

"I will do what I please," Beobrand said, his voice calm and as cool as an unsheathed blade. "Now go back to the middens you crawled out of and if Scrydan is there, tell him I will see him again soon." They did not move. Beobrand turned his head, looking at each man in turn. The moonlight glimmered in his blue eyes, like chips of ice long before the spring thaw. "Do you fools truly think you can best me and my friend here? This is the last chance I will give you. Leave now, or I promise you I will not be as soft with you as when last we met."

"Why, you whoreson," shouted Broken-Nose's son. "You do not frighten me."

Without thinking, Beobrand recognised the tensing of the muscles in the youngest of the group and was moving to meet his attack almost before it had begun. The young man surged forward, swinging his huge fists and roaring with rage. He was as tall as Beobrand and strong from years working in the fields and brawling with the men of Hithe, but the young man was no warrior. He was slow. And clumsy.

Beobrand was neither. And he had killed countless men as easily as this boy scythed wheat at harvest. Beobrand sprang forward, shrugging off the boy's punches, catching one effortlessly on his forearm and weaving underneath the other. Snapping his right fist forward, he jabbed the young man in the throat. He hit him hard, but through the sudden fire of his fury, he recalled his words to Cynan. He did not wish to kill this farm boy. At the last instant, he pulled back from hitting him with his full force and bodyweight behind the blow. Nevertheless, the boy fell to the shingle, clutching at his throat, gurgling and gasping for air. Beobrand stepped back, hoping absently that he had not in fact slain the fool.

Beside him Cynan had crouched, ready to fight.

The boy's father dropped to his knees beside his son. The other two men did not move.

Beobrand met their staring eyes with cold fire in his glare. He held their gaze for a long while, judging their resolve.

On the ground, the boy was dragging in breaths and coughing, his father tugging at his arms, pulling him to his feet. Good, the fool would live.

Beobrand looked again at the men.

"Help him up, and do not ever stand before me again," he said. "I am done with you. Next time you cross me, I will gut you all like mackerel."

And then, having taken their measure, he turned his back on the men, looking out to sea once more at the starlight flickering on the black swell far away.

Over the washing sounds of the surf, Beobrand listened to the boy's coughing. The men muttered to him, telling him to get up. Beobrand knew that Cynan would not turn his back on the threat, but Beobrand had looked into their eyes and he knew the fight had gone from them. These men were cowards, brave when drunk and bold against farmers and women. They would never dare stand before him again.

Beobrand did not turn to see them go, but he heard their footsteps crunch away up the beach. He hoped he would never see them again.

A wave broke, the foam glimmering white and ghostly. In the sky, wisps of clouds were forming around the moon like cobwebs.

Beobrand pulled his cloak about him, willing his hands not to tremble, but knowing they would, as they always did after a fight, no matter how brief.

A gravel-grinding footfall behind him made him turn back with an angry sigh. He had been sure they would not return. Now he would have to slay them. He had given them his word on it and his word was iron. He drew his seax from its leather sheath and spun around in one fluid motion. The veiled moon licked the metal of the blade.

"Gods, you must be more stupid than I'd thought. Do you truly wish to die?"

But the four men were nowhere to be seen, and someone else entirely stood before him.

Chapter 16

Beobrand took in at a glance the stocky man in front of him. The man's hand rested on the shoulder of an equally solid-looking boy. They both wore simple clothes and the man's cloak was open, hanging loose. He carried no weapons that Beobrand could discern. Beobrand flicked a glance at Cynan. He was still close by, but apparently thought a single unarmed man with a child posed no threat.

Beobrand looked back to the newcomer. As quickly as it had been rekindled, Beobrand's anger was doused. He knew this man and Cynan had been right to let him approach. He was no danger to them.

"Alwin," Beobrand said, "what brings you down here in the dark? I came for some peace away from Folca's hall, but this place is busier than an ale-wife's hut on brewing day."

Alwin let out a laugh.

"It is good to see you too, Beo," he said.

Abashed, Beobrand stepped close to his childhood friend, offering his hand. Alwin hesitated for an instant, then clasped Beobrand's forearm in the warrior grip, as they had done as boys when they had both dreamed of bearing shield and spear in service of their lord. Beobrand squeezed Alwin's muscled arm and slapped his shoulder with his left hand.

"It is good to see you, old friend," Beobrand said, and he meant it. "It's been too long."

"Aye, the years go by like the waters of a stream in spate."

Beobrand nodded, thinking of all that had passed since last he had seen Alwin. All the battles. The clamour and blood. The treasures bestowed upon him for victories.

And the deaths of loved ones.

"No man can dam the flow of time. I fear that all too often we are like twigs tossed into the water and our wyrd takes us where it will."

"And how different the wyrd of two men can be," Alwin said, his voice wistful.

Beobrand placed his hand on Alwin's shoulder.

"It seems to me your wyrd's path has led you true. You still have your farm, do you not? Andswaru is well?"

"Yes, she is well. But father died."

"I am sorry."

"Do not be sorry. He was old. His last years were difficult." He trailed off into silence.

"I am sorry," Beobrand said again, awkward at his friend's sadness. He wished to comfort him, but they were no longer the boys they had been. Too much water had flowed along the stream over the years.

"The farm does well?" Beobrand asked, hoping to turn the conversation onto happier things.

"It does well enough."

"And your family?" he said, looking pointedly at the boy standing beside Alwin.

"Andswaru has borne me two more children. Another boy, and a girl."

"And this is your oldest?" Beobrand could not remember the boy's name. He had been but a babe when Beobrand had last been in Hithe.

"Yes," Alwin's grin reflected the moonlight, his melancholy of moments before seemingly forgotten, or at least banished. Alwin had never been one to dwell on sadness. "Swithun is the reason we are here in the deep of night and we did not wait to call on you till the morn as would have been proper."

Alwin ruffled his son's hair and the boy shifted his weight from one foot to the other, embarrassed and yet content with his father's affectionate attention. Beobrand felt a dull pang of jealousy at Alwin's easy companionship with his son. He was never fully at his ease with Octa.

"Indeed? And how is it that Swithun made you come here now?"

"Word of your arrival in Hithe has travelled quickly. When Swithun heard that the great Beobrand of Ubbanford was here, he would not be still until I sought you out."

"Oh?"

"He knows that once we were friends."

"I trust we still are."

Alwin paused for a heartbeat, taken aback perhaps at Beobrand's words. But a moment later, he smiled broadly again.

"Of course we are. Even if we barely see each other, I will always count you as a friend."

Beobrand returned his smile.

"I am ever in need of good friends," he said. "Enemies are too easy to come by."

"You make enemies easily?" said Alwin, laughter in his voice. "I can scarce believe it. But you are always so easy to be around."

Cynan snorted. Beobrand sighed. Alwin was always quick to jest, usually at someone else's expense. From his memories of their childhood, that someone was often him.

"Well," Alwin went on, "Swithun knows that we are friends and he has long taken joy from the scop songs of your battles." Alwin shook his head, and sighed. Beobrand remembered when, as boys, they had listened to tales of warriors and shieldwalls. It seemed like a different life. Memories from someone else's childhood. To think that Alwin's son looked up to him made Beobrand uneasy.

"You cannot believe all the tales told by the bards, Swithun," he said.

The boy's eyes were wide and bright, glimmering in the darkness.

"Is it true that you killed Cadwallon, the king of Gwynedd?" Swithun asked, his voice high-pitched and breathless.

"No, Swithun," Beobrand replied with a sigh. How the tales of his exploits grew in the telling! The boy looked crestfallen. "It was not I who took Cadwallon's life. But I saw how Oswald, King of Northumbria took the head from his shoulders." Swithun's face caught the moonlight. His eyes were wide and shining.

"What my lord is not telling you," Cynan said, breaking his silence, "is that he chased Cadwallon from the battle of Hefenfelth. They fought at a burn and Lord Beobrand vanquished the Waelisc king, bringing him back to Oswald for the king to mete out his justice."

Swithun's eyes grew wider still and his mouth gaped open.

"Were you there?" he asked.

"No, I was not. But I have heard the tale from the mouths of men who were. It is the truth of it. King Oswald gave my lord land and the great black stallion he rode that day as gifts for his service."

"Truly?" Swithun's voice could hardly be heard over the surf.

"Perhaps your man could tell Swithun more of your adventures, Beobrand," said Alwin, raising an eyebrow. Beobrand frowned, he did not wish Cynan to fill the boy's head with tales of battle and killing. "I would speak with you," Alwin whispered, leaning in close.

So, there was more to this visit than his son's excitement at meeting a hero from song.

Beobrand nodded to Cynan who put his arm around the boy and led him away from the men.

"I can tell you more tales of my lord Beobrand," he said, "but you would be better hearing my own stories, for there is no greater gesith in my lord's warband than Cynan. I stood in the shieldwall at the battle of Cair Chaladain and it was I who saved Beobrand's life when he stood before the great giant of a man, Halga, son of Grimbold of Mercia."

Cynan's boasting was lost beneath the sound of the tide.

"Well, Alwin," Beobrand said. "What is it you would say to me away from your son's ears?"

Alwin hesitated staring out to sea. Foam-topped waves tumbled over and rushed up the shingle towards them.

"It was here where they took her," he said at last.

"Ardith?"

"Aye."

"I know. Scrydan told me so."

Alwin spat.

"She's yours, isn't she?"

Beobrand sighed. He had not wished to speak of this to anyone in Hithe.

"How did you know?"

Alwin let out a harsh laugh.

"It was Andswaru who first spoke the thought to me. I told her it could not be so. But as Ardith grew, it has become ever clearer. She looks so like you and even more like your sisters. Anyone who knew them can see the truth."

"Scrydan knows then?"

"Unless he is more of a fool than he appears, he must. But you and Udela? I never knew you had been together."

"It was only the once. Shortly before the pestilence." Beobrand's mind was suddenly filled with images he had long sought to forget. His sisters and mother, sweating and trembling. Lowering their bodies into the earth. The flames of his father's house, smoke billowing, dark and greasy, smearing the sky. "I did not know Udela carried my child. I knew nothing of this until two days ago."

"But now you know."

"Yes, now I know. My daughter has been taken, and I must find her."

"But she was not taken, Beobrand."

"What do you mean? Scrydan told me she was taken by traders. Seamen. A captain called Grimr."

"Grimr took her, but it was not as Scrydan told you, I am sure. I was on the beach that morning. I watched what happened here. I came to tell you the truth of it."

Beobrand turned to look at his old friend. His face was shadowed, hard-edged and dark like stone, but his eyes glittered with a deadly, cold light.

"Tell me," he said.

Chapter 17

"I need a ship!" Beobrand bellowed in his loud battle-voice and the chatter in the smoke-fogged hall was silenced in an instant.

The old man at the far end of the room was the first to recover his composure. He stood and peered towards the doors of his home, where Beobrand, Alwin and Cynan had entered abruptly from the darkness. The flickering flames from the hearth lit the man's face from below in a ruddy glow, casting shadows into his eyes, twisting his features like a nihtgenga. Even in the dim light Beobrand could see that the man had aged. His hair was white and his beard a wintry hoary thatch.

"Is that the mighty Beobrand, son of Grimgundi?" the man said. "We had heard you were back. I did not expect a visit, but now that you are here, come, seat yourself. There is herring, and more importantly, there is ale and mead. It has been many years since last we spoke. You must tell us all about your travels. The scops sing often of your battles. It seems King Edwin was right all those years ago."

Beobrand clenched his fists at his side. Gods, he had no time for this. He was done telling tales. He glanced at Alwin, who shrugged, a twisted smile on his lips. Beobrand's fury threatened to bubble to the surface. The knowledge of what Alwin had told him burnt within his mind. He had known Scrydan had been lying, but to have sold his own daughter! No, not his daughter. Beobrand's daughter. Had Scrydan done this terrible thing because he had known the truth of who her father was? By Woden, Scrydan had best pray to whatever god he held dear that Beobrand never saw him again.

Beobrand strode into the warmth of the hall. After the cool air of the beach, the stench of wet wool, sweat, spilt ale and stewing fish was overpowering. All the men in the room stared at him as he threaded his way towards Hrothgar. He recognised many of them. He noticed Immin, the sailor who had given him his bone-handled knife all those years ago. Immin's hair was grey now, his face lined and sagging. The passing of the years was never kind. Beobrand nodded at him, but did not pause as he approached the old man at the head of the table.

These men were sailors all. Good, earnest seamen. Fishermen and traders. Not the warriors he was accustomed to share a board with. For this was no lord's hall. This was the home of Hrothgar, son of Hebeca, the richest shipman in Hithe. He had once shown kindness to Beobrand, giving him passage from Cantware to Bernicia. He hoped Hrothgar would be generous to him again.

Beobrand accepted the cup of mead Hrothgar poured for him. Hrothgar gestured for the young man to his right to squeeze along the bench and patted the wooden seat nearest to him. Beobrand sat.

"I need a ship," Beobrand repeated.

"So you said, lassie," Hrothgar replied. "I see age and wealth have not improved your manners. You come asking for something from me. I would drink and talk a while. I would hear of the deeds of the great Beobrand who slays night beasts with his bare hands and slices the heads from treacherous kings before he breaks his fast of a morning."

For a moment Beobrand simply stared at the old man. This was foolish. Surely he did not believe the songs and tales he'd heard. At his expression, Hrothgar guffawed, his laughter rumbling up from within him to shake his whole body like a sail billowing in a stiff breeze. Some of the other men joined in and soon the hall echoed with the throb of laughter. Despite himself, Beobrand felt his rage lessen, drifting away just as the waves receded on the beach outside.

After a time, Hrothgar wiped his eyes with the backs his of gnarled, weathered hands. Reaching for the horn before him, he took a long draught.

"By the gods, Beobrand, you ever were a sombre one. I see you have no time to listen to an old sailor's tales or to spin your own yarns of the lands you now call home. What is it you want from me?"

"A ship," Beobrand said for a third time. His simple response set Hrothgar chortling once again.

After stifling his mirth, Hrothgar said, "Why?"

Beobrand looked about the room. All of the men returned his gaze. They were listening intently. Some had to crane their necks to see past the smoked herring, strips of meat, turnips and onions that dangled from the roof beams.

"You know that Ardith, daughter of Udela, has been taken by strangers?"

Hrothgar nodded.

"Of course, though they were not strangers. It was Grimr and his crew of pig-swivers and that one-eyed bastard brother of his. They stop here every so often in search of trade. But Folca has their measure and never lets them into his hall. As vile a band of ruffians as sail the Whale Road."

Beobrand fixed him with a cold glare. Hrothgar swallowed.

"I mean to seek out Ardith. I will bring her back safely if I can. But for that, I need a ship. And a crew."

Hrothgar stared at him for a time. He poured himself more mead and sipped from the horn before replying. The room was utterly still now. None of the men spoke. The only sounds came from the fire and two hounds who were gnawing on pieces of antler beneath the table.

"Why would you do such a thing? I know you were once friends with Scrydan, but this…"

"I am no friend of Scrydan's," Beobrand said. "He sold Ardith to Grimr."

A murmur ran through the room. A couple of the men grumbled. One of the dogs growled, snapping its teeth at the other that had crept too close to what it was chewing.

Hrothgar sighed.

"This is a bad business, Beobrand. For sure. She was a sweet girl. But Scrydan is her father and it is not unheard of for a man down on his luck to sell his kin thus. Surely you have more important errands to run for your king than to go in search of a child who has been sold as a house thrall. It saddens me to say it, for she was but young, too young for this bitter fate, but she may already have been sullied. She is lost."

Beobrand slammed his fist into the board with such force that the cups and plates rattled. Hrothgar's decorated drinking horn toppled over, spilling its contents over the rough timber where it trickled over the edge onto the old man's leg. He stood quickly, cursing and overturning his stool.

"Do not speak so!" shouted Beobrand. His hand had fallen to the handle of his seax, for this was no lord's hall where weapons were left at the door. There were no door wards here.

Nobody spoke.

The gathered seafarers seemed to hold their breath. Death was in the air and suddenly they all recalled the tales they had heard of Beobrand's victories. How the ravens had gorged themselves on his fallen foe-men. And, seeing him now, his eyes burning with an icy fire, his corded neck muscles bulging and his hand gripping menacingly the short but deadly blade at his belt, they believed all of the stories. Many had known Beobrand as a boy, but this was no boy who stood before them now. No, this was no farmer or sailor from Hithe. This was a death-dealing thegn, a man who would snuff the life from his enemies without a thought.

The silence drew on. At last, Beobrand let out a ragged breath.

"Do not speak so," he repeated. He rubbed his hands over his face, then took a swig from his cup. "Ardith is my daughter."

Hrothgar sat down again, slowly.

The room was as still and silent as a barrow now. Even the hounds fell silent, perhaps sensing the mood of the men. Beobrand glanced about him. None of them would meet his gaze.

Carefully, Hrothgar righted his horn, refilled it from the pitcher of mead and drank deeply.

"I am sorry, Beobrand," he said, wiping droplets of liquid from his moustache with the back of his hand. Gone was his light humour. His lips pulled down into a frown. "Kin is no laughing matter."

Beobrand waved a hand vaguely, dismissing the apology.

"You knew not," he said. "So, now you know the truth of it, can you help me?"

Hrothgar's frown deepened.

"This is a quest for a younger man than I. My bones are weary, and the claws of winter are already scratching at the door. The seas are treacherous at this time of year. You should wait till the turning of the year. After Geola. After Solmonath the winds will be softer, the waves less prone to swallow ships whole."

"I cannot wait till spring. Even if I could, Ardith surely cannot."

"Would that Swidhelm were here," Hrothgar said with a sigh. "He was never one to turn away from a challenge, and his ship was the fleetest wave-swan any man has captained."

"I remember him. His ship was fine indeed and you always said he had the luck of the gods."

"It seems even the luckiest of men run out of fortune in the end."

Beobrand nodded. He scarcely felt lucky, despite what men said about him. Still, he yet lived.

"What happened to him?"

"I do not know. He sailed from here bound for Hibernia last Hreðmonath. He never returned."

"His ship was lost?"

"None of us has seen any sign of the ship or any of the crew. As I said, it seems Swidhelm's luck ran out."

"But there are more ships in Hithe than that of Swidhelm. Surely one of you men has a ship and a crew that can serve." Beobrand scanned the faces around the hall. A couple of the older men met his gaze but shook their heads. Most of the seamen avoided his eyes. "I am not a poor man," he said. "I will pay silver."

A murmur ran though the room, but nobody stepped forward.

"It is a fool's errand, Beobrand," said Hrothgar. "The winter storms will come and even if you track these men across the sea road…" He hesitated, then raised his hand to placate Beobrand before another outburst. "You must accept that it may be too late."

Beneath the board Beobrand clenched his fists. His head had begun to throb. He was tired.

"I must try," he said, a wave of exhaustion washing over him. "But I need a ship."

"I could go."

Beobrand turned at the sound of the new voice. It was the young man beside him, the man Hrothgar had moved along the bench to allow Beobrand to sit. He was thickset, with the brawny arms and shoulders of one used to pulling at the oars. His beard and hair were an unkempt and unruly muddle of curls and tangles, as if he had never cut either. The man's eyes were intelligent and bright and the green of a summer sea. Despite his throbbing head and the tiredness that had come upon him, Beobrand liked the man instinctively.

"Indeed?" said Hrothgar. "And whose ship do you presume to command?"

The young man pushed his mane of hair out of his face and grinned, his teeth flashing in the thicket of his beard.

"Why, yours, of course, father," he said.

Hrothgar fixed his son with a stare that reminded Beobrand of when he had sailed with Hrothgar all those years before. The old sailor had been intimidating then. The years had not diminished the power of his glare.

The young man met his father's eyes and neither spoke for several heartbeats, locked in a silent battle of wills. Eventually, having reached his own conclusions as to his son's worthiness, Hrothgar smiled and offered him a small nod.

"Beobrand," Hrothgar said, "this is my son, Ferenbald."

The name conjured up distant memories in Beobrand. Images flitted in his mind of a child, laughing and swinging from the branches of trees that none of the other children had dared to climb.

"Ferenbald?" he said. "Gods, I remember you as nothing more than a whelp. You were but a child when I left Cantware."

"We have both grown since then, lord," Ferenbald answered.

Despite himself, Beobrand smiled. Ferenbald was a few years his junior, and he had never paid him much heed when he had lived in Hithe, but there was an easy confidence to him that spoke to Beobrand.

"Your beard has certainly grown," Beobrand said.

Ferenbald laughed.

Hrothgar placed his drinking horn on the board and said, "Why is it that you think you are ready to skipper *Brimblæd*, son? She is that which I value above all else, save for your mother, brothers and you. It fills me with dread to send my eldest son into winter seas aboard my fine vessel, on a quest that may well end up in a fight, if any of the tales of Beobrand are truthful. What say you? Why should I allow such a thing?"

Ferenbald stood and made his way to his father's side. He placed his hand on Hrothgar's shoulder.

"It is as you have said, father. You are young no longer, but I am older than you were when first you took a ship of your own onto the Whale Road. I have stood on the deck of *Brimblæd* since I could walk. I have sailed and rowed and guided her through heavy seas. How many long nights have you allowed me to stand at the steerboard while you slept? I am prepared for this, father. You have taught me all of my life. Besides," he squeezed his father's shoulder, "Beobrand seeks to do that which is right. What would you do if one of my brothers had been taken by Grimr?"

"Your mother will never allow it," Hrothgar said. "She will say you are too young yet to go to sea alone."

"Nonsense, husband. Those are your words, not mine."

A stout woman had entered the fug-filled hall from a doorway at the rear. The dim red light from the hearth picked out her round, heavy-jowled face. A fine brooch and necklace glimmered in the firelight.

"By the gods, woman," said Hrothgar, "I thought you abed long since."

"Well, it seems you were wrong about that too," she said.

A smattering of chuckling in the ill-lit room. Hrothgar frowned.

"But the boy is yet young," he said, a tone of pleading entering his voice.

"Young, yes. But also strong and able, husband." She walked to Hrothgar and Ferenbald, placing a hand on each man's shoulder. "Our son speaks true. It is time. And it is right. Think of the poor girl."

Hrothgar looked up at his wife. He was furious, taut as a mainstay in high winds, and Beobrand wondered if, like a stay rope that is cut loose, the old sailor would lash out. But after a few moments, the anger drained out of Hrothgar and his shoulders slumped in defeat. His wife smiled and patted his back.

"Very well, Beobrand," Hrothgar said, "you have yourself a ship, and a fine captain." Ferenbald beamed at his father's words. "I have two conditions."

"Of course, Hrothgar," Beobrand said, "speak your terms."

"The first is for Ferenbald," he turned to face his son. "Bring back *Brimblæd* to me in one piece. She is the finest ship I have ever owned and she is very dear to me."

"Of course, father. I swear I will bring *Brimblæd* back to you."

Hrothgar smiled, but Beobrand felt a prickling of unease at Ferenbald's quick oath. Hrothgar turned his attention to Beobrand.

"For you I have a different request."

Beobrand said nothing.

Hrothgar said, "Bring back my son to me."

The weight of the words hung in the air. Hrothgar's eyes flashed red, reflecting the embers of the hearth fire. Beobrand held his gaze; did not look away. The silence dragged out awkwardly. Part of Beobrand wished to blurt out his consent to Hrothgar's wish as Ferenbald had done, but he held back. In his mind's eye he saw Eowa's handsome, scarred face, as he had last seen him before the battle of Maserfelth. Eowa had sons and a wife, but Beobrand had no more been able to keep him safe than he could halt snow from thawing in the sun.

"Well?" Hrothgar asked at last.

"I cannot give you my word on this. I have seen too many good men fall, lost too many brave friends to make you a promise I may not be able to keep. But I give you my oath that I will do all that is within my power to see that your son returns to you safely. I cannot control a man's wyrd, but I will do my best to see that no harm comes to him. On that you have my word."

Hrothgar held his gaze for what seemed an eternity. Men began to fidget. One of the hounds whimpered. A log shifted in the fire, sending up sparks around the dried herring that hung from the soot-draped beams. Beobrand could only imagine what thoughts were going through the old man's mind, but eventually Hrothgar nodded.

"Very well," he said. "It is all I can ask. We all know that the sea is a dangerous mistress and even the luckiest of sailors and ships do not always return from voyaging on the Whale Road. But, Beobrand," he said, reaching out and gripping Beobrand's arm with the strength that came from years of working the rigging and steerboard, "see to it that your best is good enough and bring my boy back."

Chapter 18

Coenred pulled his robes about him. Living in the monastery on Lindisfarena had made him used to cold, but the chill breeze that blew off the Narrow Sea, whilst not carrying the same icy bite as a winter storm in Northumbria, still managed to cut through his woollen garment. The wind tugged at the hem of his robe and swirled his hair into his eyes. In the manner of the Christ's holy men, the front of Coenred's head was shaved, but the hair from the crown of his head and behind his ears fell, long and luxuriant, to his shoulders. Watching the men preparing the ship to sail, he shivered. Coenred wasn't sure whether he shuddered from the cold or trepidation at the prospect of the quest on which he found himself. Perhaps both.

On the strand, the ship, *Brimblæd* wallowed in shallow surf. Around the vessel, men heaved barrels and bales. Ropes were thrown from one man to another, each seeming to know exactly what was required of him. Ferenbald, his beard and hair blowing about his head like a forest caught in the grip of a great storm, shouted orders, occasionally pointing to reinforce his meaning. He was young, but calm and ever-smiling. He missed nothing from where he stood aboard *Brimblæd*.

Coenred shivered again.

He hunched his shoulders, pulling his robe closer in against the cold. And yet, perhaps there was something else besides the weather that made him tremble. Smiling to himself, he remembered wise men, men who now rested in heaven at the side of the Lord. Fearghas and Gothfraidh had always told him he was one who sought out adventure. Coenred had denied it. He merely wanted to help his brethren, to study the word of God, to tend to His flock, to heal the sick. Quests and excitement were for warriors like Beobrand. He smiled now at his own blindness and at the older men's wisdom. It seemed they knew him better than he knew himself.

As the ship was laden with supplies and the crew and Beobrand's gesithas clambered aboard with their chests, sacks and gear, Coenred recognised the fluttering feeling in his belly. He was not overly cold, he was excited. The unknown terrified him and intrigued him in equal measure. The thought of riding this fragile ship in pursuit of the men who had taken Ardith made him tremble.

He did not know the girl, but he hoped she could be saved. Ever since hearing the news of Ardith's capture Beobrand had been so dour, more sombre than usual, if such a thing were possible.

And if he were truthful, if he were to gaze deep into the darkest corners of his being, there was another reason Coenred wished to travel with Beobrand. Something beyond the excitement of journeying further afield than he ever had before, seeing more of the Lord's great creation of middle earth. He scarce wished to think of it, but the image of Dalston would not leave him. His dreams were filled with Dalston's last moments, throat ripped crimson, his horrified eyes staring at Coenred as he had slipped beneath the dark waves. He had prayed long on this, asking the Lord to take away the memories that haunted his nightmares. But rather than see the images fade, they had become starker in his mind, and deep within his heart a dark seed of vengeance had taken root.

He sighed and began to recite the paternoster under his breath to clear his mind of such evil thoughts. He had felt the same after Gothfraidh's killing at the hands of Mercian raiders the year before. Then he had told Beobrand to avenge his mentor's death. When Beobrand had returned with the news that he had slain Halga and all his men, Coenred had for a fleeting moment felt a rush of joy. But then, he had needed to tell Beobrand of Reaghan's death. His friend's face had crumpled and Coenred had thought he might see him cry, as he had years before when they had first met. But the boy Beobrand had been was gone and as quickly as the pain had shown on his face, so Beobrand had set his features and he had stridden out of the hall, to walk alone with his thoughts and his grief.

Coenred knew that it was wrong to seek revenge. Did not Jesu say that "whosoever shall smite thee on thy right cheek, turn to him the other also"? But did not the Lord also smite his enemies? Coenred's guilt had been a terrible burden. Beobrand had been withdrawn and sullen, closing himself to all and only showing any sign of happiness when he was with Octa. The more apparent Beobrand's grief became, the worse Coenred had felt. For there was one thought that plagued his thoughts above all else. God had failed to answer his prayers to spare Reaghan because Coenred, the instrument of His healing, had begged Beobrand to kill those responsible for Gothfraidh's murder.

Coenred was certain that he had been the cause of Reaghan's death.

Abbot Aidan had called him to his chamber one day shortly after his return to Lindisfarena.

"Do not blame yourself for Beobrand's sorrow," Aidan had said, his deep brown eyes full of understanding. He always seemed to know exactly what Coenred was thinking.

Coenred had told the abbot of how he had asked Beobrand to kill the Mercians. How he was sure that Reaghan had died because of him.

"Do you think that Beobrand would not have killed the men who had attacked Ubbanford if you had not spoken in your anger and grief at our good brother's death?"

Coenred had shaken his head. Of course he knew that Beobrand would have sought out his enemies whether he had spoken up or not.

"And do you not believe that you did all you could to save the life of the poor lady of Ubbanford?"

Again, Coenred had shaken his head.

"I did all I knew how," he'd said, "and I prayed for her day and night. I kept vigil by her bedside."

"Pride is a sin, young Coenred. Do not believe that the Lord does only your bidding. You did your best, but the Lord decided that Reaghan's time had come. As had Gothfraidh's. And if ever there was a man who was prepared to meet his God, it was Gothfraidh. For was he not a good, holy man?"

"He was, Father," Coenred had replied, his voice catching in his throat. "He was a truly good man."

"So, grieve for the loss of loved ones, but do not blame yourself, Coenred."

"But I asked for vengeance! I wished for death on Gothfraidh's killers."

"You are but a man, Coenred. All men know anger and all men are weak. It is how we confront our weakness that defines us. You are a good man. Dwell not on a moment of frailty, but pray for the strength to forgive in the future."

He had prayed and he had thought that never again would he feel the burning desire for revenge. But then Dalston had been snatched, his throat slit like a hog at Blotmonath, and the terrible urge to see his murderers pay with their lives had begun to grow deep within his soul, a twisted dark weed, knotted and thorny, strangling the life from everything that grew around it.

Coenred watched as Cynan, Garr and Fraomar trudged down the shingle to *Brimblæd*. Beobrand had sent them to fetch Scrydan, but they were returning alone. Beobrand saw them approach and jumped down from the ship, walking briskly up the beach to meet them. Coenred walked towards them. He would hear what they said.

"Well," snapped Beobrand. "Where is he?"

"Gone," said Cynan.

"Gone?"

"Udela said that the friends of his we spoke to on the beach last night visited him in the darkest part of the night. He packed up anything he could find of value, and he fled."

Beobrand's face was thunder. Coenred knew he had feared for Udela now that the truth had come out about his blood-tie to Ardith. Whatever he had thought about Ardith's father before, a man like Scrydan would never take the humiliation of being publicly cuckolded without lashing out at those he blamed. He was too much of a coward to attack Beobrand, but Udela was another matter.

"And Udela?" Beobrand asked.

"Unhurt, lord," Cynan said. "We took her to Hrothgar's hall. He said he will watch over her and her son. It will not be easy for Scrydan to do her further harm."

"He has done enough already."

"There is one thing you should know."

"Yes?"

"Scrydan took the silver serpent arm ring you gave to Udela."

Beobrand stared at Cynan for a long moment. Coenred shuddered. Such was the hatred in that glare that he almost felt pity for this man he had never met.

Almost.

He made the sign of the Christ rood over his chest and offered up a silent prayer for Scrydan, for the look on Beobrand's face spoke of more than death. It spoke of pain and suffering and of the desire to make Scrydan scream with agony before he succumbed to the release of the afterlife.

"Did he?" Beobrand said at last. "Well, I suppose he is already dead. I can only kill him once."

And with that, he turned back to *Brimblæd*, and the preparations for their departure.

Chapter 19

"Thanks be to Woden that we are finally away." Beobrand flicked his cloak over his shoulder, but the wind caught it and wrapped it about his frame. His fair hair whipped around his face, and after a few attempts at pushing the errant strands from his eyes, he ceased trying. He could not control the wind.

Ferenbald leant into the steerboard as *Brimblæd*'s sail unfurled and snapped in the stiff easterly breeze. The prow of the ship climbed up a wave and then the ship rode down the far side with the slightest of tremors along its beams.

Ferenbald grinned and said, "Forgive me, had I known before last night that I was to take you on my father's ship in search of a lost girl, I would have been more prepared." Hrothgar's son's great mane of hair and beard waved and flowed around his face.

Despite the urgency that had been building up within him like a flood behind a dam, Beobrand returned Ferenbald's smile. It had taken the whole of the morning and much of the afternoon to ready the ship, but Beobrand could not fault Ferenbald or the crew. They had worked with a determined speed and efficiency, seeming to pick up on Beobrand's own nervous anxiety at dallying in Hithe while his daughter was surely travelling ever further from him, from home. But it was no longer his home.

It was Ardith's home. And the home of these sailors.

He must not forget, these men were her neighbours, men who had known her since she was a babe in arms. Their wives would be friends of Udela. He wondered how many of the crew had been pushed by their women to go in search of Ardith.

The ship rolled over another wave. Gulls shrieked and wheeled in the sky. Grey clouds had formed on the horizon to the west, and the sun shone weakly through the rain that streaked the air beneath them. They would surely be wet soon enough, but the prospect of a dousing did nothing to dampen Beobrand's spirits. The cold wind flung his cloak about him again, pushed his hair into his eyes. *Brimblæd* rode another wave and Beobrand staggered slightly. He had never been a good seafarer, but he noticed something with surprise: he did not feel sick. Instead, he felt light and more focused than he had in days. Even in weeks, or months perhaps. Looking back at their wake he watched as the coastline receded. The lightness of body could be explained simply enough. His byrnie, helm, and the iron splints of armour he wore on his wrists and, more recently, on his shins, were all stored safely in a greased leather sack. He had become so accustomed to wearing them, that to be free of his armour made him feel at times exposed and vulnerable. Now though, with *Brimblæd*'s keel dancing over the heaving sea and the wind billowing the sail and plucking at the hem of his cloak, Beobrand felt free. It reminded him of galloping astride his great stallion, Sceadugenga. It was the feeling of power that came from unfettered speed.

The cliffs and beaches of Cantware fell away behind them, and his troubles faded with the land. He could never forget those he had lost. Memories of Reaghan and Acennan were still as raw as recent sword cuts to his flesh. And yet, as *Brimblæd* pulled away from the land, Beobrand's mind turned from the past and began to look toward the future. He would find the daughter he had never known. He would rescue her. And he would make the men who had taken her pay. There would be time enough for

Scrydan on their return. He spat over the side, careful that the gusts of wind did not blow his spittle back into his face.

"You think we will make much progress today?" Beobrand asked.

Ferenbald looked up at the sail, then stared away towards the horizon.

"With this wind we should make Hastingas before nightfall."

Beobrand felt a pang of disappointment.

"You mean to take us into land?"

"Aye, with any luck we will make Hastingas afore the wind changes and brings that rain down upon us."

"The wind will change then?"

Ferenbald glanced up at the clouds and cocked his head to one side as if they uttered words only he could hear.

"Aye, this breeze won't last. It will shift into the south and I don't like the look of the sky to the west. We will make landfall at Hastingas and will wait for the storm to pass."

Beobrand's mood darkened like the thunder heads in the distance. His joy at speeding after Ardith and her captors fled on the wind.

"If we do not plan to press on, why did we sail today?"

"My father says it is always best to sail when the winds are good. You never know what the gods will bring the next day."

"Hrothgar is a wise man and a fine sailor no doubt, but it pains me to think that we will once more be resting on land while those pirates sail ever further away from us."

"If that squall is half as bad as I think it will be, nobody will be sailing anywhere for quite some time. Besides, have you not thought that we cannot track these men over the Whale Road? There are no footprints left on the waves. We must put into shore frequently to ask for tidings of their passing."

Beobrand grunted. He scanned the expanse of slate-grey water around them. There was no other vessel in sight. The only movement came from the gulls that careened in the air above

Brimblæd. Grimr and his ships had several days advance on them and they could be anywhere that a ship was able to travel. Of course Ferenbald was right. The only way to find out about their route would be from other ships who might have seen them, or from ports and settlements.

"If the gods smile on us, we may catch them soon," Beobrand said. "For we have one thing in our favour."

"What is that, lord," asked Bearn, who had removed himself from the belly of the ship where much of the activity of sailing was taking place. His face was pallid. Evidently he was suffering from the ship's motion. Beobrand felt sorry for him.

"Why, they do not know they are being hunted," he said, clapping Bearn on the back, as he tried to rekindle the spark of his excitement at the chase.

"The sky is growing ugly quickly," said Ferenbald. "I truly hope that the gods are smiling, for if we do not reach land before that storm, we will be in for a rough and wet night. It will matter not if our quarry knows of our approach, if we are sleeping with the fish," he added, grimly.

Beobrand thought of the storm-harried night they had so recently endured and felt his mouth grow dry.

Ferenbald stood, feet planted solidly on the heaving deck, eyes a-glimmer with the excitement of his new command and a smile half-hidden behind his thick beard, Beobrand could easily see that he was of Hrothgar's blood. Here was a man who lived for the sea. It was as much a part of him as the sod and turf were part of a ceorl farmer. Ferenbald called out to one of the crew and the man adjusted a rope without comment. Ferenbald shifted balance slightly and *Brimblæd* responded to his deft touch on the steerboard, changing course almost imperceptibly. He controlled the ship as Cynan controlled a horse, effortlessly, with an ease most men could but dream of. Beobrand glanced once more at the horizon. The clouds there were thick now, black, ominous. Beobrand sighed. He must trust to Ferenbald's judgement. And if this son of the sea thought it too dangerous to ride out the storm, Beobrand would be a fool not to listen. For he could see one thing for certain: Ferenbald was not easily frightened.

"Christ's bones!" a voice exclaimed from amidships. Beobrand looked down into the broadest part of the ship, where one of the crew was wrestling with a slender form. The sailor, a bald man whose down-turned eyes and constant frown gave him a sorrowful look, tugged on the figure's arm, yanking them upright. "What in the name of all that is holy are you doing here?" he yelled.

"Cargást," snapped Ferenbald, "what troubles you?"

The sad-looking sailor pulled the figure roughly towards *Brimblæd*'s stern. Beobrand saw the figure was a boy, gangly and awkward in the way of youth. He was tall and slim, but strong of aspect, not scrawny. His forearms were sinewed and stout, like a warrior's, but he did not walk with a fighter's grace.

"Take the helm," Ferenbald said to a grizzled man who looked old enough to be his grandfather. The grey-bearded sailor nodded and stepped forward to grasp the steerboard.

"What is happening here?" asked Beobrand, addressing Cargást.

At the same moment, Ferenbald stepped forward to meet Cargást and the boy and said, "What is the meaning of this?"

Cargást's sad eyes flicked from Beobrand to Ferenbald, hesitating.

"I am the captain of this ship," Ferenbald said, his tone curt, brooking no argument, "you will answer me."

Beobrand said nothing, but he felt his face grow hot.

Cargást dipped his head.

"I found him hiding 'neath the lord's gesithas' shields."

"What is the meaning of this, Brinin?" asked Ferenbald.

The boy tugged his arm free of Cargást's grip and straightened his back, meeting Ferenbald's gaze squarely. He's a bold one, thought Beobrand.

"I had to hide," Brinin said. "I knew you would never allow me to come. And my father would forbid it, even if you had let me."

"You are right on both counts," said Ferenbald. "By the Blessed Virgin, your father will skin us all if anything happens to you."

"Who is the child's father?" asked Beobrand.

"I am no child!" shouted Brinin before Ferenbald could answer. "I am fourteen summers old."

"Almost a man then," said Beobrand, a smile touching his lips.

"I am a man!" yelled Brinin. His voice cracked, shifting into a high-pitched whistle, and Beobrand could not help but smirk. Brinin's face flushed crimson and he fell silent.

"Who is this 'man's' father?" asked Beobrand.

Ferenbald grinned.

"Byrhtísen. The smith."

That explained the strength in the boy's arms.

"Brinin," said Beobrand, "why did you hide aboard?" He half expected Ferenbald to interject, to exert his authority as the master of the vessel, but the captain remained silent.

Now, faced with the tall, battle-scarred thegn and the broad-shouldered, bearded ship master, Brinin shuffled his feet on the deck and would not meet their eyes.

"If you would have us treat you as a man, you must speak as one," said Beobrand. "I asked you a question."

Brinin looked up, misery in his eyes.

"I had to." He bit his lip. His eyes shone. Beobrand thought he might cry.

"Why?" asked Ferenbald.

"I must. I..." The boy trailed off.

Beobrand stepped forward and placed a hand gently on the boy's shoulder. He noticed that the skin beneath Brinin's shining eyes was dark. He had the look of one who had not rested in days.

"Why?" he said in a soft voice.

Brinin swallowed.

"I had to help you find her," he said, his voice so small it was almost lost over the rush of the sea beneath the hull.

"You are friend to Ardith?" Beobrand asked.

Brinin pulled himself upright once more, seeming to regain his confidence.

"I am more than a friend. We are betrothed."

"I see."

"I love her," Brinin said, and there was such ferocious certainty in his tone, that Beobrand could not help but smile again.

"Do not mock me!" said Brinin, anger flaring like fat dripped onto a fire.

"I do not mock you." In truth, there was something about the boy that he liked. An earnest sincerity. "You know who I am?"

Brinin nodded.

"Everybody knows you. You are Beobrand, son of Grimgundi."

"And I am Ardith's true father. Did you know that?"

"Word travels quickly, lord. Everybody in Hithe knows it now."

"But you did not think I would be able to bring Ardith back without your help?"

"No, lord," Brinin stammered, "I meant no such thing…"

Beobrand clapped his shoulder.

"Now, I am mocking you," he said, with a grin.

Brinin did not smile, he returned Beobrand's gaze glumly.

"If you are to come with us, you will have to prove yourself useful."

"I will, lord," he said. "I will. I am strong, and good with my hands. And if it comes to a fight, I will stand with you."

Beobrand held him in his stare, appraising him. He liked the boy's determination. And he was touched at Brinin's declaration of love for Ardith. Beobrand felt a stab of guilt. Ardith had not known enough love in her short life.

"He cannot come," said Ferenbald. "He is but a boy. He is too young. We must turn back or put him ashore and send him home to Hithe."

"Too young, is it, Ferenbald?" asked Beobrand. "Is it not true that all men must at some moment grasp the thread of their wyrd? Is that not what separates men from boys?"

Lightning flickered in the west, lighting the black clouds momentarily with Thunor's fire.

Ferenbald held Beobrand's gaze for several heartbeats. Thunder growled in the distance.

"Very well. The boy comes with us. But know this, Beobrand. If he is hurt, or worse, it is on you, not me. And you will speak with Byrhtísen on our return."

Beobrand nodded. He was no stranger to having the life of men in his hands.

"You heard the man," he said to Brinin, "you stay. But if you are to travel with men, you must make yourself of use at all times. While aboard *Brimblæd* you will do as Ferenbald says." Beobrand raised his voice, so that all the men would hear. "Ferenbald commands here. This is his ship and his word must be obeyed."

Ferenbald offered him a smile and a nod.

Beobrand leaned in close and said in a hushed tone, "The men need to know whose voice to listen to. The ship and the sea are your domain. But when the bloodletting comes, and come it will, I will lead them. Understood?"

Ferenbald grinned.

"You'll hear no argument from me there, Beobrand. I am sure there is enough truth in the songs and tales to know that you are the killer here. Each man to his own strengths. I would not set a weaver the tasks of a butcher." Without awaiting a reply, Ferenbald turned his attention to *Brimblæd*. He strode back to the helm, barking out orders. The crew reacted instantly, the excitement of finding Brinin forgotten, or set aside while the more pressing matter of seeing them safely ashore was dealt with.

"Brinin," said Ferenbald, his voice carrying easily over the sounds of the ship, "you will do as Cargást says for now. He speaks with my voice. And let me not catch you shirking your duty, or you will regret your decision to choose now to become a man."

Brinin paled and made to follow Cargást once more towards the prow. Beobrand grasped his arm, holding him back.

"And Brinin," the youth swung round to look at him, "see that you stay alive."

The storm clouds roiled on the horizon and the swell grew. Another flicker of lightning was followed by the grumble of thunder and Beobrand watched as Brinin joined the busy sailors.

Beobrand clenched his fists at his side. He prayed he had made the right decision. But watching as Brinin joined the sailors, seemingly happy to have been accepted into their throng, Beobrand could not help but wonder whether he had as good as slain the boy himself. For one thing was certain, there would surely be weapon-play before this journey was ended and no man, and no boy, was safe in the steel-storm of a shieldwall.

Chapter 20

There was a storm brewing in the west. Sparks of lightning flickered in dark clouds and the grumbling of thunder rolled over the waves to *Saeslaga*.

Ardith pulled her new cloak about her shoulders. It was well made, thick wool trimmed with beaver fur. She had never owned anything so fine before and enjoyed running her fingers through the soft, smooth fur. She was glad of the cloak's warmth and the pelt trimming was comforting to stroke. It reminded her of the sleek coat of the cat that would sometimes sneak into the house at night when it was supposed to be catching rats from the granary. It was a savage tom, with shredded ears and a scarred face. The other children had learnt to keep their distance from the beast, as it made it clear to them that it did not like to be handled. If its snarling hisses were not enough, its needle-sharp claws quickly brought home the point and many of the children bore the thin scars to remind them.

But the cat had become Ardith's secret friend one cold winter night when driving rain had lashed the house and great gusts of wind had made the timbers groan and creak in the darkness. Ardith had not been able to sleep, lying awake terrified of the dreadful storm that raged in the night. Somehow, over the noises of the storm, she had heard the pitiful mewling of the cat followed by scratches at the door. How she had heard it she did not know, nor why the animal had come to her, but she had tiptoed through the house, frightened she would awaken her mother and father, and let the bedraggled creature in. It had followed her silently to the cot where she slept and it had curled up at her feet. She had been too frightened to touch it that night, instead content to feel the warm weight of its body nestling against her.

It did not come to her every night. Sometimes weeks went by when she would scarcely see the cat, but whenever they crossed paths, if she were alone, the animal would not flee as it did from the other children. It would approach her, looking up at her with its strange green eyes, even deigning to allow her to caress it. If she closed her eyes now, she could imagine that the fur trim of the cloak was the cat and that the timber behind her was the wall of her house in Hithe.

The air was colder than it had been of late and she huddled into the protection of the cloak. She no longer went to stand at the prow of the ship. Not since Draca and the dolphin. She had been foolish, imagining that by not looking at the men in the ship behind her she was somehow free. Safe.

She was not free. And she was not safe.

However much Grimr told her he would protect her, she knew that to leave her small haven at the stern of the ship was to invite danger.

And death.

Lightning lit the darkening sky. The sudden light picked out the dark stain on the woollen material of the cloak. She pulled back her hand, recoiling from the memory of how the stain came to be made. Grimr stood at the steerboard and when she looked his way he feigned disinterest. But she knew that his eyes were often upon her. Looking beyond him, the ship's wake disappeared into the distance. Gone were the other two ships that had accompanied them for the first few days. The men on those other ships had meant her no good she knew, but seeing the emptiness of the sea behind them made her loneliness more acute.

They had parted ways after Grimr had given her the cloak. She shuddered despite the garment's warmth.

They had put to shore where a few thatched buildings overlooked the sea. A small, unfinished church, surrounded by timber and piles of stone, stood atop a hill. Heaving the ships up onto the beach, they had waited for the townsfolk to visit, to trade, to offer them their produce and to see what Grimr and his band had brought from faraway lands. Grimr had seemed happy and the men were in high spirits. The local lord himself had come to them. He was a wealthy man, garnets and gold adorning his belt and cloak clasp. A quiet, sombre man, his retinue of servants and guards had stood by while he perused the goods that Grimr's people had lain out on the sand. To Grimr's apparent surprise and obvious delight, the lord had picked up a finely decorated and bejewelled golden crucifix that nestled in a carved wooden casket, and had asked Grimr how much he would like for it. Ardith had watched the events from the confines of the ship but she had heard later that the man had barely haggled, paying much more than Grimr had expected. And he had paid silver no less, leaving his steward to weigh out chunks of metal on a small scale he carried for that purpose. When asked why the lord wanted the relic, the steward told Grimr that the man's wife had died quite suddenly from a fever and that he would have the Christ priests pray for her soul. The lord meant to give the holy relic to the local priests that they may better be heard by the one true God.

That night the men had purchased a pig, strong mead and ale from the village and had built up a great fire on the beach. One of the men had butchered the swine and soon it was on a spit beside the blaze. It was a cloudless, cold night and Grimr had beckoned to her to come down from the ship to warm herself by the flames. She did not wish to sit with the men, but the warmth of the fire and the smell of the roasting meat had called to her.

She'd made her way tentatively to sit at the furthest reaches of the fire's light. The men had watched her approach and she had regretted leaving the apparent safety of the ship. The leering eyes, grins and lewd shouts unnerved her, but when Grimr handed her a chunk of coarse bread and a dripping slice of pork, her worries had momentarily been forgotten. She had ignored the men as much as she could, instead focusing on the warm food and the unusual sensation of the ground moving beneath her feet, the remembered motion of the sea tricking her mind. The ebony-skinned sailor, teeth and eyes flashing bright in the darkness, thrust a cup of ale into her hand and said something she did not understand. He answered to the name Ælmyrca, but where he came from was a mystery to her as were most of the words that he uttered. He terrified her, but she had timidly nodded her thanks, sipping the liquid. It was stronger than the ale she was used to at home. But it was good.

As the night had worn on, so the men had become drunker and louder. Grimr seemed to have forgotten she was there. He laughed and told riddles with Draca, who she had learnt was Grimr's brother. Now, thinking back to the incident with the dolphin, when Draca had struck her, Ardith thought Grimr had only spared his life because they were kin. She knew now how Grimr treated those not of his blood when they crossed him.

She huddled more tightly into the cloak, burying her hands into the plush fur of the edging. Lightning flashed again and the wind grew stronger and colder. Beneath the thick cloak Ardith was not cold, and yet her thin body trembled as the memories of that night tumbled through her thoughts.

It had happened so quickly. She had finished her food and drained the cup of ale and her eyes had begun to feel heavy. The heat from the fire, the food in her belly and the strong ale all worked to make her drowsy. Her head had nodded a few times when she had decided she could not sleep here with the men on the beach under the stars. Her blanket was on *Saeslaga* and she missed the comfort of having the ship's solid wood at her back. So she had climbed to her feet, silently leaving the light cast by the fire and headed back to the ship.

"I had wondered how long it would be until we could be alone," a rasping voice had whispered from the darkness.

Terrified, Ardith had drawn in a breath to scream. But before she could utter a sound, a callused hand had clamped over her mouth. An arm as strong as iron had wrapped about her and she'd been lifted from her feet. She'd struggled then, kicking and scratching and squirming. She had tried to bite the man's hand but was unable to open her mouth beneath the tight, iron-like grip. All the while, as she fought, she had felt herself being carried further from the fire into the total blackness of the night. After some time she had come to understand that she was too weak to free herself.

Think, she had told herself. Do not give in to fear. If you do, all will be lost. Think!

And so she had relaxed, hoping that if her assailant believed her to be cooperative she might be able to flee. The sounds of the sailors had faded when eventually the man had set her down onto her feet. She had tensed, ready to flee, or to renew her struggles, but he had gripped her tightly and whispered again in her ear.

"If you scream or try to run I will cut you open like that pig I gutted on the beach. Understand?"

Ardith had seen how easily the animal had been slain, how its innards had slithered, glistening and steaming, onto the sand. Her terror threatening to overcome her, she'd nodded and grunted something from behind his hand. Slowly, he had released his hold of her face, but his hand was instantly replaced by the cold, unyielding iron of a knife's blade at her throat. She had been too frightened to scream then. He had pushed her down onto the ground. The sand had been cold and damp beneath her. By the distant light of the fire and the silver glimmer of the half-moon she recognised her attacker. His name was Abrecand and in the days since she had been with the ships he had never before spoken to her. But she knew him by his fine cloak with the beaver fur trim and the hungry gaze that had followed her whenever she had moved.

Later she thought of what she should have done. Perhaps she could have bitten him. Maybe she should have clawed at his eyes or kicked out at his manhood. Should she have wrested the knife from his hand and turned it upon him? Would not a brave girl have fought harder or screamed out?

And yet she had done none of these things.

She had lain, trembling in her terror as the man pushed up her peplos, his jagged nails digging into the soft flesh of her thighs. She had done nothing as he pushed down his breeches, and lowered himself onto her. He had been panting in his excitement, his sour breath washing over her face as his hands roved over her body, pinching, squeezing, probing. She had barely been able to breathe such was her fear and yet later, whenever she thought back on that night she believed she had been craven, that somehow this had been her fault, of her doing. That perhaps, in some strange way that she did not fully comprehend, she had led the man to believe that she was willing to lie with him.

She had cast about for anything, or anyone, that could help her, but they'd been alone in the darkness, the cold stars gazing down implacably on her anguish.

When Abrecand had thrust his hands between her thighs, forcing them apart, she had squeezed her eyes shut, blotting out the terror, hiding her shame from the stars and the moon. She had prayed silently, feverishly to the Blessed Virgin that she would take this horror away from her. And in that instant, the weight atop her lessened and warm liquid splashed her face.

"I told you, Abrecand," bellowed a new voice, strangely accented.

Grimr.

"I told all you whoresons that the girl was not to be touched."

She had opened her eyes then.

Her attacker was dying, his lifeblood pouring from a huge gash in his throat that Grimr had opened with Abrecand's own knife. The hot blood gushed over Ardith's face and chest and as Grimr had pulled the man from her she had scrabbled away, sobs finally racking her body.

The rest of that night was a blur in her memories. Abrecand had been dragged back to the fire. She did not know if he was dead by then, but he was certainly dead after Grimr had cut off his manhood and shoved it into his mouth. Grimr had raved at the men, slurring his words in his anger and drunkenness, his thick accent making them barely intelligible. But the meaning was clear to all. Ardith was not to be touched.

Later, Grimr had placed Abrecand's cloak over Ardith and carried her gently back to her resting place on the ship.

"You are safe now," he had whispered to her in the darkness, his words thick with emotion.

Safe.

Ardith smiled grimly to herself. She would never be safe while she was aboard this ship, with these men. She wondered whether she would ever be safe again. Staring out at the wake that trailed behind *Saeslaga* she watched a gannet spear into the water. She had offered up thanks to the Blessed Virgin, for surely it was the mother of Christ who had saved her that night. Still, as her home and the life she had known grew ever distant, she could not rely on the Virgin's protection. Grimr might keep her safe until they reached their destination. And then, who knew? Or perhaps the lust she saw in his eyes would grow until he could no longer control it and he would snatch from her that which Abrecand had failed to take.

No, she would never be safe. But next time one of these bastards came to her with thoughts of lust in their mind they would not find a coward, or a placid girl. She would be no plaything for these men or any others. For, like the cat back in Hithe, she had claws now. Beneath the warmth of Abrecand's cloak Ardith's fingers wrapped around the cold blade of the knife which she had snatched from the sand even as Abrecand's blood had pumped onto the beach, steaming just like the slaughtered pig's.

She clutched the weapon to her, tracing the sharp edge with her thumb. The metal was gelid; as final as death. It was comforting in a way that the soft beaver fur could never be. She gripped her secret claw tightly beneath the cloak and waited for the storm to come.

PART TWO

WARM WELCOMES ON THE WHALE ROAD

þær ic ne gehyrde
butan hlimman sæ,
iscaldne wæg.

There I heard nothing
but the roaring sea,
the ice-cold wave.

"The Seafarer", author unknown – The Exeter Book

Chapter 21

The wind shifted and the storm blew in just as Ferenbald had predicted. *Brimblæd* raced before the squall on surging waves that shoved against her beams, attempting to twist her from her course. Beobrand feared they would be swamped by the angry sea, but Ferenbald grinned as the force of the wind grew. These were waters he had sailed countless times before and he had clearly been waiting for this moment for a long while; when he had command of his father's ship, with a crew of able sailors who answered to his words and did his bidding without question or complaint.

The swell had risen dangerously by the time they were swept into Hastingas. The rain lashed at them like icy pebbles cast from the heavens by rancorous gods. The sky was the colour of soot.

Beobrand clung to a shroud and offered a silent prayer to Woden. The storm brought back the terror of that long night aboard *Háligsteorra* on the journey south. He was glad the tossing of the ship no longer made him sick, but the fear of plunging beneath the chill waves settled on him like a shroud. He shivered. The bitter rain flayed his face. Lightning crashed overhead. The night was filled with white light and the terrible roar of Thunor's fury.

Ferenbald stood at the helm, feet seemingly rooted to the planks of the deck. His beard and mane swirled in the wind, wreathed his head in a halo of hair and lightning flicker. The young skipper's mouth was open and Beobrand caught something over the screaming tempest. Ferenbald was laughing.

Bearn was in a wretched state, retching and reeling. Cynan, Dreogan, Fraomar, Garr and Attor had all struggled against the pitching of the ship and made their way back to stand close to their lord, as if their swords and stout hearts could protect him from the ire of the storm. It was folly, Beobrand knew. But was glad to be surrounded by his gesithas, taking some comfort from their proximity.

Attor stared aghast at Ferenbald, who was still laughing uproariously. The slender warrior pulled out the rood he wore at his neck and made the sign of the cross over his body in the way of the Christ followers.

"The man's mad," he yelled over the rushing wind, rain and surf.

Beobrand reached his free hand up to grip the Thunor's hammer amulet he wore at his throat. His hair plastered against his face and he shook his head to clear his vision.

"Perhaps not so mad," he said. "Look." He pointed into the encroaching gloom. For a moment it seemed that before them lay only foam-topped waves, an endless world of water and danger. But then they could all see what Beobrand had pointed out. It was faint, hard to see through the rain-riven darkness. The men blinked, trying to free their eyes of the after-images from the bright fire of the lightning.

Brimblæd rose up a wave. At its peak, just before the ship slid down into the trough, Fraomar let out a cry, gesturing in the same direction as Beobrand.

"A light!" he shouted. "It looks close."

"More than one light," shouted Ferenbald. "Those are the beacons of Hastingas. They light them to guide ships in." He laughed again. "Of course, you need to be close enough to see them on a night like this!" The skipper bellowed orders to the crew, his voice booming like the thunder.

"Mad or not," said Dreogan, "he knows how to pilot this wave-steed."

Bearn said nothing. He was as pale as whey.

As *Brimblæd* crested another wall of water, Beobrand had to agree with Dreogan. They were lucky to have Ferenbald at the helm of the ship. How he had steered them into the very harbour he intended was beyond Beobrand's ken. All around them lay wind-tossed water and darkness, and yet Hrothgar's son had guided them to safety.

Beobrand was about to respond to Dreogan when another shaft of lightning crackled out over the sea, followed an eye-blink later by a cataclysmic crash. It would not do to think of safety when the gods were reminding him that the flimsy vessel and its occupants were still at the mercy of the wind and the tide.

The harsh brilliance of the lightning picked out details on the beach in stark contrast to the dark sky where the clouds tumbled and rolled. There were three large beacons blazing on the dunes beyond the strand. Men were gathered on the beach, their faces white and staring in the flash of the storm's light. Beyond the dunes were several buildings. Trees, limbs stripped of leaves, reached up over the settlement with skeletal fingers.

All this Beobrand saw in a single moment of light. The images burnt into his mind and he could see them still when he blinked. *Brimblæd* was coming on too fast, pushed by the wind and the waves towards the land. Beobrand clutched the amulet at his throat and clung to the swaying shroud. How had he believed they were safe? He could almost hear Thunor's laughter in the roar of the tempest. The puny ship would be dashed against the beach, or some hidden rocks, and they would be drowned. Beobrand remembered the terror in Dalston's eyes as he had disappeared beneath the waves.

He cast about for a sign of Coenred. He had not seen the monk for some time and now, suddenly, he felt the weight of his friend's life upon him. He could not let him die as Dalston had. *Brimblæd* was buffeted by a breaking wave, bitter cold water sluiced into the ship and it listed alarmingly. Gods, they were going to capsize. But then, as if by Ferenbald's sheer force of will, she righted herself. At the same moment, Beobrand saw Coenred, quaking and huddled against the storm, but safe enough and out of the way of the sailors, who, even now rushed to fulfil their master's orders.

Ferenbald no longer laughed. His face had become a mask of concentration. But his voice was firm and carried over the tumult as he bellowed commands. The men responded and Beobrand again marvelled at the captain's sea-skill. *Brimblæd* looked to be heading side on for a collision with the land. With the strength of the waves it seemed impossible that she would not be toppled, casting the crew and passengers into the cold water. But then, with a shout from Ferenbald, a couple of the crew heaved on a sheet and he leaned on the steerboard with all his strength and weight and *Brimblæd* answered by turning towards the shingle, wave-washed beach. In a few heartbeats, the ship had ridden a wave high onto the strand. Its keel ground and rasped against the sand and pebbles of the beach and it had not ceased moving when sailors were leaping over the sides into the churning surf.

For a heart-clenching instant Beobrand thought they were abandoning the ship, fleeing from its wreck. Just as quickly he saw what they were about. They were not seeking to save themselves, they were saving the ship.

"Come on," he shouted. His voice sounded strained and fearful to his own ears. He hoped the men would not notice. He forced himself to relinquish his grip on the shroud. His hands were stiff, aching from cold. The ship lurched suddenly as the water receded from beneath its hull and Beobrand clutched again at the rigging to prevent himself from falling. Taking a deep breath to steady his nerves, he raised his voice over the roaring of the storm. "We must help pull *Brimblæd* beyond the reach of the sea." His voice was steadier now. "Come on."

Without waiting to see his gesithas' response, he released his hold on the rigging again and swung himself over the side of the ship.

He instantly plunged into water so cold that his breath was snatched from his lungs. A wave broke, cascading water over his head. He spluttered and coughed, spitting out a mouthful of brine. The water receded, leaving the sea washing about his chest. Gods, it was deeper here than he had thought. More figures splashed into the waves near him and rose out of the murk like beasts of the deep. A hand reached out to him, gripping his arm and tugging him towards the beach, into the shallows.

"Follow me, lord."

A crackle of distant lightning showed Beobrand the man's face. Cynan. Another wave crashed over them, momentarily submerging both men. Cynan did not release his grip on Beobrand's arm. Beobrand nodded, unable to talk, his mouth and nose full of water.

Together, they waded up the sloping beach to where the sailors now stood. In the time it had taken Beobrand and his gesithas to reach them through the foam and surf, *Brimblæd*'s crew had marshalled themselves. Ropes had been thrown down to them and now they set about hauling the ship up the beach.

What had appeared so light on the surface of the sea, tossed by the waves and wind like a leaf in a stream, was cumbersome indeed on land. Men came down from the dunes and picked up the ropes, lending their weight to the crew's efforts. Beobrand spat out more seawater and shouldered his way into the group of men tugging at the closest rope. By the occasional flicker of Thunor's fire and the flames from the beacons on the dunes, he saw the rest of his men take places at the ropes. Even Bearn, who had to stop momentarily, doubling over to empty his stomach, grasped the hempen cord and added his strength to the task of bringing the ship high above the tide line, where it could rest safely while the storm raged.

It took only moments to drag *Brimblæd* up the beach to where marram grass grew and the sea never reached. The men dropped the ropes to the shingle, their talk strident and boisterous. They slapped each other on the back and joked loudly. Beobrand recognised the brash tone of their jests. He had heard the same after countless battles when men would boast of their exploits. They were full of the joy of surviving when moments before death had seemed so certain.

Someone said something amusing and laughter rang out. It was a good sound. And they were right to be happy. They yet lived and, unlike after a clash of shieldwalls, none of them had lost friends or family this day.

Beobrand turned away from the gathered men and shivered. He dragged in great lungfuls of the salty air. It had not taken long to pull the ship to safety, but the terror of the storm, the freezing water and the exertion had exacted their toll on him. He wished for a dry cloak and a warm fire. His hands shook at his sides and he clenched them into fists, willing them to be still.

Absently, he noted that Cynan was close beside him. Beobrand frowned. Together they watched as more men clambered from the ship. With a sigh of relief Beobrand saw the pale face of Coenred peering over the wale. He raised a hand, but wasn't sure that the young monk saw him.

Beyond *Brimblæd*, the sea was a chaos of foamy peaks. Lightning streaked the sky far out to sea. The ire of the storm seemed to have dissipated as soon as they had found shelter on the beach. It was as if Thunor had tired of his sport now.

Beobrand spat and shuddered again. It was foolish to think such things. His mind turned to Octa far away in Northumbria. Was his son well? How was he being treated by Oswiu and his household? The image of Ardith as he had last seen her came to him then; a small child, fair hair framing a delicate face. Was she out there even now on that storm-savaged sea?

The gods cared nought for mortals. They would not protect his offspring. They left that for children's fathers. Beobrand gripped the Thunor's hammer amulet at his throat. He offered up a silent challenge to the god of thunder, his unuttered words as bitter as the salt in his mouth.

"Go on then, Thunor," he thought, "blow and rage! Call up gales and storms to stop me. There is nothing you can place before me that will prevent me from fulfilling my wyrd. I have set myself on this path and I will bring the girl back, or I will die in the attempt."

Wind gusted hard, tugging at his sodden kirtle, making him shiver. In the distance, sparks of lightning lit the clouds. He held his breath, waiting to hear the sound of Thunor's laughter, but he heard nothing over the crash of the waves and the howl of the wind.

Chapter 22

The lightning grew ever more distant during the night, until the thunder was the merest of grumbles from afar, barely heard over the tumult of the wind and rain that battered the hall where *Brimblæd*'s crew had sought shelter. Beobrand wondered whether Thunor had heard his silent challenge. With each far-off rumble he shivered and took another swig of ale. The drink was good and strong, and soon Beobrand was drunk. Thoughts of gods drifted from his mind. But the drink did nothing to brighten his mood.

They were comfortable enough in the great hall of Hastingas. It was a clean, well-run place and Lord Dudoc and his wife, Aelfgyth, a portly grey-haired couple who looked enough alike to be siblings, were hospitable and friendly. They knew Ferenbald, who had often visited them when trading with Hrothgar, and Lord Dudoc was overjoyed to entertain the famed Beobrand from songs and tales in his humble hall. The heavy-jowled lord had ordered a feast to be prepared and a beaming Lady Aelfgyth had offered Beobrand the Waes Hael cup. He had taken a long draught of the sweet mead. It was good and he'd nodded his thanks. When the food was served it was sumptuous and hearty and the men had laughed to be fed such delicacies as roast goose, its flesh dripping with fat, and a rich black pudding that had been boiled along with the pottage. All of this had been served with some of the softest bread Beobrand had ever tasted.

Despite the warm welcome, the rich food and the fine ale and mead, and no matter how much Dudoc cajoled him, Beobrand would not be drawn into telling tales of his exploits. After a time, the old man had frowned, sucking on his moustaches grumpily, and stopped asking. And yet he seemed incapable of being quiet and he quickly continued to prattle on about all manner of things. For the most part Beobrand allowed the man's words to wash over him as he ate and drank his fill. The food was well-prepared, wholesome and fulfilling and from time to time Beobrand mumbled his thanks for the selection of meats and fish on the board. He knew they would be eating into Dudoc's winter stores and would not have been surprised to detect resentment at the number of mouths he needed to feed. But to his credit, Dudoc seemed genuinely pleased of the diversion presented by his surprise guests. Beobrand felt a prickle of guilt at not giving the man what he wanted, but he could not bring himself to talk of the glories of battle. He had long since accepted that part of him craved the madness of battle; the clang and clash of sword on shield. But he had never felt at ease making light of the spear-din and horror of the shieldwall. The screams and stink and terror were not worthy of songs.

"You were there, were you not, Lord Beobrand?" Dudoc asked.

Beobrand had not been listening. He turned now to the plump lord at his side. Dudoc's eyes glittered expectantly in the firelight. With a wrench, Beobrand was suddenly aware that this portly, elderly man reminded him of Tondberct. He had the same eagerness, the same babbling exuberance. But Tondberct was long since dead. Beobrand took a great swallow of ale. Is this what Tondberct would have become, had he lived? He pushed the thoughts away. Tondberct was dead. Hanged by Beobrand for savage crimes. He had not deserved to live.

Fleetingly, he recalled the boy who had tumbled into the North Sea during the storm. Had he too deserved death? He had offered Woden the boy's life in payment for sparing *Háligsteorra*. But the boy's end had not been his doing. He knew this to be true, so why then did he feel guilty at the thought of him? Beobrand drank more ale.

"Where?" he asked, his voice only slightly slurred.

"Why, at Maserfelth, of course," replied Dudoc. "They say it was the greatest battle ever seen in Albion. The scops speak of the majesty of the two warhosts. And the magnificence of the two kings who commanded them. You served Oswald, did you not?" Dudoc seemed to scarcely need to breathe, his words came as fast as hailstones.

Beobrand sighed and held the old man in his gaze until his words dried up. Thinking of Tondberct and the young sailor had only further soured his mood.

"I was there," he said.

Dudoc plucked a slice of goose breast from the trencher before him and popped it into his fleshy mouth.

"What was it like?" he asked, spitting globules of meat as he spoke.

Anger flared within Beobrand. He remembered the corpses strewn on the hill. The ravens and wolves had gorged themselves at Maserfelth. He recalled Renweard's blood-splattered corpse. Seeing Eowa's red-and-black boar banner dip and fall, trampled beneath a tide of Waelisc warriors. Oswald's limbs and head atop the waelstengs where Penda's priest had placed them. And then his mind turned unbidden to the face of his friend, Acennan, as he had last seen it. Brave, faithful Acennan, eyes unseeing, tongue-lolling from mottled pallid flesh.

Gods, how he missed Acennan.

"What was it like?" he snapped, and his voice held the steel edge of murder. Dudoc's chewing slowed and he swallowed with an effort. The older man nodded, quiet and uncertain now in the face of the rage that washed off Beobrand.

"I'll tell you what it was like," Beobrand went on, his voice growing in volume as his anger pulled him with it. All eyes in the hall turned to him then. Conversations faltered. "It was terror and death, blood and shit. Have you ever stood in the shieldwall, Dudoc?" The man shook his head slowly. "Then you have no right to ask those who have done so what it was like. Just thank whatever gods you pray to that you have grown old and fat without having to see your shield-brothers cut down beside you. To hear the screams of dying boys wailing for their mothers." He placed his hands upon the board, holding them still and taking a deep, shuddering breath. As quickly as it had flared up, so his ire dissipated. He lowered his voice to a whisper. "I sometimes awake at night to the sound of screams from boys who will never grow into men." He sighed and reached once more for his ale.

Before he lifted the horn to drink, Dudoc placed his hand on Beobrand's outstretched arm.

"I am sorry," the old man said. Tears welled in his eyes.

Beobrand drained the horn of ale and pushed himself up from the table.

"No, it is I who should be sorry," he said. He was suddenly filled with shame. His face burnt hot. "I am poor company tonight."

Without waiting for a reply, he strode from the hall. The door wards swung the doors open and he stepped out into the wind-blown night. The birch trees that towered over the hall creaked and rattled, the sound of breaking bones. From the black distance beyond the shadows of the dunes came the churning roll of the waves breaking on the beach. Laughter echoed loud from inside the hall.

Beobrand took a deep breath. The air was cold and clear after the smoke-thick atmosphere of the hall. Stepping out from the porch, he lifted his face to the sky, welcoming the rain, allowing it to wash over him. A presence behind him made him half-turn before he realised it was Cynan. Whatever the man's failings, there was no denying that he took his role as Beobrand's protector seriously.

Beobrand shook his head, again wishing that Acennan yet lived. When he was alive, Beobrand had never truly understood how much he had confided in his friend, but since his death, he felt more alone than ever.

"I can take a piss without you watching over me, Cynan," he said, forcing any frustration from his voice. Cynan was a good man. None of this was his doing.

"I will wait here," Cynan replied and stepped back under the shelter of the small porch that covered the hall's double doors.

When Beobrand returned from relieving himself, he found Cynan to be as good as his word. He stood in the shadows, alert and poised. Beobrand noticed how the tension went out of Cynan as he saw him coming back out of the rain. There was another figure in the porch with him now.

"Coenred," said Beobrand, "are you well?"

The monk stepped from the shadows of the door and pulled his robes about him against the chill of the night.

"Yes, I am well," he replied. "Are you?"

The spark of his anger threatened to rekindle, but Beobrand suppressed his ire with an effort of will.

"I am well," he said. "I just wish this storm would blow over and we could be on our way. I hate being closed in here in the warmth and comfort of Dudoc's hall when Ardith... my daughter..." His voice caught in his throat and the force of his emotion surprised him. "When she is out there." He waved his mutilated left hand at the stormy darkness.

Cynan pressed his back to the doors and pretended not to be listening. Coenred placed a slender hand on Beobrand's shoulder.

"No ships can be abroad on such a night. Our quarry will not be making any headway tonight."

Beobrand nodded. He knew it was true, but still his frustration burnt within him. There was nothing they could do but to wait out the storm, but he could feel the pressure of their inaction building up within him.

"What if they were caught out on the sea when the storm struck?" he asked. He thought of the night they had been driven from the shore into the teeth of a storm aboard *Háligsteorra*; the face of the boy who had looked like Tondberct. The rest of them had been lucky to survive.

"Try not to think such things, Beo," said Coenred, his tone comforting and soft. "I have been praying for Ardith's safety every day since we heard of her plight. God will keep her safe."

Beobrand snorted. He offered Coenred a thin smile. Though he found the monk's blind faith in his god galling, he could not be angry with his friend.

"I give you my thanks. Perhaps your god will listen to you, Coenred. But it will not be the nailed Christ who will bring my daughter back. And it will not be your god who slays the men who have taken her. Now," he said, clapping Coenred on the shoulder harder than he needed to, "I need another drink."

Before Coenred could respond, Beobrand pushed his way back into the smoke-filled hall.

Chapter 23

The storm raged for a whole day and two nights before blowing itself out. In its wake it left uprooted trees, fallen branches, flattened fences and damaged buildings. But on the morning of the third day in Hastingas the sky was clear and the land looked fresh and new, scoured clean by the force of the elements.

On the first night in Dudoc's hall, Beobrand had continued to drink heavily until he at last wrapped himself in a coarse woollen blanket by the hearth. Some of Ferenbald's crew, exhausted from the trials of the day at sea and full of Dudoc's meat and mead were already asleep. Others were still talking and drinking. His gesithas sat at one end of the board and shared a pitcher of strong mead with *Brimblæd*'s sailors. From time to time a voice would be raised in jest, but Beobrand had no patience for humour.

He felt eyes on him as he lay down, hopeful of the welcome release of sleep. He half expected an offer of a sleeping chamber from Dudoc or Aelfgyth, but nobody spoke up. Beobrand grunted as he made himself comfortable. His thoughts and movements were fuzzy, blurred and dulled by drink, but he knew he had been a poor guest, cantankerous and surly. On the morrow he would seek to repay Dudoc's hospitality at least with a smile and some kind words. He was a lord of Bernicia now, not a farm boy. He must learn to curb his temper and frustrations and act the part of a thegn. Sleep overtook him without warning as he berated himself for his churlish behaviour.

Reaghan came to him in his dreams. It was warm by the embers on the hearth stone and her small hands were cold against his skin as she lifted the blanket and pushed her body against him. Her cool fingers gently caressed his neck and chest. He groaned softly. An animal sound. He had missed her. His body thrilled at her touch and he felt himself hardening in an instant. He moaned as her soft lips fluttered against his and he tasted mead on her tongue as it probed his mouth. The sensation was so real. He clung to the dream, pressing his eyes closed, not wishing to let it vanish into the night. His groin throbbed. He ached for Reaghan. It had been over a year since he had last lain with her.

She raised the blanket, allowing the night-cool air of the hall to waft underneath. For a moment he was chilled, but in an instant she had straddled him, her body-warmth engulfing him, the weight of her hips pressing against him. Long hair fell over his face and her slim fingers pulled his strong callused hands up to her breasts. He squeezed her flesh gently, feeling her nipples stiffen. The breasts were full and heavy, unlike Reaghan's slender, fragile form.

His eyes flickered open. This was no dream.

And this was not Reaghan.

By the dim light of the dying embers he recognised the woman atop him as one of those who had been serving at the feast. She was comely, and had smiled when he had looked her way during the evening. He had thought no more of her, instead focusing on the ale and mead until the welcome escape of sleep had come.

It seemed she had plans of her own for him.

"What are you—" he whispered, but she smothered his mouth in another kiss. Despite himself he moaned again at the taste of her and the grinding of her hips against him.

Breaking off from the kiss, she said, "Hush, my hero," her breath hot and sweet.

"I am no hero," he whispered, but she silenced him again with her mouth and her hands reached down to free his manhood.

Beobrand's heart hammered in his chest. He had been so long without a woman. She guided him, grunting deep in the back of her throat as he pushed inside her. His passion mounted as quickly as his anger had earlier that evening. He grasped her hips and thrust into her. She continued to kiss him, their tongues exploring, lips pressed so forcefully together that they were bruised the next morning. With each heave of his hips she let out a small moan, hidden and muffled within their locked mouths.

Only a few heartbeats later, Beobrand thrust inside her for the final time, his body jerking and shaking. For a short while afterwards, they clung to each other, panting and trembling despite the warmth of their bodies. And then, she rose and vanished into the gloom of the hall without another word.

*

The next morning she served him porridge. She smiled, but made no display of what had happened in the night. He recalled the warmth of her body against his and felt his face grow hot. He glanced about at the men seated around him, but there was no knowing look, or lewd comment. If anyone had witnessed their coupling, nobody spoke of it.

The day passed slowly. The men riddled and played tafl. Beobrand sipped ale and talked to Ferenbald about where he thought Grimr might be headed and what they could expect as they sailed further down the coast. The skipper said he had spoken to Dudoc the night before and Grimr's three ships had stopped there not a sennight earlier. They had arrived at sundown, traded the following day and then set off at the turn of the tide the next morning. That meant they were only a few days ahead of them, said Ferenbald. And he seemed happy with that. If Grimr continued the pattern of halting at each wic and harbour, Ferenbald was certain they would close with the pirates soon enough.

"And if they have crossed the Narrow Sea?" Beobrand asked.

Ferenbald grinned, seemingly undaunted by the prospect.

"It is just more water for *Brimblæd* to cut through. I have sailed to Frankia many times. Do not fear. We will catch up with them."

Beobrand looked into the flames of the hearth fire. Outside the rain beat against the hall, falling from a slate-grey sky. The wind gusted and moaned in the eaves.

And when they catch them, he thought, what then? And what of Ardith? What horrors might she be enduring?

He took a draught of ale, gripping the cup so tightly that the willow wood creaked.

At the far end of the hall, near the double doors, his gesithas had cleared away the tables and benches and now Cynan and Dreogan set about teaching Brinin the rudiments of weapon-skill. The boy was earnest and solemn, biting his lip in concentration as the warriors shouted encouragement. All of the men, sailors and warriors alike, seemed to look upon the boy fondly, and whilst Beobrand was still concerned over what might happen when they caught up with their quarry, he was pleased with the decision to let Brinin join them.

Bearn came and sat near Beobrand, filling a drinking horn with ale and leaning back, stretching out his feet to the fire with a grunt of pleasure. He had recovered quickly once they were on land and Beobrand was sure that he was pleased of the chance to eat and drink without the fear of emptying his guts the moment the food touched his stomach.

Bearn indicated with his chin at where Cynan was showing Brinin how to hold his shield arm and sword for the best chance at defence and counter attack.

"What do you think?" Bearn asked. "Will we make a Black Shield of him?"

Beobrand studied Brinin for a while before replying.

"He's no natural fighter, that's for certain." Cynan gave the boy an order and Brinin leapt forward, clattering his blade down hard on Cynan's black-painted shield. "But he is strong," said Beobrand, "and willing to learn. I think we'll make a warrior of him yet."

They watched in silence as the boy continued to beat his borrowed blade against Cynan's shield. The Waelisc warrior parried each blow easily, stepping lightly to the left and right until he tired of taking the brunt of Brinin's clumsy attacks. Without warning, Cynan stepped inside Brinin's over-reaching swing and placed the edge of his sword gently against the boy's throat. There was a moment of silence, before Cynan stepped away.

"Reminds me of Eadgard with those great swings," Cynan said, laughing. Eadgard was one of Beobrand's warband who had remained in the north, guarding Ubbanford. He was a huge brute of a man, who wielded an axe in battle, cleaving through his enemies as if he were chopping timber.

Beobrand rose and made his way over to them.

"Brinin," he said, "all those days spent helping your father at the forge have given you great strength. That is good. But just as when you are forging a blade, you need skill and finesse too. Practise, and listen to Cynan and Dreogan. And when the time comes, perhaps you will be ready to stand with us."

"Thank you, lord," said Brinin.

Beobrand frowned.

"Do not thank me. This is no gift I am giving you. But if it comes to it, I would rather you knew which end of a sword to stick into our foe."

When Dudoc joined them shortly after, Beobrand found the man's company more agreeable than the night before. He thanked him for welcoming them into his hall and the old man beamed, Beobrand's poor humour seemingly forgotten. They talked at length and Beobrand found himself speaking of Ubbanford, of Sunniva and Reaghan and Octa. Dudoc grew sombre, nodding gravely at hearing of Beobrand's misfortunes and smiling at his successes. He did not push for more than Beobrand was willing to tell, and so the day wore on pleasantly enough as the storm continued to bluster outside. The rushes on the floor near the door became sodden and squelched underfoot from all the coming and going of the men to the midden, but the hall was warm and dry and they were all glad not to be out on the Narrow Sea on such a day.

Dudoc wished to play tafl and brought out a fine board of oak and pieces fashioned from bone and antler. Beobrand cared little for the game, but there was nothing better to occupy his time, so he moved his pieces around the board dutifully attempting to ensnare the king. His thoughts turned to Oswiu and the pieces that shifted position around the king of Bernicia ever since Oswald's death. He wondered how long Oswiu could play the game and whether the stakes were too high now. His heart wasn't in it, as he imagined the pieces on the board to be the players in the great game of kings and thrones. Which piece was he? Was Oswine on the board? And Eanflæd? They played all through that long afternoon, Beobrand losing more than he won, while the lord of the hall grinned and clapped his hands at his good fortune.

When the women came to serve them food and to replenish the pitchers of ale, Beobrand caught himself watching out for his buxom night-time visitor. He was disappointed not to see her during the day, but as evening drew in and the hall was prepared once more for a feast, she was there again. She went about her business, carrying platters of mutton and salted fish, bringing a great tray of freshly baked loaves and then refilling the jugs. Beobrand listened to Dudoc, nodding absently, but his eyes followed the woman's movements. Her clothes were well made, but simple enough. A cream under-dress beneath a green peplos. She was perhaps a few years older than Beobrand, with an alluring swing to her hips and a bounce to her bosom that attracted the gaze of several of the men. At her waist she wore a girdle of woven linen, and iron keys hung from the belt. Was she widowed perhaps? He thought about asking Dudoc, or perhaps Aelfgyth, but he did not know how without inviting them to question his interest. So he merely watched her as she poured ale and served food, smiling demurely as she went. He thanked her when she filled his drinking horn. She did not look him in the eye, but dipped her gaze.

The mood in the hall on that second night was more convivial than the first. The men were rested and were no longer strangers to the hall's inhabitants. The wind had lessened, the storm giving way to straight sheets of rain that slicked the thatch and cascaded from the eaves. The board was again plentiful. The greasy mutton and salty herring was filling and tasty and the ale was yet fresh. Beobrand wondered for how long Dudoc could continue to host them in such a fashion, but the old lord smiled and appeared happy enough.

When the fire had burnt down and men were nodding over their cups, Fraomar stood and began to tell the tale of Maserfelth. He had a clear voice and though he was no scop, his telling was good. Fraomar told of the clash of shieldwalls atop the hill overlooking the wide expanse of the Maerse. To hear the tale from his lips, it sounded as though Beobrand and his black-shielded warriors were the only ones with mettle who had been brave enough to stand with their king. For a moment, Beobrand was embarrassed. Many were the men who had stood strong that day, and many had fallen in defence of the land and their king. But he heard the pride in Fraomar's tone, saw the glint of memories in the eyes of his gesithas and the rapt expressions on the faces of Dudoc and the men of his retinue. Who was he to stand in the way of his men recounting their well-earned battle-fame? They were his sworn men, shield-brothers, steadfast and doughty and had every right to be proud. He was their hlaford and gave them gifts as was his duty. In return he expected their loyalty and their service. Their fame-hoard was theirs to do with as they wished.

Just as the flames of the hearth fire died away into glowing embers, so the noise of the feast slowly ebbed away and was replaced by snores and murmured, drunken conversations in shadowed corners of the hall. Beobrand's head ached where he had been hit by a sling shot in the battle of the great ditch in East Angeln. It troubled him thus whenever he was tired or drank too much mead. But despite the throb in his forehead, he was content. He found a place further from the fire and far from the draughts that came from the doors. Wrapping himself in his blanket, he lay down. The dry rushes crackled beneath him and high above, out of sight in the darkness, the rain hammered against the roof, creating a muffled, rolling drone. He thought of the previous night and how his sleep had been interrupted. He smiled to himself in the gloom. Listening to the sounds of the night, he waited in anticipation, hoping she would come to him again.

He did not know for how long he had slept when she slid beneath his blanket, but the fire-glow was gone and the hum of the rain was different, lighter and less constant. Beobrand was instantly awake and could feel himself grinning in the darkness. Gods, he had not realised until the previous night how much he had missed having a woman.

As on her first visit, she did not speak, instead awakening his body with her hands, her lips and her tongue. He would have liked to savour the moment, to draw it out and enjoy each touch, every caress. But there was an urgency to her, and in what seemed like only a moment, she had lifted up her skirts and taken him inside her. She kissed him furiously, as she heaved and rocked atop him and any thoughts Beobrand had of slowing down were forgotten. He pushed into her, revelling at the slick tightness, feeling the building pressure within him.

Without warning, she broke from the deep kiss and whispered close to his ear, "I would have the seed of a hero in me."

Beobrand halted his rhythm with difficulty. Her words were jarring, threatening to extinguish the fire of his passion. By all the gods, his seed?

"I am no hero," he whispered to her for the second time.

But she kissed him again, silencing his words. She rolled her hips with increasing speed, with each motion taking him deep inside her. He grunted. By Woden, there was no holding back now. If she wanted his seed, she would have it.

Moments later, gasping and panting, he gave her what she craved.

When he awoke, she was gone and it was morning. The storm had blown over and the day was clear.

Chapter 24

They left Dudoc's hall on the morning tide. Beobrand had searched the faces of the women who served them when they had broken their fast, but she was nowhere to be seen. He felt an unexpected pang of regret as they trudged down to the beach.

A line of flotsam and debris showed where the storm tide had reached, but beneath that point, the sand and shingle was pristine, clean and smooth. Waves lapped up the beach, the vehemence of the storm a distant dream.

Ferenbald and his crew busied themselves about *Brimblæd*, checking her rigging and hull for damage. Beobrand and his gesithas carried the sea chests and other stores down from the hall where they had been secured against the rain and wind. And then, as soon as Ferenbald had declared the ship seaworthy, they helped to heave *Brimblæd* into the surf. The water was icy cold on their legs, making them gasp. Beobrand clambered aboard, his breeches clinging wet and cold to his legs. He already missed the warm smoky hall of Hastingas.

Dudoc's people came down to the sea's edge to bid them farewell. Beobrand again searched the crowd, but there was no sign of his nocturnal visitor.

"Thank you for your welcome and your hospitality," Beobrand called out from the stern of the ship, where he stood near Ferenbald. "The name of Dudoc will forever be woven into the tale of Beobrand of Ubbanford and you will always find a warm welcome in my lands." Dudoc's round face broke into a broad grin and he hugged Aelfgyth to him. Beobrand could not help but return the man's smile, such was his infectious happiness. As the oars bit into the water, pulling them out to sea, Beobrand raised his hand and shouted, "Farewell!"

Dudoc waved back for a long while until the figures on the beach were hard to discern. All the while, Beobrand watched the gathered throng beneath the dunes and swaying marram grass until they were lost in the distance.

Ferenbald ordered the sail to be unfurled and with a crack the cloth billowed and the ship picked up speed, leaving Hastingas behind them.

"Well, Lord Beobrand," Ferenbald said in a loud voice, "it is just as well we left when we did."

"You think we will catch up with Grimr soon?"

"Well, yes," Ferenbald replied, a smile tugging at his mouth, "we must not waste time if we are to catch our quarry. But that is not what I meant."

"No?" enquired Beobrand, unease prickling at the back of his neck. "What was your meaning?"

"Just that if we had stayed any longer I am not sure you would have had the strength to continue."

"What?" Beobrand's face grew hot, despite the cool wind from the sea.

"And even if you had the stamina," Ferenbald continued, his grin broadening, "I don't think Wilnoth would have been too pleased when he returned from hunting on the downs. He was due to return when the storm hit. Probably holed up in the forest somewhere, but now the weather has turned…"

"Who is this Wilnoth you speak of?"

"One of Dudoc's gesithas. A fine hunter, or so they say." Ferenbald's eyes twinkled with barely contained jollity. "And I hear he is a jealous one. I am not sure how he would have taken to learning of his wife's night-time visits to a certain thegn of renown."

Beobrand's mouth grew dry and his face flushed.

"You... you mean..." he could not find the words.

Ferenbald laughed, throwing his head back and shaking with mirth. In that moment, he looked just like his father.

"You thought we did not hear you rutting like lusty boars?" Ferenbald wiped his eyes with the back of his hand. "Oh, by Christ's bones, Beobrand," he said, relenting at the sight of Beobrand's distraught expression. "I am sorry. You are not the first man to fall under Leofgyth's spell. But most men are too scared of her husband to accept her advances. You are made of sterner stuff, it seems. The tales of your bravery must all be true."

Dreogan stepped up and clapped Beobrand on the shoulder.

"You needed a good woman to plough, lord. It's been too long."

Beobrand glared at Dreogan and Ferenbald, his anger surging up within him.

"You knew!" he spat. "She is married and you said nothing."

Dreogan made an effort to appear serious, but the tattoo soot lines on his cheeks twitched. Ferenbald stifled any further chuckling and said, "I didn't think you would have taken kindly to me spoiling your fun."

Cynan strode down the length of the ship, walking with sure-footed ease over coils of ropes and past bales and chests.

"Do not be angered, lord," he said, a grin spreading across his face. "It is as Dreogan says, you were in need of a good fuck."

Beobrand felt foolish. He would never have lain with the wife of another man had he known. But he had seen her in the hall; had seen the keys hanging from her girdle. He had not thought to question her or anyone else. Still, these were his men, his gesithas. If they had known, they should have told him. Was it not their duty? Beobrand was set to reply with an angry retort, but then he noticed Coenred looking on with such a pained expression of disapproval that he could not hold onto his ire. His thoughts turned to Leofgyth's warm curves, the taste of her kisses, the passion of their coupling and the shuddering relief of climax.

"You should have told me," he said, making his tone and face hard. "But I cannot deny that I will remember the warm welcome of Dudoc's hall for many a year."

"It will not be the warm welcome you'll remember," laughed Bearn, who, even though they had only just left shore, was already pale, open-mouthed and clutching to the sheer strake. "It will be the warm cunny!"

Laughter rippled over *Brimblæd*. Beobrand looked at Coenred. The young monk's eyes and mouth were wide open in shock. Beobrand could no longer keep up the pretence of seriousness. He laughed with the rest of them as the ship pulled ever further from Hastingas and headed west on a placid sea.

Chapter 25

They made good time that day. There was scarcely a cloud in the sky and the breeze was light, without the bite of winter. Spirits were high as *Brimblæd* sliced through the water of the Narrow Sea. Ferenbald kept them close enough to the coast that he was able to guide them by what he saw. There were the Seven Sisters, great hump-backed hills atop sheer white cliffs that rose high above the sea. He pointed out the barrows and earthen mounds of the old settlement that stood on the brow of one of the Sisters. Ferenbald told Beobrand that soon they would be in the shadow of the isle of the Wihtwara. They travelled west, the land always on the side of the steerboard.

Ferenbald piloted into the harbour of Bristelmestune and spoke to the fishermen who were fixing their nets on the beach. They had seen Grimr. His three ships had moored there not four days before the storm hit.

"He's a wrong 'un, that bastard with the beast-skull helm," said one of the fishermen. He was bald, with a stubbly grey beard and skin as weathered and lined as old wood. He sucked his lips over the few teeth that nestled, brown and sickly, in his fish-pale gums. Nobody had answered him or asked for more, yet he continued to speak. "He's not the kind of man one goes in search of," he said, spitting into the sand. All the while his fingers, old and gnarled as twigs, worked deftly at the nettle-hemp lines, threading through with the help of a worn wooden needle before knotting them and moving on to the next part of the net. Beobrand thought of the Sisters who weaved the wyrd of men. He held back a shudder. "And you with only one ship and him with three," the old man went on. "I hope you know what it is you will do when you find him. He has some devils in his crew. Black-skinned demons from lands far beyond our ken. Further away than Hibernia, if you can believe it. Make no mistake, they will gut you like mackerel given half a chance."

Beobrand stepped forward then, pulling himself up to his full height. Beside him loomed Cynan and the tattooed warrior, Dreogan. All of them bore their weapons and had donned their iron-knit byrnies before coming ashore. Beobrand fixed the man with an ice blue stare. The taut and stretched skin of his scar stood out beneath his left eye. The old fisherman shivered, as if the beach had grown suddenly cooler.

"We will not give them half a chance," said Beobrand, his voice as cold and hard as his glaring eyes.

The fisherman said no more. He looked down at his hands as they continued to work with their uncanny speed and agility, weaving his nets as the gods wove the destinies of men.

They slept aboard *Brimblæd* that night. The moon was up and the sky clear, so Ferenbald said they would continue at half sail. Beobrand had struggled to sleep, the creaking of the ship and the rush of water beneath the keel unnerving him rather than lulling him to slumber. In the middle of the night, when the moon was high and bright in the cold sky, Beobrand had fancied he'd heard a wailing, ululating call, echoing up from the deep, through the timbers of the ship. It pierced the still of the night, a plaintive moaning cry that made his skin prickle. This was no sound of man. He lay there for a time, listening. The other-worldly sound came again and Beobrand rose, sure that he would not sleep again that night.

The night was cold and quiet. The sail flapped against the light breeze as *Brimblæd* slipped ever westward through the darkness. In its wake trailed a pale line of foam on the black sea. At the prow of the ship was the shadow of one of the crew, looking out for any obstacle or enemy. To stern, Beobrand recognised sad-eyed Cargást at the rudder. Also at the rear of the ship huddled two men. Their whispered voices came to him on the cool air, but he could not make out the words. Wrapping his cloak about him, Beobrand made his way past the shapes of sleeping men towards the two figures. He nodded at the helmsman, receiving a grunt by way of reply.

The nearer of the two men turned and he recognised the shaved forehead, long hair and slender features of Coenred. The moonlight fell on the face of the other man. It was Brinin. The boy's wide eyes shone in the night.

The unearthly cry echoed up from the sea again and Beobrand had to stop himself from shivering.

"What is that?" asked Brinin, fear sharpening his tone.

"I know not," replied Beobrand.

"Could it be a devil?" said Coenred, his whispers excited and fearful in equal measure. "A night creature from hell?"

Brinin shuddered.

"Coenred said it might be the voice of sea-women, calling for us to join them in their watery world."

"Did he indeed?" answered Beobrand. "Perhaps it is." Truth be told, he too feared the strange sound. It conjured up dark images of women swimming up from the depths, seaweed in their hair, beckoning to them to come to them, to feel their cold, wet embrace. He willed himself not to shiver. Scanning the moonlit sea all around them, there was no movement save for the rolling waves. "I think if it were demons come to enslave us, the seamen would be showing more concern. They do not appear to worry. Come, let us ask one who will give us answers."

They stepped close to Cargást. He flicked his eyes at them, but did not move, holding the rudder as still as if he were part of the very timbers of the ship.

"What is that wailing?" asked Beobrand.

"Nobody rightly knows," answered the sorrowful-looking helmsman. "Some say it is the singing of women of the deep, calling out for husbands from men of middle earth."

Brinin gasped.

Cargást chuckled quietly.

"Do not fear, Brinin, they would not want one as skinny and young as you."

"You say nobody knows what makes the sounds," said Beobrand.

"Nobody I have met."

"What do you think it is?"

Cargást hawked, leant over the side, and spat.

"I think it is the song of whales."

Beobrand searched the dark surface of the sea around them again for sign of one of the great creatures. But the dark surface was unbroken.

"But we have seen no whales."

"No, not this trip. But I have seen plenty in my time. And they are bigger than anything you can imagine. As long and broad as a mead hall. So big that if one sang, I think you would hear its voice halfway across middle earth."

For a time they were all silent, listening to the night and the soft sounds of *Brimblæd*'s hull pushing through the water. Again, they heard the thin, moaning song. Coenred and Brinin stiffened. Coenred made the sign of the Christ rood over his chest and murmured words in the tongue of the Christ followers.

"You don't think it is creature of evil then?" Brinin asked.

"As I said, boy," replied Cargást with a grin that looked out of place beneath his doleful eyes, "nobody knows what it is, but I will tell you something, I have never seen no watery woman in the sea." He paused, staring out into the darkness. "And another thing," he said at last.

"What?" Brinin asked, eager for reassurance.

"I have never heard the singing when a storm was nearby, so I would say we are in for a quiet night. That is if you would shut up your chattering and leave a man in peace."

Chapter 26

"**I** think we have them!" shouted Fraomar from where he stood at *Brimblæd*'s prow. He had keen eyes and as soon as Ferenbald had announced they would be at Seoles soon, Fraomar had pulled himself up, clinging to the ropes and the carved prow to peer into the misty morning. Beobrand tried to see through the veils of mists that hung over the water, but all he saw were shadows. There was something out there, but his eyes were not sharp enough to make out any details.

Ferenbald took a quick glance and nodded.

"I think you're right," he said before hurrying back down the ship, barking orders.

"What do you see?" asked Beobrand, his frustration and lack of sleep adding a sharp edge to his tone.

"There are ships beached there," answered Fraomar, jumping down from his perch. "I recognise at least one from when we were attacked. I think we have them."

"Arm yourselves," Beobrand called to his men. Bearn groaned. He had spent much of the night puking and was the colour of the foam that topped the waves that broke before *Brimblæd*'s bow. But he knew his business and heaved himself up and began to wriggle into his byrnie. Garr, Dreogan, Fraomar and Cynan joined him in his preparations. Attor did not wear a shirt of metal, so there was nothing for him to do apart from check the seaxes sheathed at his belt. His savage grin showed Beobrand he was ready.

Beobrand went to the leather sack where his gear was stored and began to pull his iron shirt out. It was greasy and cold, but as he shrugged it on, he welcomed its weight on his shoulders. His body thrummed with the anticipation of battle. Thank Woden they had found them so quickly. A sliver of hope came to him then that perhaps the girl would still be whole, unharmed and unsullied. A surge of rage flooded through him as he strapped his belt tightly around his middle, taking some of the heft from his byrnie. He placed his half-hand on Hrunting's pommel, the touch of the sword familiar and reassuring. It would sing its song of death soon enough.

All around the preparing warriors, the ship bustled with activity. Ferenbald called out and men responded instantly. Beobrand smiled to see the control the young man had of the vessel. *Brimblæd* was closer to the beach now, and Beobrand could discern the hulls of ships and boats that were resting there, pulled up beyond the reach of the sea. The mist was clearing as the sun rose. There were a couple of small fires on the beach, their smoke drifting lazily on the soft morning air, mingling with the mist. Men moved about between the fires. Beobrand thought that one waved to the incoming *Brimblæd*.

"Beobrand," said a small voice behind him. He turned from the beach and saw Coenred, his face pale against his dark robes.

"What is it, Coenred?" he asked. "We will soon be ashore and I must prepare myself for the coming fight, for I doubt they will give up Ardith easily."

"That is what I wanted to talk to you about."

"What do you mean?" Beobrand answered, reaching for the bands of metal he strapped to his shins. "Speak quickly. There is not much time."

"I do not think you should fight them," Coenred said.

"What?" Beobrand was incredulous. "Why? These men killed Dalston and have taken my daughter. And from all we hear, they are scum. They deserve nothing more than death."

Coenred swallowed.

"That may be so, Beo," he said, "but look and think."

"What do you mean?"

"Look at your gesithas. How many do you see?"

Beobrand did not need to count them, there were seven warriors aboard counting him. He began to take Coenred's meaning.

"So we will be outnumbered," he said, "it will not be the first time. Besides, they will not be expecting a fight."

"Perhaps, perhaps not. But how many of the three crews we seek are fighting men?" He lowered his voice. "Do you think Ferenbald's men will stand and fight?"

Beobrand looked about him. The men were strong, willing and able. They might well fight if pushed to it, but he did not see warriors. They were men of the sea, not the shieldwall. Grimr's crews had fought with violent abandon when they had boarded *Háligsteorra*.

"Seven men against three crews of pirates, Beo," whispered Coenred. "You will be no use to Ardith dead."

The sudden surge of joy at finding their quarry so quickly was replaced with a nagging doubt. No matter his battle-skill and the bravery of his gesithas. Those odds were insurmountable. Was this how the song of Beobrand would end? Cut down by men of no honour on a beach? His body stripped of valuables, his armour and blades sold in some windswept wic somewhere down the coast?

"What would you have me do?" he asked.

"I have an idea."

"Tell me," said Beobrand.

Chapter 27

"**Y**ou think this will work, lord?" Cynan whispered, as they trudged along the beach.

"It might," replied Beobrand. "But not if you call me 'lord' in front of those men."

Behind them rested *Brimblæd*, canted to one side where they had pulled it ashore. Ahead of them were several small vessels on the strand and, beyond them, the larger ships that Fraomar and Ferenbald had recognised as belonging to Grimr's band of pirates. The morning mist had lifted and the thin smoke from the driftwood cooking fires did not obscure their view of the ships or the men who were camped in their shadow. As they had beached *Brimblæd*, Beobrand had cursed to see only two of Grimr's ships. They were hunting three, yet just two were on this beach, sharing the sand with the fishing boats of the village-folk. The largest vessel they sought, the sleek fighting ship with the blood-red sail, was nowhere to be seen.

"Remember," said Coenred in a small, pinched voice, "you are my men, guarding me from earthly attacks. And Beobrand is no lord. Not here today." This had been the young monk's plan, but now Beobrand wondered at the sense of it. Coenred was pale and clearly terrified.

"As Coenred says, you will call me Octa. The name of Beobrand is too well known. And remember, these men have not seen us before today, apart from briefly in battle, and we were armoured then. And we were not aboard *Brimblæd*. With any luck, they will believe the tale we tell." He shot a glance at Coenred and frowned. The monk was biting his lip and his eyes flicked this way and that, nervously searching the beach for signs of danger.

"It is a good plan, Coenred," he said, lowering his voice so that only his friend would hear him. "But it will only work if you act the part you chose for yourself. You are our master, and you must act as such."

Coenred took in a deep steadying breath and nodded. Striding forward, the young monk shouted at them, "Come on, you lazy maggots. I do not wish to tarry here longer than I must. The tide will turn soon and the bishop is expecting us by the holy day of Saint Columba the Virgin."

Some of the men gathered around the smoking fires glanced in their direction, clearly curious as to who disturbed them so early in the morning. A few of them rose and Beobrand noticed how they spread out, giving themselves options should the approaching men prove a threat.

Beobrand caught Cynan's eye and each of them grinned as they trotted after the monk, their heavy byrnies jingling, swords and seaxes slapping against their thighs. Garr, Bearn, Dreogan, Fraomar and Attor picked up their pace, jogging to keep up. They had chosen to leave their shields and helms aboard *Brimblæd*, for fear that they would give them away. For surely these men would not have forgotten so easily the bloodletting at the hands of Beobrand's Black Shields.

A grizzled man with thick, meaty ears and a wide, crooked nose, stepped forward. Some of the men who had stood joined him, their hands menacingly resting on the hilts of their seaxes. A couple held short axes. One of them, a slim man with the features of a weasel, slapped the iron head of his axe into the palm of his hand. Beobrand fixed him with a cold glare, but the weasel's eyes were devoid of emotion as he continued to whack the metal into his hand over and again.

The grizzled man appeared to be the leader. He held up a hand.

"What would you be wanting from us on this fine morning, priest?" he asked, his voice rasped and rumbled like boulders rolling down a mountain.

Coenred halted. Without a word, Beobrand and his gesithas formed a defensive line behind the monk.

"I heard you men were trading in all manner of goods," said Coenred. To Beobrand's ears his tone sounded high-pitched and reedy with anxiety.

The leader's eyes narrowed and he looked along the line of warriors who were arrayed behind Coenred.

"You heard right," he said at last. "We are traders. But why bring so many swords to a wic. If you mean to barter and haggle, silver is what you need, not steel."

For a moment, Beobrand was worried that Coenred would not answer, but the monk straightened his shoulders and returned the man's gaze.

"The land is ever dangerous for one carrying valuables. The almighty God protects me from evil, but I have found that strong arms and swords protect treasures better than prayer alone."

The sailor weighed his words for several, uncomfortable heartbeats, before grinning broadly.

"If you seek trade and you bring valuables with which to barter, then you have come to the right place," he said, stepping aside and waving them towards the fires. The weasel-faced man's eyes followed Beobrand as they walked forward. Beobrand forced himself to ignore him.

"You are well come," said the crooked-nosed leader. "I am Wada. *Brimwulf* is my ship." He waved an arm at one of the vessels, a fat-bellied trading ship. Beside the nearest fire stood a stocky man with an expensive-looking fur-trimmed hat. His red cloak was held in place with a golden clasp. "This is Thurcytel," said Wada. "He is the captain of the *Waegmearh*. We travel together."

"I thought you travelled with a third ship also," said Coenred.

Wada tensed, looking at the monk askance.

"What is it you seek, priest?" asked Thurcytel. "And what is it to you who we travel with?"

Beobrand cursed silently at Coenred's clumsy question. He scanned the men around them. They were heavily outnumbered, but none of the seamen wore armour. If they attacked quickly and with determination, Beobrand thought they would be able to cut themselves free and rush back to *Brimblæd*.

Coenred shook his head and smiled.

"I care nought for your travelling companions," he said. "It is just that when we stopped at Hastingas, Lord Dudoc told us of three trading ships that had travelled west a few days earlier and I had presumed you to be said ships. As to what it is I seek, well, Dudoc's wife, the Lady Aelfgyth, said she had seen a fine example of a relic, an exquisite rood encasing a most holy item, amongst the things you had offered her husband. Now it just so happens that I have been sent by my bishop, his most holy Utta, in search of artefacts with which to adorn his new church. He has vowed that it will be the finest house of God in all of Albion. And he will spare no cost to furnish it in all the splendour he can find."

Beobrand looked at Cynan, who raised an eyebrow. It seemed he was as surprised as he at Coenred's quick thinking. Beobrand was not sure what Utta or Aidan would have to say about the ease with which the monk lied, but he had nothing but admiration for his friend's cunning.

"There was a third ship with us," said Wada, an unreadable expression on his face, "but we had a difference of opinion with the captain and we have parted ways."

Beobrand let out a slow breath, struggling not to let the disappointment show on his face. There was no sign of Ardith or Grimr on the beach. Both must be on the missing ship.

"I see... and the rood?"

"Well, that too was true. At least it was when we moored at Hastingas. But it would seem you are not the only Christ priest in search of such."

"Indeed?" said Coenred.

"Yes, we sold it to the priest of yon church not two days ago," he gestured up a rise to where a small timber structure stood.

"How unfortunate," murmured Coenred. "I would so have liked to see it. Lady Aelfgyth said that it was of exquisite craftsmanship."

"Why don't you go up to the church and see it?" said Thurcytel.

"You never know," grinned Wada, exposing yellow teeth, "he may sell it to you for the right price."

"What a splendid idea," said Coenred. "Come, Attor, let us take a look at this relic and see what price we might strike with the priest."

"Shall we go with you?" asked Beobrand, uneasy at having to defer to Coenred. The gaze of the captains and their crews was heavy on him. He did not wish to remain here with these men who had attacked and plundered *Háligsteorra* and, until recently, held Ardith captive. His hand itched to drag Hrunting from its scabbard and to lay about him, slicing and rending these seamen. With an effort, he clenched his hands at his sides.

Coenred turned to him, a small smile playing on his lips. He seemed to be enjoying himself now, thought Beobrand. He could scarcely believe it, but he should not have been surprised, he knew his friend was brave and quick-witted once he pushed his fear to one side.

"I do not need to sully the sanctity of God's holy house with all of your swords and seaxes, mighty Octa," Coenred said.

"Remain here with these good men and share with them the mead we brought, if it is not too early for such drink."

"It is never too early for mead," chuckled Wada.

Beobrand wished to speak out against Coenred's decision, but he knew he could not without exposing their pretence.

"As you wish, master," he said, dropping his gaze. Fraomar handed him the skin of good mead they had brought with them, a gift from Dudoc. Beobrand weighed it in his half-hand for a moment, before tossing it to Wada. The older man caught it easily. Unstopping it, he took a long draught.

"And, Octa," Coenred paused and said over his shoulder, "you can look through the other things these men have on offer while I am away. You know what sort of things I am looking for."

Coenred gave Beobrand a meaningful nod before turning and walking away.

"Yes, master," said Beobrand.

Unease scratched down his back with chill fingers as he watched Coenred walk away purposefully with only the unarmoured, lithe warrior, Attor, to protect him.

Chapter 28

It was gloomy in the small chapel. The building creaked in the wind, even though there was only a light breeze blowing in off the sea. Lines of light shone between the thin planks of the walls and the whole place smelt of resin and sawdust. It reminded Coenred of the chapel Beobrand had ordered to be built for the Christ followers of Ubbanford. That was a flimsy building too, little more than a hut, not a church fit for the Almighty. Here though, it seemed the lord of Seoles had plans to erect a more lasting construction for the edification of God. For outside the shaky timber chapel Coenred and Attor had passed slabs of dressed sandstone. Trenches had been dug for the foundations of the walls of what would become a mighty building overlooking the Narrow Sea. Coenred had measured it out in paces – the finished church would be at least the length of five men lying end to end. This would be a house of God to rival that within the fortress walls of Bebbanburg, or the stone building at Eoferwic or the new construction at Inhrypum.

It would certainly be a solid structure, a fitting testament to God's greatness. Not a feeble, rickety wooden affair like this, or the building Beobrand had deigned to have built for them in Ubbanford.

Gothfraidh had always rebuked Coenred for being ungrateful. "It is warm enough," the old monk had said. "If it is luxury you seek, you have chosen the wrong calling." Coenred had seen precious little luxury in his life and when he spent time in the halls of lords and kings, he found the warmth, rich food and plentiful drink little consolation for the intrigues and politics that frequently led to conflict, suffering and death. The machinations of nobles were like a game to them. A deadly game in which he too often found himself playing a role, or at least observing from close quarters.

Once more he found himself far from home and in the company of warriors. Coenred smiled as his eyes grew accustomed to the darkness. What would Gothfraidh have thought of this latest adventure? Coenred could scarcely believe how easily he had acted the part of the master of Beobrand and the other warriors down on the beach. His hands were shaking as he had walked up the hill towards this timber building. His mind reeled at the temerity of it all. What would have happened if the seamen on the beach had seen through his ploy? Would they have fought Beobrand's gesithas? Dalston's pale face, blood gushing from his throat, eyes wide and terrified, came to him then in the gloom. Of course they would have fought. These were murderers. Death-dealers who thought nothing of killing. He had known their kind all his life.

Peering into the darkness of the chapel, his mind turned, as it so often did to another shadow-filled church many years ago. He could remember walking, as if pulled by some hidden force, into the gloom, each step taking him closer to the white, bloodless form on the altar. The horror and revulsion he had felt at seeing his sister's broken body had overwhelmed him. Tata had been violated and slain by men such as those who had ripped the life from Dalston and stolen the casket meant for Eanflæd.

Gothfraidh would have believed him mad to attempt to hoodwink such killers. Dalston, with his nerves and uncertainties, would have been appalled. On several occasions, Beobrand had told Coenred he was brave. He did not feel brave, but he could not deny that part of him thrilled at the deceit. Besides, it must be better to avoid bloodshed, if possible. Jesu would surely forgive his lies.

If He could forgive robbers and murderers, what would a few lies matter, when they were employed to do what was right?

Coenred shuddered, unsure if from the cold or from the excitement of what had transpired on the shingle shore.

"Are you well?" Attor asked. The warrior stood close by, hands resting on the hilts of his seaxes, body taut, ready for battle.

Coenred realised he had halted in the doorway of the church and had remained immobile there for some time, lost in his memories. He could not imagine there would be cause for Attor to use his blades in this holy place.

"I was just thinking," he said and stepped into the dark interior of the chapel.

It was still and quiet inside, the floor merely packed earth. The room was empty, save for a table at the far end. The table was covered with a white cloth. Atop it rested the finely carved casket Coenred had last seen plucked from Dalston's grip before the monk was pushed, bleeding and terrified, into the dark waters of the North Sea.

Coenred shivered again and walked towards the table. The dark memories of Tata's pallid form threatened to fill his mind, each step taking him further into the past and the chapel in Engelmynster. He took a deep breath, pushing the thoughts of his sister away with an effort. As he reached out a trembling hand to open the box, he saw again Dalston's fear-wide eyes. There were too many memories in this place. His thoughts beat and flapped in his mind, black and dirty, like soot-streaked raven wings. Coenred closed his eyes and shook his head to clear it of the horrors of the past. He whispered the paternoster under his breath and his breathing slowed.

Opening his eyes, he pushed up the lid of the casket, wondering if the relic would still be within. It was. Just as he remembered. A small Christ rood, fashioned of gold and inlaid with precious stones, rested on a bed of silken cloth. Reaching in, he pulled out the cross, turning it so that the thin shafts of light in the church caught it, picking out the garnets and emeralds and the intricate scroll work of the metal.

Attor gasped.

"This is truly a thing fit for a king," he said.

"Or for a queen," replied Coenred. "The gold and gems have their value, of that there is no doubt, but this holds something of much more worth."

"What could be worth more than the gold and the stones?" asked Attor, his tone hushed and incredulous.

"Behold," said Coenred, and with his fingernail he prised open a tiny compartment that rested beneath the largest emerald. The hinges of the minuscule box were of the finest craftsmanship, and the box that lay within the body of the cross could easily be missed if one did not know it was there.

Attor peered into the dark recess in the reliquary. It seemed empty until Coenred tilted it into the scant light that filtered in through the doorway.

"What is it?" Attor asked, his voice barely more than a whisper.

Inside the hidden recess was a small twist of dried thorny twigs. Around them was wrapped a strand of hair, fair and long.

"This is part of the very crown of thorns pressed upon the brow of our Lord Jesu when he gave his life for you and I." Coenred repeated what he had been told by Abbot Aidan, but he could not help wonder at how the thorns were still intact. They must have been hundreds of years old. A miracle, he had been told.

"Is that a hair?" asked Attor, his voice filled with awe. Ever since Aidan had healed him from a festering arrow wound, saving him from certain death, Attor had been a devout follower of the Christ.

Coenred smiled despite himself to hear Attor's innocent amazement and joy. He chastised himself for his lack of faith. Who was he to question the abbot?

"Yes," he said. "It is a hair from the very head of the son of God."

He glanced at Attor. The slim gesith's face was rapt, his mouth open, eyes wide and glistening.

"May I hold it?" asked Attor.

"With care." Coenred offered the cross to Attor who, after hesitating briefly, took it in his hands. His eyes and face seemed to glow with the reflection of the gold.

"What are you doing?" a harsh voice snapped from behind them. The room darkened as a bulky figure filled the doorway, blocking out the early morning light.

Coenred spun around, guilt and terror gripping him. Attor turned more slowly and calmly took a step away from Coenred, into the shadows.

Coenred squinted to make out the features of the newcomer to the chapel, but his face was in shadow. The man was broad, but not tall. He wore a long woollen robe not dissimilar to Coenred's own, but his hair was cut differently, with just the crown of his head shaved, leaving a circular bald patch surrounded by a ring of dark hair.

Coenred let out a breath.

"We were merely looking at this holy object," he said.

The stocky priest stepped further into the chapel. The movement felt like a threat of violence. His eyes flicked at Attor, taking in the golden cross in the warrior's rough hands.

"Put that back," he spat. "It is not for the likes of you to touch."

Attor allowed his left hand to drop to the hilt of one of the seaxes that hung from his belt.

"Am I not good enough to touch this?" he asked, his voice rasping like a whetstone dragged along a blade. "Am I not one of Jesu's flock? I have been washed of my sins by the holy Abbot of Lindisfarena, and I have oft partaken of the body and blood of the Christ in memory of his sacrifice."

The priest's eyes widened at Attor's words. The hand on the seax and the talk of blood as clear a threat as a blade pulled from a scabbard.

"Put it back," he said, with less venom in his voice. "It is not yours. It is a most holy relic."

Attor held his gaze for a long moment, before stepping to the table and placing the rood into the casket. Coenred noted that he also carefully closed the secret door in the artefact.

Coenred stepped toward the priest, his hands open in an attempt to ease the tension in the gloomy church. From outside came the sound of men talking and the harsh crack of chisel on stone.

"As you can see," he said, "I too am a man of God. I have come from the holy isle of Lindisfarena, far to the north."

The priest said nothing.

"As a follower of Christ," continued Coenred, "I am sure you would like to know from whence this relic comes." He paused, hoping for some acknowledgement of his words or of their shared beliefs. He was disappointed. "The cross is stolen," he said at last. "It was sent from Northumbria by my lord King Oswiu as a gift for his bride to be Eanflæd of Cantware."

"I care not from where it comes," said the priest, his words as harsh as a slap. "Or for whom you say it was destined. It is my lord's now. Bought with his silver. And it will rest here forever. Have you not seen the stone outside? My church will be magnificent. Pilgrims will come from all over Albion and beyond to see the crown of thorns and hair of the Lord Jesu the Christ." His eyes shone in the gloom, sparkling with his greed and ambition.

Coenred took a deep breath and swallowed back his anger.

"We were attacked by pirates," he said. "One of my brethren gave his life protecting this holiest of gifts."

"Well," said the priest with a sneer, "he didn't do a very good job, did he?" He pushed past Coenred, evidently keen to check that nothing was amiss with the cross and its carved casket.

A coldness wrapped around Coenred as suddenly as if he had been plunged into the autumn sea. Dalston must have felt as cold, the instant before he died, as he had drifted down into the chill depths of the Whale Road, the light dimming as he fell ever further from the sun and the air, the salt of his blood mingling forever in the cold brine of the ocean.

The church grew dark and Coenred's ears rushed with the sound of his own blood pumping through his body. He yet lived, Dalston would never again know what it was to feel the wind ruffle his hair, or the touch of the rough wool of his robe against his skin.

Fury at the injustice of it and the priest's cruel words bubbled within him and, as if witnessing another, Coenred watched his own long-fingered hands reaching for the priest's dark robe. He saw his fingers grip a fistful of the rough spun cloth, but he felt nothing. His body was as numb and unfeeling as the sea, as cold as winter and as unforgiving as death.

Coenred was as surprised as Attor and the priest when he yanked the man backwards. Hard.

The priest staggered and fell sprawling to the earthen floor at Coenred's feet.

"Why you..." he spluttered.

Coenred blinked, looking down at him in confusion. What had he done?

The priest struggled to regain his footing, but Attor fell on him as quickly as a gannet spears into the surf in search of prey. One of his wicked-looking seaxes was in his right hand, and his left grasped the priest's hair, pulling his head back, exposing his throat. The sharp blade of the long knife pressed against the flesh. A bead of blood trickled down to soak into his robe.

"You'll not be wanting to add your blood to that spilt for this relic now, would you?" Attor hissed.

The priest's eyes were as wide and white as duck eggs. He did not move.

Shocked, Coenred looked on. What had he done? Oh sweet mother of God, what had he done?

"Pick up that casket, Coenred," said Attor, his voice as calm as if he had been asking him to pass a jug of ale during a feast.

"But... but..."

The priest wriggled, but Attor shook him roughly, pressing the blade against his throat so tightly that the man whimpered. Fresh blood ran down his neck.

"Stay still," Attor whispered. The priest stopped moving and made no further sound.

Outside, the sound of a chisel chipping away at sandstone continued.

"You said yourself, Coenred," insisted Attor, once again in his matter of fact tone, "this relic was destined for King Oswiu's bride, not to line the pouch of this priest and his lord with pilgrims' silver."

Coenred closed the casket and picked it up. It felt very heavy in his grasp.

"Not a sound," hissed Attor, releasing his grip on the priest. Without warning Attor pierced the man's robe with the point of his sharp seax. The priest whimpered. Attor held up a finger for silence. Using his blade, he tore strips of cloth from the robe. All the while the priest watched him with white-rimmed eyes, but made no sound.

Coenred stared in amazement as Attor quickly bound the priest's limbs and mouth with the woollen rags. The warrior then dragged the man into the shadows behind the table. He whispered something to him in the darkness that Coenred could not hear. The priest shook his head furiously. Attor sheathed his seax and slapped the man on the cheek a few times, almost affectionately.

"Ready?" Attor asked Coenred.

Coenred just stared at him. What had he done? The box in his hands rattled with his trembling.

"We'll just walk back down to the ships now," Attor said. "Walk as if you belong here."

Coenred could barely breathe. He did not belong here. The stolen casket shook before him. What had become of him?

"As if you belong," repeated Attor and stepped out into the daylight.

With a last glance at the cowering form of the bound priest, Coenred drew in a ragged breath and followed Attor.

Chapter 29

Beobrand slowly began to relax. Anxiety had gnawed at him as he'd watched Coenred and Attor trudge up the beach, their feet crunching deep into the shingle. He'd followed them with his gaze until they'd reached the small timber church overlooking the sea. The building stood out starkly against the blue morning sky and the silhouettes of Attor and Coenred had been small in the distance.

The rest of the men seemed oblivious of his worries. Wada passed around the good mead and soon Beobrand's gesithas were sitting by the fires, apparently as at ease with these men as if they had grown up with them. Cynan had found one of his people, a swarthy-skinned man from the craggy coast of Gwynedd and now the two of them were sprawled on a blanket, exchanging bawdy riddles in their sing-song, lilting tongue. Beobrand understood little enough of their words, but their laughter grated. Bearn and Fraomar had quickly joined a game of knucklebones. Dreogan and Garr were more subdued, but they too sat and drank the mead when it was passed to them, each giving the semblance of resting while their master was absent.

They were doing better at the deception than Beobrand. He glanced back at *Brimblæd*. Ferenbald's crewmen had built their own fire, the smoke wreathing the beached ship as if it rode on a swirling sea of mist. *Brimblæd*'s sailors lounged around the fire, no doubt taking advantage of being ashore to prepare some hot food. Beobrand had warned Ferenbald to be ready to leave quickly. The gods alone knew how this encounter with the crews of *Brimwulf* and *Waegmearh* would end.

"Gods, you're a jumpy one," Wada said. "Your priest will be fine. If you were so worried about him, you should have gone with him."

Beobrand smiled thinly. Wada was right. He should never have let Coenred go to the chapel. Still, he had Attor for protection and there was no braver or deadlier warrior.

"He is prone to get himself in trouble," Beobrand said.

"Well, be thankful he left you down here with us then." Wada grinned and passed him the mead. "What else did you say you were after? We have many fine things. From the fens of East Angeln, the great halls of Frankia, the green hills of Hibernia…"

And so Beobrand nodded and talked, but said little, as Wada and Thurcytel had their men pull out chests and sacks of goods. Beobrand wondered how much of it was stolen. And how many innocents had been killed in its taking. He looked up from a fabulous silver drinking horn. It was a thing of great beauty, with a horned beast clutching the point of the vessel in its metal talons. Through the woodsmoke he saw the weasel-faced man glowering at him. As he watched, the man once again whacked the flat of his axe head into his palm. Beobrand held his gaze for a moment. The man did not blink. Beobrand turned away. Let the man have his petty victory, he was not here to prove he could outstare these pirates.

"The quality of this is fine," he said, turning the drinking horn in his hand so that the sun caught it. With a shake of his head, he handed the piece back to Thurcytel. "But it is not what my master seeks."

"We don't have any more objects of Christ magic," replied the stocky skipper. The sun glinted from the clasp at his shoulder, the red of his cloak was as dark and warm as blood.

"The relics are for my master's bishop. He wishes to furnish his Christ house," said Beobrand. "My master's tastes are less holy and more of the flesh," he said with what he hoped was a knowing grin. Thurcytel looked bemused and Beobrand silently cursed himself. Gods, he was not one for this subterfuge. His skin prickled with his unease, but the ships' masters were both now staring at him. He had to speak. "My master seeks something warmer and softer than a golden cup or rood, if you take my meaning."

Thurcytel lifted the edge of his hat and scratched beneath the fur. He shared a look with Wada and said, "If it be slaves you are seeking, we have none."

"Pity," said Beobrand, taking a swig of mead and handing the flask to Thurcytel. "My master pays very well. Especially for young ones."

"It seems once again your master is just a couple of days late," he said.

"How so?"

"We had a girl with us until we parted company with Grimr and *Saeslaga*. She was fair-haired, like you, and as ripe and unsullied as you like. Couldn't be more than twelve or thirteen summers. I prefer them older and fatter myself. Something to hold on to. A woman who knows what she wants from a man," he winked. "But some like them young and tight."

Beobrand clenched his jaw. His hand gripped Hrunting's pommel so hard that his knuckles popped.

"She sounds just the sort of thing my master likes," he said. The words were sour in his mouth. He wanted to spit, to vomit. He longed to drag Hrunting from its scabbard and lay about him with the sword's patterned blade. These men deserved nothing more than death.

"She'll be half the way to Frankia by now," said Thurcytel.

"Frankia? That is where they are heading?"

But before Thurcytel could answer, the man with the weasel face sprang up with a roar.

"I know you," he shouted.

Swinging both his hand axes menacingly, the slender seaman advanced on Beobrand through the drifting smoke.

All around the fires, faces turned to see what was the cause of the commotion. Beobrand swallowed. If he could convince the man he was mistaken, perhaps he could avoid bloodshed. Much as the idea of slaying all of them sang to him, victory would be no certain thing. Besides, Coenred and Attor were still up at the chapel. If Beobrand and his gesithas had to retreat, they would need to leave the monk and Attor behind. That he would not do.

"I don't think so, friend," Beobrand said, standing quickly.

"I am no friend of yours, you Northumbrian bastard," said the axeman.

"What is the meaning of this, Stanmear?" asked Wada. Beobrand noted that he had laid aside the flask of mead and his hand now rested on the handle of his seax.

The weasel-faced Stanmear hesitated.

"I knew I'd seen this big one before. When I saw his half-hand, it came back to me. He slew Gerold. He was aboard that Northumbrian ship. He wore a great helm and had a black shield, but I noted that hand as we pulled away from them after the fight."

Wada and Thurcytel were staring at Beobrand, searching for something in him that would spark recognition. He could sense the eyes of the men around the campfires on him. Some of the sailors were rising. He flicked a glance at Cynan. Their eyes met and the Waelisc warrior gave an almost imperceptible nod. Turning back to the two captains, Beobrand saw their memories bringing back the skirmish where Beobrand and Cynan had stridden down the pirates' ship, hacking and hewing a path through them as easily as their wave-steeds cut through the cold waters of the North Sea.

Recognition dawned on Wada's face first. At the same instant one of the other sailors cried out in anger. The time for talk was through. Sensing his leaders' approval, Stanmear came at Beobrand, his two vicious axes spinning and wheeling before him. Behind him the camp was a sudden mass of confusion as Beobrand's gesithas leapt up, springing to defend their lord.

But there was no time to wait for them. The danger was too near, those sharp axe blades too deadly. Beobrand ignored the tumult of the camp, the shouts and grunts as men grabbed for the Northumbrians and were pushed or kicked aside. Instead he focused all of his attention on Stanmear. The man's eyes were dark and filled with hatred. His mouth twisted in a savage snarl and before him, his axes were a blur. Beobrand's iron byrnie was strong, its links well-forged, and he believed it would hold against a blow from the small axes. But his head and neck were exposed and he did not want to leave it to chance that Stanmear would not strike his flesh. The man's skill with those axes was obvious.

Beobrand fixed his attacker with a piercing cool stare, allowing the calm of battle to fill him. Now was not the time to unfetter the beast within him, but his fury and focus were what set him apart from other warriors. So he loosened the chains of his animal rage just enough to deal with this threat.

He hoped.

Stanmear must have been expecting Beobrand to draw his sword or seax, for his eyes widened in surprise as the tall, fair-haired warrior sprang to meet him without a weapon in his hands. Beobrand saw the shock in Stanmear's face, and he noted the slightest hesitation in his attack.

Beobrand needed no more than this momentary lapse. Closing the gap to Stanmear in a heartbeat, his hands flashed out and caught the seaman's wrists. The man was wiry and strong, and

Beobrand's left half-hand grip would not be strong enough to hold him for long. But he did not need long. He carried on his forward momentum, at the same time yanking Stanmear towards him. With gritted teeth, Beobrand snapped his head into Stanmear's nose. Through his skull, Beobrand heard a sickening crunch of cartilage and Stanmear became as limp as a doll in his grasp. A spike of pain drilled into Beobrand's head from the blow, reminding him of his dazed retreat from the battle at the great ditch. His stomach churned and his vision blurred as he stepped back, allowing Stanmear's inert body to slump to the sand.

He swallowed back bitter bile, shaking his head to clear it. He instantly regretted doing so as fresh agony lanced behind his eyes.

Feeling a hand on his shoulder, Beobrand smiled grimly, despite his pain. On his right stood Cynan, and beside him, Fraomar and Garr. To Beobrand's left were Dreogan and Bearn. Somehow, they had all reached him and even without shields they were a formidable sight in their iron shirts, their deadly blades catching the morning sun.

Around the campfires, the sailors had been slower to react, but now they were all on their feet and forming some semblance of a line. Beobrand spied swords, axes and seaxes, and a handful of the men had found shields from somewhere. There were many more of them than the small Northumbrian band.

"With me, brothers," Beobrand snapped. His vision had cleared, but his head throbbed. Looking down, he saw Stanmear's face was awash with blood that streamed from his smashed nose. He grinned and took a step forward. His gesithas moved with him, their training clear in the fluid movement. Beobrand kicked Stanmear in the face for good measure. The sinewy seaman did not react.

Pulling Hrunting from its scabbard, Beobrand halted. His band of warriors stopped as if they thought with one mind. Before them, Thurcytel and Wada had fled back to join the unruly ranks of their men. The sailors were still arraying themselves. They glowered at Beobrand and the Northumbrians with a mixture of fear and loathing.

"I am Beobrand of Ubbanford," Beobrand bellowed. "My Black Shields will spill your guts and feed you to the ravens." His battle-voice sliced though the noise of the preparing sailors as easily as a seax blade pierces an eyeball. "Do you think you can stand against us?"

The seamen fidgeted and shifted, but none moved to answer or to attack.

"Forward," Beobrand yelled, and as one the Bernicians took another step.

"Do you wish to die?" he shouted. "Hrunting is thirsty for blood." He raised his fine sword high above his head. The serpent skin markings of the blade seemed to ripple. "I can offer you all death, if that is what you seek. But you do not need to die this day."

"What do you want?" asked Wada, and Beobrand knew in that moment there would be no further fighting. These were not warriors they faced. Killers, yes, but not men of honour who would face armed foe-men with bravery. Perhaps Stanmear was the bravest of them. Or the most foolhardy.

"I seek the girl. Where is she?"

Wada blinked and swallowed.

"Grimr took her. If you seek her, you must follow him." Wada spat into the sand before him.

"And where is he bound?"

"Frankia. To the hall of Lord Vulmar."

Beobrand's head pounded as if a smith were using it for an anvil.

"How can I trust you?" he asked. "Too easily have you given up your friend, this Grimr."

Wada spat again and sheathed his seax. Evidently he too believed a fight had been avoided.

"I cannot make you trust me, Beobrand Half-hand, but Grimr is no friend of ours. If you find him, I hope you kill the whoreson. I told him not to take that girl. Womenfolk are nothing but trouble."

"So why did he take her?"

Wada shook his head.

"He was certain she would be a tasty enough prize to make Vulmar take him back into his service."

"Who is this Vulmar? And why would he want the service of a nithing like Grimr?"

"Vulmar is a lord of Rodomo. A nasty one, with a vicious streak, but he is a generous gift giver. His gesithas want for nothing. Grimr was once his man. I don't know what he had done, but he was always talking about returning to Rodomo and repaying his debt."

Beobrand's stomach twisted and his head ached. He took a deep breath of the cool sea air and prayed silently to Woden that he would not disgrace himself by puking in front of these men.

"And he thought to do this with the girl? Surely this Vulmar could find his share of thralls in Frankia. Why take one from Cantware?"

Wada frowned, perhaps sensing that his words could reignite Beobrand's anger.

"He likes them young and unspoilt. He has large appetites and it is ever more difficult for him to find ones to his liking. Grimr was sure this one would have pleased him."

Beobrand's mouth filled with spit and bile. He hawked and spat. Gods, his head felt ready to crack open.

"So you say we will find them at Rodomo. If you are lying to me, I will hunt you down and I will find you and I will kill you."

"I do not doubt it, lord," replied Wada, his face pale. "All I can tell you is that Grimr was heading to Frankia, to Rodomo. You will find him at the hall of Vulmar. But if I were you I would hurry. Vulmar is not gentle with his bed thralls."

Through the pain and queasiness Beobrand felt his ire straining at its chains. These men had slain Dalston and taken Ardith from Hithe. They were no innocents. Beobrand's grip on Hrunting tightened. He took a deep breath, trying to calm himself, but the fresh air only seemed to fan the flames of his fury. He knew he should retreat with his men back to *Brimblæd*, but a voice within him screamed out for blood. He recognised the voice, it was low and mellifluous. It tempted him with frenzy and release. But before he could shout out the command which would unleash his warband, a cry came from the hill. And the church.

Coenred and Attor were sprinting down the incline. Coenred's robes flapped about his thin, pale legs and Beobrand thought he looked set to trip and fall. But sure-footed Attor reached out to the monk and hauled him forward. Behind them came several figures, men brandishing hammers, axes and chisels. The men were shouting.

Beobrand chanced a look down the beach and offered up a silent thanks to Woden for Ferenbald. The skipper knew what he was about. The men around *Brimblæd* were rushing about like ants whose nest has been kicked. Already they were heaving the ship back down towards the surf.

"It seems it is time for us to be going," Beobrand said.

Thurcytel gave a lop-sided grin.

"Thank you for the mead," he said.

Beobrand did not reply.

He took several steps backwards, wary of a sudden change of heart from the sailors. But none had the courage, or was foolish enough, to attack. All the while the pirates glared at them, but they made no move.

When they were a safe distance, Beobrand spun around and began running back towards *Brimblæd*. His gesithas fell in beside him, matching him stride for stride.

"Dreogan, Fraomar and Bearn," he barked, "see to it that Coenred and Attor make it back to the ship. Hurry now!"

Without a pause, the three men sped up the beach towards the fleeing men. Coenred and Attor had seen what was happening on the beach and they had changed their course to take them directly to *Brimblæd*.

Moments later, Beobrand and Cynan were lending their weight to the crewmen shoving the ship into the surf. Beobrand's head hurt with each wave that broke and rolled up the strand. He cursed as the water splashed cold over his ankles and then his knees. Soon it was over his thighs, and the waves splashed chill and bitter up to his chest. He gasped with the sudden cold of it, thinking absently that his byrnie would be a ruin of iron-rot before long if he was not careful. He reached up and touched his forehead, wincing at the bruise there, but surprised that his fingers came away clean. He had half expected to see blood, sure that his head had been split on that whoreson Stanmear's thick skull.

The ship was afloat now, and the sailors, as nimble as squirrels, scampered up and over *Brimblæd*'s low wales. A hand appeared before him and Beobrand looked up to see Ferenbald, teeth flashing from within his thick thatch of beard. Beobrand grasped the proffered hand and allowed Ferenbald to pull him up. When he was able to get a grip on the side of the ship, he clambered over the side and collapsed onto the deck, panting.

"Welcome aboard," Ferenbald said, laughing, before running to the stern, shouting orders.

From somewhere, Cynan appeared at Beobrand's side. His hair was wet and plastered to his scalp, as if he had taken a dunking. Around them the crew went about their activities calmly and efficiently. With an effort, Beobrand pulled himself up so that he could peer over the side. With a sigh of relief he saw that the men who had been chasing Coenred and Attor had changed their minds when confronted with Dreogan and the others. The craftsmen watched forlornly from some distance as the monk and the warriors waded into the waves and were pulled aboard.

Beobrand was only mildly surprised to see that Coenred held above his head and safely clear of the water, the carved box that Grimr had taken from Dalston.

At Beobrand's side, Cynan was staring down the beach at where *Brimwulf* and *Waegmearh* still rested, their crews evidently content to let Beobrand and his retinue leave unhindered.

"By the gods, lord," said Cynan, "and there is you always saying you aren't lucky. By my oath, if those brigands had rushed us together, we would have been food for the gulls by now."

Beobrand snorted and looked at him askance.

"You think that was luck?"

Chapter 30

Ardith stared out over the slate-grey sea. She was huddled under the thick, fur-trimmed cloak that had been Abrecand's. It was warm beneath the woollen cloak, but the chill in the wind cut at her face and brought tears to her eyes. Angrily, she wiped at her cheeks, cursing the breeze. She would not weep. In her hand, like a talisman, she clutched Abrecand's knife. She was terrified that Grimr or one of the crew would find it and take it away from her. All the time she had the secret – her claw – she knew she could defend herself. Nobody could hurt her while she had the hidden blade.

A quiet voice whispered to her in the creaking, yawing darkness of the night that she was just a girl, that any of these men could do whatever they wished with her. But she ignored the voice. What did it know? She had seen Abrecand's throat ripped open with the knife that was now hers, had felt his lifeblood splatter her. The small weapon had saved her once, and now that she possessed it, she would be safe.

There were dark clouds on the horizon again, presaging another storm. Grimr had taken them into a secluded cove before the last storm had struck and they had camped on the beach, beneath a jutting cliff, in the wind-shadow of *Saeslaga*'s hull. They had fashioned a shelter from the sail and had managed to keep a fire burning despite the wind and rain. It had been a miserable couple of days, but none of the men had approached her, save for Ælmyrca, who brought her food and drink. He still frightened her, with his eyes and teeth that shone so brightly in the soot-dark skin of his face. But she accepted his fare. She needed to keep her strength up if she had any hope of freeing herself.

You? Free yourself? The small voice inside mocked her. How do you plan to do that? She pushed the voice away, refusing to listen.

Even if she could escape though, where would she go? They would be in Frankia soon, the Blessed Virgin alone knew where that was. All she knew was that it was far away from Cantware and that without a ship to carry her back home, she would never see her mother, brother or Hithe again. Fleetingly she thought of her father. Would she cut him with her knife if she saw him again? She shuddered, unsure of her own feelings. For what he had done, he surely deserved to be cut and stabbed, killed perhaps. She looked into herself. Would she be capable of hurting him? She could not say, and her uncertainty filled her with impotent fury.

And what of Brinin? Perhaps he would find out what her father had done and confront him. She shivered at the thought. Her father was always surrounded by his brutish friends and whilst she was sure Brinin was brave and sure to seek out Scrydan if he were to learn the truth of how she had come to be enslaved, she was also sure that the smith's son would be no match for her father's bullies. But perhaps Brinin would never know the truth. What lies must her father have told? She imagined Brinin, with his strong hands and soft eyes, grieving for her for a few weeks. Months perhaps. But he would move on. He would probably end up married to that bitch, Gytha.

A fresh tear tracked a cold line down her cheek and she swiped it away. The wind pulled at her hair and Ardith gazed longingly towards the prow. She no longer risked standing there. She was too keenly aware of the men watching her, so she remained in her safe place beneath the cloak. She missed the sensation of the wind and spray on her face and the open sea rolling away before her. The sense of freedom, that there was nothing behind her, that she was alone and flying on an endless ocean. Her memories and thoughts had not clamoured so loudly for attention then. She had been able to believe the fantasy. Until Draca had shattered her fragile peace with the death of the dolphin. Then, after Abrecand's attack, she was too terrified to move from the stern.

When she slept, her dreams were filled with rough hands and hot, splashing blood and she would often awaken with a scream on her lips. Grimr would come to her then, if he was at the helm, and whisper that she was safe, that there was nothing to fear. She did not believe him, but she allowed the words to smooth away her jagged night-time terrors. Just as she had chosen to trust her father's words when she knew he was lying. Not to do so, was to confront the true horror of the reality of who her father was. And now, it would mean giving in and listening to the voice of despair within her that grew louder with each passing day.

She gripped Abrecand's knife in her tiny hand and prayed silently to the Blessed Virgin. She was safe. She was safe. She would survive. She would escape.

Close to her, Grimr stood at the steerboard, guiding *Saeslaga* with a deft touch. Grimr liked to be in control of his ship whenever possible, and he slept little. Gone was his savage-looking beast helmet, replaced by a woollen cap. He looked less terrifying without the tusks and iron of his great helm, his jowly face was soft even. But she recalled Abrecand's gurgling screams and the ease with which Grimr had slain him and knew the softness was an illusion. He sensed her looking at him and glanced in her direction. He offered her a small smile, but she turned away, to the iron sea and the gathering dark clouds on the horizon. Ardith had wondered whether he would have spent so long at the helm if she had not been aboard, as even when her eyes were closed, she felt his gaze crawling over her. The hunger in his look was unsettling, so, as with so much else, she chose to ignore it. He had said he would keep her safe.

From the edge of her vision she saw Draca approaching his brother. She sensed rather than saw the brooding glower Draca aimed at her.

"I don't like the look of those clouds," he said.

"We'll be safe in the mouth of the river before the storm hits," replied Grimr.

Draca stared at the darkening sky for a long time, then squinted up at the sail with his single glaring eye.

"I hope you are right," he said. "There is snow in those clouds and that wind is going to change soon. If we are not in lee of the shore, we will have the devil's own time tacking against a south-wester."

Grimr leaned into the steerboard as *Saeslaga* slid up a huge roller of a wave. There was no doubt that the sea was rising.

"I am right," Grimr said with finality.

Draca nodded, apparently trusting his brother's word. "It will be good to get some of that freshly grilled mackerel they cook there. Remember there is that one man who cooks them down on the beach. I wonder if he yet lives. He was as old as the sky years ago. But his fish were the tastiest thing I have ever eaten. The men of Albion don't know how to prepare fish. Their women are tasty, I'll give them that, but their fish... Gods, how hard can it be to make fish have flavour?"

"Perhaps it is the fish here that have more taste," offered Grimr, before shouting out at the men in the belly of the ship to adjust the sail and to prepare to tack.

After the flurry of activity, as the ship was swung onto a fresh course that took them ever nearer their destination, a sailor at the ship's bow pointed and hollered, "Sail ahoy!"

Ardith peered forward, along the length of *Saeslaga*, following Grimr's gaze. There, still far ahead of them, bobbed the shape of a small vessel. It had a sail up, but seemed to be struggling against the strengthening wind. Grimr grinned, his mouth open like a wolf scenting a stag.

"They don't look to be making much headway," he shouted. "Let us show them how well *Saeslaga* can beat into the jaws of the wind."

The men rushed about the business of sailing the ship towards the small boat. They scurried about the deck, pulling ropes and adjusting rigging and sail. They needed to tack a few times, but it soon became clear that they would overhaul the smaller boat. Eventually, Grimr brought *Saeslaga* in close. From where she crouched at the port side stern, Ardith had a clear view of the vessel and the upturned faces of its crew. There were four of them, the oldest had hair as white as the foam of a cresting wave, the youngest could not be much older than Ardith herself. All of them had the same flat-nosed, thick-browed features to mark them out as kin. The belly of the ship was full of glistening silver. A modest catch of saithe and ollack were heaped there.

"Hail," called the old man. And then he streamed off many words in a tongue she could not comprehend. She thought she heard the word "Rodomo", but could not be sure.

Draca responded in the same tongue. The white-haired man glanced at the younger members of his family, hesitating. They exchanged a few hushed words, the eldest of the others, his son perhaps, becoming agitated. Draca called out something and the old man silenced his son with a sharp retort. With a solemn nod to Draca, he beckoned to him. One of *Saeslaga*'s crew was ready and threw the man a coil of rope. It snaked out over the water, the middle part splashing into the cold sea. The youngest of the boys on the boat caught the end and quickly secured it to their craft. *Saeslaga*'s crew pulled them alongside. The two vessels rubbed and creaked together as if their hulls were conversing in a secret language of timber and resin and brine.

Draca threw down a bucket attached to a rope and one of the Frankish fishermen half-filled it with sleek, sparkling fish. Draca said something, his voice harsh. The fisherman added some more saithe to the bucket. Draca spoke again, but this time the man replied and shook his head. Though she could not understand the words, the meaning was clear. They would give *Saeslaga* no more fish than what they had already offered.

Draca spoke again to the fishermen at length, his tone now becoming softer, conciliatory. Behind him, Ardith could see several of *Saeslaga*'s crew arming themselves. The iron and steel of seax blades and hatchets glimmered dully in the brooding light that filtered through the low, snow-filled clouds. She shuddered and wished to call out to the fishermen, to warn them of the attack she was sure would come.

But she remained silent. To speak out would be to draw attention to herself. She must survive. She clutched the small knife in both her hands and watched, wide-eyed and still.

The conversation with the fisherman did not last long. Draca nodded as the old man explained his position with open hands. His white hair fluttered about his head as he gestured to his boys and then pointed to the shore that they could make out, a dark shadow beneath the dark clouds.

Draca pulled up the bucket that was now almost full of fish and then, placing it carefully on the deck, he barked out an order.

Ardith was shocked at how quickly the chill afternoon was filled with death and blood. The armed seamen surged over the side of *Saeslaga* and into the cramped boat. The fishermen had clearly anticipated such an attack, and they lashed out with their knives and a large hook. The hook bit deeply into the forearm of one of the pirates. But there was no reversal of fortune for the fishermen. The wounded pirate screamed out, yanking the hook from the hand of the wide-eyed youth before burying a sharp axe into the boy's skull. None of the fishermen's other blows landed. With a frenzy of stabbing and hacking, all four Frankish men were dead in as many heartbeats, their warm blood mingling with that of the ollack and saithe that slithered in the broad belly of the boat.

Ardith clamped a cold hand over her face, holding in the scream that threatened to billow up from deep within her. Through the laughter of the pirates as they quickly searched the corpses and then tumbled them into the grey waters, she could hear the voice in her mind cackling. It sounded hysterical to her.

Safe, are you? Safe?

Draca ordered the rest of the fish to be brought on board. There was a brief discussion amongst the men whether they should strip the vessel of its rigging and sail, but Grimr cut them off with a curt word. The storm was too close, the risk not worth it. So the small craft was holed with an axe and cut loose. It was already lying low in the water, its sail flapping forlornly as they sailed away. It would sink beneath the waves soon enough, no trace of it, or the family of fishermen, would ever be found.

Ardith could not stop shivering now, in spite of the warm cloak that encircled her form.

Draca said something to Grimr, who laughed. The sound, so sharp and wrong after the screams and grunts of dying men, made her start. The atmosphere on the ship had lifted, the men chattered and boasted as they went back to their tasks.

Ardith looked back just in time to see the last sad flap of the sail as the stricken boat slid beneath the surf.

"Fresh fish for supper, lads," shouted Grimr, his voice full of joy and amusement.

Ardith's gorge rose. Shaking and filled with shame, she emptied her stomach over *Saeslaga*'s side.

Chapter 31

The pain in Beobrand's head lessened as they headed westward. Soon after the oarsmen had pulled them out to deep water, the need to puke had dissipated and now, as they ploughed through placid waters, the searing agony had dulled to a muted throb.

Beobrand stood with Coenred at *Brimblæd*'s prow, watching the distant land slide by to the left and right. They sailed the Soluente between the mainland of Albion and the isle of the Wihtwara. Ferenbald had said it would be more sheltered than the open sea. Once they were past the island, they would turn southward, towards Frankia. Beobrand had never travelled beyond the island of Albion and knew not what to expect in the strange southern land. All he knew of the distant place was that its inhabitants spoke in a different tongue and they drank wine. The few times he had tried it, he had liked the sweet, rich drink, so that was something. Of the Frankish people he knew next to nothing. The few stonemasons he had met in Eoferwic had come from Frankia and had seemed decent enough. Normal men, who drank, ate, laughed and fought as any other. They were not a bad people from what little he had seen, even if one of their lords liked to bed young girls.

And hurt them.

Beobrand gripped the oak of the sheer strake tightly. The brief skirmish on the beach had done nothing to dispel the fury that boiled within him. If anything, his throbbing head served to further anger him, like a hazel switch painfully goading a beast into action.

Absently, he reached up and touched the lump on his forehead. He caught himself doing this frequently. Each time he winced, as if surprised it was still there and that it yet hurt. He flinched from the touch of his own fingers, cursing silently at his own foolishness. It would hurt for days, he was sure.

"Does it pain you?" asked Coenred, his long hair curling about his face in the brisk, cold wind. One of the sailors had given the monk a dry cloak, which he had wrapped about his thin frame. Despite the thick wool, he still shivered, his face pale and pinched.

"What do you think?" answered Beobrand, his voice harsh.

They were silent for a while. The sail cracked noisily as a gust filled it. A gull shrieked in the sky. Beobrand sighed.

"I am sorry," he said. "It hurts, but that pain is nothing. It will pass. But I worry. I cannot help that, and that will not pass until we find her." He did not say his daughter's name, somehow hoping that not saying it would make her and her plight less real. It didn't work. His mind returned to the image he had in his mind of the small girl running along the path from her house in Hithe.

"I keep praying we will find her," said Coenred. He pushed his hair out of his face with thin, pale fingers. "And that she will be unharmed."

"Do you think your God listens to your prayers?"

Coenred bit his lip and stared out to the horizon.

"I am sure God listens," he answered.

"But he does not always answer," retorted Beobrand. He shook his head. "Your god or mine, there is little difference it seems to me."

Coenred sighed, his breath steaming momentarily before it was snatched away on the wind.

"I am too tired to argue, Beo," he said. "I will continue to pray for Ardith. It is all I can do."

At the mention of her name, Beobrand's mind turned to his daughter once more the way his fingers continually touched the lump on his forehead despite knowing that nothing had changed and that to touch it would only bring renewed pain. He tried to think of something else, and muddled in with his thoughts of Ardith, he saw the face of Udela, sorrowful and stolid. He wondered what would become of her without a husband. Perhaps he should wed her, he pondered. He had no wife, and after all, she was the mother of his daughter. The idea of it filled him with a dread deeper and darker than the fear of standing in any shieldwall. Unbidden and without warning, he thought of Eanflæd, the shining braids of her hair, the intelligent glint in her eye, the smirking twist of her lips when she was making fun of him. He felt a different dread then. Would she yet be waiting for his return? Or would Fordraed and Utta have forced the issue with Eorcenberht? Perhaps she was even now travelling to Northumbria.

To Oswiu.

Again he cursed himself for a fool. What did it matter if the princess had been taken to Oswiu already? She would be wed to the king of Bernicia regardless of Beobrand's feelings on the subject. Neither he nor Eanflæd could change a thing. Mayhap it would be better if he were not there to witness the wedding.

He pushed all these thoughts away with an effort. Gods, he was mad to think of Eanflæd at all.

To change the direction his mind was taking him, he turned to Coenred and said, "Attor tells me you are quite the brawler."

Coenred flushed.

"It was a sin," he said. "I should never have struck that man. He was a fellow brother in Christ."

"You were angry. And Attor says the priest was an ass." Attor had been proud of Coenred's actions when he had recounted the story for the others to hear. He told the tale with a light-hearted pride in his tone, as if Coenred were his younger brother.

"That is no excuse," answered Coenred, flustered. "I should not have laid a hand on him."

"Well, I think Utta will be pleased with you. You've recovered the casket and that relic."

Coenred's face was a picture of misery.

"But when he finds out how I came by the cross…" He gripped Beobrand's arm. "Oh by the holy rood, what will I do?"

"Don't tell him and he'll not hear of it from me."

Coenred looked thoughtful, as he puzzled over his predicament.

"Besides," said Beobrand, keeping his face sombre, "won't you be leaving the brethren of Lindisfarena now?"

Confusion played across Coenred's angular features.

"What? Why?"

"Well," said Beobrand, allowing his smirk to show now, "I thought that a fighter such as yourself would be joining my warband. If it comes to a fight, we would have one more doughty warrior to join us in the fray."

A myriad of emotions vied for supremacy within Coenred, the struggle evident on his face that had once again turned the hue of curdled milk. He settled for a mixture of sorrow and outrage that made him look somewhat comical.

"Coenred will be a fine shield brother," called out Attor, loud enough for everyone aboard to hear. "Just as long as we only fight priests who have their backs to us." Laughter rolled across the ship.

Coenred's cheeks reddened. He opened his mouth to reply, then thought better of it. Pulling his borrowed cloak about him, he made his way to the stern, ignoring the men who called out to him.

The men were in good spirits and the light-hearted mood continued for the rest of that day as *Brimblæd* sped along the

Soluente. On the far westerly tip of the isle of the Wihtwara rose huge shards of rock from the waves, like the teeth of some massive beast. Perhaps a sea serpent, thought Beobrand, though if there were truly a wyrm large enough to have teeth that size, it would be capable of eating most of middle earth. Fleetingly, he imagined he could hear Acennan's voice in his mind. They're only rocks, the voice said and Beobrand smiled to himself. He missed his old friend's sense; his calming influence on him.

Leaving the Wihtwara's island behind, *Brimblæd* sailed into the Narrow Sea once more. The men took advantage of the time and fair weather to dry their armour and weapons. They chatted and laughed and Beobrand almost forgot his foreboding anxieties.

There was little room aboard the crowded ship but Cynan had Brinin run through a series of thrusts and swinging attacks with a sword. The boy was getting better, faster and more assured, but he still held his shield too low. As Beobrand thought it, so Cynan rapped Brinin's shoulder with a stick he had found somewhere. "Hold it up," he said. Brinin glared at him, but shifted his stance, raising the black-daubed linden board.

"You'll make a fighter of the boy yet," said Dreogan, who watched from where he slouched amidships, running a whetstone over the blade of his seax.

Beobrand watched the boy practising for a while longer. He hoped Dreogan was right. But the truth was that no man could tell which way the warp of his wyrd was woven. He feared Brinin would find out all too soon.

They made good progress over tranquil waters and there was still much of the afternoon left when Ferenbald changed course for land.

"How long till we reach Rodomo?" asked Beobrand.

Ferenbald leaned on the rudder, peering into the distance to be sure of his course before replying.

"I am taking us in to land. We will sleep ashore and make the crossing to Frankia tomorrow."

Beobrand wished they could just turn to the south now and be done with this caution. With each day that slipped by, the chances of finding Ardith unharmed grew slimmer. But he knew better than to question Ferenbald's judgement on this.

Perhaps Ferenbald saw the disappointment on his face, for he said, "With good weather and a favourable breeze, we'll make the mouth of the Secoana, the river that flows to Rodomo, before dusk tomorrow."

*

They beached *Brimblæd* and camped on the sand. An alder had been washed up in the recent storms, roots and all, so they built a great blaze. As dusk fell Fraomar pointed out a few boys in the distance, their white faces peering down at the men on the shore. Fraomar beckoned to them, but they did not approach and as night came they vanished into the gloom.

Beobrand ordered guards be set around their camp, but they saw nobody else after the boys. They had seen tendrils of smoke rising from behind a stand of elm, but decided not to seek the hospitality of the locals. The fire made from the washed-up alder was warm, and the mood of the men was buoyant. Even Coenred had stopped his sulking and smiled thinly as the men joked with him, understanding, Beobrand hoped, that they would only jest so with a man they liked.

Beobrand took one of the watches and listened to the sounds of the men around the campfire. The night was still and cold, the darkness a thick blanket that provided no warmth. The soft song of the night washed over him. The murmur of the waves from the Narrow Sea and the wind sighing through the branches of the elms, lulling him into a dazed waking-slumber. His thoughts were like dreams. Images and ideas, fears and longings, played in his thought-cage, as jumbled and muddled as the surf tumbling onto itself on the beach. An owl's shrill call split the quiet and Beobrand came fully awake. He stared into the darkness, the skin on his neck prickling. The bird screeched again and then all was still.

It was only a bird. For the second time that day he heard the echo of Acennan as if his friend's shade stood beside him in the darkness. He shivered, but was not afraid.

Later, when he lay down on the sand, wrapped in a blanket and his damp cloak, he was surprised that his mind seemed devoid of worries, as if he had had his fill of dreaming whilst awake. He fell into a deep, untroubled sleep and awoke to the camp being packed away.

Cynan saw him rousing and smiled.

"A quiet night for once," he said. "It makes a difference from storms."

Beobrand looked up to the sky. It was a clear, egg-shell blue, with barely a wisp of cloud in the east.

Later, he wondered whether the gods had been listening when Cynan spoke. Or perhaps it had been Ferenbald's assertions the day before that had reached their ears, for, despite the clear morning, as the day drew on, they had neither good weather nor a favourable breeze.

They set off on the rising tide, thrust southward into the Narrow Sea by a strong northerly wind. There was winter in that wind, and those men who had them, pulled on mittens. The others stuck their hands under their arms when they did not need them to perform some task. Beobrand noticed Cargást taking a thick pair of woollen gloves and trailing them in the frigid water that rushed past the hull. Seeing his quizzical look, Cargást said, "You'd think it would make your hands colder, but you'd be wrong. They'll be as toasty as a babe by a fire soon enough."

They were well out of sight of the coast of Albion when the sky began to darken and the wind turned. Ferenbald did not seem concerned, taking the shift in the weather with a wide grin and a shrug.

"It looks like we're going to have to do some real sailing again, lassies," he shouted, reminding Beobrand once again of Hrothgar.

The sailors knew what they were about, and they followed their captain's orders without hesitation. Beobrand was pleased to see Brinin following in Cargást's shadow, pulling on ropes and tying knots with increasing confidence.

For a while they tacked southward, but the wind continued to swing until eventually they were attempting to beat into the very jaws of the increasingly powerful breeze. The sky before them had grown an ugly bruised hue and the waves around them were white-peaked, their crests snatched away by the quickening wind. The men continued to do Ferenbald's bidding, but Beobrand could see that they were tiring, and despite not being a seasoned seaman, even he could tell *Brimblæd* had ceased to make any headway.

"It's no good," shouted Ferenbald, over the growing roar of the wind, "we'll never make Frankia in this." For the first time his smile had faded and beneath the shaggy mane of hair and beard, Beobrand thought Ferenbald looked pale.

"Then what?" Beobrand yelled.

"We must run before this storm," Ferenbald said. "And, Coenred," he said, turning his attention to the thin monk who clung to a stay, "pray that we find a safe harbour."

Beobrand's heart sunk to think of another day wasted, but one glance at the louring sky told him there was nothing for it.

Ferenbald swung *Brimblæd* back towards the north and for the rest of that day they raced before the rising gale. At sunset, great flakes of snow, thick and wet, began to fall, engulfing them in a swirling world of white. The cold bit at their faces with jagged, spiteful teeth, and their beards frosted from their breath. As darkness surrounded them and with the snow already thick on the wales and the rigging, Beobrand staggered and slipped across the pitching deck to Ferenbald. He clung to a rope, his hands so cold it felt as though his fingers might snap off like icicles.

"How can you see where we are going?"

Ferenbald's teeth flashed in his familiar grin. Gone was the pale fear of earlier, replaced by a savage intensity that made Beobrand wonder if the man was moonstruck.

"I cannot see anything!" he roared. "But we will reach land soon enough, by my reckoning."

"And then what?"

"Let's hope that monk of yours is praying and that his God is listening."

Beobrand moved back to where his gesithas huddled under a hide awning. It provided some shelter, but the wind still probed beneath it with its icy claws, and when *Brimblæd* crashed through a wave, the spray washed over those who hunkered there.

"How bad is it?" asked Dreogan.

"Bad," said Beobrand.

Bearn didn't even acknowledge them, instead retching noisily over the side. Fraomar held onto Bearn's belt, just in case he should lose his balance or be struck by a wave.

Garr opened his mouth to speak, but before he could utter a word, a cry went up from the lookout posted at the prow.

"A light!" he cried. Then, after a pause, "No, two lights!"

"Where?" shouted Ferenbald.

The man signalled where he had spotted the lights and everyone who was able peered into the snow-riven night. Beobrand could make out nothing beyond the crashing surf and the blizzard, but after a few heartbeats, Ferenbald let out a whoop.

He barked out some commands and leaned on the steerboard. With a groaning of timbers, the ship began to turn.

"It seems the monk's prayers are answered," yelled Ferenbald, his gaze never leaving the teeming gloom. He leaned forward, seeking out details of the coast. And then Beobrand heard a new sound, something different in the voice of the stormy sea. A crashing roar boomed to starboard, and suddenly, in the thin light of the night Beobrand saw the waves breaking in great white torrents over jagged rocks as big as the teeth he had seen on the isle of the Wihtwara. A wall of water crashed over *Brimblæd*, soaking them all. Beobrand watched aghast as the slick, black, jutting shards of rock slid past, a mere arm's length away from the hull.

Looking forward, the points of light of the fires that the lookout had spotted were clear to him now.

"Hold on!" bellowed Ferenbald. "Ready, men."

The lights drew closer, but they were off to the port side of the vessel now. The wind howled, throwing *Brimblæd* towards the rocks. For what seemed a long time, there was no sound save the rush of the water and the wind, and the rumble of the waves smashing into the craggy shore. Beobrand thought he saw another rock, jagged and deadly, slip past, but he could not be certain. Nobody spoke. Beobrand's lungs began to burn and he realised he was holding his breath. His hands were locked frozen and unfeeling on the taut backstay that thrummed with the pressures of the storm.

With a sudden shouted command from Ferenbald, the crew burst into action as the skipper heaved on the rudder. The ship slewed to port. Beobrand was thrown to one side. Bearn, so sick he was oblivious, almost tumbled over the edge. With a grunt, Fraomar hauled him back, away from the dark, hungry, roiling sea.

For a heartbeat, all was still, as if the storm itself took a breath, and then they were flung forward as the keel struck rock with a terrible grinding crunch.

Chapter 32

The world was a chaos of biting wind, swirling snow and freezing surf. Men rushed all about Beobrand and he was momentarily confused. Pushing himself upright, he watched as Cargást and several other sailors ran to the prow and leapt over the side. With each incoming wave, *Brimblæd* heaved, rocking and wallowing on whatever rock had split its keel.

Ferenbald was at Beobrand's side in a moment.

"Come on!" he yelled over the roar of the waves and the storm. "Get your men over the edge and help to secure the ship."

Beobrand did not understand.

"How long until she goes down?"

For a merest instant, Ferenbald stared at him open-mouthed. Then he let out a barking laugh.

"*Brimblæd* is not going anywhere, if we can get her up the beach." He laughed again at Beobrand's confusion. "She has not been holed. At least I hope not, by God! Did you truly doubt my skills? With the prayers of our young monk, how could I have failed to make land?" He slapped Beobrand on the back and bounded forward, as sure-footed as if he had been taking a stroll on a summer beach. At the prow men were throwing ropes over the side.

Beobrand looked around him, still not fully comprehending what had happened. Another wave hit the stern of the ship, causing it to slew around and he almost lost his footing on the ice-rimed deck. Staggering to the wale, he gazed out into the night and finally, by the dim light of the moon and the flickering light from the fires on the shore, he understood. Despite the storm, the darkness and the heavy seas, Ferenbald had brought them ashore. The hull had ground over pebbles, not rocks, and even now those sailors who had already thrown themselves into the frigid waters were tugging hard on ropes to bring *Brimblæd* up onto the beach out of the clutches of the turbulent sea.

Beobrand shook his head. How the man had steered them to safety, he had no idea. Perhaps Coenred's god truly had listened and answered his prayers, for this seemed to be the work of gods. A miracle.

The waves pounded the small beach and *Brimblæd*, still mostly afloat, canted to one side dangerously. Close by to the cove Beobrand discerned the shadows of rocks rearing up out of the surf; their locations clear by the white foam and spray thrown up from the waves breaking upon them. *Brimblæd* had evaded those rocky teeth, but Beobrand imagined they were yet hungry and would revel in ripping gaping gashes in her timbers.

"My gesithas!" Beobrand bellowed in his battle-voice, loud enough to slice through a shieldwall's crash and a storm's roar alike. "To the prow and over the side. If we do not get the ship out of these waves soon, she will be smashed to kindling and Ferenbald's sea-skill will have been for nought. Up! Up!"

The men responded to his command. Even Bearn, as pallid as the snow that flurried all about them, surged to his feet and half-ran, half-fell towards the prow. Beobrand smiled grimly at their loyalty and faith in him. The prow was crowded with men clambering over the side and he was forced to wait until the way was clear. As he watched, he saw movement on the cliffs that loomed over them. Men were scrambling down the escarpments that surrounded the cove. Was that the glimmer of steel?

The dark figures from the cliffs climbed down the snow-lined faces of rock and then ran across the sand and shingle towards the toiling crew who heaved on *Brimblæd*'s ropes. Beobrand shouted out a warning, but none of the men on the beach heard him. The attackers would be on them in a heartbeat. Beobrand shouldered his way past Dreogan and pointed.

"Beware!" he shouted as loudly as he could. Surely his hardened battle-voice would carry down to the men on the beach. Indeed, a couple of them looked up now, their faces questioning. But before he could warn them further, he saw with a stomach-twisting wrench that it was too late. The first of the strangers was upon the crewmen.

But they did not attack.

Instead they grabbed onto the ropes and aided *Brimblæd*'s crew to haul the ship out of the raging sea.

A slap on his shoulder made him start. It was Ferenbald, his grin showing wide within his frosted thatch of beard. Beside him stood Coenred, draggled and miserable in his borrowed cloak.

"I tell you, Beobrand," said Ferenbald, "I think I will have Coenred join my crew so that he is with me on every voyage." The abject terror on Coenred's face at the prospect almost made Beobrand laugh.

"How so?" replied Beobrand.

"See? His prayers are so strong that he not only finds us a safe haven from the storm, but God summons up men to help us bring *Brimblæd* to safety."

*

The men who had come from the cliffs and helped them secure *Brimblæd* against the wind and the sea came from the hall of one Lord Mantican. They were led by a gaunt man named Tidgar.

He had sharp cheeks and eyes that never ceased moving as he spoke. It was as if he was trying to count the snowflakes in the sky, Beobrand thought, but later, inside the warmth of his lord's hall, his eyes still flicked and roved, never still, always searching for something.

Mantican's men were a surly lot. They had been quick enough to lend their strength to the task of bringing the ship up out of the tide, but they spoke little and said less. By the time they reached the hall – a long, squat, sod-roofed building, already blanketed in a thick layer of snow – Beobrand knew next to nothing of where they were, save for the name of the group's leader and that of their lord.

"We must thank you for the beacons you had lit," Beobrand said to Tidgar, as they trudged up the winding narrow path that took them to the top of the cliff.

Tidgar merely grunted.

Beobrand turned to Ferenbald, raising an eyebrow, but *Brimblæd*'s master seemed subdued, as if the exertion and excitement of surviving almost certain death had taken its toll on his spirits. That was no surprise to Beobrand. He always felt somehow deflated and empty after an action. Battle exhilarated him as nothing else, but afterwards, when the bodies were growing cold and the ravens were gorging themselves on the feast left on the field, any feeling of battle-joy fled and was replaced by a hollow sensation of futility and doom. Perhaps it was the same for Ferenbald.

Arriving at the hall, Tidgar ushered them into the smoky interior and introduced them to Lord Mantican. The lord of the hall was tall and bony, with arms that seemed too long for his body and hands that looked too large. He jerked upright when they entered the building, disturbing the stillness inside with a great stamping of feet and coughing. Men shook out their cloaks and sighed to be away from the blustery chill. Mantican rose from his gift-stool and scuttled forward, in a way that reminded

Beobrand of a crab. But after a moment's surprise at suddenly having so many strangers in his hall, and so many new mouths to feed, Mantican was gracious enough.

"You are well come to my humble home," he said. "Come sit by my side and tell me of the tidings of the land. We hear little of the world beyond the borders of the Dornsaete."

Mantican led Beobrand and Ferenbald to the high table and snapped at a thrall to bring food for his guests. The slave scampered off into the shadows, no doubt wondering how she was to find food for so many at such short notice.

Beobrand seated himself on Mantican's left. On the lord's right was a spindly woman whose face looked as though it could have been carved from the rocks of the cliffs. She did not meet Beobrand's gaze, but stared fixedly at the table before her.

"Mead for our guests," growled Mantican and the woman flinched. Without a word, she rose and followed the thrall into the shadows.

Relishing the tingle of warmth returning to his fingers and toes, Beobrand glanced around the hall. As Mantican had said, it did appear humble. There were few lights, rush wicks that gave off but a dim glow, guttering and smoking with the thick scent of mutton fat. The beams of the hall were bare wood, solid enough, but with no carving, and no painting to give them life. The hearth fire was small, with a meagre supply of logs stacked beside it. Beobrand had seen larger fires in a ceorl's hut.

Some of Tidgar's men pulled out benches and boards from where they had been pushed up beside the long walls. There was ample space for Beobrand's gesithas and *Brimblæd*'s crew, but everything about the hall was plain. If Beobrand had only observed the building, it would have been easy to imagine that Mantican was a poor man.

But while Mantican clearly did not put stock in the construction of his hall, when Beobrand looked upward it became clear this was no poverty-stricken minor lord. For the walls and beams of

Mantican's hall were bedecked with a veritable hoard of ornaments and objects, as rich and valuable as they were diverse. Animal pelts and finely woven hangings adorned the walls. Between them, at intervals along the length of the hall, were dotted shields of all colours and designs. Ornate iron and bronze bosses glimmered dully from hide-covered linden boards painted with all manner of sigils. From the pillars of the hall were suspended weapons fit for a king's retinue. Swords as fine as Hrunting, with gold and garnet pommels and the pattern of the sea in their blades, glittered beside langseaxes and axes of the best quality. One pillar was surrounded by great boar spears, each blade of the deadly patterned steel only a master smith could forge. Other columns were home to intricate carvings, of wood, bone and antler. All around the hall, such chiselled likenesses of animals and monsters hung from the soot-stained beams. In the flickering glow of the hearth and the meagre rush lights, the faces seemed to scowl, their features writhing. Beside him, Beobrand sensed Ferenbald tensing. The skipper's face was pale beneath his shock of dark hair.

"Once you get some mead in you, you'll warm up," said Beobrand.

Ferenbald turned to him, and there was something in his eyes that unnerved Beobrand, but before the skipper could reply, Mantican's thrall bustled back to the high table and placed green-tinged glass beakers before the newcomers. Beobrand had seen their like before, on the table of King Oswald. These were not the drinking vessels of a poor lord.

"Forgive us our lack of hospitality," said a meek voice from behind him, "we had not been expecting visitors." Beobrand started. It was Mantican's wife. She had returned with an ornate bowl, which she now proffered to Beobrand with two hands. It was filled to the brim with a liquid as dark and rich as blood. "I bid you Waes Hael," she said.

Beobrand took the bowl. It was heavy and cold. To his amazement he realised it was solid silver, with cunningly worked images of men, women and animals running along its rim. He raised it to his lips, hesitating at the tangy scent that filled his nose. This was not mead, it was wine. He drank deeply, savouring the complex flavours and aromas. There was flint and sun, ripe fruit and long summer days in that bowl. It was the most wonderful drink he had ever tasted.

"My thanks, lady," he said, passing the bowl reluctantly to Ferenbald. "That wine is fit for a king." Mantican's woman dipped her gaze and said nothing.

Mantican smiled broadly, an oddly predatory expression.

"It is fine, is it not? From the lowlands of the valley of the Liger. You will never taste finer."

Beobrand could believe that.

The old lord chuckled and clapped his hands, clearly pleased with himself and Beobrand's response to the wine.

"I fear the food I can offer you will not be as rich and fine. Had we had time to prepare, we could have slaughtered a sheep for a feast. Alas, there is only pottage tonight. Still, at least you are warm and dry, safe from the sea and the storm."

"And we thank you for the shelter and whatever food you give us."

Mantican waved the thanks away as if it were a cobweb that had draped his face.

"I see you like my trinkets," he said. "My wife tells me I do not need more things to add to my trove, but I cannot bear the thought. I do so love to have new treasures."

Beobrand looked at the lord's wife. She sat timidly, unspeaking and with head bowed. He wondered that she would ever berate her husband about anything. He did not seem the kind to listen to advice, especially not a woman's.

The thrall stepped forward and filled the glass goblets. Beobrand was pleased to see it was more of the wine. He took a deep draught and was immediately disappointed. It was not of the quality of the drink the lady of the hall had offered him.

Still, it was smooth and spicy and better than many drinks he had endured before.

Bowls of thin pottage, vaguely fishy in flavour, were placed on the board. He would have preferred meat, but it was warm and it was sustenance. He took a mouthful with a wooden spoon, chewing absently as he once more gazed at the richly adorned walls and roof beams of the hall.

"It is something, isn't it?" chuckled Mantican. "Hard to keep your eyes from wandering over it. Like seeing another man's wife who's prettier than your own." He giggled to himself. Beobrand glanced at Mantican's wife, but she seemed unaffected by her husband's words. "Don't look at her," said Mantican, "there are prettier baubles hanging from my roof than that silly old mare."

Beobrand looked away. He felt sorry for the woman. But he was a guest here and no good would come of speaking out and angering their host.

"Which one catches your eye?" Mantican asked.

Beobrand frowned, unsure how to respond.

Mantican said, "Which of my treasures do you like the most? It is not easy to choose, I know. So much to see, so many memories hanging up there. But I always like to ask my guests for their favourite. It tells me a lot about a man."

Beobrand scanned the weapons, his eye roving over the burnished patterned blades of the spears and then on to a particularly grand sword. Its blade was broader and longer than Hrunting's, its ringed pommel glittered with intricately shaped garnets inlaid in a mesh of gold. The sword's grip was made of the darkest wood, interspersed with the whitest bone. It was the most fabulous sword he had ever seen. He wondered where the Dornsaete lord in this far south-western reach of Albion had come by it. And more importantly, whether he would consider selling it.

But before Beobrand could speak, Ferenbald broke his silence.

"What of that carving?" he said, gesturing to a great wooden creature. It was a fantastical animal, fanged and with protruding tongue painted blood red. It reminded Beobrand of the prow beasts on some ships, serpents and dragons set at the front of vessels to watch for spirits and to scare them away from the rivers and lands where the ships might travel. There were several other prow figures dotted about the rafters and pillars of the hall, and this one was by no means the finest workmanship. In fact, the carving was somewhat crude, chisel marks still noticeable through the paint. The craftsman showed some skill and had captured the beast's ferocity and motion cleverly, but there were many finer pieces on display.

"What of it?" replied Mantican. "Of all my collection is that the object that most pulls at your heart?"

For a moment Ferenbald seemed disinclined to answer. He peered at the dragon head, studying it intently.

Outside, a sudden gust of wind shook the hall. Some of Mantican's trinkets rattled in the rafters, and a shower of dust and soot fell like black snow from the sod roof.

"Where did you come by it?" asked Ferenbald at last.

"That prow carving?" Mantican squinted at it. "Why, I have had that piece for years. Since I was your age. I bought it from a Frankish merchant, if I recall. Swapped it for a good salt ham. Isn't that right, Tidgar?" he called out to the other boards where his gesithas sat mingled with Beobrand's warriors, Coenred and *Brimblæd*'s crew.

Tidgar looked up from his drinking horn.

"What, lord?" he said.

"That dragon," said Mantican, pointing, "do you remember how I bought it from that Frankish trader? That was nigh on twenty years ago, wasn't it? We were yet young then, and this old cow's tits," he gestured to his wife, "were still worth a squeeze." He looked wistful. Beobrand shifted in his seat uncomfortably, but Mantican's wife was evidently used to his insults, for she did not so much as twitch.

"As you say, lord," said Tidgar, a sour expression on his face.

"You want it?" said Mantican, taking a swig of wine and wiping his moustaches with the back of his fingers. His eyes glittered in the dark. "I would sell it to you for a good price. Wouldn't it make a nice addition to that ship of yours?"

Ferenbald met the old man's gaze. He was very still, eyes unblinking, beard bristling from his jutting chin.

"I have no need of a prow beast," he said. He looked away and drank a sip of wine.

Mantican stared at him for a heartbeat, before shrugging.

"What about you, Beobrand of Ubbanford? You have your eye on that sword yonder, do you not?"

"It is a blade like none other I have seen."

"A fine weapon indeed," said Mantican, with a twisted smile. "It would serve well a mighty warrior such as you."

Beobrand's mouth grew dry. The thought of owning the weapon sang to him. But he did not wish to appear too eager. He spooned more pottage into his mouth. It was mealy and chewy. He drank some wine to help him swallow.

"You would sell it?" he asked, after what he hoped was a suitable pause.

Mantican laughed, as if he could see Beobrand's very thoughts.

"Let us not spoil this night with talk of prices and silver. Tomorrow, we can speak of trade, but tonight, let us drink and eat."

From the lower board, Dreogan shouted out, "You call this eating? I've seen more meat on a grasshopper than in this stew." The men laughed. Mantican's face darkened, his brow furrowing. Beobrand pushed himself to his feet, glaring at his men. He agreed with Dreogan that the fare was not good, but they were warm and dry and Mantican had not expected them. Besides, it would not do to anger the man. Beobrand could sense his chance of buying the wondrous sword ebbing, flowing away on Mantican's annoyance at the slight.

"Enough," he snapped, his voice cutting off the chuckles and jests. "We are guests in this hall. We have drunk of the Waes Hael bowl and we are dry and warm. Do not forget yourselves. Would you rather be out there, in the snow and ice? Perhaps you would rather be sleeping with the fish in the dark depths of the Narrow Sea." The men murmured and would not meet his glowering stare. "Dreogan," Beobrand said in a tone that would broach no argument, "you will apologise to Lord Mantican at once."

Dreogan stood, awkward with all the eyes in the hall on him. He approached the high table and dropped to his knee.

"Lord Mantican, I am sorry for my words," his voice quiet, but clear enough that all could hear, "I meant nothing by it. I thank you for your welcome, your wine and your food."

Mantican grinned and flapped his hands, waving Dreogan away, as if shooing away a bothersome moth. Dreogan rose.

"Fine words, but it is nothing. We all say things we do not mean when we are young. And we do some stupid things too, eh, Tidgar?"

Tidgar grunted.

"It has been known, lord," he said.

Beobrand said, "Once again I thank you for your welcome, Lord Mantican. Without your hospitality, we would be spending a very cold night, or worse. And thank you for your understanding. Dreogan is a doughty warrior, skilled with spear and sword, but his mind is less sharp than his blades." He scowled at Dreogan, who looked ashamed, the tattooed lines on his cheek somehow accentuating his hangdog expression. The warrior mumbled another apology.

Mantican smiled expansively.

"Nonsense," he said, "there is nothing to apologise for. Sit yourself back down, brave Dreogan. Drink! At least my wine is fine, eh?"

Dreogan returned to the bench and soon the men were once again talking and laughing.

"You have my thanks," said Beobrand. Mantican seemed embarrassed and once again flapped his hands, waving away

Beobrand's words. "Your modesty does you credit, lord," Beobrand continued, "but truly, without your men's beacons leading us to shore, I fear we might all be dead now. Coenred, the Christ monk there, was praying for deliverance, and I am tempted to believe that his god listened and answered his pleas, for we would have surely been lost without Tidgar and his fires to guide us to safety."

Mantican was drinking from his goblet, and now choked on the liquid, coughing and spluttering uncontrollably. After a few heartbeats, as the man's face was growing dark, Beobrand leaned over and slapped him hard on the back. Mantican's coughing subsided at last.

"Gods, never mind the storm," he said, wiping the tears from his eyes with the back of his large hands, "I thought I was to end my days just then. That would have been a poor way to go, choking on Frankish wine." He took a tentative sip from his glass and grinned.

"I am glad to see you survived to drink again," said Beobrand smiling.

Mantican roared with laughter, which set him coughing once more.

Beobrand patted him on the back, but this time, the coughing passed quickly and was replaced with mirthful chuckling.

Beobrand raised his own goblet and offered a smile at Ferenbald, who had been quiet for some time. Beobrand was truly glad they had seen the fires and found this hall and this strange magpie lord. But the smile faded on his lips as he looked at *Brimblæd*'s captain. For Ferenbald did not return his grin. His features were brooding and dark and he looked as though he would rather be anywhere on middle earth than in this hall. He was gazing into the shadowed rafters and without looking, Beobrand knew what his stare was fixed upon.

What was it about that dragon carving that had so unnerved him?

Chapter 33

Beobrand had almost forgotten about the dragon prow carving and Ferenbald's fixation with it when he stepped out into the night. His head was muzzy with Mantican's wine and the cold air made him gasp. The snow was still coming down thick and fast, and the great gusts of wind that blew from the sea were pushing it into banks and drifts. He trudged a few paces away from the hall, his feet sinking into the deep blanket of snow. Beobrand instantly regretted coming outside to relieve himself.

He had considered staying inside, but decided it was better to brave the cold than risk causing trouble. Earlier in the evening one of Mantican's men had pissed in a corner. A fight had quickly erupted when another warrior saw that his shield, which had been leaning against the wall, was being splashed. Later, Beobrand had seen some of the men pissing into a bucket in the corner of the hall nearest the door. But one of them had drunkenly kicked it over, soaking the rushes and making that end of the hall reek. The womenfolk had shouted at the man, pushing him away and cleaning up as best they could. The men had jeered at the man, but the women had glared at them and forbidden any more of the drinkers from relieving themselves inside.

Beobrand's feet were already cold, and he could feel the icy wet seeping through his leg bindings and shoes. But he had needed to clear his head, and part of him was glad of the clear chill air after the cloying smokiness of the cluttered hall, with its dangling treasures. The inside of the hall felt like the lair of some great, trophy-taking bird, as if a giant shrike had hung gilded keepsakes rather than prey from the thorns of its bushy home.

Mantican had been a congenial enough host, but the constant dismissive jibes and barbs he aimed at his wife had grated on Beobrand. More than once he had found himself about to respond with an angry retort in the lady's defence. But each time, he reined in his anger and swallowed the words. This was not his hall, or his wife. The man could speak to her as he wished. By Woden, the man could beat her if he so chose and it was none of Beobrand's concern. But something in the way Mantican spat such incessant insults in the lady's direction needled Beobrand and he began to wonder if the old lord was not doing it on purpose. As if he could sense his reproach and was goading him for a reaction.

With each taunt, Beobrand's smile grew thinner and more fixed. He would take another sip of wine and nod absently, and then draw the conversation in a different direction. They talked of the storm, and how heavy the snow was likely to be at this time of year. Later they spoke of trading and Frankia. It seemed Mantican had travelled there several times in his youth and Beobrand questioned him about Rodomo. Mantican told him little though, except to say that it was a large town that had been built by the Romans on the great river Secoana.

They had talked and drunk wine until Beobrand's thoughts were blurred and he feared he might disgrace himself by losing his temper. He'd looked down to the lower tables and wished he could sit with his comitatus and the other warriors. He would have enjoyed their company better, he was sure. But he was their lord, so he must sit with the lord of the hall and endure his ramblings interjected with hate-filled attacks at his wife.

From time to time, Beobrand had found his gaze drawn back to the great sword. He'd wondered whether Mantican would allow him to buy it from him and if so, what price he would ask. Each time he'd contemplated the weapon, he would turn back to find Mantican looking at him with a knowing twinkle in his eye and a smile tugging at his mouth.

A huge buffeting blast of cold air rushed in from the south, slowing Beobrand in his tracks with its force. The ash trees near the hall shook and rattled. Devoid now of any leaves, their skeletal limbs were dressed in an ever-thickening shroud of snow. Above the moaning of the wind and the muffled sounds of laughter from the hall, he could discern the roar of waves crashing on the beach and rocks far in the distance. He shivered, wishing he had brought his cloak. Still, he would only be outside for a short while.

Stumbling through another drift of snow, he almost fell, as his foot found a hidden dip in the ground. He managed to keep upright and staggered around the side of the long, squat building. In the wind-shadow there was much less snow, and the rage of the storm was muted. But it was still bitterly cold. He quickly unlaced his breeches and sighed as he started to piss.

Movement to his left made him tense. He was suddenly acutely aware that he had no weapon. And he was alone out here in the freezing darkness. A heartbeat later, he allowed himself to relax. There was enough thin moonlight reflecting from the snow to allow him to make out the figure of Ferenbald, his great shaggy mane of hair and beard making his head appear other-worldly, almost monstrous in the gloom.

Beobrand grunted by way of a welcome and continued with the business of emptying his bladder.

Ferenbald stood close to him and his voice hissed in the dark.

"Lord, we have little time," he said, and something in his tone went further to sobering Beobrand than the cold air.

"What do you mean?" asked Beobrand, and he heard the slur in his words and cursed himself for a trusting fool. He should never have drunk so much in a stranger's hall.

"Mantican. These men." Ferenbald spoke in a rush. "They mean us no good." Clearly he had been waiting for just such a moment to be able to speak to Beobrand away from the men in the hall.

Beobrand shook his head, seeking to clear it of the fuzziness of drink.

"Why do you speak so? Mantican has fed us and given us wine. I grant you the pottage was poorer fare than you could expect from a ceorl in Solmonath, but at least it was warm. Something which I am not, out here in the snow."

"Do you not wonder at the fires?" asked Ferenbald. "Think, lord. Mantican said they were not expecting visitors. They had no reason to be there on the cliff with those beacons and so many men."

In the darkness, Beobrand frowned. His mouth was suddenly dry.

"They light those beacons to guide ships surely…" he said, but even as he said the words, he heard their hollowness.

"I do not think the fires we followed were meant to lead us to safety," said Ferenbald, lowering his voice now, so that Beobrand had to strain to hear him. "I think they were meant to lead us to our deaths."

Beobrand thought of the huge teeth of rock that had narrowly avoided rending *Brimblæd*'s hull to splintering ruin, of Ferenbald's sea-skill in manoeuvring the sea-steed onto the shingle beach of the sheltered cove. He recalled how the men at the beacons had hesitated on the clifftop before climbing down to aid *Brimblæd*'s crew.

Beobrand now understood Ferenbald's taciturn silence during the evening.

"But you cannot be sure. It could just be as they say," he said. "That they light the fires to guide ships in when the weather is poor. Just like the men of Hastingas."

"No, I am sure of it. Mantican and his men mean us nothing but ill. I fear that they had thought to see *Brimblæd* wrecked. But now that we live, they will seek to slay us as we sleep."

Beobrand shivered. It would explain much. Even the bad food. Why feed someone well when you plan to kill them shortly afterwards?

"But how can you know this?"

"You remember back in Hithe we told you how Swidhelm had gone missing last spring?"

"Of course. Lost at sea, with his ship and all his crew."

"That dragon that Mantican said he bought from a Frankish merchant a score of years ago was on the prow of Swidhelm's ship."

"Perhaps you are mistaken," said Beobrand, but he heard the deadly certainty in Ferenbald's voice. And the skipper did not strike him as a man prone to fanciful fears. Still he did not want to face what was quickly becoming the obvious truth. Gods, all he wanted was to be warm and to rest. Was that so much to ask? "Couldn't that carving be from another ship?" he ventured.

"No," replied Ferenbald, "I am sure. There is no doubt. That is Swidhelm's prow beast."

"How can you be so certain?" asked Beobrand, desperately hoping that he could somehow refute Ferenbald's assertion. That they could go back and wrap themselves in blankets and sleep peacefully until the morning when the storm would have blown over and the land would be bright and light. But Ferenbald quickly dashed his hopes.

"I carved it for him," he said, his tone as chill and bleak as the snow-riven night.

Beobrand sighed and then spat into the snow.

Two things were suddenly clear to him. There would be no peace for them that night, and before the dawn, blood would be shed in Mantican's hall.

Chapter 34

They came for them in the darkest part of the night. It is the moment when men are sleeping at their deepest, furthest from the light of the dawn. It is the time for hall burnings and treachery, secret murders and silent villainy. Tidgar and his men had expected to find Beobrand's gesithas and the crew of *Brimblæd* lost in the embrace of wine-soaked slumber. They had thought they would find easy prey, that the visitors to Mantican's hall would struggle up from sleep as heavy as the thick blanket of snow that smothered the land outside.

They were wrong.

Beobrand drank no more wine after Ferenbald's revelation. And, as the night drew on, they managed to pass word of Mantican's treachery to the men, so that when the time came, they were all ready. It had not been easy to spread the ill tidings through the group without arousing the suspicions of Mantican or Tidgar, but Ferenbald managed a few whispered words to Cargást, and Beobrand joined Coenred and Attor at their prayers. Both men had known something was wrong the instant that he knelt beside them. He called out to Mantican that he never missed his night-time prayers and asked if the old lord would care to join them.

Mantican sneered.

"I've not time for your soft Christ," he said. "Woden was good enough for my father and his father before him. The one-eyed one is good enough for me."

Coenred and Attor looked at Beobrand askance, but they had enough presence of mind not to voice their surprise. Beobrand whispered warnings and plans in between the offices and prayers that Coenred recited. The only acknowledgement he received from Attor was a grimly whispered, "We will be ready, lord." Coenred said nothing, but nodded his understanding.

Shortly after, Mantican withdrew with his wife behind the partition at the rear of the hall and the rest of the men and women in the hall prepared to sleep. As they wrapped themselves in their blankets by the pitiful fire that had almost completely died down to ash-covered embers, Beobrand fretted. Had the word been spread? Would Mantican's men strike in the night, as he suspected? If they did, would his gesithas be able to stand against them, unarmed as they were?

As the storm continued to batter the hall with great, roof-shaking gusts of wind and the snow piled ever deeper against the walls, he watched from hooded lids as his men positioned themselves around the hall into small groups. Dreogan and Garr and a couple of sailors rolled out their blankets beside the rack of spears. Fraomar and Bearn and some more of the crew lay down nearer the hearth, within reach of shields, seaxes and axes. And Attor and Cynan, along with Coenred, made their resting places closer to the hall's wide doors.

One of Tidgar's warriors called out something to them about sleeping so far from the fire.

Cynan laughed and replied, "There is not enough heat in that fire to make us want to sleep close to Dreogan and his farts. It may be colder here, but trust me, you'll realise why we prefer a bit of fresh air from the door by the time morning comes."

Laughter rippled through the men of the hall. To Beobrand's ears it sounded forced, false and jagged, but nobody spoke again and the men settled themselves down for the night.

To await the blades in the darkness.

The night dragged on longer than Beobrand would have believed possible. The sounds of the dark threatened to drag him down into sleep, and he wondered how many of the men, both his and Mantican's, had drifted into the realm of dreams. A few men snored. The hall creaked. The wind moaned, gripping the hall in its invisible grasp and shaking it until more dust fell from the roof.

In the darkness Beobrand felt specks of soot caress his face. His eyes snapped open. Had he been sleeping? His heart hammered and he lifted his head to peer into the gloom. He could sense that time had passed. Gods, he had been asleep. Cursing himself, he thanked Woden and all the gods that the hall was yet quiet and still. The only sounds were from the storm outside and sleeping men and women. Mayhap Ferenbald was wrong. Perhaps Mantican was what he had seemed all along, just a lonely old lord who ordered beacons lit on his coast to guide hapless ships to safety.

Then he saw the movement. Shadows, barely discernible in the faint glimmer of the hearth's embers, rose up, silent as barrow wights. The shades slipped stealthily about the hall. After a few moments, it was clear that they were positioning themselves. Preparing themselves. Readying for a bloodletting they believed would be as easy as Blotmonath sacrifices.

Beobrand sensed movement behind him. Was that the quiet rasp of a blade being drawn from a scabbard? From the other side of the embers, close to Dreogan and Garr, there was the briefest lambent glimmer of steel in the darkness. The moment was upon them.

Throwing back his blankets, Beobrand surged to his feet with a bellow.

"Now!" he yelled. "Treachery is upon us!"

Mantican's gesithas had believed they would slaughter sleeping drunks. Instead, they were met with a storm of steel.

All around the hall men who had appeared to be asleep leapt to their feet. And the very treasures that Mantican and his band of wreckers had surely stolen from their previous victims became the salvation of Beobrand's warband and *Brimblæd*'s crew. For, despite having left their weapons at the door, as was customary, they now snatched up spears, seaxes, axes and shields from the plethora of items dotted about the beams and pillars of the hall.

The stillness of the darkened building was shattered with the clangour of metal on metal and the grunting shouts and oaths of fighting men. Women screamed. Flashes of light flickered as sparks flew from clashing blades. But Beobrand could not pause for a moment to see how his men fared. Even as he sprang up, he sensed death coming for him from behind. He spun around and more by instinct than any conscious thought, avoided the wicked knife that sliced through the darkness towards him. Before his assailant could recover his balance, Beobrand shoved the man backward and hauled Ferenbald to his feet.

Beobrand could make out the shapes of three attackers. The man he had pushed crashed into one of the others and Beobrand seized the opportunity to twist away. In two quick steps his hand was upon the hilt of the fabulous sword that had so captivated him. He wrenched it free of the leather thongs that supported it and swung it in a great arc towards the three opponents. As they had planned, Ferenbald snatched up a small Frankish axe that had hung nearby and the two of them moved to stand back to back. Their enemies closed in, wary now of these men who were no longer defenceless.

Someone threw a stool onto the hearth stone, stirring the embers into life. Small, tentative flames began to lick at the wood. They provided scant light, but after the near complete darkness of the hall, the new illumination seemed bright, making the men blink.

The new glow of light seemed to spark their attackers into action and one of the men, armed with a vicious-looking langseax, jumped forward. He swung his blade at Ferenbald's side, but Beobrand spun on the balls of his feet and hacked the sword's broad blade into his shoulder. It cut deeply, smashing through flesh, sinew and bone. The man let out a mewling cry, like a newborn lamb born in a blizzard only to die. Sobbing and gasping, the man slumped to the rush-strewn floor.

Beobrand twisted the sword, tugging it clear of the bloody wound and swinging it around once more to ward off the attack he knew would come from the man before him. The flickering flame light picked out the features of Tidgar, who was smiling sardonically. In his hand he held a sword that was the mirror of the one Beobrand now wielded. It too was finely wrought, long and broad with a ringed pommel encrusted with gold and garnets. Tidgar's blade was also of the finest patterned steel and, thought Beobrand, if it was the sister of the sword in his own hand, it was perfectly weighted and thrummed and sang at the taste of blood.

"We are not such easy prey as if we had been shipwrecked upon the rocks!" shouted Beobrand, allowing all of his anger, his frustrations and worries, to boil up within him. The hall was a cacophony of killing now. Men screamed and women wailed. The flames caught the chair on the hearth and the shadows of the battling men danced, tall and dark around the hall. Beside him, Ferenbald was locked in a fight with a scrawny-looking warrior clutching a seax. Ferenbald could deal with him, Beobrand decided.

Beobrand did not take his gaze from Tidgar.

From the way that Tidgar carried himself, Beobrand could see he was a killer, a man to reckon with. They both dropped into the warrior stance, swords raised, their weight on the balls of their feet.

"I knew we should have killed you on the beach," Tidgar said, spitting.

"The sea will not do your killing this night, Tidgar the craven," Beobrand said, provoking his foe and circling away from Ferenbald. "Tonight you must stand against men and fight!"

The hall rang with the weapon-clash and the howling wind outside matched the moaning of the bleeding and the dying. Outside, the snow was piling in drifts against the walls. Here, in the gloom, cooling corpses were heaped in drifts of death. Whether those of his men, or of Mantican's, Beobrand did not know. He could not spare a moment to look. Despite his words to Tidgar, taunting him for a coward, he could tell from his gait and the way in which he moved, that he was a skilled swordsman, a man who was no stranger to the sword-song or death-dealing.

As though he were listening to Beobrand's thoughts and wished to prove him right, Tidgar grinned and launched himself forward, scything his deadly blade towards Beobrand's throat.

Chapter 35

Tidgar was as fast as a striking adder. And as slippery.

Beobrand needed all his skill to avoid the warrior's first swiping blow. Ducking, he threw his new sword upward to parry. The blades met and the shock of the collision made Beobrand's arm throb. Tidgar was stronger than his wiry frame would have suggested. Neither of them were armoured and without byrnie, helm or shield to soak up damage, any strike would almost certainly end the contest.

This fight would not last long.

Without hesitation Beobrand changed his footing and, twisting his blade, he brought it down in a brutal thrust. Tidgar skipped out of reach, grinning, his teeth obscene yellow stumps in his fish-pale gums.

The hall resonated with the clash of weapons. The roaring gale shook the building, but the men were more concerned with the steel-storm within than the snow and ice. Ferenbald grunted close by, but Beobrand could not turn to see how the skipper fared. His eyes were fixed on Tidgar.

"I do not need the sea to slay my enemies," Tidgar hissed and, without warning, he sent another probing attack darting at Beobrand's unprotected legs.

Beobrand parried easily, and took a quick step backwards. But Tidgar had anticipated the move and changed the focus of his strike to Beobrand's face. Beobrand leapt backward. His left foot landed on an overturned drinking horn. It slipped beneath him, skittering across the rushes and Beobrand fell to one knee. The firelight caught in Tidgar's eyes and Beobrand saw the joy of victory there.

Tidgar raised his sword and stepped forward.

"I thought you were a great warrior," he said, almost with disappointment in his voice, and swung his blade. Beobrand flung his own sword up to meet the attack, but he knew that he was beaten. He would not be able to defend against a swordsman of Tidgar's skill from a kneeling position. It would be only a matter of time before the viper-fast fighter was able to knock his blade aside and land the killing blow.

Tidgar chose to swing his blade in an arc aimed at Beobrand's left side. Without a shield and without being able to manoeuvre, this was the easiest target, against which it was most difficult to parry with his sword. Beobrand threw himself to the right, and swept his sword to the left, but he knew it was useless.

And yet, Tidgar's blade did not bite into his side. Nor did their blades collide. At the same instant as Tidgar launched his attack, so Ferenbald shoved his own assailant backward, into the deadly path of Tidgar's sword. The man grunted as the steel of Tidgar's blade tore into his shoulder. The glee of victory vanished from Tidgar's eyes. He struggled for a moment to free his sword from his ally, but it was too late.

Shielded now by Ferenbald's wounded opponent, Beobrand surged up and lunged forward with a great bellowing roar. The fine sword blade buried itself deeply in Tidgar's belly, hardly slowing as it sliced into his flesh as easily as if he had been made of curds. Beobrand's charge was fuelled by his rage and the fear that he had known moments before. This was the true joy of battle. To feel the breath of death on your neck and then, in a heartbeat, to cheat the end your wyrd had seemed to already have woven into your life threads. Beobrand continued to scream his ire and relief as he pushed forward. Once again he had used the sharpness of a sword to cut the weft of his wyrd. The three Sisters would not put an end to him so easily.

His charge carried him into Tidgar and his sword sunk ever deeper in the man's body. With his left, half-hand, Beobrand pushed Ferenbald's adversary out of his way. His sword trembled as it hit bone within Tidgar's frame, and then it was through his body and ripping the cloth of his kirtle at his back. By Woden, but the blade was as sharp as it was beautiful.

They tumbled to the ground, Beobrand allowing his body weight to land heavily upon Tidgar, driving any remaining fight out of him in a great rushing sigh of breath. Tidgar's sword had fallen from his grasp. He blinked up at Beobrand. For a moment, they were as close as lovers. Tidgar's mouth was moving. Beobrand pulled back, removing his weight from the dying man. There was no reason to inflict further pain on him now. But as Beobrand's shadow left Tidgar's features, Beobrand saw in the flickering light from the burning stool, that the man was not crying out. Nor was he gasping for breath.

He was laughing.

"By all the gods, it is true what they say about you," he chuckled, but his laughter turned to coughing. Blood stained his lips.

Beobrand pushed himself onto his knees. He was still clasping the sword's grip. The blade that protruded from Tidgar's body was strangely clean, catching the firelight in a golden glow.

"And what is it they say about me?" he asked.

"That you are a lucky son of a whore," said Tidgar, and his words choked in his throat as he tried to laugh again.

Reaching across Tidgar's prostrate form, Beobrand retrieved his sword and placed it in his hand. The slim warrior's fingers gripped the hilt feebly.

"My mother was no whore," Beobrand whispered and pushed himself to his feet. In the same motion he yanked his sword free of Tidgar's flesh. Blood gouted, quickly drenching the man's kirtle. Tidgar's eyes widened and he grunted. He began to laugh again, blood bubbling at his lips and soaking the rushes beneath him. He was still laughing as death stole the light from his eyes and he became still.

Looking around the hall, Beobrand saw that the skirmish was over. The white-faced women cowered in a hushed group at one end of the building. His gesithas and *Brimblæd*'s crew had drawn together into a defensive wedge near the doors. He scanned their number for a moment, and felt a rush of relief to see Coenred's shaved forehead standing out from the mass of men. Bodies were scattered about the floor, some were dead, eyes open and already dusted with the soot that still shook down from the rafters with each buffet of the storm. Others yet lived, their groaning and crying loud in the sudden stillness of the hall.

Only Ferenbald and he had remained separated from the rest of the men. Movement nearby made him tense, dropping into the warrior stance, ready to fight once more. But it was no fresh danger. It was Ferenbald. As he turned, Beobrand saw the shaggy-haired seaman bring down his Frankish axe in a crunching blow into the man Tidgar had wounded. The axe caved in the man's skull and he jerked for a few heartbeats, like a chicken when its head has been severed and it does not yet know it. Then he collapsed and moved no more. Ferenbald spat and came to stand beside Beobrand.

He was pale and Beobrand saw there was blood running from a gash in his right arm.

"Bad?" he asked.

Ferenbald glanced down at his arm and seemed surprised to see the bloody wound.

"I'll live," he said and spat again.

Beobrand nodded.

"What is Woden's tithe?" he called over to the men who stood with shields and weapons still at the ready.

Cynan stepped forward. There was blood on his face, but he seemed unhurt.

"Ermenred and Brorda are fallen." Beside Beobrand, Ferenbald sighed. The two sailors were both good men, with wives and children back at Hithe. "And Dreogan has taken a nasty cut to his leg."

Dreogan hobbled out of the ranks. His right leg was dark and glistening with blood. The soot lines on his face were stark against the snow-white pallor of his cheeks.

"I will live to drink another day," he said with a grimace. From his bearing and the strength of his voice, Beobrand believed it, but there was a lot of blood.

"You had better not die, Dreogan," he said, forcing a smile, even as his hands began to shake. Droplets of Tidgar's blood showered from the tip of his sword's blade as it twitched in his trembling hand. Placing the point on the rush-covered floor, he gripped the pommel tightly, in an effort to hide his weakness.

"Coenred," he barked, "tend to Dreogan at once. There is much blood and I have seen such wounds claim a man in moments."

Coenred hurried forward to help the large warrior, and Dreogan did not protest as he was laid upon the rushes and Coenred began ripping cloth to bind his wounds.

"There has been much killing tonight in this hall," said Beobrand. He stepped towards the hearth. From a beam above his head dangled a prow carving of interlocking birds and animals, each seeming to bite the tails of the others. With a swipe of his blood-smeared sword, Beobrand cut it down. It clattered onto the floor, Beobrand scooped it up and threw it onto the hearth. It splintered the burning stool and sent up a shower of sparks twinkling between the trophies that yet adorned the roof beams. "But there is yet one who must pay the price for his villainy, for

I see not the corpse of Mantican. Cynan," he snapped, his voice as deadly and sharp as the bloodied blade in his grasp, "fetch the lord of the hall out here to face us. I would show him what becomes of a lord who offers the cup of Waes Hael and then betrays the trust of his guests."

Cynan, Fraomar and Bearn strode across the hall. Cynan kicked aside the door to the partition. There was a moment of absolute hush, and then a woman's wailing filled the air.

Chapter 36

"Please, lord, do not slay him."

From where she knelt before him, Mantican's wife clutched at Beobrand's arm. He pulled away from her. Her pleading both saddened and angered him. Beside her, also kneeling, was Mantican. Cynan had punched him a couple of times to quieten him and blood trickled from the old man's nose and split lips. But the lord of the hall had not accepted defeat, no matter how evident it was to all those who stood around him. The old man stared up at Beobrand with hope glimmering like a newly kindled flame in his eyes. Four of Mantican's gesithas knelt alongside their master. They were all injured and pale. Their hands were tied behind their backs. There was no hope in their eyes. Nothing but fury and hatred burnt in their glares. Beobrand and his friends had slain their spear-brothers and they longed to avenge the fallen.

Beobrand ignored them. They would not be having their revenge in this life.

"Why should I show mercy?" he asked the lady of the hall.

"You have killed most of the men. What will we do without them? We need them to protect us." Her voice took on a whining, tremulous tone that grated on Beobrand's exhausted nerves. "We need men to hunt for us."

"These are no men," he spat. "These are nithings. You can find better men than these. Perhaps the next ship you seek to wreck on your rocks will bear men with more honour than these."

Outside, the storm had calmed, as if the violence within the hall had satisfied the blood lust of angry gods.

"Lord Beobrand," said Mantican, "we should discuss this like men of worth. You could—"

"Silence!" shouted Beobrand, his ire flashing hot and deadly, as fast as lightning from a cloud-laden sky.

"But lord—" Mantican continued, his voice honey-sweet.

"Enough!" said Beobrand, his tone hard and sharp as steel. "Cynan, if he speaks again, silence him." Glowering, his face flecked with dark spots of blood-spatter from the fight, Cynan stepped closer and placed a hand on his seax handle. Mantican fell silent, and some of his bluff arrogance dropped from him like snow from a roof in spring.

"You are truly a fool," said Beobrand, "if you believe your words can alter your fate. The time for words fled when blades were unsheathed in the darkness. A man can cut the threads of his wyrd with bravery and a good sword." Beobrand hefted the great sword he had taken from Mantican's hanging hoard. "You have neither."

He took a deep, steadying breath. The battle-stench of smoke, spilt bowels and slaughter-sweat stung his nostrils. Beobrand had ordered his men to drag the corpses of their enemies into the snow, but the smell of their death lingered on. The hall was well-lit now, bathed in the glow of the fire that had been heaped high with timber. The stark shadows cast on Mantican's upturned face twisted his features, giving them a bestial aspect.

Beobrand turned his attention to Mantican's wife. She stared up at him, her lip trembling and eyes glistening with unshed tears. He reached out a hand. After a moment's hesitation she took it in hers and allowed him to pull her to her feet. Her hand was small and bony, fragile, dry and cold as autumn twigs.

"You will be better without this swine and his retinue of pigs," he said to her. "Dreogan, time now to pay the lord back for his welcome."

Dreogan, his soot-black tattoos dark against his pallid skin, limped forward. Coenred had bound his leg tightly. But Beobrand noticed blood was already seeping through the bandage.

"Make it quick, Dreogan," he said. "I am tired and you need to rest that leg."

Grim faced, Dreogan dragged his sword from its scabbard. Its blade was blood red in the light of the flames.

"No!" shrieked Mantican's woman, once again clinging to Beobrand, clawing at his kirtle, her bony fingers scratching his arm.

As quickly as he had calmed himself, so his anger returned, raging within him, hotter than any hearth fire. He gripped her shoulders and shook the woman until she was still. Her eyes widened, but still her tears did not fall.

"Would you rather I put your hall to the torch too, woman?"

"Please," she pleaded, her voice small and fearful, like a child's, "let him live."

Through the veil of his anger, Beobrand recognised that this woman was braver by far than her treacherous husband. He pushed her away from him, but did not release her shoulders. His head ached.

"Your husband will die in this hall, this night. It is his wyrd, as sure as the sun will rise in the morning. You will be better without him. I know it. But would you be homeless in the winter as well as husbandless? For know this, I make no battle with women, but I will burn your hall before we leave, if you do not shut your mouth."

Despite his words, she seemed about to speak again. Part of him was impressed with her courage. But before she uttered a sound, Mantican let out a mocking laugh, like the bark of a seal.

"If you can get her to shut her mouth, you are a better man than I!" he said.

Cynan slapped him hard with the back of his hand, rocking his head back. Mantican fell sideways onto the ground.

For a long while nobody spoke. The flames crackled on the hearth stone. A knot of wood caught with a popping sound that was loud in the hall and sparks danced in the smoky air. Someone coughed. A child sobbed and one of the women pulled it close to her chest for comfort.

Mantican pushed himself back onto his knees and spat blood into the rushes.

His wife broke the silence.

"You are right, Lord Beobrand." Her voice was firmer now, harder and colder, like soft snow that has become crusted with brittle, sharp ice. "We women are resourceful. We will manage without men."

One of the women huddled in the corner let out a moaning cry.

Beobrand held Mantican's wife's gaze for a long while. Her eyes had turned flinty and dry. Turning to Dreogan, he nodded.

Dreogan stepped forward.

"He is," he growled, his words carrying throughout the hall.

"What?" asked Mantican, spitting more blood. He was pale now, his bluster fled.

Dreogan raised his sword.

"A better man than you," he said, and sliced downward in a flame-flickered arc.

PART THREE
DESPITE AND DESPAIR

Hwær cwom mearg? Hwær cwom mago?
Hwær cwom maþþumgyfa?
Hwær cwom symbla gesetu?
Hwær sindon seledreamas?
Eala beorht bune!
Eala byrnwiga!
Eala þeodnes þrym!
Hu seo þrag gewat,
genap under nihthelm,
swa heo no wære.

Where is the horse gone? Where the rider?
Where the giver of treasure?
Where are the seats at the feast?
Where are the revels in the hall?
Alas for the bright cup!
Alas for the byrnied warrior!
Alas for the splendour of the prince!
How that time has passed away,
dark under the cover of night,
as if it had never been!

"The Wanderer", author unknown – The Exeter Book

Chapter 37

Ardith awoke slowly. Her head was full of fog and for a time she was unsure where she was, or what her eyes were seeing. But with each passing moment her surroundings became clearer, as though she was climbing through thick clouds wreathing a mountaintop, pushing herself ever upward toward the sun, towards light and clarity.

Blinking, she cast her gaze around the room. She was lying on a soft mattress and the walls around her were smooth whitewashed plaster. Gone was *Saeslaga*'s ever shifting deck. And in place of the sounds of the sea rushing beneath the keel and the creak of the strakes flexing against the waves was the stillness and hush found inside a solid structure. At the angle of the wall was a pillar that rose into the ceiling. Her eyes widened in amazement. The column was made of cut stone, cunningly crafted and cemented with mortar. She looked at the white wall again. Part of the plaster was cracked, a spider's web of fine fractures ran up the wall and into the ceiling. Where the plaster joined the stone column, some of it had flaked away. Where she had expected to see mud and straw daubed over a wooden framework she now saw more worked stone. She had never been inside a stone building before. She looked up at the cracks in the plaster and saw how the fingers of those cracks splayed into the ceiling. She wondered how high the building was. How heavy it must be. She shuddered at the thought of the oppressive weight above her.

She made to rise, but before she had lifted her head more than a hand's span from the mattress, she slumped back. She was so weak. It was cool in the room and she noticed for the first time that she was naked beneath a linen sheet and a luxuriant pelt. She plunged her hand into the lush fur, relishing the touch despite her confusion and anxiety. It reminded her of Abrecand's cloak. In a sudden moment of acute terror that twisted her stomach the reality of her situation washed over her. How had she come to this place? Who had undressed her? She could feel the scream welling up inside at what might have been done to her. Had she been violated? Her mind filled with dark thoughts in an icy, heart-wrenching instant. She moved her limbs, ran her hands over her body. There was no sensation of pain. Her breath came in gasps as her fear mounted. Scared of what she might find, she gingerly reached down between her thighs, tentatively touching, probing for bruises, but still she felt no pain. No sign that she had been hurt in any way. Relief replaced her fear, but her confusion remained. Ardith's head spun. By the Blessed Virgin, where was she and how had she come to this place?

She closed her eyes for a moment, taking deep breaths to steady herself against the sudden dizziness that had come over her. Images flashed before her mind's eye, fragments of memories she barely recognised as her own. It was as though she was watching the dreams of another girl.

There she was, trembling and shivering in the belly of *Saeslaga*, her stomach heaving until she was empty and spent. Strong arms carrying her between tall buildings. Gulls squealing in the thin sliver of sky beyond the dusky form that carried her. Voices speaking in a tongue that made no sense. The shades of faces leering and looming over her. A grin pressing close to her face, the long teeth white and sharp between red lips. And all the while she had been cold. So cold.

*

Ardith awoke to the sound of a woman's voice. This time her mind was less clogged with the cobwebs of dreams and sleep. The woman was singing quietly to herself words that meant nothing to Ardith. But her voice was pure and musical and the sound of it soothed Ardith, as if she had awoken to find her mother sitting at her side. Gone was the fear of before. Ardith opened her eyes and saw the slender back of the woman. The room was in shadow, what scant light there was came from a brazier in which glimmered red embers. The room was warmer now.

The woman was slim and tall. She moved around with a purposeful, lithe grace. Ardith watched her silently. Questions about where she was still filled her head, but she was content for the moment to bask in the warmth under the bearskin and to watch the beautiful woman. Though she had not seen her face, Ardith was certain that the woman was comely. Her voice was as sweet as the summer flowers of woodbind and there was something in the way her hips swayed, how her hair, long and dark, fell like a midnight brook down the curve of her back. It had been so long since she had been in the presence of a woman. Ardith thought of her mother. She would be terrified for her. Tears stung Ardith's eyes. She swiped them away with her hand.

At once, the woman turned to her. Her eyes were shadowed pools that held the glitter from the embers. She moved closer to Ardith and she saw she had been right: she was beautiful. Nothing like her mother at all. She felt a pang of guilt at the mean thought. But it was true. This lady was younger, slimmer, with delicate angular cheekbones and a straight, thin nose.

To Ardith she looked like a princess; a peace-weaver daughter of a mighty king.

"So, you awaken at last, little one," she said, and her voice carried an accent, lilting and fluid.

"How…" Ardith croaked. Her throat was so dry.

"Hush," the woman said and helped her to rise into a sitting position. Ardith's body ached and was weak, but she was suddenly overcome with thirst and hunger. She pulled the fur up with one hand to cover her breasts and accepted the cup the woman offered her. She sipped. It was cool, fresh water.

Sensing her unease, the woman said, "Do not fear, child, it was I who undressed you. None of those brutes touched you." She took the empty cup from Ardith. "Are you hungry?"

"Yes," replied Ardith, her tone firmer now. "I feel like I have not eaten in weeks. How did I come to be here and how long have I been asleep?"

"All in good time, little one," said the woman. "I will fetch you some food and I will tell you all you would like to hear."

"Thank you," Ardith said, in a small voice.

The woman rose. She opened the door, hesitating in the doorway. Raucous laughter echoed into the chamber from deep within the stone building. Ardith tensed at the sound. She thought she recognised the voices that were laughing and shouting somewhere nearby. The woman seemed about to speak, but instead, she slipped through the door, closing it behind her, leaving Ardith in the quiet warm darkness. In the moment before she left the room, Ardith thought the woman's expression had changed. It was for the merest instant, the flutter of an eyelid, no more, and perhaps it was a trick of the shadows. But for that moment Ardith thought she had looked unutterably sad.

Ardith lay back against the soft pillow and awaited the beautiful woman's return. The muted sounds of revelry invaded the stillness of the room. Despite the warmth from the brazier and the furs, Ardith shivered.

She did not think she would like to hear all that the woman would tell her.

Chapter 38

Coenred's mouth hung open as *Brimblæd* slid into Rodomo. All around him, the men were seated at the oars. They pulled in perfect time. Coenred did his best to match them, leaning forward while raising the oar from the water, then lowering the wooden blade into the river and heaving backward. He was not weak; the brethren of Lindisfarena worked hard in the fields and toiled to help those of their flock who needed their aid. But his body was not used to this activity. With each pull his back screamed. His hands were raw too, making every oar stroke a misery of pain.

On one of the nearest benches Brinin also toiled at an oar. Ferenbald had told them both to take the place of Ermenred and Brorda. Brinin seemed to be much more suited to the work and did not complain. The youth saw Coenred looking at him and he offered the monk a wide smile. Coenred smiled back, yet he couldn't help but feel envious of the young smith's easy strength. He was barely sweating, whilst Coenred's face was slick and his robe was dark with sweat, in spite of the cool wind that blew down the river. Coenred turned his attention back to rowing and grunted. He'd almost fallen out of time with the others. Groaning, he rapidly dipped his oar into the water and pulled.

Despite the agony of the rowing, Coenred twisted and turned his head, trying to take in all that surrounded the ship as it made its way up the Secoana river. He had never left the shores of Albion before and didn't want to miss a thing.

The monk glanced at Ferenbald, who stood at the steerboard. The skipper grinned over the heads of the crew.

"I'd wager you've never seen so many ships in one place before, eh, Coenred?" he shouted.

"I will not take that wager," Coenred panted in reply. "And not just because the good Lord frowns on gambling." He stopped talking for a moment so that he could match the other rowers' timing. He heaved back on his oar, and then, when leaning forward once more with the oar out of the water, he said, "I would lose such a bet. I do not believe I have seen this many ships in all my life."

On either side of the broad Secoana were moored ships and boats of varying forms and sizes. Wallowing merchant ceapscips, broad of beam and cumbersome in the water, rubbed strakes with sleek serpents of the sea. Flexible hydscips, favoured by the men of Hibernia, seemed almost to be living creatures, as their stretched leather hides shifted with the tide and currents, making them appear to breathe. Light, agile wherries ferried passengers across the wide river, their oarsmen expertly navigating between the myriad docked and anchored craft.

The largest and richest vessels were moored along a wooden quay on the north bank. Behind the forest of jostling masts and rigging, lay the city of Rodomo. It was a vast, sprawling array of buildings and a great pall of smoke hung over the place like a low-lying cloud. The stench hit Coenred's nose then and he all but gagged. After the cold, fresh wind of the open sea and the broad estuary of the Secoana, the smell of thousands of cooking fires, muddled with the waste of the thousands of men, women and children of Rodomo was like an assault.

Ferenbald was peering around, clearly looking for a place to moor. They edged past sandbanks, quagmire islets where many ships were anchored in the middle of the river. Small boats ferried men and goods across from the islands to the city of Rodomo. Sailors shouted to one another, but Coenred could not understand their words.

One slim boat approached *Brimblæd* with purpose. Its oars dipped and rose quickly as it was rowed across the water from the north shore towards them. The dull winter sun gleamed on the helms of the boat's passengers. Ferenbald shouted an order for the crew to slow their rowing and to back up, changing the direction of their rowing so that now they should push when before they had pulled. He wished for them to hold their position against the flow of the river and await the oncoming boat.

As one, on Ferenbald's command, the crewmen shifted their rowing. All except Coenred, who had not understood the order. His oar snagged with those of the men ahead and behind him. He almost lost his grip on the wooden shaft of his oar as its blade clattered against the others. Men shouted at him and Coenred felt his cheeks grow hot. He struggled to correct his mistake, but it was difficult now, as others tried to mend the situation too, each hesitating and then pushing and pulling their oars out of time with one another.

Brimblæd began to flounder, to spin slowly to larboard.

"What in the name of all that is holy do you think you are doing?" Ferenbald bellowed, his face pale with sudden rage. "We come here in the finest ship, laden with treasures to rival the king of Frankia and you disgrace me thus." Spittle flew from his lips, such was his fury. Coenred's face flushed yet further and he felt tears prickling his eyes. He had never seen *Brimblæd*'s captain so angry before.

Coenred concentrated on matching the rhythm of the other rowers, but still he failed to do so, rattling his oar once more into the one in front. The sailor spat a curse at him. Coenred did not know what to do. He blinked back his tears. He could feel the weight of Ferenbald's ire on him; sense the gaze of Beobrand and the other warriors resting on him from where they watched from the prow. He could imagine their sneering at his incompetence.

A soft voice spoke in his ear.

"The skipper is nervous. There is nothing a seaman likes less than to be seen to be lacking in skill before other sailors. And there are a lot of ships here. Just raise your oar out of the way and let the others fix it."

It was Cargást, who sat at the bench behind him. Coenred felt a wave of relief at the sad-eyed sailor's words. He pushed his oar down, lifting the dripping blade high into the air, freeing the other oars to move unhampered.

"Right, lads," said Cargást in a loud voice, "with me." And as he called out, the oars were once more rising and falling in harmony.

"I thank you," Coenred whispered, but he was not sure if Cargást heard him. Coenred took a deep breath. Not for the first time, he wished he had not so readily accepted the role of sailor when Ferenbald had asked him on the morning they left Mantican's hall. But Brorda and Ermenred were dead, and the rest of the crew had been brooding and sullen. When they had trudged down to the beach through the melting snow, their bitterness and anger had rolled off them like the waves crashing onto the rocks. They had loaded the ship in a surly silence. It had been unsettling and so, when Ferenbald had said that Coenred should take Brorda's place on the crew, he had not complained. He was not scared of a bit of work and he hoped that the men's mood would lift once they had set sail for Frankia again.

He watched the oars lift and fall in perfect unison now, making quiet splashes into the dark waters of the Secoana, and smiled at his own naivety. The crew had lost two of their number and they felt it was a price too high to pay for what was beginning to look like a doomed quest.

They had taken a long time to carry Mantican's riches down to the ship and to secure it all on board. There were piles of weapons, shields and armour, silver and gold ornaments and plates, finely wrought goblets of glass and all manner of jewels and brooches. It was a mighty hoard and the sun was high in the sky and the ship low in the water by the time they were ready to once more set off across the Narrow Sea towards Rodomo.

But before they left the cove, surrounded by jagged rocks and sheltered by the snow-clad cliffs, Sigulf, one of the younger crewmen, a burly man, with thick neck and short legs, had stepped forward. His hands were on his hips and he'd faced Beobrand directly. Sigulf was no coward. He had fought hard in the hall and yet Coenred still marvelled at his boldness to stand before Beobrand so. Beobrand had looked down at him, his ice pale eyes reflecting the steel-grey of the sky and sea.

He said nothing.

Sigulf swallowed.

The men all watched on. Coenred noted how Beobrand's gesithas moved silently to stand beside their lord.

"My lord," Sigulf began, his voice cracking. He cleared his throat and started again. "My lord. The men and I have been talking."

Still Beobrand said nothing.

"We think we should turn back to Hithe." He paused, perhaps expecting a response. He got none. "Two men have died…" His voice trailed off.

Beobrand stared at him for a long time.

At last he said, "We stood together last night against Tidgar and the rest of Mantican's murderers, did we not?" Sigulf swallowed and nodded. "We mourn the loss of Ermenred and Brorda, but they, like you, Sigulf, and every one of you," Beobrand cast his gaze over all of the gathered sailors, "knew what this voyage was for." He paused, looking at each of them in turn. "I did not demand that you come. No, you chose to board

Brimblæd because one of your own had been taken. Ardith is but a child. In need of the strength of men. Brave men, like you all. I hope that we will find her and bring her safely back to her mother…" Beobrand's voice broke for a moment, and he halted, drawing in a deep breath before continuing. "But know this. Whatever happens, after last night, we no longer stand together as men. We stand together as brothers." Cynan, Dreogan and the other gesithas nodded at this, and some of the sailors hoomed in their throats. "And make no mistake, the plunder we have taken from Mantican's hall is worthy of many battles. And the spoils will be shared evenly between each of you. And I give my word, here, before you all and all the gods, that for any man that falls helping me to bring back my daughter, his kith and kin will receive twice the amount of a man's share of the treasure." He stepped forward and clasped Sigulf's forearm in the warrior grip. "I know you are all brave men," he said. "Now you are all rich men too."

Still gripping Sigulf's arm, Beobrand looked over the squat man's head at the other sailors.

"So, what say you?" he said, holding the gaze of each in turn. "We know now where Grimr has taken Ardith. Shall we finish what we started? As rich men? As brothers?"

Cargást was the first to answer.

"Aye," he said, his voice carrying over the crash of the waves that tumbled up the shingle beach. The other men quickly added their voices to Cargást's. Beobrand had slapped Sigulf on the shoulder and released his grip on him.

They had soon been on their way, and this time, no storm pushed them back or threatened them with mountainous waves. The sky remained leaden and overcast and squalls of bitter rain spattered them as *Brimblæd* crossed the Narrow Sea, but when night drew in around them, the shore of Frankia was in sight. They had sheltered in the estuary of the Secoana that night, before rowing up the river on the dawn tide towards Rodomo.

The gentle bumping of the boat against *Brimblæd*'s port side brought Coenred back to the present. Without the hindrance of his oar, the crew had straightened *Brimblæd* in the current and then held it in place as the slender vessel rowed close. It nudged alongside the larboard bow and Fraomar reached down and took hold of a line. There were seven men in the boat. Six wore simple polished helms. The seventh was a portly man of middling years. He had a hat of thick beaver fur and a blue cloak held in place with a large silver clasp. The hat looked too small for his fat head, thought Coenred, making it seem as though a small animal had curled up and fallen asleep on his pate.

"Welcome to Rodomo," he said in Anglisc, his voice a whiny wheeze. Just as his hat did not fit his head, so the man's voice did not suit his chubby body. He stood, and with surprising nimbleness, he jumped up into *Brimblæd*. Two of the guards followed him as quickly as they could. None of Beobrand's gesithas made a move to help them. The temperature aboard seemed to drop, *Brimblæd*'s crew bristling at the sudden intrusion. The fat man appeared not to notice, or not to care.

"My name is Gozolon and I am the port reeve of Rodomo," he said, with an obsequious smile that did not reach his eyes. "You come from Albion, do you not?"

Ferenbald strode down the length of the ship, easily making his way over the benches and past the rowers. All sign of his recent anger was gone now, and he returned Gozolon's smile.

"That is right," he said, reaching out his hand. "We sail out of Hithe, in the kingdom of Cantware."

Gozolon looked down at the proffered hand for a long moment. His mouth twisted, as if he had been offered a rotting trout, but he clasped Ferenbald's hand briefly and his smile grew broader.

"Good, good," he said. "I thought I recognised the ship. It is late in the year for *Brimblæd* to be trading. But where is

Hrothgar? I pray to God and all the saints he is well." Coenred thought he could not have sounded less sincere.

But Ferenbald smiled and said, "My father is well, master Gozolon. My thanks. He has honoured me with command of *Brimblæd* for a special voyage."

Gozolon's eyebrows shot up.

"Indeed?" he said, his voice growing even more high-pitched. "You bring something special to trade with us?"

Coenred looked over his shoulder and saw Beobrand's face darken. He clearly did not like the way this conversation was going.

The ship drifted now, spinning languidly as the current pulled at it. A wherryman bellowed his ire at the larger vessel, as he was forced to row quickly to avoid a collision against *Brimblæd*'s oak hull. Some of the sailors dipped their oars into the river and gently corrected *Brimblæd*'s position, holding the ship steady in the water. Coenred thought it best not to try and aid them.

"We bring nothing of importance to trade, Gozolon," Beobrand said, stepping forward and squaring his shoulders.

Gozolon turned, disdain oozing from him. Beobrand pulled himself up to his full height. His half-hand rested on Hrunting's pommel and his eyes burnt with a cold fire.

Gozolon seemed unperturbed by the threatening presence.

"And you are?"

"My name is Octa," said Beobrand.

Gozolon glanced down at Beobrand's mutilated hand.

"Indeed," he said, his tone flat. "And you bring nothing to trade in Rodomo?"

"Nothing of interest to you, little man," Beobrand said. "But we have travelled far and we wish to moor."

Gozolon smiled thinly. He turned back to Ferenbald, dismissing Beobrand as though he were a child.

"You can moor on the Isle of Múgr," he pointed to a massive sandbank in the middle of the wide river. "And remember, son of Hrothgar, that whatever is brought ashore for trade and whatever you laden into your ship from Rodomo, is subject to payment of the Hlaesting."

"Of course," said Ferenbald, accepting the mention of the loading tax with a flick of his hand, "but could we not dock on the north bank? We would rather be closer to the city than over there surrounded by those slovenly hydscips and ceapscips. They are not fit to moor alongside the likes of *Brimblæd*."

"I am truly sorry," Gozolon said, not sounding the least bit apologetic, "but the northern moorings are for the richest ships and those lading the heaviest goods."

"Listen, you fat toad," said Beobrand, his voice as sharp as a seax, "we have said we wish to moor on the north bank and if you do not give us your leave, we will tie *Brimblæd* to the dock with your guts for a rope."

The two guards moved to stand protectively before Gozolon. Their hands dropped to the long knives they wore at their sides. The crowded prow of the ship was suddenly full of the threat of death.

"Lord," said Ferenbald, in a pleading tone, "please."

Beobrand ignored him. He glowered at Gozolon. Most men would cower under the force of that gaze. But not Gozolon. The fat official sighed. He appeared bored with the proceedings. He looked Beobrand up and down.

"Do you truly believe you can intimidate me?" he said at last. "This is the great city of Rodomo, not some farmstead in Bernicia." Coenred started at Gozolon's use of the name of the northern kingdom. "If you threaten me again, or strike me, or even, heaven forbid, slay me, dozens of warriors will descend upon you. This wonderful ship would be forfeit, as would your life, and that of your men, most likely. At best you would all become thralls, niedlings aboard a trade ship, pulling on an oar until death would claim you, offering sweet relief from the pain and suffering. Is that how you wish to depart this life, brave," he paused for a heartbeat, "Octa?"

The muscles on Beobrand's jaw clenched and bunched, but he said nothing.

"Good," Gozolon said, when it was clear Beobrand was not going to reply or attack him. "Now, enough of this unpleasantness. From the look of it, you have a lot more to offer me than violence."

For a long time nobody spoke. Somewhere on the Isle of Múgr someone laughed. Gulls flew down close to the deck, shrieking and observing them with their empty, dark eyes. Over on the northern dock, there was a sudden commotion. A barrel was dropped with a splintering of wood, followed by shouts and curses. Coenred jumped at the sound. His neck ached from where he was craning round to see Beobrand and Gozolon.

Beobrand was staring unblinking at the fat Gozolon, violence coming off him like a stink. Coenred's mouth went dry. He was certain then that his friend would attack, that he would spill blood and in so doing end their quest and quite possibly, their lives.

As he watched, Beobrand nodded slightly, and beckoned to Gozolon to step closer. The two guards clearly agreed with Coenred's assessment of the situation for they did not move. They blocked Gozolon's way. Their eyes were nervous, darting this way and that as they sought to see from where the next threat might emerge.

"Come," said Beobrand at last, his voice softer now. "I would make you an offer."

Coenred wished to scream out, to shout a warning to Gozolon. He loved Beobrand as a brother, but he was sure that his old friend's next action would plunge them all into chaos. But he did not utter a sound. Instead, he held his breath as Gozolon pushed his way past his guards and allowed Beobrand, half-hand resting on his seax hilt now, to step in close.

Chapter 39

A light touch on her shoulder awoke Ardith. Sleep must have claimed her again as she waited for the woman to return. Her eyes flickered open. A shadow loomed. Fear engulfed her.

The distant voices of Grimr and his crew were harsh and strident in the dark stillness of the room. Had one of the seamen come for her, creeping into the chamber? Ardith's breath caught in her throat. She wanted to scream, but no sound came. Who would come to her aid anyway? Her mind whirled with terror. There was nobody here to help her. She was alone with nobody to care if she lived or died.

"Hush, little one," said a soft lilting voice.

Ardith's eyes finally made sense of the shadows she saw in the room. This was no grizzled sailor come to violate her, this was the beautiful woman, black hair framing her delicate face. "You are safe," she said. "Nobody will harm you here tonight."

For a fleeting instant Ardith wondered at the woman's words. Here? Tonight? What of tomorrow, in another place? But she pushed the dark thoughts away. The woman set down a steaming bowl on a small table and helped Ardith to sit up. Ardith felt as though her body belonged to another. Her hands trembled but she was in no pain.

"Who are you?" Ardith asked.

"My name is Erynn," answered the dark-haired woman.

She picked up the bowl and, dipping a wooden spoon into its contents, offered a mouthful to Ardith. After a brief hesitation, Ardith opened her mouth, allowing Erynn to feed her as though she had been a babe. The stew was hot and salty and flavoured with a spice Ardith had never tasted before. Warmth trickled into her and her stomach growled. It was as loud as an unhappy hound in the quiet room. Ardith met Erynn's gaze and they both smiled.

"Eat, little one," Erynn said spooning more of the pottage into Ardith's mouth.

Ardith chewed and swallowed.

"My name is Ardith," she said. She reached out and took the bowl and spoon from Erynn. "I can feed myself." Erynn's brow wrinkled at Ardith's abrupt tone. "Thank you for the food," Ardith said around a mouthful of meat and vegetables. "For everything."

She spooned more of the warm stew into her mouth, chewing quickly, enjoying the rich spiciness. Somewhere within the building a voice was raised in song. She did not recognise the melody but soon those gathered at the feast picked up the tune. The noise grew as the singers took up the beat of the song. Ardith could imagine them beating time in a threnody of stamping feet, crashing fists and knives into boards that groaned with delicacies and rich, bloody cuts of meat. The rhythmic thunder unnerved Ardith.

"Where is this place?" she asked.

"This is the palace of Lord Vulmar," Erynn told her. Seeing Ardith's blank expression, Erynn continued. "He is a powerful man of Neustria. This is Rodomo. Do you remember nothing of how you came to be here?"

Ardith shook her head.

"I remember being at sea. I was sick." She remembered her father walking away, his feet crunching in the shingle as Grimr's men had dragged her aboard *Saeslaga*. She remembered the cold creaking loneliness aboard a ship filled with men with nothing but lust and death in their eyes. "I think someone from the ship carried me here. The one they call Ælmyrca, I think." She remembered Abrecand, his hard hands bruising; his sour breath, his hot blood. She shuddered. "But I can recall little else."

The singing and stamping cacophony ended in a crescendo of laughter and applause, rumbling through the stone walls like waves crashing on distant a beach. Ardith winced. Erynn seemed not to notice the sound.

"Yes, the black-skinned man brought you here," she said. "But it was Grimr who asked me to care for you."

"He must have been worried that he would not get such a good price for a sick or dead bed-thrall," Ardith said, her tone as bitter as bile.

Erynn took the now empty bowl from Ardith. The dim glow from the embers and the single rush light she had brought with her showed the sadness on her face.

"Little one," she said, and then, at seeing Ardith's frown, "Ardith, I see you are no fool."

"I am young. Not an idiot."

Erynn sighed.

"I am sorry."

"Sorry about what?" Ardith almost spat the words. The anger she felt directed like a blade at the only person who had shown her kindness.

Erynn shrugged. Her eyes glimmered, but her face was in darkness.

"That you are here. That you were born pretty. That your breasts mark you as a woman when perhaps your years do not."

Ardith's mind reeled at Erynn's words. She had known what fate awaited her in Frankia, had heard Grimr talking to the others. Gods, if there had been any doubts, Abrecand had made it all too clear. And yet somehow, she had never truly believed. Now, Erynn speaking of her body so frankly, made it real for the first time. She had prayed to the Blessed Virgin over and over and yet here she was, a gift to the lord of this hall. Tears stung her eyes. She scrubbed at her cheeks angrily.

"Gods," said Erynn, lowering her gaze. Her black hair fell over her face.

For a long time neither of them spoke. Ardith could feel the warmth of the pottage oozing into her limbs. The embers in the brazier hissed. The sounds of laughter and singing were quieter now, muted and dull like rainfall thrumming in a dense forest. Despite the fear that gripped her, Ardith felt her eyes grow heavy. She willed herself not to succumb to sleep. Not yet. Forcing her eyes open she stared at Erynn.

"What is to become of me?" She was sure that she knew the answer but she needed to hear it from Erynn. If the dark-haired beauty said the words it would make them true. She didn't want to hear the words; she needed to.

Erynn met her burning stare. For a long while she said nothing. Then she drew in a deep breath.

"I think you know," she said, her voice flat.

"I think so too. I'm afraid." As Ardith said the words fresh tears spilt down her cheeks. She made no move to wipe them away this time.

"Don't be afraid, little one. Lord Vulmar will not be wanting you if you are ill, will he?"

"But the fever has gone," Ardith said.

"If I were you," Erynn said, "I would be ill for a few more days. I will say it is so."

"How bad will it be?" Ardith asked, her voice catching in a sob. The terror that had been hidden deep within was now rushing out of her. There was no stemming the tide of the tears now, her face was slick with them.

"Let us not talk of that now," said Erynn. Leaning forward, she reached for Ardith and embraced her. Her fragrance was sweet, her skin the perfumed scent of roses. Her dark hair covered Ardith's face as the girl allowed her grief and fear to consume her. Ardith's body was wracked with sobs as her anguish poured forth. She had long prayed to the Blessed Virgin Maria that she would be rescued, that she could return to the safety of her mother's arms. The Virgin had not set her free from her tribulations and, as far as Ardith knew, her mother was still back in Hithe.

And yet perhaps the mother of Jesus had answered her prayer by putting her into the care of this woman who held her, giving her comfort where before she had none. Ardith wept, her body trembling and shaking while Erynn stroked her back and whispered soft words to console her.

After a long time, when the sounds of feasting had vanished into the silent darkness of the night, Ardith pushed herself away from Erynn's embrace. Her eyes were puffy and she sniffed. Her head throbbed but she felt as though the tears had washed some of the dark stain of fear from within her; from her very soul.

A sudden thought came to her then in the darkness.

"Erynn, when you undressed me did you find…"

Erynn placed a finger on Ardith's lips to silence her.

"Hush," she whispered. "I found your secret. It is safely hidden."

"I must have it."

"In the morning," said Erynn. "Sleep now, little one. I will watch over you and keep you safe."

Ardith lay back down with a sigh. Her tears cooled on her face in the gloom. She closed her eyes and in her mind's eye she saw Abrecand's final moments, saw the ruin on his throat, sliced deeply with his own blade. In the darkness of her memory she once more felt the burning splash of his lifeblood covering her.

Tomorrow she would reclaim the sharp knife. Her claw. Perhaps the Blessed Virgin had answered her prayers by providing her the means of her own salvation, she pondered, and fell into a deep, dreamless sleep.

Chapter 40

"And then he said, 'I want to make you an offer.'"

Those gathered around the boards listened intently to Ferenbald as he recounted the story of how *Brimblæd* came to be docked at the choicest mooring spot on the northern bank of the Secoana.

"I thought Beobrand was going to gut the port reeve like a mackerel," Ferenbald continued with a toothy grin.

"I almost did," said Beobrand, smiling grimly at the memory. Woden knew he had been tempted. The officious toad of a man had tested his patience and it had taken all Beobrand's strength of will to avoid striking him.

The room bubbled with laughter. Despite the anxiety that gnawed at his innards, twisting and growing like a tumour as each day passed, Beobrand found himself chuckling with them.

"That preening cockerel, Gozolon, would try the patience of Saint Hruomann," said the silver-haired man sitting at the head of the table. He spoke Anglisc without a trace of a Frankish accent. In fact, his voice could have belonged to any of the inhabitants of Cantware. For he was originally from Addelam in Cantware. Ferenbald had introduced him as Feologild, an old trading partner of Hrothgar's.

Leaving most of the crew on board to guard the plunder from Mantican's hall, Ferenbald had led them through the twisting, noisy and noisome streets of Rodomo. The streets thronged with people and Beobrand was giddy with the twists and turns of the route they had taken, the cries of the vendors and the smells of food on offer mingled with the ordure that ran in a thick, stomach-churning sludge through the streets. He had never known such a place. The buildings were packed in almost as densely as the inhabitants, and even though it was a fine day, in places the alleyways they traversed were gloomy. Little light could filter past the jumbled huts, shacks and houses. Beobrand longed for open spaces, hills, moors and fields. And clear air. Not this thick miasma of too many people crammed into tight proximity. Even the open sea would be preferable to Rodomo and its stink. Ferenbald seemed unperturbed by the busy streets and he walked determinedly, unerringly leading them with an almost uncanny sense of direction into an area of the city where the buildings were grander and the streets were cobbled with stone. They had arrived at a large brick house which nestled safely behind a wall and a stout timber gate.

It was not yet midday by the time they'd arrived at Feologild's villa. Ferenbald had told the door ward who they were and they had not had to wait long before the master of the house himself had come to the courtyard to greet them. Feologild had embraced Ferenbald as if he had been a long lost son and quickly offered them lodging in his house. He had insisted that they stay to eat before they went about organising to have their goods brought to his warehouse.

Beobrand liked the man instinctively. He was direct and forthright, with a twinkle in his eye that spoke of a fine sense of humour. Ferenbald had introduced Beobrand to Feologild as Octa, but after the merchant had taken in Beobrand's stature, scarred face and the missing fingers on his left hand, he had laughed. "Octa, is it?" He had grinned. "What with the black shields of your companions and your half-hand, I would have thought you were one whose brother had been called Octa."

They had dropped the pretence after that. Feologild had set them at their ease, offering them warm water to wash and then having them ushered into his main hall, where the boards were laid out as if for a feast.

Feologild had asked for news of Albion and had listened quietly, nodding as Ferenbald spoke of recent events, of rival merchants, the price of wool and the cost of good wine. Feologild seemed impressed that they had a monk with them and bowed his head solemnly when, at his behest, Coenred blessed the food.

"You know that today is the feast of Saint Hruomann?" Feologild had asked Coenred, when he had finished praying.

"Alas, I have not heard of this saint," answered Coenred. "Is he local?"

"Indeed he was," replied Feologild, taking a bite of glistening, succulent pork that he had skewered on the tip of his eating knife. "They call him a saint, but I don't really understand these things. He was the bishop of Rodomo." He took a swig of wine to wash down the pork. "He only died a few years ago. A nice enough man, but now they say to touch the hem of his habit will cure the blind."

"The Lord works His miracles in many and varied ways," said Coenred. "And you say that today is Hruomann's holy day?"

"Yes. The poor will flock to the church. There is a procession and an awful lot of praying."

Coenred was wide-eyed.

"I would most like to see this," he said. "I may never be in Rodomo on the day of Saint Hruomann again."

Beobrand gave Coenred a long look.

"Very well," he said at last. "But you will not go alone. Take Attor with you, and perhaps our host could provide you with a guide."

Feologild nodded and signalled to a lean, pale man.

"Gadd," the merchant said, "take our friend the monk to the church of Our Lady of the Assumption."

The servant bowed, but seemed less than pleased to have been assigned this task.

As they were leaving, Beobrand called to Attor, who was quickly plucking food from the different platters on the boards as he walked the length of the hall.

"See to it there is no repeat of what happened last time you visited a church!"

Attor grinned around a mouthful of food and waved.

Feologild looked perplexed, and raised an eyebrow quizzically, but Beobrand did not explain his words.

After they had tasted enough of the dishes on offer to dull their appetites, Feologild had enquired about how they came to Rodomo. Ferenbald had been vague, saying only that they had come to trade. Feologild nodded, but said nothing, instead changing the subject to how it was that they had found a place to dock on the northern waterfront.

"Still," said Feologild now, his eyes yet full of laughter at the tale of Beobrand's altercation with Gozolon, "I am glad you did not feed the whoreson to the fish. Who knows how corrupt his replacement might be?"

Beobrand frowned.

"I did not strike the man so as not to draw attention to myself," he said. Feologild surveyed Beobrand, taking in his warrior bearing, the broad shoulders and great height, his mutilated hand, the ice-chip blue eyes glaring from beneath a shock of fair hair. He let out a barking laugh.

The man's amusement annoyed Beobrand, made him feel foolish. He thought back to his anger at Gozolon, the man's sure knowledge that he could not be touched had made his stomach churn.

"I can think of few men more worthy of being struck," he said. "And surely if somebody killed the bastard he could be replaced with an honest reeve."

"Nonsense," said Feologild. "It is always much better to have a man you know you can bribe. An honest man is so much more difficult to deal with."

Again, the men laughed. Cynan smiled and raised his cup. Bearn nibbled at his food gingerly, seemingly content to have arrived safely on land. Beobrand nodded at Feologild, forcing a smile. The warmth of the man's hospitality was welcome, but Mantican had also fed them and given them fine wine.

"So, Feologild," Ferenbald said, ale foam flecking his thick beard, "I see you have already fathomed the ending of this story."

"Well, as you say Lord Beobrand here did not open the man's belly, I can only see one outcome. So," he turned his gaze to Beobrand, "how much did you give him?"

Beobrand shrugged.

"A silver chalice."

Ferenbald held out his hands to show the size of the object.

"It was fine too," he said. "Carved with the most elaborate work you have ever seen. Animals and trees intertwining. A thing of true beauty."

Feologild whistled quietly.

"By Christ's bones!" he exclaimed. "Gozolon would have moved half of the ships in the river for such a thing."

Ferenbald grimaced.

"I told Beobrand as much. But he gave the man a fortune, just to get us a good berth."

"You are happy with the mooring, are you not?" asked Beobrand, bridling.

Ferenbald chuckled.

"Aye," he said, "you should have seen how quickly Gozolon made room for us on the dock."

There had been much shouting with the captain of a ship which Ferenbald had told Beobrand had sailed from a southern kingdom called Baetica. The captain and his crew all had dense black beards and skin as dark as leather. Beobrand could not understand the words they spoke, but the captain was clearly furious, waving his arms and gesticulating wildly. He was no fool though, it seemed, for he ceased his protesting quickly enough when the port warden called out to the guards on the dock. Six more quickly joined those from his boat. A dozen armed warriors was ample to convince the Baetican that he would be better off moored on one of the islands.

"That is the difference between a merchant and a warrior," said Feologild. "Neither you, Ferenbald, nor your father, nor I would have given that bastard more than we could get away with."

Feologild's words needled at Beobrand.

"I do not need to haggle to get that which I want," he said. "As you say, Feologild, I am a warrior, not a merchant. I do not count my coins and pieces of silver. If I seek to bribe someone, I make sure it is an offer he cannot refuse. Just as when I face an enemy with my sword, I do not plan to lose."

"Nobody plans to lose, lord," Feologild said, his eyes crinkling with mirth. "But I admire your mettle. You see what you want and you take it. It might just be at a greater cost than I would be willing to pay. But we are not so different, you and I. So, now that you have sated your hunger and thirst, what is it that really brings you to Rodomo?"

Chapter 41

"I will do no such thing!" Ardith trembled with anger and tears stung her eyes.

Erynn reached out to her, but Ardith shook her off.

"Do not touch me!" she hissed, lowering her voice now for fear the noise would attract others to come to the small parlour where they sat. Erynn withdrew her hand as if it had been bitten.

She sighed.

"You must, little one," Erynn cooed, but where her voice had soothed Ardith in the night, now its honeyed sweetness was cloying and turned her stomach.

Ardith's vision wavered as her eyes brimmed with tears. She cuffed the tears away. She would not cry again in front of this woman. All of the warm comfort she had felt when she had awoken in the darkness of the night before had been dashed away in the morning light. Erynn had brought her clean clothes, a pale green woollen peplos over a simple shift of linen, and then led her to this small room near the kitchen. From time to time servants and thralls bustled through, but, after bringing them some bread, cheese, apples and a strange reddish fruit that she had never seen before, they had left Ardith and Erynn alone.

The room was cool, the shutters open. Mid-morning sun lanced through the windows, illuminating the parlour and dispelling shadows. Her mother always said that problems looked better in the light of day. But Ardith could find no consolation from the cool wintry sun. The chill, watery light allowed nowhere for her to hide her grief.

As she had fallen asleep last night, she had been sure that in Erynn she had found an ally, a beautiful guardian angel sent by the Blessed Virgin herself to look over and guide her. How quickly dreams fled with the rising sun, to be replaced by the stark realities of the day.

"Little one…" Erynn said, her tone seeking to mollify Ardith, but only succeeding in further angering the girl. "Ardith…"

Ardith turned away from the beautiful woman. She could not bear to look at her. The betrayal was so painful it felt as though Erynn had stabbed a knife into her chest. But there had been no blade, just harsh words delivered in that sweet smooth voice.

"You told me I could have my knife," Ardith said, a sob catching in her throat. She heard the pleading tone of her voice and hated it. Such a tone would have garnered her a slap from her father and even her mother would have been angry with her for whining. But Ardith's ire seethed and boiled impotently within her and it was all she could do to speak without crying. She wished she could remain strong and aloof, but as the prospect of escape fled, so did her self-control.

A thin man with a balding head and sparse, wiry beard, hurried past carrying a stack of platters. He flicked a glance at the two of them. Perhaps he had overheard Ardith's words about the knife. Good, she thought. Perhaps the Lord Vulmar would hear of it and… And what? Have her killed? Her head was filled with black thoughts. Blessed Maria, Mother of God, could it be true?

"Hush, Ardith," Erynn said, waiting until the thrall had passed out of earshot. She lowered her voice to a whisper. "He would kill you," she said, exasperated. This was not the first time they had spoken of this since the sun had risen. She continued in a placatory tone, entreating Ardith to see sense. "He would kill us both."

"I would rather that than what is planned for me," snapped Ardith.

Erynn let out a sigh.

"No, you do not mean that. You know not what you say."

"I know well enough that I do not wish to be his... his..." She did not wish to say the word. She swallowed. Her mouth was filled with the bitter acid taste of bile. "I will not be his whore," she said at last.

"You must learn to give him what he wants," Erynn said. "I know you are scared, but it is not so bad. It might hurt for a while, but some girls find they enjoy it. If you behave well, he will not be too hard on you."

Ardith's stomach twisted at Erynn's words. She tasted bile in her throat and thought she might puke.

"I am betrothed," she said, her voice again the timid squeak of a child. She thought of Brinin then. Of his sombre, thoughtful eyes and his strong, but gentle, callused hands. Of the stolen kisses behind his father's forge. Of the Thrimilci feast, where the summer night sky had been spattered with the flying sparks from dozens of bonfires. They had sat together on the beach that night, talking and laughing and in a moment of awkward silence she had allowed him to slide his hand up under her peplos while he had clumsily kissed her. She had thrilled at his touch, this boy-man who would be her husband. And now she would never see him again.

"I am sorry, little one, truly I am."

"Stop calling me that," hissed Ardith. "If I am old enough to be a lord's bed-thrall, I am not so little any longer."

Erynn lowered her gaze for a moment.

"You must forget your betrothed," she said.

"I will never forget him," said Ardith. "But I know he would never want me. Not after this." She took a shuddering breath, willing herself not to weep. She was done showing weakness. She realised that Erynn had been wise not to give her back her knife, for such was the fury Ardith felt, she would certainly have used it on the beautiful woman who had seemed to be her friend and had become her captor.

"If you are good," Erynn said, "if you listen to me and learn what I have to teach you, the lord will be happy with you. It will not be so bad and in time he will find someone new and you might be allowed to stay here. Like me."

Something in her wistful tone made Ardith turn back to the woman. A breeze blew through the room and from the distance came the sound of shouting from the streets of Rodomo. Erynn's dark hair wafted about her slender face in the draught and her eyes shone.

"I was once such as you, Ardith," she said.

Ardith's ire and fear was suddenly replaced with an overwhelming sadness. She met Erynn's gaze and saw her face reflected in the dark mirrors of her eyes.

"I see no other girls here," she said. "How many have come here, to Vulmar's bed, since you were a child? Where are those other girls?" Her words were heavy; stones dropped into the stillness of the parlour. The ripples of the words clearly had an effect on Erynn, for she blanched.

But before she could answer, a man approached them. Despite his middling years, he was tall and straight-backed, with a close-cut beard. His eyes were dull, cold and unfeeling and his thoughtful, lingering appraisal of Ardith sent a cool shiver along her spine.

"Richomer," said Erynn, "how can I help you?"

She spoke to the man in Anglisc and he frowned. Ardith thought that perhaps he did not speak her tongue, but then he replied with words she could understand. His voice had the music of the Franks, but he spoke the language of the Anglisc well enough.

"You know all too well how you could help me, whore," he said, and his eyes roved over Erynn. Ardith noticed Erynn tense, but she did her best to hide her revulsion. "Alas," Richomer continued, "I have no time for such things now. Perhaps tonight, when the Lord Vulmar is himself too busy to need me."

"Tonight?" asked Erynn.

"Yes," he replied. He looked Ardith up and down and said something in his native Frankish tongue.

Erynn shook her head and replied in the same language.

He reverted to Anglisc with a smirk and a wink at Ardith. She felt her bowels turn to water under the man's scrutiny.

"She seems well enough to me," he said. "Get her prepared, for tonight this pretty thing will meet our master."

Chapter 42

"So you have goods to sell," said Feologild, smiling and rubbing his chin, "but, unless I am blind to the nature of man, that is not the main purpose for your visit. Am I right?"

"We have things of great value and beauty aboard *Brimblæd*," Beobrand answered, ignoring the second part of the merchant's question.

Beobrand was being deliberately vague. He was unsure of his footing here, in this strange place. The multitudes of people outside in the teeming streets filled the air with their gibberish language. The sounds of the bustling city wafted in through the open shutters of the hall. But rather than clearing the air of the crowded feast, allowing the scent of food, drink and the sweat from so many gathered men to drift away into the cool day outside, the open shutters seemed to Beobrand merely to bring in more smells. It only served to further unnerve him. He was used to a hall becoming hot, the fug of bodies and smoke from the hearth fire stinging the eyes of those gathered until the doors or shutters were thrown wide, bringing in the still and fresh air from outside. When he opened the doors of his hall at Ubbanford he would hear the wind rustling the branches of the oak where Sunniva had liked to sit. If he stepped outside during daylight and strained his ears he might make out a shepherd whistling to his dogs, or perhaps the distant thunk of an axe into timber. One thing was certain, unless a mighty storm raged across the land, it was more peaceful without the hall than within.

Outside Feologild's house there was a sudden crash, a cart overturning perhaps, such was the din produced. This was followed by screams and shouts of many people. Beobrand half rose from his seat, expecting the master of the hall to send them all running outside to see what had caused the commotion. And yet Feologild did not seem to even notice the new noise.

"Indeed," he said, raising his cup to Beobrand in a slightly mocking toast. "I would see these items you speak of soon. We can discuss whether there are any things I am interested in purchasing. I normally deal in simple commodities," he waved a hand airily, "wool from Wessex, glass from the Sasanids, cinnamon and pottery from Ægypte, but I might be persuaded to dabble in things of a more, shall we say, exotic nature." He took a sip of his drink, holding Beobrand's gaze. "But tell me, what is it that truly brings one such as you to Frankia?"

Beobrand sighed. Feologild would not let the matter rest. Beobrand had done his best to ignore the merchant's probing questions, or to deflect them and to change the subject. He did not know the man well enough to trust him. He had hoped that Feologild would be satisfied to discuss trade, but the man was as persistent as a wasp buzzing about a rotting apple. Gods, the man seemed to enjoy Beobrand's discomfort. It was as though he saw their conversation as a test of his skill. As a warrior would relish crossing blades with a worthy adversary, so Feologild seemed to enjoy the cut and thrust of words. Beobrand was growing increasingly frustrated. He was not made for these intrigues. He would sooner draw Hrunting and fight Feologild or any champion of his choice than to endure this constant needling of words from the man.

Beobrand shook his head at the idea of fighting the merchant. Feologild was no more a warrior than Beobrand was an orator. A contest of strength and battle-skill would have been an unmatched competition. He would be able to cut Feologild down after a few clumsy parries from the trader. Beobrand felt he would be defeated equally easily in this sparring with words.

Gazing out through the window to the overcast sky, Beobrand took a long draught of ale. Outside, the raised voices had died down, replaced instead by the constant hubbub of the city. A titter of female laughter pierced Rodomo's rumble and, unbidden, Beobrand was instantly reminded of Eanflæd. Despite the tension he felt, he smiled into his drinking cup. No doubt Eanflæd would have relished the opportunity to wield her wit against that of Feologild. Beobrand thought of her youthful exuberance; the keen intelligence and iron will that lay trapped in the lithesome body of a girl. No, not a girl: a woman, a peace-weaver. The daughter of a king. Eanflæd would quickly have got the better of Feologild in a war of words, and Beobrand was certain the merchant would have offered her whatever she asked of him. It seemed men were incapable of denying her. He took another swig of ale and felt his face grow hot as he pictured her golden hair and the curve of her hips. He missed her, he realised with a start.

Gods, he was a fool. To think of Eanflæd at all was folly. But deep down within him, a quiet voice whispered that perhaps he was not foolhardy. Mayhap he was brave. And a brave man could take what he desired. Anger flashed through him at his own stupidity and he slammed his wooden cup down on the board, causing many of those seated at the table to glance in his direction.

"I have angered you with my questions, I see," said Feologild. "I meant no harm."

Beobrand's face grew hotter still.

"I apologise, Feologild. It has been a trying journey and I am tired."

"Of course, forgive my endless prying. I just had an inkling that there was more to your journey than you had at first chosen to share. Perhaps I could help you, if I knew of your mission. I am not without influence in the city."

Beobrand hesitated. For a moment he considered telling Feologild everything, but instead, he reached for a pitcher of ale and refilled his cup.

Still he sought to hold his secrets close. He was a stranger here in Rodomo and it seemed to him that, despite his warm welcome and hospitable manner, Feologild was a trader and therefore governed by his love of gold and silver. Any such man could be bought, and Ferenbald had told Beobrand that the Lord Vulmar they looked for was the richest man in Rodomo. Beobrand did not want his adversary to know he was coming before he had even learnt the location of Vulmar's residence.

Feologild frowned for a moment, like a cloud passing across the sun before he once more beamed a smile at Beobrand.

"Well, thegn of Bernicia," he said, "I will leave you to your secrets. Perhaps in time you will grow to trust me, for surely I am your friend here. And," he went on with a knowing nod, "nobody can ever have too many friends."

Beobrand inclined his head at Feologild.

"I thank you for your friendship and I offer you mine in return," he said.

"I will drink to that," Feologild replied in a loud voice. He held out his cup and a thrall refilled it immediately. He maintained Beobrand's gaze as he raised the cup to his lips and drained the contents. Beobrand matched him and both men slammed their drinking vessels down on the board at the same instant. Despite himself, Beobrand grinned. Feologild laughed and the atmosphere in the hall lifted.

Still smiling, Beobrand allowed his cup to be filled again. Perhaps he would confide in the merchant after all. As the man said, he had few friends here and Feologild might be able to assist him.

Beobrand was about to speak when the sound of a new commotion came to them from outside. This time it was from the front of the house. Beobrand heard a banging, as someone hammered on the timber gate to the courtyard. Feologild pursed his lips, frowning slightly and clearly listening intently. This was not a noise to be ignored, this came from within the merchant's property. Conversations died away in the hall, as the men stilled. For a time there was silence, with nothing but the sound of the city's streets coming to them on the breeze from the open shutters. And then the door to the dining hall swung open.

One of Feologild's door wards stepped into the hall. Behind him came a slender, middle-aged man.

"A messenger has come, master," said the door ward. "He demanded to speak to you."

Feologild's brow furrowed, but he beckoned to let the man enter. The messenger stepped into a shaft of the thin afternoon light that spilled through an open window. He walked proudly, head held high, as one accustomed to being listened to. He looked about the room, taking in the men thronging at the boards, the copious amounts of food and drink, the thralls waiting on the diners. His eyes were dark and impassive above his trimmed beard.

Focusing his attention on Feologild, the messenger spoke a few words in the tongue of the Franks. Feologild turned sharply to gaze at Beobrand. After the merest hint of a hesitation, Feologild replied to the messenger. The man nodded, said something more, and then, bowing, withdrew from the hall.

Feologild watched him leave, before turning to Beobrand with a quizzical expression.

"Well, Beobrand," he said, "it seems tidings of your arrival have already travelled widely."

Beobrand was confused.

"How can this be? What did the messenger say? Who sent him?"

Beobrand's head swam and he regretted drinking so freely of Feologild's ale.

"A man such as yourself does not pass unnoticed. But perhaps you do not need my friendship quite as much as I thought."

"What do you mean? Speak clearly, man."

"Well, it would seem you already have at least one friend in Rodomo who is a lot more powerful than I."

"I know nobody in Frankia."

"Well, if that be true, someone here knows you. And they request that you attend their hall immediately for an audience."

Beobrand's head began to throb. How could this be? Who knew he was in the city? They had not even been moored at the dock for a whole day.

"But who?" asked Beobrand, wondering what man on middle earth wished to see him.

"I hope for your sake that the man who has sent for you is a friend and not a foe-man, for he is not an enemy that anyone would wish to have."

"Why?" replied Beobrand, a coolness flowing through him as if he had drunk ice water. "Who sent the messenger?"

Feologild stared at him, perhaps trying to ascertain whether this huge fair-haired thegn was playing him for a fool.

"The messenger came from the greatest palace of Rodomo, Beobrand," the merchant said at last. He picked up a small cloth and wiped his lips and hands before scrunching the linen into a ball and tossing it onto the board. "He has come from the hall of Lord Vulmar, cousin of the king himself."

Chapter 43

"I see from your expression," said Feologild, "that you have heard of Vulmar."

Beobrand said nothing. His head was pounding now. He set aside the cup of ale. There would be no more drinking this day. He would need his wits about him.

"Your business is with him perhaps," continued Feologild shrewdly, squinting at the thegn as if he could divine whatever secrets he held within his thought-cage by staring into his mind.

Beobrand ignored him. He turned to the nearest thrall, a slim, swarthy-skinned young man.

"Water," Beobrand snapped. The thrall turned to do his bidding, but Beobrand stopped him, pulling him back by the arm. "Bring water for me and all my men." He released his grip and the slave scampered off. Beobrand raised his voice for his gesithas, Ferenbald and *Brimblæd*'s crew to hear. "No more drinking ale, wine or mead. You need your minds straight. Drink some water now to clear your heads." Some of the men groaned. "There will be time enough for feasting later," Beobrand went on. "When all this is done, I will see that you have your fill of meat and mead."

"Vulmar is not a man to be kept waiting," said Feologild, fidgeting in his seat. Was his face pale?

Beobrand frowned and rubbed a hand across his forehead in a vain attempt to reduce the throbbing pain there. Beneath his fingers he made out the now-familiar lump where the Mercian sling shot had almost taken his life.

Gods, how could Vulmar have known of their arrival? And even if he had heard of Beobrand coming to the city, why was the lord interested in him? They had not even been in Rodomo for a day. Could some of the men they had encountered in Seoles have travelled here before them, warning Grimr that they were on his trail? Beobrand shook his head. They had seemed to have no love for their erstwhile leader, and besides, surely the storm would have kept them in Albion. He thought through their trip along the coast, past the isle of the Wihtwara and then towards Frankia, being beaten back by the sea and wind northward to the rocky cove and Mantican's hall.

The skinny thrall returned, labouring under the weight of a great jug. He filled cups for Beobrand and Ferenbald then staggered to where the rest of the recent arrivals from Albion sat.

Beobrand filled his mouth with the cool liquid, swilling it around to rid himself of the souring taste of ale. Or was it perhaps the flavour of fear and uncertainty he sought to remove? He turned to Ferenbald, who was sipping his own cup and looking at Beobrand with a questioning twitch of his eyebrows.

"What do you think?" Beobrand asked in a low voice. "Could Thurcytel and Wada have made the crossing to Frankia, if they had left immediately after *Brimblæd* had departed Seoles?"

Ferenbald tugged at his beard gently and pondered the question. Beobrand could imagine him mapping the routes and the currents in his mind's eye. After a few moments he shook his head.

"I think it is unlikely, lord," he said, and the use of the title reminded Beobrand of Acennan with a twisting pang of pain. He'd always called Beobrand "lord" when he was worried. By Woden, how he missed his friend.

"How then does Vulmar come to send a messenger for me to this place?"

Ferenbald frowned and then his face clouded, downcast.

"I fear I am to blame," he said.

"How so?"

"It was I who told Gozolon we were on an important journey. He knows where I hail from, and I think he recognised you from the tales and songs. Believe it or not," he said, with a twisted smirk, "you are not a man to go unnoticed and it seems even in Frankia they know of Beobrand the half-handed."

Beobrand sighed.

"But do you not see?" said Cynan, who had joined them from the lower benches.

"See what?" asked Beobrand.

"Until now we have been following the trail we hoped would lead us to Ardith. This gives us proof that she is where we believed."

Beobrand indicated for the Waelisc warrior to continue.

"Surely it must be the fact that both the girl and *Brimblæd* come from Hithe that has caused this Vulmar to act. He must have heard from Gozolon the reeve that we had moored and then pieced together the story of what brings us here. By summoning you, he seeks to confront a potential enemy on his terms. In his own hall."

Beobrand turned Cynan's words over in his mind, nodding slowly.

Feologild had risen from his seat. Gone was his calm control of earlier, replaced with a nervous energy. He licked his lips and sucked his teeth as he moved in close to where Beobrand and the others spoke in hushed tones.

"It is as they say," he said. "There are no secrets in Rodomo once Gozolon knows of them. Vulmar pays well and Gozolon reports to him daily all the comings and goings at the port. And Vulmar is no fool. If you come seeking something," he paused, perhaps weighing his words, "or someone, that he possesses, he will not allow you time to plan or think. He will do his utmost to keep you off balance. And know this, I do not believe you will get what you have come for."

"Indeed?" said Beobrand. He could feel his anger swelling within him and forced himself to be calm. This was not something he could solve with the sword. He would need guile if he was to play the game of this noble and to leave Rodomo with his daughter.

"Vulmar is rich and powerful," said Feologild. He bit his lip and shook his head. "He did not get that way by being stupid or by backing down and admitting defeat."

Beobrand bridled.

"I am no man's fool," he said, wondering silently whether that was true. Too often he feared he had been the plaything of powerful men. "And I also do not back down from a fight."

Feologild nodded and raised a hand to placate Beobrand.

"Of course, lord," he said. "I do not accuse you of foolishness or cowardice. But this is Vulmar's land, not yours. You are far from home and Vulmar holds Rodomo in his fist. I have no love for Vulmar, but I must speak true, I cannot afford to make an enemy of him. He knows you have visited me here, which already places my interests in danger should you confront him."

Beobrand's head ached. He closed his eyes and took in a deep steadying breath.

"It is as you say, Feologild," he said at last, meeting the merchant's gaze. "I cannot make an enemy of this Lord Vulmar any more than you can. I will meet with him and hope I can resolve matters with him smoothly."

Feologild held his stare for a long while, appraising the veracity of Beobrand's words as a trader weighs the value of a gemstone. After a time, he nodded.

"That is wise," he said. "Might I make a suggestion?"

Beobrand waved his half-hand impatiently for Feologild to continue.

"I have a warehouse," said Feologild, "and armed men, loyal to me, who guard it. Anything you have aboard *Brimblæd* would be safe there and we can discuss trade when you have more time. It is clear now that you have more pressing matters to attend to."

Feologild's words caught Beobrand off guard. He had not thought of the ship and its contents. Could it be that the vessel was in danger?

"I thank you for the offer," he said, "but the ship is not mine. Let me speak with her skipper before making a decision."

"Of course." Feologild had visibly relaxed now. He was back onto firmer land, a path that he understood well. That of trade and alliances, the movement of goods and gold.

Beobrand drew Ferenbald and Cynan away from the merchant, turning their backs on him.

"What do you think?" he asked Ferenbald in a hushed tone.

"The ship is not so easy to defend if that bastard Gozolon plans anything. I have heard tales of ships being raided at night. Perhaps it would be safer to move the goods now, before darkness."

Beobrand felt as though he had stumbled into a rats' nest of treachery and intrigue. The brick walls of the house seemed to close in on him and he longed to be far away, riding Sceadugenga at a gallop over the hills of Bernicia where the air was clean and life was simple. He snorted in quiet amusement at his own thoughts.

When had his life ever been simple?

"Do you trust Feologild?" he whispered. He could not make out the trader's true intentions.

Ferenbald ran his meaty hand through his long hair, tugged at his thatch of beard.

"He has been my father's friend for many years."

"That is not what I asked of you, Ferenbald," Beobrand said, his voice taking on a hard edge of iron. "Do you trust him?"

Ferenbald hesitated for the merest heartbeat before nodding.

Beobrand held his gaze for a moment, then turned to Cynan, who shrugged.

"Very well," Beobrand said, addressing Ferenbald once more, "make it so. And Ferenbald," he said, keeping his voice low, "see to it that the ship is ready to sail at a moment's notice."

Ferenbald nodded.

"Thank you for your hospitality and generous offer, master Feologild," said Beobrand in a clear voice. "Ferenbald will see to the unlading of the ship. I will follow Vulmar's messenger, along with my comitatus, and we shall see what he has to say."

He made to leave the hall. Cynan fell into step beside him. Fraomar, Bearn, Dreogan and Garr rose and joined them. Brinin suddenly jumped up from where he sat with the crew and rushed to join Beobrand and the warriors. In his hurry, he tripped on a bench, overturning it with a clatter, and stumbling forward into Beobrand's path. Curses and shouts rang out in his wake as he left others to right the bench and to sort out the mess he had caused.

The gangly youth stood, flush-faced and wide-eyed before Beobrand.

Beobrand placed a hand on his shoulder, meaning to push him aside.

"Go help Ferenbald with the ship, boy," he said.

Brinin squared his shoulders and pulled himself up to his full height. His jaw jutted stubbornly but he still needed to gaze upward to look Beobrand in the eye.

"If you go to where Ardith is," he said, his voice thin with anxiety, but resolute nonetheless, "I am coming with you."

Beobrand took a step forward, applying pressure to his shoulder and all the while holding the boy in his cold blue stare. Brinin leaned against Beobrand's hand and did not budge.

Despite himself, Beobrand smiled. Gods, but he liked the boy. He was brave and steadfast.

"Very well," he said, "but you will keep silent and you will do as I say. Understand?"

Brinin returned his smile, nodding.

"Yes, lord."

Beobrand reached the doors and the wardens moved to open them for him and his companions. Just before the doors swung open, Feologild called to him.

"I do not know what trouble you have with Vulmar," the trader said, "but be very careful, Beobrand. The man is a snake."

Beobrand did not reply. If only it would be as simple as dealing with a single serpent. A quick slice of a blade would sever the head, removing any danger. But, as he swept from the room, Beobrand could not shake the cold feeling that he was about to step into a pit filled with writhing, venomous vipers.

Chapter 44

Coenred shivered as he entered the darkness of the church. Like many of the buildings in Rodomo it was made of stone; grey and sombre. The solidity and height of the huge structure made him think of the power of the Almighty. He gazed up at the shadowed ceiling as he and Attor were ushered in by a young clergyman. Candles dotted the darkness and cunningly carved statues nestled in niches. They seemed to watch Coenred as he passed. He could sense their eyes upon him. The flickering flames of the candles made the shadows cavort. The statues' faces frowned, menacing and angry at the intrusion into their domain. Coenred held back another shudder with difficulty. They were but stone. Perhaps what he felt was the pressure of the eyes of the Lord on him. Ever since the incident at Seoles, Coenred had been racked with guilt. He had struck a brother priest! And stolen from a church! No matter how many times he told himself the relic was not the priest's to keep, he could not dispel the truth that he had sinned. He had prayed endlessly, offering up to God silent words of contrition and sorrow, but the heavy feeling was still draped on him like a physical weight.

He hoped that if he were able to confess his sins to the bishop of Rodomo, he might find some peace. When he had heard Feologild speak of the church here, his heart had leapt and Attor and he had eagerly followed the merchant's servant, Gadd, through the crowded streets to the small open area before the imposing stone edifice.

The previous day, while aboard *Brimblæd*, Coenred had approached Attor. He wondered whether the warrior too felt anything like the guilt that pressed down upon him, but Attor had smiled thinly and said, "You know we did what we needed to do. I am proud of you, Coenred." There was more warrior of the old ways in him than follower of Christ, and he seemed to relish the spontaneous savagery of Coenred's attack on the priest. But Coenred noted how quickly Attor had jumped up and offered to join him when he voiced his desire to go to the church. Perhaps the wiry gesith understood sin better than he made out. Perhaps. Despite the feeling of overpowering foreboding that was upon him, Coenred smiled at the idea of Attor expressing feelings of guilt. Whatever the warrior felt, he would never admit weakness. That was not his way; not the way of a lord's spearman.

When they had arrived at the church of Our Lady of the Assumption, the sun had been low in the sky, and the streets were shadowed and cold. In spite of the lateness of the day, the square of cobbles that stood before the church's great oak doors was thronged with a multitude of people.

"It is Saint Hruomann's day," Gadd had said. "Pilgrims come from afar in the hope of touching the relics of Hruomann. The saint often heals the sick. It will be difficult for you to obtain an audience with Bishop Audoen today, I fear."

Dismayed and awed, Coenred had nodded, taking in the heaving mass of humanity that seethed before the church like a many-coloured roiling ocean. A cripple on twisted crutches of wood was shoved aside by two burly men carrying cudgels and using them liberally on the packed crowds. They were clearing the way for two other stout men, carrying a man atop a board. The cripple stumbled and Coenred reached out to prevent him from falling. The invalid would surely have been trampled beneath the feet of so many worshippers had he fallen. The man on the timber board looked dead, his mouth lolling, eyes unseeing, and yet the two brutes cried out urgently, kicking and pushing their way through the crowd and wielding their staves savagely when someone was slow to move.

A woman screamed in Coenred's face, her breath foetid and dank. He did not understand the words, but she proffered a greasy hunk of meat at him, its juices trickling down her bony, dirt-encrusted fingers. Coenred's stomach heaved. Attor pushed the woman away. He grasped a handful of Coenred's robe and tugged him along in the wake of the men carrying the invalid on the makeshift stretcher. Feologild's servant trotted behind them. In this way, keeping close to the men who barged their way through the throng before the crowds closed in again behind them, Coenred, Attor and Gadd were able to get near the steps of the church.

They passed all manner of sickness and disease. Faces with festering sores, flesh black and sickly sweet with the wound rot, the blind and the raving, eyes rolling around in their heads and foam frothing at their lips. For a hideous, stomach-twisting moment Coenred wondered whether this was not punishment for his sins. Perhaps God had created this hell on middle earth for his torment. Or maybe he had already died somehow, unshriven and unforgiven and this was in fact the domain of the devil. For surely, apart from the biting cold, this was hell.

But soon enough they had reached the steps that rose up to the huge timber doors of the church. There were guards there, holding back the crowds with crossed spears. One of the warriors shouted at the throng as they shoved. Again, Coenred could not comprehend the Frankish words, but the venom in the man's tone made him sure they were not words of forgiveness and love such as the Christ would have spoken to the poor and infirm.

Gadd had caught the angry guard's attention and spoken a few words and after only a brief moment of hesitation, the guard had given the order to his men to let them pass. They had walked up the stone steps, rising out of the shade of the surrounding buildings and into the cool afternoon sunshine that reached the uppermost steps and this western facade of the church. They had stood there, blinking and breathless, gazing down at the heaving sea of sickness and desperation. So many ill, so many needing care, seeking a miracle. Coenred had swallowed against the lump in his throat and rubbed a hand over his face. He was a healer. One of the best of the Northumbrian brethren. Had God sent him to this place with a purpose? Surely it must be so. This was not his personal hell, this was his salvation. He would show his penitence by giving succour to the poor and the lost. Taking a deep breath, Coenred had stepped back down towards the shadows and the swaying tides of pilgrims. But a hand had pulled him close. Attor. The warrior had given a small shake of his head and then indicated to where the great doors of the church had opened, letting out a slim figure of a young man. The newcomer was a cleric dressed in black robes. He had stepped into the afternoon light and ushered them inside.

Unlike Coenred, the man's hair was shaved at the top of his head, making his hair like a crown about the bald pate. But he smiled at Coenred as one brother in Christ to another. He glanced at Attor, taking in the rood necklace he wore about his throat and nodded his approval.

For a moment, Coenred did not move. The noise of the crowd pulled him back. Screams and shouts, bellowed exhortations aimed at the two holy men on the steps. Surely God had sent him here to tend to His flock. But Attor had kept a firm grip on his robe and shook his head again.

"This is what we came for," he whispered close to Coenred's ear, and, as if he could perceive what Coenred was thinking, "you cannot heal them all."

Coenred had sighed and reluctantly followed the priest into the dark stillness of the stone church.

Once inside the priest pushed shut the thick iron-studded doors. With the doors closed behind them, muffling the cacophony of the crowd to a dull roar, like a storm raging in a distant forest, or waves crashing on a far beach, the clergyman turned to Coenred, speaking quickly and animatedly. Coenred held up his hand to halt the man's tirade. At the same moment Feologild's man said something in Frankish, presumably that Coenred did not speak their tongue. The priest nodded, paused with a slight frown. Then he spoke again, but this time in a strongly accented Latin. Coenred had never been the best student, and he still remembered old Fearghas' despair at his lack of attention, but he had grown to be a good scribe and his grasp of Latin was now better than he would ever have imagined all those years before when Fearghas had needed to punish him almost daily.

"The boy here tells me you are come from Albion?" the man said.

"Yes," Coenred replied, also in Latin. "I am of the brethren of the holy island of Lindisfarena."

The man turned to stare at him, the light of candles glittering in his widened eyes.

"You have travelled very far indeed then. And what brings you to Rodomo?"

They walked further into the gloom of the church. The noise of the crowd outside subsided to a murmured memory.

"That is a very long story," said Coenred. "I had hoped to speak with the bishop." He swallowed and ran his long fingers through the hair that hung down to his neck. "I would like him to hear my confession."

"I am afraid that will be impossible today. His Excellence Bishop Audoen is otherwise engaged."

Coenred was unable to hide his dismay. He had not dared to believe he would be allowed to speak with the bishop on such a day and with no prior arrangement, but after the ease with which they had gained entry into the church, he had begun to hope.

"Do not be downhearted," the cleric went on. "If you are in need, I would hear your confession."

Coenred frowned, confused.

"Are you a bishop then?" For Coenred had heard that the Christ followers on the continent only allowed bishops to hear confession.

The priest smiled.

"No, I am no bishop. My name is Walaric and I am vicar here at Our Most Holy Lady of the Assumption."

"Then how can you hear my confession? Is it not the case that only bishops can hear confession and offer penance?"

"That was true, friend, until the Council at Cabilonen. There, new canons were agreed."

Coenred tried to make sense of the words. He knew nothing of this Council, but back in Lindisfarena, priests would hear each other's confessions. He longed for the release of forgiveness. Penance and absolution.

"My confession would be secret, as if I spoke directly to God?" Coenred asked. His voice wavered slightly and he knew that his words might make Walaric suspicious for what he was about to tell him.

They had reached the altar now. An ornate silver cross stood there. Walaric held Coenred's gaze for what seemed a long while, as if he was weighing up the young monk's sins. At last he nodded.

"Of course, brother," he said. "The seal of the confession is sacred and cannot be broken."

Relief rushed through Coenred, making him light-headed. He could be free of this guilt. He let out a long, shuddering breath.

"Very well, Walaric," he said, "I accept your offer to hear my confession and I thank you."

Leaving Attor and Gadd to wait for them by the altar, Coenred and Walaric made their way into a small chapel at the rear of the church.

A wooden bench was propped against the wall, a sliver of dull, winter afternoon light trickled through a small window. Walaric seated himself and motioned for Coenred to do the same.

Making the sign of Christ's cross over his body, Walaric said, "*In nomine Patris et Filii et Spiritus Sancti.*"

Coenred moved his hand automatically, head, chest, left shoulder, right shoulder. The words came bubbling up from within him too, as if they had been straining behind a dam.

"Bless me, Father, for I have sinned. It is many weeks since my last confession. And these are my sins."

The light had dimmed to dusk outside by the time he had finished. He stood up quickly, as if his body was lighter now, allowing him to move more freely. He had told Walaric everything – the lustful thoughts of Leofgyth in Hastingas, lying about who he was to the men at Seoles, and then striking the priest and stealing the reliquary. He felt as though a great weight had been lifted from his shoulders. But there was more than that. He was giddy, almost light-headed, thrilling now with the certainty that God had meant him to come to this place; that he had been right to turn away from the poor and sick thronging outside the church. For Walaric had not only offered him penance to absolve him of his many sins, the priest had given him something so unexpected and valuable that it was all Coenred could do not to run from the church yelling.

When he emerged from the chapel, his excitement must have been plain on his face, for Attor leapt up from where he was sitting in the gloom beside the dozing servant.

"What is it?" Attor asked.

"Come," said Coenred, without waiting, already half-running down the nave towards the double doors, "we must find Beobrand immediately."

Attor frowned in confusion, but followed without hesitation. Together they rushed out into the gathering night of the city.

Chapter 45

"Do you think Vulmar will listen to you?" asked Cynan. His voice was hushed, though why he bothered lowering his tone, Beobrand could not understand. They might as well have shouted for all the interest being paid them by the people in the hall. A sudden guffaw of laughter, like the harsh croak of a raven, made Beobrand start. The hairs on his neck prickled.

"He will listen to me," he said, forcing calmness into his voice; a certainty he did not feel.

On the bench beside him Brinin fidgeted and squirmed. Beobrand placed a hand on the boy's shoulder.

"Easy," he said. "Never show your enemy you're nervous. Here, drink." He reached for one of the fine glass beakers that rested on the linen-draped board. When they had first been invited to wait here at the end of the long hall, Beobrand had sipped of the dark liquid in a show of relaxed insouciance. The wine was wonderful, rich and warm as blood. Brinin gulped the contents of the glass and Beobrand pulled at his arm. "Easy, now. Do not make me regret allowing you to come with us."

The boy's cheeks flushed and he bit his lower lip.

On the lad's left, Dreogan smiled through a mouthful of some dainty pastry that had been offered to them by a pretty slave girl.

"Try one of these, boy," he said, spitting crumbs. "It'll settle your nerves."

Brinin gaped at the usually scowling warrior. Dreogan's chewing made the soot lines on his cheeks writhe like serpents. Brinin shook his head and murmured something about not being hungry.

Garr, Fraomar and Bearn seemed to have no such problem, and they each took handfuls of the sweetmeats and pastries proffered on silver platters.

Beobrand looked at Bearn askance.

"Did you not eat your fill at Feologild's?" he asked.

"Well, I had saved some space for more ale and mead, but you told us not to drink any more." He picked up another treat and popped it into his mouth. Crumbs flecked his beard and he brushed his fingers through the hair. "You are not going to tell me I shouldn't eat now too, are you, lord?"

Beobrand snorted, shaking his head.

"Good," said Bearn. "I've puked so much these past days at sea, I feel I could eat my own weight in meat."

"Don't get so full you can't fight," said Beobrand.

Fraomar shot him a glance.

"You expecting trouble then?" he asked.

"I always expect trouble," said Beobrand. "No matter where I am, I always seem to find it."

"Well, let's hope this Lord Vulmar listens to you," said Cynan, taking the smallest of sips of his wine. He scanned the hall, and Beobrand followed the Waelisc warrior's gaze, taking in the laughing men and women, the thralls and servants, the guards at the doors and the nobles in their finery, sitting at the high table around Vulmar himself. "If Vulmar does not wish to listen to you, and there really is trouble, we might as well eat and drink now, for we won't fare well. We are too few to make much of a stand if it came to that."

Beobrand made himself smile, despite the chill he felt. He wasn't sure Cynan did not see through his bluff. There was a sharp intelligence behind those Waelisc eyes. And ever since the fight at the Wall, and Sulis, Beobrand often felt the weight of Cynan's judgement of him.

"Don't forget," he said, "Vulmar sent for us. If he did not wish to talk, why bother?"

Cynan did not reply, instead taking another sip of wine and offering Beobrand a twisted expression someway between a smirk and a glower.

Beobrand couldn't deny he shared Cynan's concerns. The uncertainty of their situation, in a foreign land, surrounded by intrigue and powerful foes, had threatened to engulf him as they'd ridden to Vulmar's palace.

Feologild had loaned them horses from his stable and the six of them had followed Vulmar's messenger and a small escort of armed warriors through the busy city as the sun sank in the grey western sky. Their escorts all bore cloaks of yellow, which clearly marked them out as men of Vulmar. The lord's power was evident and he was obviously feared. The people of Rodomo parted before them without complaint. They looked away or cast their gaze downward, so as not to catch the eye of one of Vulmar's guards or the visitors to the city who rode behind them.

They had soon ridden far from the bustling crowds and after passing through an area of crumbling ruins, all fallen columns and spindly winter weeds, they had reached a whitewashed wall that surrounded a collection of buildings. The wall was high and in good repair. They rode along its length until they came to a great gate, stout oak reinforced with iron. More yellow-cloaked guards allowed them entry and they had been admitted into a courtyard. In the distance, from the city, came the doleful clangour of a bell. At Beobrand's questioning look, the messenger, swinging down from his saddle, had said, "It is the bell of Our Lady. It calls the faithful to prayer."

Beobrand had looked at the watery setting sun and thought of Coenred, wondering fleetingly how the monk fared. Better than us, riding into the dragon's lair, he'd thought.

They had dismounted and the horses were led into a large stable on one side of the courtyard. On the other side of the enclosure was a massive structure, built of sandstone and red brick, its roof shingled in ruddy clay tiles. It was grander than any hall he had ever seen. The courtyard was lined with statues and carefully trimmed plants and bushes, reminding Beobrand of the hall of King Eorcenberht in Cantwareburh. Both buildings must have been constructed by those long-vanished giants of Roma, but as with everything here in Rodomo, Vulmar's palace was more grandiose than what Beobrand had seen in Albion, more redolent of riches. They had needed to hand over their weapons at the entrance and had then been ushered into a huge hall. Stone columns ran down the building's length, like a forest of petrified trees, reaching up to arch their stone branches to the ceiling.

The hall was filled with noise and the sour-sweet scents of a feast. And all the people gathered there seemed to Beobrand to be beautiful. Their hair shone and their clothing glowed. Gold and silver glittered from the light of candles and braziers that warded off the gathering gloaming of dusk. Beobrand felt shabby and dirty in his travel-stained breeches, kirtle and cloak. He looked over his men, imagining what these nobles of Frankia would see. Bearded, broad-shouldered, greasy-haired brutes. Fearsome in battle perhaps, but here, surrounded by wealth and silks, they stood out like a handful of flint pebbles in a box of gold and pearls.

The messenger had offered them places at the table furthest from the lord of the hall and his retinue. Beobrand, now a mighty thegn in his adopted home of Bernicia, had grown accustomed to being seated at the high table. He had the ear of kings and was one of the richest men in the north of Albion. To be so obviously snubbed would usually have kindled his infamous temper. He would have strode down the hall and demanded to be given the respect due to one of his station. But now, with the salt of the sea still griming his beard, and his clothes stiff with dried sweat and dirt, he had merely nodded and allowed his men to be seated close to the doors. The messenger had walked the length of the hall and leaned in to speak to Vulmar. The lord, a squat, broad-faced man, with dark, gimlet eyes, had gazed down at Beobrand and his gesithas for the briefest of moments before dismissing the messenger with a flick of his hand. He had turned back to the man at his right and continued his conversation.

Shame and indignation had rippled through Beobrand, but as he sat, he'd forced a smile for his men. He had felt Cynan's gaze upon him then, incredulity in the arch of his brows. Beobrand had ignored him.

"It seems we shall have to wait a while," he had said, in a cheery tone. "But the food looks good, and I think we can allow ourselves a little of this wine."

If the rest of his gesithas felt his discomfort, or if they too noticed the implied insult from Vulmar's lack of acknowledgement of their lord, they said nothing. Perhaps they too felt out of place, shabby and dirty in this hall of splendour. Cynan's gaze lingered though, needling Beobrand.

The evening wore on and Beobrand and his men grew weary of smiling and acting as though nothing was wrong.

Brinin drank the rest of the goblet of wine and his cheeks grew red. His eyes gleamed and he began to raise his voice in indignation at their treatment. He leaned across the board for a pitcher of wine to fill his glass, but Beobrand pulled it from his reach.

"No more wine for you, Brinin," he said. "You will eat and you will be silent."

The boy opened his mouth, perhaps readying an angry retort, but one icy look from Beobrand was enough to silence him. He looked down at the stained linen cloth on the table before him, his eyes sullen, his lips quivering.

Beobrand sighed. He was just a child. And everything was felt more keenly by children. Without warning he thought of Octa, saw in his mind's eye his son's earnest eyes, his fragile slender limbs. He missed the boy. They had never been close, but Octa was his son and to imagine him in Oswiu's hall, far away and lonely, filled him with anxiety. Gods, how had it come to this? And he had not one, but two children. Suddenly, as if awoken from a deep sleep, Beobrand's anger roused within him, instant and terrible as lightning. Ardith too was a child, by Woden. What was he doing sitting here, cowed and passive, while the man he believed had her prisoner drank and ate and laughed with his silk-draped and jewel-festooned cronies?

He placed a hand on Brinin's shoulder.

"Remain silent and drink no more," he said. The boy gazed up at him, brow furrowed and eyes brimming. "This ends now," said Beobrand.

He pushed himself to his feet. A slave girl stepped close, offering him a tray of oysters. He stepped past her without a glance.

"Lord?" asked Cynan. Beobrand ignored him. He had made up his mind now and there would be no hesitation.

He strode purposefully down the long hall, past the guests sitting at the long tables. The columns slid by, their shadows marking time to his determined walk. He fixed his cold blue eyes on Vulmar.

As the huge, fair-haired warrior with the dusty cloak and the scarred face made his way down the hall, the conversations stuttered and sputtered out. Beobrand smiled grimly to himself as his men hurried to catch up with him and, unbidden, formed an escort behind him. He did not need to look back to know that their faces were dour, hard and sombre. Done was the time of jests and laughter. His gesithas were at his back and they were prepared to follow their lord come what may. They were unarmed and surrounded by enemies, but they commanded the room with their presence. Silence followed in their wake and by the time they reached the foot of the raised dais where Vulmar and his closest retinue sat, the hall was as still as a barrow.

Vulmar opened his mouth to speak, but Beobrand was adamant now that he would give the man no such honour.

"I am Beobrand, son of Grimgundi," he said, his voice steely edged and loud enough that none other would be heard until he allowed them, "thegn of Bernicia, lord of Ubbanford and servant of Oswiu, son of Æthelfrith, King of Bernicia. I would speak with you, Lord Vulmar of Rodomo."

Silence in the hall. Far behind Beobrand, back near the doors, someone coughed.

Vulmar looked vaguely amused by Beobrand's display. But he did not reply. After a moment, he clicked his fingers and the messenger scuttled forward. He said a few words and Beobrand heard his name. Vulmar nodded and spoke, all the while holding Beobrand's gaze. Vulmar was not a tall man, not powerful of build or handsome. He was of middling years, his hair greying at the temples, his cheeks jowled and heavy. Of all the men at the high table, he was perhaps the least sumptuously dressed and by no means the grandest in physical appearance.

And yet he exuded power. His eyes were dark and somehow empty; deep, cold caverns filled with nothing but darkness and the promise of death. Vulmar's eyes were devoid of feeling, like those of a snake.

Beobrand's mouth went dry in that viper-like stare.

Just as heat rolls off a forge, so Vulmar radiated malevolence. The force of the man's gaze threatened to make Beobrand doubt himself. He clenched his fists at his side and vowed that he would leave Rodomo with Ardith, or he would not leave at all.

The messenger translated his lord's words:

"I am Vulmar, son of Vulmaris, Lord of Rodomo. Welcome to my hall."

Impatiently, Beobrand waited for the man to finish speaking. He nodded to acknowledge the man's words.

"I know not why you summoned me here, Lord Vulmar, but I have a matter I would discuss with you. A matter of urgency."

The messenger translated, listened to Vulmar's response, and spoke again to Beobrand. All around the hall, the faces of the men and women were pale and staring, avidly listening to the exchange between the two lords.

"My lord says," replied the messenger, "that he had learnt of your arrival in Rodomo and he wished to meet the great Beobrand with half a hand." He paused, and offered Beobrand a small smile. "He says he did not believe all that he had heard of your exploits, so wished to see you for himself."

Beobrand bridled.

"And what does he think now that he has seen me?"

A pause while the messenger translated. On hearing Vulmar's reply, a titter of laughter ran through the guests in the hall. Beobrand gritted his teeth, the muscles in his jaw bulging, as he awaited the messenger's translation.

"My lord says that if the tales are true of the men you have killed, then the warriors of Albion must be a poor lot indeed for you to slay so many."

Dreogan made a step forward, growling deep in his throat. Beobrand held out his mutilated left hand and stopped him. His eyes never left Vulmar's. The lord was grinning, but no humour reached those soulless, empty eyes.

Beobrand forced himself to smile.

"Well, in Albion we fight with spear, sword and shield. It is with steel and iron that I have won my battle-fame, not with words and jibes delivered in a hall surrounded by men who dress like maidens."

The messenger frowned and began to speak Beobrand's words to Vulmar. Murmurs of anger and outrage along the benches. Vulmar's expression did not alter. His grin never wavered. He began to voice a reply, when Beobrand continued, cutting him off.

"And when I wage war, it is against men. Warriors. Proud spear-men, shield-men, who are brave enough to fight for their lord and king. I do not fight against women." He paused, squaring his shoulders and raising himself up to his full height. His eyes pierced the gloom of the hall with an icy glare. "And I do not suffer those who harm girls."

Silence. No mutterings now as the messenger translated Beobrand's words.

Vulmar, still unblinking and smiling, listened. Did his expression harden slightly? Had Beobrand's words struck home? Beobrand noticed that a couple of the men at the high table looked away from their lord, as if they wished nothing to do with what was to be talked of now.

Vulmar spoke. The messenger interpreted.

"Now my lord says he sees the iron in you that makes you a formidable foe. Perhaps the poems are true. But what is this matter you mentioned? What would you like to discuss with my lord?"

All along the length of the hall, there came the scrape and shift of benches and stools as men and women changed their positions to get a better view of the confrontation between Vulmar and this tall, angry Anglisc foreigner.

Beobrand took a deep breath and swallowed against the dryness of his throat. He wished he could take a drink of water or wine, but dismissed the idea instantly. It would make him look weak. And this was no time or place for timidity.

"I would speak with Vulmar of a girl," he said, pleased that his voice remained strong and clear. "A girl I believe is here. In this household."

Vulmar's smile broadened. The messenger spoke his reply.

"There are many girls in my lord's household," he said. Someone laughed. Beobrand did not see who.

"This is a young girl. Fair hair, like mine. And she would have been brought here very recently. A man named Grimr took her from her home in Cantware. I would take her back. To her family."

Vulmar listened to the words relayed by the messenger in Frankish, but from the slight pinching around his eyes as Beobrand had spoken, he began to suspect that he understood more of the Anglisc tongue than he was letting on, that perhaps the interpreter was all for show, to ensure that all those gathered could follow what was being spoken of.

Vulmar twisted in his seat, finally breaking eye contact with Beobrand.

"Well, Grimr," Vulmar said in accented, but understandable Anglisc, confirming Beobrand's suspicions, "what say you? Did you take this girl?"

A thickset man heaved himself up out of a chair someway down the table. Beobrand's eyes narrowed as he took in the man's strong limbs, muscled shoulders and gnarled, shovel-like hands. He tried to picture him without the fine red kirtle he wore, imagined him instead wrapped in a heavy leathern cloak and a helm fashioned from the skull of some great tusked sea creature. Yes, this could be the man who had led the ships against them all those days ago. For the merest instant the man's gaze met Beobrand's and he was certain of it, this was the pirate who had attacked *Háligsteorra*. Beobrand recalled Dalston's pallid terror. The blood fountaining as he dropped into the deep for all eternity. Renewed rage flashed within him so suddenly that he was almost overcome by it. He took a step forward, only halting at Cynan's touch on his arm. Beobrand's hands were trembling at his sides and he cursed his weakness as he clenched them into fists so tight that his knuckles cracked.

"The girl is a gift for you, my lord," said Grimr. His words were guttural, not the soft tune of the Franks. "I paid good silver for her."

"So, there it is, Beobrand of Bernicia," said Vulmar. "It would seem your visit here has been for nothing. Still, I am glad to have seen the mighty Half-hand in the flesh." He grinned.

"The girl was not the man's to sell," said Beobrand, his expression cold, flat.

"I bought her from her father," said Grimr. "She was his to do with as he pleased."

"No," said Beobrand, his tone harsh and final, "he was not her father." He fixed Grimr with his gaze. The man frowned. "I am her father," Beobrand said and his words fell like rocks into a pool.

Whispers and mutters rippled around the hall as the words were translated.

Grimr pursed his lips, but said nothing. Vulmar sat up, as if genuinely interested in this conversation for the first time.

"Oh, that is good," he said, staring at Beobrand with increased intensity. "Yes, I can see it now. The hair. The eyes." He smiled, pleased with this discovery. "I do hope she has inherited her father's spirit." He licked his lips.

Bile rose in Beobrand's throat. Could he leap forward and slay this toad before he himself was struck down? He measured the distance, took in the eating knives strewn carelessly on the table. It would be a simple matter to snatch one up and drive its iron point into the man's throat, or his heart, or even his eye. Yes, he believed he would succeed in taking Vulmar's life should he try. He tensed, moving his weight onto the balls of his feet. At his side, he flexed the fingers of his right hand.

As if sensing his thoughts, perhaps reading them on his face and his change of demeanour, Vulmar shifted back a way in his chair. Beobrand forced his muscles to relax. If he did this thing, what then of Ardith? And what of his gesithas? They would all be slain and his daughter would fare no better at the hands of Grimr or one of the other lords in the hall.

And what of Octa? The boy would never see his father again. He would grow to adulthood in the thrall of Oswiu.

"I am a rich man," said Beobrand, tasting acid in his mouth as he spoke the words of a merchant rather than leaping into the fray as befitted a warrior. But he could see no other way. He took in a deep breath and continued. "I have treasure and wealth. I will pay you for her. Name your price."

Vulmar chuckled.

"Oh, my barbarian friend," he said, "look around you. Do you truly believe I have need for more gold or silver? I could drown in the stuff. There is nothing you could offer me that would make me return the girl to you. Unless you happen to have two young maidens to hand. Unspoilt virgins are so hard to come by."

Beobrand's ire at Vulmar's words was such that he was almost panting. His breath came in short, sharp gasps and it was all he could do not to spring onto the dais, smashing through the boards and squeezing the life from the lord.

Along the high table, the red-bearded man sitting beside Grimr raised his cup in mock salute to Beobrand. The man had the look of a warrior and might have been handsome once, had it not been for the ruin of his left eye. Where the eye had once been, now just a burnt and scarred pit of puckered skin remained.

"Do you have some virgin girls to trade for your daughter, Beobrand?" asked Vulmar, clearly enjoying seeing his guest's anguish. "No? Well, I trust you understand. I have been waiting for one such as her for a long time. As I said, it is not about riches. I have more than I could ever want. But some pleasures are still elusive. The, how do you say it?" He paused, waving his hand as if hoping the smoky air might bring the inspiration for the words he sought. "The flower can only be picked once, no? You comprehend? I live for these small pleasures. And do not fear, Beobrand. I will treat the girl well." Vulmar showed his teeth as he grinned broadly.

For an instant then, Beobrand thought he would lose control. His vision dimmed and his hearing became muffled. All he could see was Vulmar and his smirking face. The man was an animal. A monster. A snake that should be killed. Cynan and Bearn both reached for Beobrand, held either arm, steadying him. Slowly, he willed himself to breathe. His sight brightened and once more he could hear the whispers of those gathered in this den of vipers. He fixed Grimr with his steely gaze. Then he glowered at the one-eyed man. Finally, he met the empty eyes of Vulmar. The Frankish lord did not blink.

"Very well," said Beobrand, his voice quiet, almost timid. He swallowed down the bile that stung the back of his throat. "I understand."

Beobrand spun on his heel and prepared for the long walk down the hall. His gesithas parted before him, but Brinin stood in his way.

"Step aside, boy," Beobrand whispered.

Brinin did not move. Beobrand could feel the eyes of all those in the hall upon them.

"We cannot leave her with that man," Brinin said, his voice was high and wavering, he was close to weeping, his cheeks flushed and eyes liquid with tears.

Beobrand gripped the boy's shoulders roughly and leaned in close. In a harsh whisper that only the boy could hear, he said, "We can and we will. You think I want this?"

The boy looked lost, unable to speak. Beobrand shook him. The boy's head rocked back and forth.

"Do you?" Beobrand hissed.

"No," muttered Brinin. A tear trickled down his cheek and he rubbed it angrily away.

"No," replied Beobrand, his voice softer now. He let the boy go. "Now follow me," he whispered, "I do not want to stay another moment in this place. The reek of it is making me sick."

Beobrand stepped past the boy and walked straight-backed and stiff-legged down the length of the great hall towards the huge doors. His gesithas followed behind their lord, as faithful in defeat as in victory. Brinin sniffed, scrubbing at his tear-streaked cheeks and stumbled after the men.

Chapter 46

All about them loomed the shadows of collapsed giants. The mouldering bones of decayed edifices, once magnificent, statements of the grandeur of their creators, now just the tumbled ruins of forgotten memories in the dark. The sun had long set and clouds covered the sliver of moon that hung in the sky. There was no light here in these rubbled remnants of rock and Beobrand had ordered the men to dismount and lead their horses. The rough cobbles were cracked and broken, and a hoof slipping into an unseen hole in the darkness would lead to a lame beast and a bad fall. The clatter of their animals' hooves echoed from the stone that surrounded them. It sounded as though they were being followed by shades, invisible wraith horsemen who rode just out of sight, in the black of the night.

Beobrand's neck prickled at the thought.

"We will be followed," said a voice from the gloom.

Cynan.

In the darkness Beobrand nodded, then, realising the movement would not be seen, he said, "I do not doubt it."

They walked on in silence for a time, trying to hear any sound beyond the crunch and crack of their mounts' hooves and their own booted feet on the cobbles. There was a faint glow in the distance, perhaps from some open shutters down in the sprawl of Rodomo. Beobrand wished they had thought to bring torches to light their way. But they had been in haste to leave Vulmar's hall. And, the truth was Beobrand had expected trouble long before they left the Frankish lord's palace enclosure. It had been with surprise that he had found the doors unbarred, and nobody blocking their way to the stables. All the while as they had readied the horses that they had borrowed from Feologild, Beobrand had expected the rasp of steel in the shadows of the courtyard. He could not imagine that Vulmar had invited them to his hall only to let them leave again. Perhaps Vulmar had been uncertain as to his intentions, but surely after Beobrand had confronted him, let him know that he was Ardith's father, the lord of Rodomo would not simply allow the men from Albion to ride away.

The hostlers had quickly brought out their steeds and they had led them to the great gates, closed tight now against the night. But doors that shut out the darkness, just as well stopped those inside from leaving and Beobrand had been tense and nervous as they had made their way across the courtyard, torches illuminating the bushes and statues that lined the enclosure.

He had said nothing, for there was nothing to say. He had been certain that Vulmar's yellow-cloaked guards would descend upon them and hack them down, there, inside the palace walls, while Beobrand and his gesithas were unarmed. It would be slaughter and Beobrand's shoulders and neck had ached from the tension of knowing death awaited and he would be unable to prevent it. He would fail, his men would die and Ardith would be left to face her fate, alone and abandoned. And he would never see Octa again. He knew that his men believed the same. This was where their wyrd threads would end, cut in the cruellest way, in a welter of blood in the night. None of them had said anything as they approached the gates, but Beobrand could sense them all tensing muscles, could hear their breathing quicken.

They would not shy away from death when it came, but they would put up such a fight as they could. Even without weapons they would fight with their fists and eating knives and they would sell their lives dearly.

And yet the guards had merely handed them their swords and seaxes and then swung the great gates open. The gates squeaked slightly on the iron hinges, loud in the dark silence. Beobrand had clasped Hrunting's cold pommel disbelievingly as they had ridden out of Vulmar's domain, past the watching, shadowed faces of the guards, and into the cold darkness.

For a short while he had felt a surge of relief to be away from the place, but then, as the night wrapped about them like a shroud he had cursed himself for a fool and a craven. Yes, they were free of the palace, but this would not be the end of things with Vulmar. And how could he feel relief when his daughter still languished within the palace? The gods alone knew what the girl had already endured, but one thing was certain in Beobrand's mind. He could not rest while she yet resided in the thrall of that toad, Vulmar. And then there was that bastard, Grimr. He would have to pay the blood-price for poor Dalston. And for taking Ardith from Hithe. And if that gloating one-eyed whoreson was with him, Beobrand would slay him too. And be glad of it.

But as they had ridden further into the black chill, Beobrand's mind gnawed and scratched at his thoughts. By all the gods, how could he free Ardith and seek vengeance for Dalston? Thoughts of great deeds were easy, but he could see no path from the thinking of it to the doing. They were few, in a strange land, and Vulmar was surrounded by walls and loyal warriors.

They had ridden in silence for a time, each lost in their thoughts, until it became too dark to ride safely. They had dismounted on the edge of the ruins and trudged through the echoing gloom, disconsolate and seething at the impotence of their position. They were men of action, warriors all, who burnt with the fire of vengeance against those who had wronged them or their kin. Or their hlaford's kin. Even Brinin, young and untried in battle, would gladly fight and give his life to see Ardith safe. But there was the rub. They could all give their lives, but for what? To die here for no gain was pointless. To throw themselves onto the points of Vulmar's guards' spears would avail nothing.

They plodded on and the infinite darkness above them reflected the blackness of Beobrand's thoughts and mood.

"Vulmar will send men to kill us," said Cynan, again speaking over the quiet, cutting into Beobrand's dark thoughts.

Beobrand said nothing.

A sudden flare of light before them caused him to blink. After-images in the darkness, the shapes of the sprawled ruins. Were those men? For an instant he thought it was the flicker of lightning, but then, just as quickly, he saw the truth. Several fire pots had been uncovered, throwing pools of light flooding out onto the path. Long black shadows danced and trembled in the night.

Beobrand and the others halted, blinking against the new brightness. Beobrand was aware of more light behind them. Men stepped from the ruins and blocked their path. The light gleamed from their byrnies, helms and shield bosses. The steel of sword and seax blades glimmered in the darkness.

Beobrand reached for Hrunting, thrilling at the touch of the sword's hilt. If it was to end here tonight, at least he could carve a bloody swathe through his enemies' ranks. He might provide one last tale for the scops to sing of, and send some more men on to Woden's corpse hall to serve him in the afterlife. He looked sidelong at Cynan who had also drawn his blade.

"It seems Vulmar already has," Beobrand said.

Cynan's teeth flashed white in the dark.

"I hate always being right," he said.

And then, without warning, the men attacked and the night was filled with the bitter music of battle: the keening of sword-song and screams.

Chapter 47

Coenred was panting. Out of breath, he looked about the smoke-hazed room. The place was packed full of men and the air was thick with the odour of sweat, ale, sour wine and, underlying it all, the brackish tang of river water. Across the steamy fog of the room, a flash of pale flesh caught Coenred's attention and for a few heartbeats he found himself unable to look away from a scrawny woman who, skirts hitched up to reveal skinny legs, straddled a bearded seaman. The woman returned his gaze and stuck her tongue out at him, waggling it lasciviously. He shivered, turning back to the man on his left.

"Are you sure this is the place?" he said to Gadd.

Feologild's servant nodded, his expression pinched and eyes narrowed. Perhaps against the smoke, or maybe as an indication of his anger at having been coerced into leading them here. Gadd had agreed to accompany them into the night only after Attor had whispered to him in a dark corner of the merchant's yard. Coenred had seen Attor's hand rest on the handle of his seax, and the smile on his face had been absent from his eyes. The servant had swallowed and grown pale at the Northumbrian's whispered words, but had nodded his agreement to lead them once more into Rodomo.

On leaving the church, they had rushed through the darkening streets back to Feologild's home. Coenred had buzzed with excitement at what he had learnt from Walaric. But when they had arrived, they'd found that Beobrand and the others had left. Coenred had been dismayed to discover that Beobrand had been summoned to Lord Vulmar's palace, though to what end he could only guess. It had not taken him long to convince Attor that they should venture out into the evening streets in search of this hovel where cheap ale and wine were served to those who did not have a hall to go to. It seemed that despite his protestations, Gadd knew of the place's whereabouts, for he led them unerringly through the now quiet streets and they had arrived without incident.

It was a leaning, timber structure, that seemed about to sink into the mud of the Secoana. It overlooked the shifting, gently creaking herd of wave-steeds that thronged, moored and anchored along the docks. Most of the men who lined the benches within appeared to be sailors.

"Can you see our man?" Coenred asked, half to himself. None of them knew who they were looking for.

A swarthy man, with a thick, curled black beard, shouted something at them. Coenred gawped at the man, not understanding.

Gadd touched Coenred's arm.

"He asks if we are coming in or going out, for now we are letting in the cold air." It was not such a bad thing to let some fresh river air into the reeking place, thought Coenred, but he nodded and stepped inside the crowded ale house. Attor and the servant followed and they dragged the door closed behind them. It hung on leather hinges, and there were large gaps at its edges where it did not sit true in the frame. But the black-bearded man seemed mollified and turned away from them, back to his friends and his ale.

"There," said Attor, pointing across the room to a corner less crowded than the rest. In the shadow, far from the hearth, sat a man in a yellow cloak. He was hunched over the board before him, staring into a wooden cup as if all the secrets of middle earth lay within.

Gone was Coenred's excitement of earlier, replaced with a sense of gloom and worry. When he had been talking to the priest, Walaric, it had seemed a simple thing to seek out this man. He could provide them with a solution to their predicament. But now, with Beobrand and his gesithas at Vulmar's hall, the lustre of the idea had vanished. How could this man, huddled in a corner of this slovenly hovel, help them? Coenred offered up a silent prayer to the Lord, asking forgiveness for his lack of faith and began to thread his way across the room.

A sailor suddenly leapt to his feet beside Coenred. The man was tall and slim with hair braided into a long plait that hung down his back like a serpent. Swaying, he careened into Coenred, almost knocking the monk from his feet. Attor leapt forward and shoved the drunk man away with a snarl. The man's friends, all dark eyes and braided hair, caught him and cursed Attor in their foreign tongue. Beside Coenred, Gadd had grown very pale and quiet, as if he did not expect to ever see the light of day again.

A straw-haired woman, who was draped over a barrel, looked up at their passing and made a desultory effort to pull down the front of her dress to expose her white, doughy breasts. Her nipples were large and dimpled, the colour of clouds on a summer's sunset.

Coenred's mouth grew dry and Attor chuckled, pulling him along.

"Come on, young Coenred," he said, "no time for that tonight."

At last, they reached the solitary man in the mustard-coloured cloak and Attor rapped with his knuckles on the scarred and splintering board before him.

The man looked up without haste. His expression was dull and disinterested as he took in Attor and Gadd. But when he spied Coenred with his dark woollen habit and his shaved forehead, he pulled himself up on the bench, making an effort to straighten his back. He said something, and following an elbow in the ribs from Attor, Gadd translated.

"He asks what it is you want," he said. The yellow-cloaked man continued speaking. "He wants to drink in peace."

Coenred swallowed.

"Tell him we need his help."

Gadd spoke. The man listened, then shook his head and drained the contents of his cup. Coenred did not need to understand the words of the reply for the man's meaning to be clear.

"Tell him I have a friend who needs his help."

The servant translated. The man gave a short answer.

"What friend?" asked Gadd.

"A man who has travelled all the way from Albion to Rodomo," Coenred said, and Gadd continued to translate. "A lord of Bernicia."

The man spoke then, anger creeping into his tone.

"He says he cares nothing for lords."

"This lord is a good man," continued Coenred, "and he has something in common with you, Halinard." He pronounced the man's name with care, just as Walaric had taught him.

The man's eyes widened. His mouth twisted, making him seem even less inviting than before, if such were possible.

"He says he has nothing in common with any lord of Albion. And he asks how you know his name."

"Tell him the priest of the church of Our Lady of the Assumption gave me his name and told me where I might find him. Walaric, the priest, believed he had something in common with my friend."

"And what is that?" asked the man through the servant's interpreting. He was angry now, but unnerved too, wary and expectant, evidently wondering what the priest had told this young monk from Albion.

Coenred took a deep breath.

"My friend has a daughter too."

Gadd spoke Coenred's words in Frankish, but before he had finished uttering them, Halinard burst up from the bench. His face was thunder. His eyes blazed. The bench tumbled over onto the sodden rushes of the floor. Halinard raged, spittle flying from his mouth.

Coenred took a step back, scared that the man meant to attack him. He jostled into the board behind him, rattling cups and spilling ale. Curses and cries of anger from the men seated there.

By the Lord Almighty, I will be slain here now, thought Coenred, quite sure that between Halinard and the angered sailors, he would not be leaving this noisome hut alive.

Attor seemed unperturbed. He pulled Coenred away from the table of irate sailors, then, with a nod and not a word, he slammed his hand onto the ale-spattered board. The crash of it silenced the men for a heartbeat and Attor withdrew his hand. Beneath it he left a small sliver of silver; enough to buy drinks for all the men for longer than they could remain awake. He met their gaze and after a moment, one of them shrugged, nodded and palmed the silver. Satisfied, Attor turned back to Coenred and Halinard.

Gadd was as white as a newborn lamb's wool, clearly terrified at the yellow-cloaked man's outburst. But it seemed that Halinard's anger had blown out as quickly as it had kindled, snuffed out like a tallow candle carried into a gale. He stood, breathing heavily, shoulders slumped, eyes downcast.

Despite not understanding the Frankish words the man had spoken, Attor appeared to comprehend the man's pain. And his need. Casting about the ale house, he spotted the innkeeper, a short fellow with white hair and bushy eyebrows. Attor picked up Halinard's empty cup in his left hand, and held up four fingers on his right. The innkeeper grinned and hurried to bring them more ale.

Attor righted the bench and from somewhere dragged over a couple of stools, and soon the four of them were seated at the board, with freshly filled cups before them. Attor handed the old gnome of an innkeeper a piece of hacksilver and the man's grin broadened. The silver disappeared into a fold of his apron and he bustled away.

Halinard reached out trembling fingers for his ale. Before he could raise the cup, Attor's hand flashed out, fast as thought, and gripped his wrist. Halinard pulled against Attor's grasp, his face darkening once more. Attor held him fast with an iron strength. His face just as hard, eyes narrowed.

"Tell him," Attor said, "that he would do well to listen to my friend here. And that the ale is his, and more too, if he will help us."

He held Halinard's gaze and his wrist while Gadd stammered words in Frankish. After a moment's hesitation, Halinard nodded. Attor released him. Gingerly, as if expecting a trick, Halinard reached out for the cup again. Attor did not move. Halinard raised it to his lips and drank deeply.

The innkeeper appeared with a platter of bread and a bowl of steaming broth. There were lumps in that broth, and Coenred tentatively fished one out with the wooden spoon provided. He had thought it would be meat, pork or mutton, but it was neither. His stomach twisted to see what lay in the spoon's depression. It was a dark snail, shell and all.

"By all the saints," he said, startled.

For the first time since they had arrived, Halinard relaxed. There was even a hint of a smile on his lips. He plucked the snail from the spoon, and sucked the broth from its shell with a slurp. He then used the tip of his eating knife to prise the meat from the shell. For a moment he had the brown, twisted gobbet of meat dangling from his knife point, and then he popped it in his mouth. He chewed with obvious relish.

When he spoke again, Gadd translated.

"He says that Amadeo cooks the best snails in the world. You'd be a fool not to try them." To reinforce the point, the servant took a snail from the bowl and ate it. "They really are wonderful," he added, visibly relaxing now that it seemed they might escape this place with their lives.

Attor shrugged, took a snail and emulated Halinard.

"Not bad," he said.

Coenred's stomach churned. He had not been hungry before, and the idea of eating a slimy snail revolted him. But Halinard nudged the bowl towards him and was watching expectantly. To refuse would risk insulting the man, so Coenred took a snail.

He shook it, so that broth dripped back into the bowl. The snail's dark, meaty body, wobbled from the shell. Coenred hoped he could eat this without vomiting. Halinard nodded, urging him to try it.

Quickly making the sign of Christ's cross over his body and offering up a silent prayer that he would not empty his stomach moments later, Coenred tugged the snail meat from its hard, curled home and, without pausing to reconsider, he put it in his mouth.

It was more solid than he had expected. And rich with the oily broth, spicy and flavoursome with whatever recipe Amadeo used for the liquor he cooked the snails in. Coenred's eyes widened and he nodded his approval to Halinard.

In turn, Halinard raised his cup to the young monk. He drank, ate another snail and then mumbled something.

Around a mouthful of snails and bread, Gadd said, "He says you should not speak of his daughter. You know nothing of her."

"I know enough," Coenred said. "Walaric told me."

Halinard slammed his cup down onto the board. The bowl of snails rocked and Gadd steadied it before it could topple.

"The priest should not have told you," Halinard said, the servant interpreting. "He told me whatever I said was secret," his eyes were haunted, recalling memories perhaps best left in the past, "that it was between me, him and God." He took a shuddering breath, ran his dirty fingers through his tangled hair. "He said he could tell nobody."

Coenred recalled his own shock as Walaric had spoken of Halinard's tale and the plight of his daughter. Like Halinard, he too had told the priest that a man's confession was secret. The sanctity of the seal of confession could not be broken. Walaric had sighed in the gloom of the chancel. But he'd had an answer for Coenred.

The monk used Walaric's own words now to reply to Halinard.

"Would God have a priest remain silent if by speaking out he could prevent suffering and sin? I believe Jesu would rather help people than to keep secrets."

Halinard stared at Coenred. All about them men laughed. Raucous talk and bawdy chatter rolled over them. But Halinard's face was that of a man who has lost everything. His eyes were hollow, bruised and dark from lack of sleep. His skin was sallow and sickly. Coenred wondered then if Walaric had been wrong. This man was broken. Halinard would do nothing to help a stranger. But then Coenred thought back to the fury that had overcome the man only moments before. A man who could yet be stirred to such anger surely still cared. Maybe enough to help others in need.

Coenred said, "Walaric told me you were a good man." Halinard said nothing at hearing these words translated. He cast his gaze down into his cup, as if searching there for an answer to what kind of man he was. Coenred pressed on.

"He said you are a man who would not stand by and allow evil to occur again." He hesitated. "To the daughter of another."

Coenred did not look away from Halinard. The man's features twisted as he wrestled with his emotions. Trembling, he lifted his cup to find it was empty. Attor passed him his own. Halinard snatched it from him and drained it.

When Walaric had told him Halinard's tale, Coenred had at first been horrified at the breaking of the sanctity of the seal, but then, as the priest had spoken in the cool shadowed church, his heart had gone out to this man he had never met. A warrior in Lord Vulmar's guard, Halinard had the misfortune to have a pretty young daughter. Lord Vulmar would never have seen her if it had not been because one day, Halinard, late to rise after drinking too much the night before, had rushed to his duty, only to forget his knife. As Vulmar's retinue was leaving the palace enclosure, Halinard's daughter had run after them, calling for her father, and causing the procession to halt. Vulmar himself had ridden along the line of men to see what had caused the commotion and at first Halinard had been pleased that the lord had smiled at the girl, magnanimous and not angry as Halinard had feared he would be. Vulmar was famed for his violent temper, but that day, he had seemed affable and had not rebuked Halinard or his young daughter.

And yet, Walaric had told him, Vulmar was just as well known for his dark tastes and the twisted ways in which he would repay men, or women, who crossed him. And as Halinard's tale continued, it became clear that Lord Vulmar had taken an unnatural liking to the guardsman's daughter. Over the weeks that followed, Halinard had been dismayed by the attention his daughter was receiving from his master. At first he had been flattered, half-imagining his girl marrying into nobility, but these were the dreams of a fool. A drunk. His daughter was yet a child and everyone knew of Vulmar's dark desires. The lord did not seek out girls for marriage, he was already wed to the cousin of King Clovis himself. No, Vulmar had a terrible urge to prey on tender flesh, and there had been more than one occasion when Halinard had been on duty warding the hall, when cries of anguish had echoed through the night from the lord's bed chamber.

On one such night Halinard had recognised something in the screams. He had rushed through the corridors, all the while more convinced that the cries he heard were those of his own kin, his daughter. By the time he had arrived at Lord Vulmar's chamber, the crying had ceased and the guards there, men he had thought his friends, had pushed him away. He had raved at them, threatening to fight them. But in the end Vulmar had come out of his room, to ask what was happening. Suddenly unsure, Halinard had muttered about his concerns. Vulmar had laughed, saying that the cries were of pleasure and he could not mention the name of the lady he was with for fear her husband would find out.

When Halinard had arrived home the next morning, he had found his wife and daughter weeping by the hearth. There was no bread baking, no ale brewing in the pot, and he knew then that he had been right in his fears. He'd asked them what had happened, but they would not speak of it. For days he tried to get his wife to tell him what had occurred that night, but she would grow surly and silent. He knew what had happened, and he knew she blamed him for it. He blamed himself too, for the love of God. He continued to do his duty, but his drinking grew heavier and more frequent, and even though he confessed his sins and spoke to Walaric often at the church of Our Lady, his self-loathing grew and no penance or absolution seemed to touch the raw wound in his soul.

Walaric had said to Coenred, "I believe you were sent here by the Almighty. This is the Lord's way to give Halinard an opportunity to redeem himself, and for your friend, Beobrand, to rescue his daughter from Vulmar's clutches. Halinard can help your friend gain access to his hall and perhaps in this way, Halinard will find some peace."

When Coenred had asked him if he did not fear Lord Vulmar, Walaric had replied, "Vulmar is a monster who will surely burn in the pits of hell. He is powerful and it is possible he might cause me some harm, but the bishop has his own ways to control him, and I think I will be safe. Halinard though, if he helps you and is discovered, will surely face the wrath of the beast."

Now, gazing across the board at the haggard features of this tortured man, Coenred wondered what would befall them all. Had God led him to Our Lady of the Assumption? To Walaric and Halinard? Was it possible Beobrand could rescue Ardith from such a powerful foe? If anyone could, Coenred knew it would be Beobrand. His friend seemed to know no fear, to face every adversity head on and to prevail. One day, he supposed, he would meet an adversary he could not vanquish. He hoped that day had not arrived.

"So," Coenred spoke at last, "will you help my friend?"

Halinard frowned.

"Where is your friend's daughter?"

Coenred looked him straight in the eye and said, "Lord Vulmar has her." He felt sorry for the man, as Halinard flinched at the name. "Will you help us?" Coenred asked.

Halinard shook his head.

"I care nothing for you or your lord friend," he said, his tone hollow, bereft of feeling.

On hearing the words translated by Gadd, Coenred sighed. All this for nothing then. God alone knew what would happen now.

"You will not help us?"

Halinard shook his head again. Then, reaching for Coenred's cup, he emptied it of ale.

Pushing himself to his feet, Halinard said, "Come, we must hurry if we have a chance to open the gates for your friend tonight."

"But you said you would not help."

Gadd called Coenred's words after Halinard, as the man strode from the ale house, suddenly filled with vigour and purpose.

The sailors and whores parted for the yellow-cloaked guard and he shouted something back over his shoulder.

"What did he say?" asked Coenred, scrambling to his feet.

The servant slipped one last snail into his mouth and stood also.

"He said he will not help you."

"Then where is he going?" Coenred was confused, but had begun to hurry after Halinard.

"He said he will not help you or your lord," the servant said, trotting alongside, "but he will help the girl."

Chapter 48

The night was filled with noise and dancing shadows. The flickering flames from the uncovered fire pots provided but a dim light, yet it was almost blinding after the barrow mound blackness of the ruins.

Beobrand released his horse's reins and slapped the animal hard on the rump. In a heartbeat, the beast had bounded away from the sudden light and the threat of the men looming from the rocks. As they closed on them, Beobrand saw that their attackers had made two dreadful mistakes. They had provided light, which benefited those being ambushed as much as the ambushers.

And there were only a dozen of them. Fewer than double the number of Beobrand's band.

In an instant, the worries and concerns of moments before disappeared, dispelled into the darkness by the prospect of battle. Dragging Hrunting from its fur-lined scabbard, Beobrand bellowed.

"To me, my brave gesithas!"

Looking to his right, he saw Cynan, a savage grin upon his face, send his own mount galloping back towards the men who were closing in from behind. Bearn, Garr and the others followed their lord's lead, and the terrified horses caused the men behind them to curse and jump aside, giving Beobrand and his companions a moment to form a defensive line of sorts, even though none of them bore shields. The men fell into position quickly on either side of him and Beobrand was pleased to see Brinin take up his own position between Dreogan and Bearn. The boy brandished a seax as though he knew how to use it. His face was pale and grim in the gloom.

Trusting to the animals to disrupt the attack from the rear a moment longer, Beobrand rushed forward to meet their assailants. There could be no hesitation. To think would be to falter. To falter would mean death. The men who stood before them were armed with shields, spears and a couple of swords. He could not give them time to form a shieldwall.

"Death!" screamed Beobrand, filled with a sudden terrible glee at the wide-eyed fright on the faces of these fools who had dared stand against him.

One man tripped in his haste to place his linden board beside his companion's. He fell to one knee, and Beobrand's laughter echoed into the night, deadly and cold as the steel that flashed in the darkness. Before the man could stand Beobrand was upon him. Hrunting sliced down. The blade cut deeply into the man's neck and blood bubbled black in the dark. The Frankish warrior beside him tried to bring his spear to bear on Beobrand, but with almost languid ease Beobrand caught the haft in his left half-hand, pushing it up and away from his face. His forward motion carried him onward and, twisting Hrunting from the first man's flesh, Beobrand spun to the left as he passed, delivering a vicious swiping cut into the spear-man's outstretched and unprotected arm. Beobrand was not able to bring his full power to the blow, but Hrunting bit deeply, rasping against the man's bone. His grip on the spear loosened and Beobrand wrenched it free from his grasp.

And then he was through the attackers. He had left two men dying in his wake in as many heartbeats and he saw that his gesithas had cut a swathe through the Franks. He turned quickly, kicking the spear-man in the side of the knee. Still confused and dazed from the suddenness of Beobrand's attack and the gash to his forearm, the man grunted and collapsed as his left leg gave way. Beobrand scythed Hrunting into the man's face, feeling bone and cartilage shatter beneath the blade.

Dreogan, though limping from the wound he had received in Mantican's hall, was still fast. He ducked beneath one Frankish man's spear and crashed bodily into his shield. The tattooed warrior roared with battle-fury and both men tumbled to the cracked cobbles. Bearn, having slain his own enemy, made to help Dreogan, but before he could close with the two wrestling men, Dreogan heaved himself to his feet, his seax dripping gore.

Beobrand swelled with pride. Even unarmoured, his comitatus were formidable. A quick glance told him that all of his men yet stood and appeared unharmed. Six Frankish warriors were dead or dying on the ground; ruined man-flesh to adorn the rocky ruins of the old Roman remains. From where they had come, the horses had all fled into the darkness and the rest of Vulmar's ambushers had now formed a shieldwall. They advanced slowly, wary now of the blood-drenched killers before them.

"Arm yourselves," shouted Beobrand.

The first man he had struck yet lived, gurgling and mewling in pain. Beobrand plunged Hrunting into the man's throat, silencing his whimpering.

He looked to the men approaching. They were almost upon them. Frowning, Beobrand sheathed his sword. There was no time to wipe the blade free of blood; it would make an appalling mess of his scabbard.

He plucked the dead man's shield from the ground where it had fallen. The iron boss handle was still warm from the man's grasp. In his right hand Beobrand hefted the spear he had taken. Its tip was long, sharp and deadly. He adjusted his grip so that he could stab down over the shieldwall.

The enemy advanced, faster now, perhaps hoping to seize advantage of the moment that Beobrand and his retinue were taking up shields and spears. But they were not fast enough. With the speed come from years of drills and countless skirmishes and battles along the frontiers of northern Albion, Beobrand's men jostled into well-practised positions, ready to meet these men who would creep in the dark like some wretched kindred of Cain.

"See, men," shouted Beobrand, his voice carrying easily over the stamping feet of the approaching warriors, "even when attacked from the darkness by cravens, we prevail against our foe-men. For we are men of Bernicia and the gods smile upon us. Let the gods hear you now!"

And they roared, inchoate screams of such rage and fury that the yellow-cloaked men who were only paces away checked their step, questioning the wisdom of attacking these savage men of Albion.

And in that moment, Beobrand thrust his stolen spear forward and charged.

It was over in moments, and soon the night was quiet once more.

For a time the only sound was the panting of the Bernician warriors, their breath steaming in the cold night air. A couple of the Frankish men moaned, groaning in their tongue, though what they said, Beobrand could not tell. He had heard similar cries oftentimes before, in many languages. They were always the same, those last calls before death claimed the wounded. They cried for their loved ones, for their wives, children or mothers. They called out against the cruelty of their end. Some railed against the gods for allowing them to die.

But none of their entreaties could ever save them from the cutting of their wyrd's thread.

Bearn and Garr stepped into the gloom and moments later, the moaning cries were silenced.

Brinin staggered a few paces into the ruins and vomited noisily. Fraomar and Cynan met each other's gaze. Nobody spoke, each lost for a moment in their own thoughts. The elation of battle slowly ebbed from their bodies and the truth of what lay at the end of each of their life's journey filled their thought-cages.

When Brinin returned, wiping his mouth sheepishly with the back of his hand, Beobrand clapped him on the back. The boy flinched.

"You did well," Beobrand said. The boy stared at him, eyes wide and shining.

"I did nothing," he said.

"You stood with your brothers and you survived," said Beobrand. "That is no little thing, Brinin. Now, help Cynan and Fraomar to round up the horses."

The men trotted off into the darkness, calling quietly for the mounts that had run into the night.

Beobrand took a deep, cool breath, clenching his hands into fists at his side against the familiar trembling. He sighed, his breath smoking in the dark.

Dreogan joined him. He hobbled on his bandaged leg and gripped his left forearm. Blood oozed from between his fingers. At Beobrand's questioning look, he said, "It is but a scratch."

It looked worse than a scratch, but Beobrand knew better than to argue with the man.

"Get Garr to bind it. We'll be needing you hale before we are done this night."

Dreogan grunted.

"The boy did well," he said.

Beobrand looked at the shapes of the corpses scattered on the cracked cobbles.

"Gods, you all did well."

"We did our duty, lord."

"Aye, and I thank you for it."

In the night, they heard the clatter of hooves as Cynan led one of the horses back towards the pool of light that yet glowed from the ambushers' fire pots.

"Vulmar will know soon enough that his men have failed," said Cynan, stepping close to them and handing the reins of the beast to Beobrand. "We must hurry to the docks and *Brimblæd* if we are to escape Rodomo this night."

"I do not mean to flee," said Beobrand. "Surely you know me better than that after all these years."

Cynan sighed, clearly not overly surprised by his lord's answer.

"But how can we do otherwise?" he asked. "The palace is walled and guarded, and we are few where Vulmar has many dozens of gesithas at his command."

Beobrand glowered at the Waelisc warrior. He clenched his jaw, grinding his teeth. His mood was as dark as the endless sky above them. He could see no way forward and yet he was certain that he could not run away, leaving Ardith behind.

Biting his lip, he gazed up at the black heavens. A thin drizzle began to fall, light and chill like the breath of death.

Woden, Father of all the gods, he prayed silently, show me the way. I have ever brought you glory and I offer you the blood of these fallen in sacrifice, slain by the blades of my warband. We have soaked the earth with hot lifeblood for you.

A voice, loud and close and just beyond the light from the pots, made them all start. Without thought, Beobrand tugged Hrunting from its scabbard. Its befouled blade came out with difficulty, the blood that coated its length congealed and sticky.

"In the name of all the saints," said the voice, "it seems we have missed the fun."

Beobrand let out his breath with relief. He knew that voice.

"Come into the light, friend," he said.

The slender form of Attor stepped from the darkness. He was followed by the robed figure of Coenred and two others.

One, a pinched, sallow man, Beobrand thought he recognised as Feologild's servant. The final figure made him raise Hrunting and take a step forward. For the last man was broad and strong, with the bearing of a fighter.

And he wore the long yellow cloak of one of Vulmar's men.

"This is Halinard," said Coenred.

The man was looking about him, his face pallid, mouth wide. The bodies of the slain must be known to him. Dismay and horror played over his features.

"What is the meaning of this?" asked Beobrand. "He is Vulmar's man, and in case you were unclear," he indicated the bodies, pointing with Hrunting's gory blade, "Vulmar is our enemy."

Coenred looked wan and frightened in the gloom, but Beobrand saw something else. Something he recognised in his old friend. A determination and resolve. And a gleam of hope.

"Yes, Vulmar is our enemy, but our enemy's enemy is our friend."

"But this Halinard is but one man, even if he turns against his lord for some reason to help us, I do not see how we can hope to wrest Ardith from Vulmar. You have not seen his hall. The walls and gates are tall and stout and he has many men in his warband."

Coenred placed a hand upon Beobrand's shoulder.

"You really should have more faith," he said. "I too was unsure, but now the Lord God has shown me the way."

Beobrand frowned. Was it the Christ or Woden who spoke to the monk that night? Did it matter?

"Tell me," he said.

Chapter 49

Ardith gazed about the room and trembled. The exposed skin on her arms and legs prickled like a plucked goose's flesh. The clothes Erynn had dressed her in were thin, made from a fabric so soft and sheer, it seemed no heavier than if it had been woven from a spider's gossamer. The silks were beautiful, but she shuddered at their touch on her skin, as if they were an unwanted lustful caress.

That would come to pass all too soon, she thought, shivering again, though the room was not cold.

Two braziers smouldered, and sickly smelling smoke wafted from the bronze bowls, where some sort of herb had been crumbled onto the coals. The scent was cloying and sweet. She tried to breathe lightly, through her mouth, wondering what magics might lie in the burning wyrts. But she could not hold her breath for long and the room was hazy with the smoke. Soon her head was woozy, her thoughts slow and blurred.

She walked around the room, looking at everything. She was certain there would be no way for her to escape, but she would not resign herself to accepting her fate. Perhaps she could find a means to thwart her captors. Casting about the room, she searched for something. Anything.

She took in the large bed, its ornately carved timber frame surrounding what was surely a soft mattress. Softer than any she had ever slept on before, she was certain, but she did not approach the bed, did not reach out to touch the linen sheets, or the numerous cushions and pillows that were strewn about it. She did not wish to feel comfort. Not in this room.

The walls were draped with fine arrases. The wall hangings depicted animals and people, cunningly embroidered in vivid colours that glimmered in the ruddy glow of the braziers. She pulled back the drapes. Behind each one there was solid, whitewashed stone. No windows to climb out of. No hidden doors from which she could escape the room.

Room? No, she corrected herself, not just a room, a luxurious cell.

On a small, polished table rested a silver platter, a jug and a pair of dainty cups. The platter's gleaming surface held a loaf, a small cheese and some fruit. She had seen some of those fruits that morning. Spherical and the colour of a setting sun. Their skin was dimpled and shiny and as tough as leather. Ardith had been surprised when Erynn had shown her how to eat one. She had sliced into the hard skin, peeling it away, leaving a soft, juicy interior that she then pulled apart. The succulent flesh ripped into mouth-sized segments and despite her misery, Ardith had marvelled at the sour sweetness of the fruit. Erynn had said they came from lands far to the south, where the sun shone warmly even in the winter.

At seeing the round fruit on the plate, Ardith's mouth filled with saliva. The smoke from the braziers stung her eyes. She blinked and took a step towards the food, before pulling herself back. She would not eat in this place. Nor feel the comfort of the soft bed.

While Erynn had dressed her in the diaphanous silks, the beautiful slave had exhorted Ardith to relax.

"Take deep breaths. Drink some of the wine. And when he comes to you, smile and offer yourself to him." As she had spoken, Erynn, eyes dark with sadness, had brushed Ardith's hair in long strokes until it shone like gold. The soft touch had reminded Ardith of her mother and her eyes had brimmed with tears. How she longed to be home, in Hithe. Far from this place. And yet, as the comb slid through her shimmering tresses, with each tangle that snagged and then gave way, Ardith felt her past life being pulled ever further from her.

Her stomach had churned at Erynn's touch and her words. She had refused to reply to the woman, instead sitting sullenly as the thrall had bathed her, dressed her and prepared her hair. Eventually, Erynn had given up and fallen silent, only offering her one last piece of advice as she had left her at this windowless room, deep within the great stone palace.

A frowning, yellow-robed guard had opened the door. He had not met Ardith's gaze as she entered the room.

"Do not fight him," Erynn had whispered. "You do not have the claws for such a battle, little one," she'd murmured, with a final squeeze of Ardith's shoulder. Then the door had closed behind her. And she had been left alone in this sumptuously appointed dungeon.

She thought of the ageing Frankish lord coming to her here. Pressing her down into the cushions, his weight upon her. His breath sour with wine. His hands roving and clawing at her flesh.

Her body trembled with the strength of emotions she felt.

Disgust.

Fear.

And anger.

She had fleetingly believed that Erynn was a friend. An ally. But she was just another of her captors. And Erynn clearly knew nothing of her if she truly believed Ardith could simply surrender herself without a struggle. Ardith took a deep breath, trying to calm her hammering heart. The smoky air caught in her throat and she coughed.

She glanced around the room again, wondering whether in fact it would be better to sit on the edge of the bed rather than stand here, shaking in the middle of the floor. Erynn had told her she would probably be waiting for a long while. Vulmar was feasting, she had said, and he would not come to Ardith until much later.

But before she could decide on whether to sit or to succumb to her hunger and try one of the strange southern fruits, a scraping sound snapped her attention to the room's single door.

For several heartbeats, she did not breathe, listening intently for any hint of what might be occurring outside.

Was that muffled talking? She could not be certain.

She was beginning to believe she had imagined it, when her flesh crawled anew, as if a cold wind had blown through the cell. For, with the barest hint of creaking hinges, the entrance swung inward and a man strode in, pushing the door shut behind him.

Chapter 50

The helmet was too large for Coenred. With each step it slipped forward over his eyes, and, despite knowing that it obscured a large portion of his face, and that the dark further masked his identity, he felt terribly conspicuous. The yellow cloak he wore dragged in the mud and was growing ever more burdensome as it soaked up the thin rain. The low cloud was dark and thick above them. The cobbles of the road they followed were slick and reflected the flame-flicker from the fire pots that Halinard and some of Beobrand's gesithas carried.

Ahead of them, Coenred could make out a looming blackness. The wall that surrounded Vulmar's palace, he assumed. The shifting light from the small fires they bore cast flickering shadows on the solid wall, as they made their way along it towards the gatehouse. Terror filled him as he stared up at the brick wall. It was an imposing sight, much too high to climb.

"We'll never get in," Coenred whispered to Cynan. "The plan will not work." The Waelisc warrior walked close to the monk, leading one of the horses.

"Hush, Coenred," he said, keeping his voice low. "We are Frankish guards now, remember. And it was your plan, after all. Too late to worry now."

Coenred nodded, worrying nonetheless and regretting proposing to don the fallen guards' clothing in order to gain entrance to the palace grounds. They were sure to be found out as soon as they approached the gates. And even if they got in, those walls would trap them inside just as well as they held enemies out.

The shield in his left hand was heavier than he would ever have imagined. He paused for a moment to shift its bulk and to push back the slipping helmet with his right hand. It was awkward, as he could not release his grip on the spear he carried. The weapon's iron tip swung close to Cynan's horse's face and the beast shied away with a snort. Cynan shoved the spear away with the flat of his hand and cursed quietly.

"By all that is holy, be careful," he hissed.

Coenred felt his face grow hot beneath the overlarge helmet. Please, Lord, do not let us all be walking to our deaths. Protect us from our enemies as you protected Daniel when he was cast into the den of lions. But the guards at the gate were not dumb animals. Surely they would see through the thin disguise of the bedraggled band that now made its way up to the great metal-studded timber doors.

Coenred and most of the others halted out of reach of the light from the fire pots and the braziers that burnt and steamed in the guardhouse. Halinard stepped forward.

The man had shaken off his drunkenness and seemed to have grown in stature now that he had made up his mind to act. Before they had left the ruins, Halinard had addressed Beobrand while Gadd interpreted. He had asked if he could join Beobrand, if they managed to rescue Ardith. Rodomo would not be safe for him. Beobrand had stared him in the eye and grasped his arm in the warrior grip. He had given his word that Halinard could accompany them and his family was also welcome, as long as he could get them to *Brimblæd* in time.

Halinard spoke in a clear voice to the guards at the gate. His wyrd was now twisted with that of Beobrand and this band from Albion. They would succeed in rescuing Ardith together, or they would die together.

Close behind Halinard, Coenred saw the pale face of Gadd. After the fight in the ruins, the servant had wished to return to his master's hall, but Attor had pulled him back. They could not risk him giving them away, he'd said, and besides, they needed an interpreter. Feologild's servant had been terrified, his eyes wide and face pallid in the gloom. But Attor had drawn him aside, speaking to him in harsh whispers. Soon after, Gadd had returned, saying he would come with them to Vulmar's palace. At a knowing glance from Attor, he had shuddered. He was still frightened, that much was clear, but it seemed he was more frightened of Attor than anything else. Coenred could not say he blamed him. Though as they stood now, the drizzle pattering on the cold iron of the helmet and his fingers aching from hefting the bulk of the linden board, Coenred wondered if even Attor, Beobrand and the rest of them, could really see them safely away from this place.

Closing his eyes against the fear of discovery, Coenred recited the paternoster silently. The familiar words echoed in his mind, calming him. Who was he to doubt God? It was a priest who had directed him to Halinard. As he had said to Beobrand, he must have more faith.

He had a sudden urge to piss. Was this too something sent from the Almighty, he wondered. He bit his lip to hold back the giggles that threatened to bubble up from within him. He ran through another paternoster, before taking a calming breath and opening his eyes.

He could scarcely believe what he saw. Before them, the gates were being dragged open and Halinard and Beobrand had already entered the enclosure beyond. The others followed, walking slowly past the watchful door wards. Coenred half expected it to be a trap, for the guards to fall upon them as soon as they were safely inside the palace. But the monk instantly offered up a prayer for forgiveness. Why did he doubt the power of Christ? He should have come to trust in the Lord after all these years, but he was yet weak and fearful, despite having witnessed God's majesty at work so many times.

Besides, he thought with a twisted smile, it was too late now to turn back. To do so would see him left alone standing in the rain outside the palace gates. Coenred lifted the spear and shield, and, pushing the helmet back on his head so that he could see where he was walking, he hurried after his friends.

As the gates swung closed behind them with a clang of metal and rasp of wood, Coenred could not shake from his mind the image of a great dragon, its deadly jaws snapping shut on its unsuspecting prey.

Chapter 51

After all of her thoughts of escape, imagining somehow slaying the lord of this palace, or even taking her own life, in the end, Ardith merely stood, trembling in the flimsy silks and watched as the man entered the smoke-filled room. He stood with his back to the door for a long moment, leering at her in the dim light from the braziers.

Her breath snatched and she coughed. All of her thoughts of fighting or fleeing had left her as quickly as mice scurrying from burning thatch. She could hear her heart, pounding hard and fast in her ears. The man stepped towards her with a lecherous grin. The light from the coals glowing in one of the bronze braziers illuminated his twisted features, his red, plaited beard. His single eye that burnt with animal intensity.

Ardith's eyes widened as she recognised him.

Draca.

The sailor grinned, his teeth large and savage-looking; stained slabs that would have appeared at home in the maw of a wolf, or some beast from the depths of the sea.

"What's wrong?" he slurred. "Not expecting me?"

He took another step closer and the stink of ale wafted before him. He smelt like her father. Horror and revulsion washed through her like a poisoned draught. At last, she found she was able to move, the spell of terror broken. She staggered further from Draca, twisting away from the bed. If she turned her back to the mattress and cushions, she knew he would overpower her in an instant, throwing her down and using his weight against her.

Blessed Virgin mother, she prayed silently, help me now in my moment of need.

He reached for her, slow and clumsy in his drunkenness, but still it was only a matter of heartbeats before he would catch her. She could not evade him for long in this small space. His muscled arms were long, his hands huge and hard. He would grasp her and then she would be powerless to stop him doing what he might with her. His gaze slid over her scantily covered body. She shuddered, all too aware of how much of her nakedness he could discern beneath the gossamer-light cloth.

"Come here, little one," he said, spittle showering from his lips. "You deserve better than that bastard Vulmar. You deserve a real man. Did she tell you all about me?"

Ardith danced away from a fresh lunge, banging her hip painfully against the table. The platter rattled and the pitcher toppled over, spilling its contents of wine. The red liquid soaked into the linen that covered the board. Some of the wine dripped onto the tiled floor, crimson as freshly shed blood. She placed a hand on the table to steady herself.

"Who?" she asked, her voice small and terrified. She could see no way out of this, but perhaps if she could keep him talking... She dared not think of what would happen then, but at least if he was talking, he was not sating his lust with her.

He paused, seemingly confused by her question. His eyes were unfocused for a moment before comprehension dawned.

"Erynn, of course," he said, his words falling from his slack lips.

"She told me nothing of you," Ardith said. "Why would she?"

Draca hesitated then, took a step back. Was that disappointment on his face? Or sadness? But after a moment, his face stiffened. The gaping socket where his left eye should have been yawned dark and senseless. He grinned, but without humour.

"You never forget your first time with a man," he said. "Erynn will never forget me." He lashed out with his right hand. He was a big man, but his speed belied his size. His huge hand gripped her wrist and he pulled her towards him. With her other hand, she tried to cling to the table, reaching for anything that might stop her, but she was powerless to resist his strength and he yanked her forward. "And you will never forget me either," he said.

His left hand groped for her breast, squeezing, pinching. She gasped, fear threatening to engulf her. "I don't mind if you struggle," he said, his foetid breath making her gag. "I like a filly with spirit."

Ardith pulled away from him, her free hand once more grasping at the table for purchase. He snarled, yanking her towards him. But her scrabbling fingers had caught on something cold and hard. Hope suddenly washed through her like a spring tide. She glanced down and saw what her hand had fallen onto. It was a knife. No, not just any knife. It was her knife, the one she had taken from Abrecand. Her claw. It must have been on the platter with the fruit. Had Erynn placed it there? Ardith's mind whirled. Was the slave woman her friend after all?

There was no time to think of these things now. She grasped the familiar knife handle and then, with all her anger and fear behind the blow, she twisted her body and sliced into the hand that held her.

Draca screamed in pain, releasing her. She made to dart past him, but he caught her hair, tugging viciously. As she staggered backwards, he slammed his bloody fist into her cheek. His hot blood splattered her face, mixing with hers as a cut opened up on her eyebrow. She sprawled onto the bed, breathless and dazed. Her head rang and her vision was blurred.

Draca looked down at his bleeding hand. The knife had flensed his skin to the bone.

"You whore," he said. "Now I am going to make you scream." He stepped toward her, bunching both his hands into fists. Blood ran freely down his right arm, dripping onto the tiles beside the pool of spilt wine.

Without warning, the door crashed open. Draca spun around to see who this new intruder was. The threshold was filled with the bulk of his brother, Grimr.

"Are you mad?" Grimr said, his voice as cold the sea. He glanced about the room, taking in the scene in an instant. "Would you lose your other eye? Gods," he fumed, stepping into the room, "after all these years, you would ruin everything. And for what? So that you can swive this virgin? Returning to Vulmar's comitatus is worth more than that. You can have all the girls you want, but not this one, you fool."

Ardith shook her head, trying to be rid of the ringing in her ears. Her cheek and eye throbbed, and her scalp ached from where Draca had pulled her hair, but her vision was clearing and she still had the knife.

"I care nothing for Vulmar!" Draca spat.

"Then you are truly a fool," replied Grimr. "Leave the girl and come away. We can yet make this right. But if Vulmar finds you here again, you know what will happen."

"I will fuck her and any other girl that Vulmar wants just for himself," said Draca.

"He will blind you!" Grimr said. He shook, struggling with an effort to control his rage. "Come, leave here and I will get you some more drink. We can find some other girls."

"I will not leave!" shouted Draca, spit flecking the air before him. He shook his fist at his brother and fresh blood splattered one of the embroidered drapes. "I will not run from Vulmar, and I will lose nothing! When he comes looking for this one," he flicked his bleeding hand at Ardith for emphasis, "I will take from him both his eyes and his balls too!" He laughed then, and there was madness in the sound.

"You are moonstruck," said Grimr. He moved away from the door, towards his brother, hands outstretched. "Come, brother," he said. "Do not do this thing. You will see us both killed, or worse."

Behind Grimr the door swung slowly open. Ardith could see the corridor beyond. There did not seem to be a guard outside any longer.

"Think of all we had to give up these last years," said Grimr, his voice softening, as one who talks to an angry animal. "Now, when we have come so far, to throw it all away again is madness. And for what?"

"You have lost nothing!" screamed Draca. "Vulmar took my eye, not yours!"

"I stopped him taking your life, Draca," Grimr said.

"If you had been a true brother, you would have slain him for what he did."

"No, brother, we were oath-sworn," said Grimr, moving closer, "it was all I could do to keep you alive. You broke your oath."

"And you allowed him to do this to me," Draca bellowed, tears tumbling from his one good eye. He flailed at Grimr and the two brothers crashed into the table, overturning it. The silver plate and cups clattered to the floor. The linen cloth, once white, fell into the blood and wine, a sodden, stained rag now. The fruit tumbled and rolled across the tiles.

Draca was raving, striking at his brother, blood from his cut hand spattering the wall hangings and floor. Grimr wrestled with him. Neither was paying any heed to Ardith.

For a moment she watched the fighting brothers, wondering at their words, at their story of broken oaths, rape and mutilation.

Had Draca violated Erynn when she was but a girl? Could it be so? And Vulmar had put his eye out for the offence?

But there was no time to think of these things now. And as suddenly as if she had been slapped again, her eyes settled on the open door.

Both men seemed to have forgotten about her.

Clutching her blood-stained knife tightly, Ardith clambered over the mounds of cushions, hoping that neither of the brothers would notice. The pillows and mattress were just as soft as she had imagined they would be. She hoped she would never feel their luxurious softness again. Stepping silently onto the cold tiles of the floor, she fled from the room.

Behind her, the sickly scented smoke wafted into the corridor, followed by the grunts and curses of the fighting men.

Chapter 52

As the gates clanged shut behind them, the rain suddenly fell with a fresh vehemence. Two of the door wards hurried inside the gate house, away from the cold wet night. Beobrand nodded at Attor and Bearn, and the two of them slipped into the guard hut behind the men.

The other two guards turned from the gate at the same instant that Beobrand and Cynan closed with them. Without hesitation, Beobrand sprang forward and smashed his head into the left man's face. Beobrand wore a simple helm that he had taken from one of the fallen at the ruins, and the iron hammered into the door ward's nose. The man staggered for a heartbeat, flailing with his arms, as if to find his balance, before crumpling onto the wet cobbles of the courtyard.

Beobrand did not see how Cynan had dealt with the other guard, but when he looked, the Waelisc warrior was lowering the Frank's insensate form to the ground.

Halinard stepped forward, his words sibilant and fast in the darkness.

Gadd, his face paler than the moon that was hidden behind the clouds, began to translate, but Beobrand silenced him with a wave of his hand. Beobrand waited nervously for a moment, watching the open door to the guard room. Still no sign of Bearn and Attor. He dropped his hand to his seax and stepped quickly towards the warm light that tumbled from the room. Cynan, Garr and Dreogan fell into step with him without comment.

His body thrummed with the fear and thrill of what they had done. It was surely madness to enter their enemy's lair so unprepared, but there would never be a better time. Vulmar had sent men for them in the darkness and he would believe them slain. Once the Frankish lord learnt that Beobrand had prevailed against his thugs, there would be no way to approach the palace. He was sure it was the best time to strike, and yet he was almost as certain that it was folly. He worried that he should have turned away from this path. But it was too late for regrets now.

Beobrand was not concerned for himself, if he was to die this night in search of a daughter he had never known, so be it. But his men had followed him blindly into the wolf's maw, and Beobrand did not wish to see their lives thrown away cheaply.

He reached the door in a few paces and pulled his seax free of its scabbard. Hrunting would be a hindrance in the cramped space of the gate house. The shorter blade of the seax was better suited for the butcher's work that would be needed to help his men. Or to avenge them, he thought bitterly. He cursed the promise he had made to Halinard. If it had got his men killed...

As he readied himself to burst through the door, half-expecting Attor and Bearn to have been overpowered in the hut, the two gesithas stepped out into the rain.

Beobrand let out a long breath. He nodded to them, displaying none of the anxiety he felt.

"Just the two?"

"Aye," replied Attor. "It would have been easier to kill them."

"We may well need to kill before this night is over," said Beobrand, "but I gave my word."

Turning to Gadd, he said, "Tell Halinard my word is iron. We will do our best not to slay the men who guard the palace. But if it comes to a fight, we will feed their guts to the gulls."

Gadd's eyes bulged and he breathed through his mouth, as if he might vomit or pass out. He did neither. In a small, tremulous voice, he spoke Beobrand's words in Frankish.

Beobrand glanced about the courtyard. He felt very exposed out here in the shadow of the gate. But it seemed Halinard had told them the truth when he had said there would only be a handful of door wards on duty this late at night. Nobody moved out there in the gloom of the courtyard and for a moment, Beobrand listened intently. One of the horses whinnied, perhaps pleased to be close to its stable. His gesithas whispered and grunted as they lifted the two unconscious guards and carried them to the gate house. Inside, he knew they would bind them and gag their mouths as they had agreed while walking here through the drizzled night.

So far the plan was working better than he could have hoped, but from now they were moving into the unknown. Halinard had told them there would be only one hostler in the stables. Beobrand hoped he was right.

"Coenred, Attor," he whispered, "see that the gates are ready to open for us. I would not wish to be trapped in here with Vulmar's men at our heels. And then see to the horses, as we agreed."

Coenred looked ridiculous in the stolen helm that had slipped down over his slim face. But he turned to the gates without a word and, with Attor's help, set about lifting the bar that held the timber doors closed.

Trusting Attor and Coenred to ensure they would be able to escape, Beobrand strode across the courtyard as if he belonged there. There was no point in hiding now. They must trust to the night and their yellow cloaks to give them cover. The others followed in his wake. Reaching the lee of the hall, Beobrand paused. When Halinard and Gadd had caught up, Beobrand asked, "Where is the entrance Halinard spoke of?"

Gadd whispered to Halinard, who replied.

"He asks for your word that he and his family can come with you to Albion."

"There is no time for this now," hissed Beobrand. For a fleeting moment, he imagined reaching out and cracking the two men's heads together. Instead he took a deep breath and said, "I have already given my word. If we get out of here with our lives and he can get to our ship before we sail, he has a place in my hall. But if he does not help me find my daughter now, we will all die here. And I swear this also," Beobrand lowered his voice to a rasp and fixed Halinard in his icy stare, "if he hinders us, no matter how many foe are upon us, I will take his life before I leave middle earth. Now," his words hissed like the now seething rain, "where is the door?"

After a quick series of whispered words from Gadd, Halinard looked Beobrand in the eye for a moment, before indicating that they should follow him. Behind them, in the puddled courtyard, came the clatter of hooves. Beobrand took a deep breath. The horses were walking, being led. There was no urgency in the sound.

Woden, let this plan work.

Without looking back, Beobrand followed Halinard along the length of the stone palace, away from the large doors that opened into the main hall.

They came to a smaller door in the side of the building. Halinard nodded. He did not speak, but Beobrand clapped the man on the back. He had spoken true and for the first time, Beobrand began to believe they might actually succeed. He waited for a moment for the others to reach the door, and then indicated to Halinard to open it.

But before the Frankish guard placed his hand upon the door, it burst open.

Chapter 53

Ardith tumbled into the rain-soaked night. The corridors had seemed cool with nothing to cover her but the silks. But the air of the courtyard was cold enough to make her breath catch in her throat. The rain drenched her instantly, plastering her thin clothes to her skin. She shivered, but still she felt a surge of relief and hope.

She was out of the palace.

Grimr and Draca had continued to fight behind her and she had padded quietly and quickly through the stone corridors of the building and the Blessed Virgin must surely have been guiding her feet, for she had seen nobody and had found this door to the outside. To fresh air. To freedom. For a moment she did not worry about how she would survive the cold night, all she could think was she had escaped, and her heart leapt in her chest with unexpected elation.

The feeling was short-lived.

A heartbeat after rushing out into the night, Ardith realised she was not free after all. Not only was she still within the walled enclosure of the palace, but she was surrounded by a group of Vulmar's yellow-cloaked guards. They must have been waiting for her, for they were crowded around the doorway. In a panic, she spun about, seeking a way past the men, but there was none.

There were too many of them. They loomed tall and frightening about her.

By all the saints, was it to come to this? She would be dragged back to Vulmar's soft bed. There would be no escape from her wyrd. She would be a bed-thrall, just as Erynn was.

Despair replaced hope then. She would never be free. Clutching the knife in her hand, she brandished it at the men around her. They backed away from the blood-streaked blade, but she knew it was only a matter of time before they would take the small weapon from her and carry her back to her fate.

No! She would not suffer further at the hands of these strangers, these men intent on hurting her. She would allow these men to take no more from her. With a scream of rebellious rage, she turned the knife in her hands. She would plunge it into her own chest and be done with it all. This horror would be over in a moment.

"Ardith, no!" screamed one of the guards.

Words meant nothing to her now. They could not stop her taking her own life. She pulled the deadly knife towards her breast.

"Ardith!" came the cry again, and one of the guards launched himself at her. Strong, callused hands grasped the knife, pulling it away from her body as the two of them fell to the freezing, wet ground. The breath was driven from her lungs and she gasped for air, all the while struggling against the man who sought to take her freedom from her once more. He was pulling the knife away from her, and she felt the warmth of blood splattering her skin. His or hers, she knew not. She squirmed and tried to raise her knee into his groin. Unable to hold onto the knife any longer, she relinquished it with a sob. But still she would not surrender. Biting and scratching like the tomcat she had known in Hithe, she fought with all her strength, desperate to be rid of the man whose weight pressed down on her.

"Ardith, cease your fighting," the man gasped. His words were in Anglisc and something about the voice cut through the fog of her fear and despair. "It is me," the man went on. She tried to make out his features, but it was too dark.

She still felt light-headed from the smoke in the room, perhaps her mind played tricks on her. She recognised the voice. But it belonged to one she knew to be many days' travel away, far to the north, back in Cantware.

It could not be.

She ceased fighting for a moment.

"Brinin?"

"Yes," the guard nodded, his smile clearly visible in the gloom, "it is me, Ardith. We've come for you."

Ardith's mind reeled and she felt as though she might swoon.

"How?" she ventured, finally giving up her struggle and allowing Brinin to heave her to her feet. She noted with a pang of guilt and worry that his right hand was warm and slick with blood, where the knife blade had cut deeply into his fingers and palm. There was little light here, save for a thin glow of a candle from the corridor that spilled out of the still-open door. And yet she could see that beneath the iron helm and the yellow woollen cloak, this really was Brinin.

He seemed to have aged in the weeks since they had last been together, his face was thinner, harder, but his eyes were the same. Her Brinin.

She gulped in the cold air. Her face was wet, as much from her tears as from the rain.

"How?" she repeated.

But before he could answer her, a huge man shoved them both away from the door.

"Get her to the horses," he growled.

She looked up at the massive warrior. She had so many questions. Who were all these people? How had they known where she was? How had Brinin come to be here? But there was no time. As the huge warrior's bulk almost filled the doorway and Brinin tugged at her arm, she understood their urgency. From within the stone corridors of the palace echoed the crashing footfalls of running men, and she was just able to make out the shape of Grimr thundering towards the open door, with other men at his back.

She allowed Brinin to pull her away, leaving the area outside of the door free. Her rescuers drew swords and seaxes from their scabbards and turned to face the oncoming threat.

"Come," hissed Brinin, "follow me."

Still confused, she turned her back on the great warrior and the armed men around the door. Brinin pulled her, shivering and dazed, across the courtyard. Behind them, the night was suddenly loud with the clash of blades and the grunts and cries of fighting and dying men.

Chapter 54

Beobrand's first instinct was to make himself a barrier in the doorway, an immovable object armed with linden shield and his deadly seax. But the instant after he had sent Ardith and Brinin splashing across the courtyard through the driving rain he looked into the candle-lit corridor and saw that her pursuers were but few. Better to allow them outside and dispatch them quickly than to permit more to reinforce them from the bowels of the stone hall. If any of his fabled luck was with him, perhaps they could kill them quietly without alerting more of Vulmar's guards. And kill them they would. The time for subduing and binding their enemies had passed. Now was the time of blade and blood. And even if he had been able to merely incapacitate, Beobrand would have sought to slay. For he recognised the leader.

Stepping back from the doorway, he said to his men, "Let them out here. Bearn, when you can, secure the door behind them."

There was no time for more preparations. No sooner had Beobrand spoken the words than Grimr burst from the building, followed by five men. They wore knives at their belts, but were otherwise unarmed. Moments before they had been chasing a girl, not expecting to fight grim-faced warriors. There was a moment of hesitation as the men blinked, peering at the faces of the yellow-cloaked men about them. For a heartbeat nobody moved, and then, three things occurred simultaneously.

Beobrand saw recognition dawn in Grimr's eyes. The pirate leader opened his mouth to yell out a warning, but it was too late.

At the same moment, one of Grimr's men, a tall man, with long, grey-streaked hair and plaited beard, stepped forward and began to say something in Frankish. His voice was gruff, his demeanour angry. Surely he was wondering why they had let the girl run past them.

He never received an answer or even finished his question.

For Cynan put into motion the third action in this dance of death. The Waelisc man was already moving as Plaited-Beard spoke. The pirate's words were cut short in a gurgling moan as Cynan plunged his seax into the man's throat.

As if awoken from a dream, everybody moved at once. Dreogan, still limping, but seemingly unhindered by the wound to his arm, despite the bandage Garr had wrapped about it already being soaked through with blood, stabbed one of the men whose skin was as dark as pine pitch. Dreogan's blade punctured the swarthy-skinned pirate's chest and blood fountained in the night, as black as the sailor's skin in the darkness. His eyes were wide and white-rimmed as he sank silently to his knees.

Another man, with hair and beard the colour of weapon-rot and skin as pale as the other's had been dark, tried to retreat away from Garr, but he collided with one of his companions and was brought up short, still trying to tug his knife from its sheath. Garr stepped in close. He clamped his hand around the red-haired man's fumbling fist, preventing him from bringing his blade to bear. Garr was tall and slender, but was stronger than his willowy height would suggest. With the power of an arm trained from a lifetime of spear throws, Garr slammed his seax into the man's belly with such force that he lifted him from his feet.

Fraomar, seax already in his hand, leapt into the confused fray. His blade whirred and flashed in the gloom and a fourth man was choking on his own lifeblood as the strength left his limbs.

The rain still fell, but colder now. There was ice and snow not far behind. The hot blood pumping onto the cobbles steamed.

All of this Beobrand took in as he stepped forward to confront Grimr. But the thickset pirate had not survived by being slow, or unduly bold in the face of bad odds. He grabbed the rain-sodden kirtle of the last man that stood between him and certain death and shoved him forward, towards Beobrand. The man staggered, off balance, while Grimr spun around to flee.

The last warrior regained his balance quickly. He drew a wicked-looking langseaxe and flung himself at Beobrand. Beobrand cursed and parried the blow easily. Sparks flew in the night. Beobrand punched forward with his shield, pushing his opponent back. Beobrand feinted again, punching high with the shield boss and the man flinched. Taking advantage of the hesitation, Beobrand cut Hrunting into the man's unprotected thigh and he collapsed, crying out. A savage, hacking blow silenced him before he hit the cold, slick ground.

It grew darker suddenly and for a moment, Beobrand was confused. He cast about at the shadows. Where was Grimr? Had the whoreson escaped? The battle fury was upon him now and all he wished for was to rip the man's life from him. The metallic tang of iron and blood filled his nostrils and he thought of Dalston, blood gushing from his slit throat; his body disappearing into the deep.

Faint light from the distant braziers by the gate finally showed him what had happened.

Bearn had slammed the door shut, as Beobrand had ordered. And Grimr had been trapped outside. Alone now with Beobrand and his death-dealers. Their breath plumed in the cold as the rain continued to beat down upon them. Beobrand noted that Gadd and Halinard stood off to one side. Both were pale. Gadd looked about to puke, but Halinard was stern, his jaw set, mouth a thin line.

"You!" Grimr said, placing his back against the palace wall. He held a seax the length of a man's forearm in his meaty right hand.

"Yes," Beobrand said, stepping forward. Hrunting was gore-smeared, the blade long, notched and deadly. "Me." They stared at each other in the darkness and each knew that one of them would die that night.

"Go to the stables," Beobrand said to his men, not shifting his gaze from Grimr. "All of you. Help Coenred and Attor with the horses and get ready to leave. You know what to do." He could scarcely believe that the plan had worked. Woden was smiling on him it seemed, happy to see slaughter and mayhem. Or perhaps merely waiting to bring about a terrible end. Who could say? Woden was called frenzy, and he revelled in chaos and blood.

"But lord—" said Cynan.

"Do not argue with me, Cynan," Beobrand snapped. "Get the horses."

"Send the others. I will stay with you."

Beobrand sighed. He had known Cynan would never do what he was bidden. He chose not to pitch his will against the Waelisc man. There was no time.

"Fraomar," he said, "see to it."

Fraomar paused for a heartbeat, before nodding. Without a word, he turned and led the rest of them across the courtyard towards the stables. The thrum of the rain covered the sound of their footfalls and they were soon lost to view behind the sheets of spite-filled rain.

Beobrand had not taken his eyes from Grimr.

"I will kill you now, sea-rat," Beobrand said.

Grimr held up his seax. It was deadly, but no match for Hrunting in combat.

"I have no sword," he said. "Will you not give me a fair fight?"

Beobrand hesitated.

"Very well," he said, then to Cynan, "Throw him your sword."

"My lord," said Cynan, incredulous. "This is madness."

"Do exactly as I say, Cynan," Beobrand said. His tone was as chill as the rain and as hard as steel. It brooked no argument. "Throw the man your sword."

Cynan stared at his hlaford for several heartbeats, before eventually nodding. Slowly, he drew his sword from its scabbard. Once it was clear of the leather-bound wood, he adjusted his grip and tossed the sword high in the air towards Grimr. It was a good throw, high and true. The blade glimmered dully for a moment and Grimr reached for the sword's hilt. He was a burly man, but agile and dexterous. He plucked the sword from the air, catching its grip in his grasp as if it had been handed to him, rather than thrown.

He grinned.

But the smile vanished almost before it had truly formed, to be replaced by confusion and then shocked horror, as the truth struck him. For in the same instant that Cynan had thrown his sword, so Beobrand had bounded forward with the uncanny speed that had made him one of the deadliest swordsmen of Albion. At the very moment that Grimr's hand gripped the sword's hilt, so Hrunting sliced into his rotund belly. The blade was sharp and Beobrand had swung it with all his rage-fuelled strength. It cut through Grimr's unarmoured flesh as easily as if he had been made of soft curds.

The smile died and slipped from Grimr's face like snow falling from a roof in spring. The stocky pirate stared down in dismay. Aghast, he watched his gut-rope begin to slip from him like so many writhing, steaming eels. He fell to his knees. More of his guts poured from the gaping wound in his stomach.

"Not fair," he said, looking up at Beobrand, eyes wide with the fear of his imminent death.

Dalston's eyes had held the same terror as he had fallen into the waves of the North Sea.

"No," Beobrand said. "Not fair."

He turned his back on the dying man and strode towards the stables.

Cynan retrieved his sword from the dying man's hand. Grimr, unable to speak now, gasped, his eyes pleading. His hands flailed weakly, reaching for something, anything that might hold him to this life.

Cynan ignored him and hurried after his lord.

Chapter 55

They rode into the freezing rain and darkness, leaving fire and chaos behind them.

Coenred clung to his horse's reins and prayed the beast would not step into a rut and break a leg. It was all he could do to stay in the saddle as they galloped into the night through the tumbled ruins. Soon they were clattering along the winding streets of Rodomo. The rain had churned up the muck on the paths and the stench of ordure and rotting refuse hung over the place like an invisible mist. Coenred gagged. His stomach churned, as much from the fear they would be caught by Vulmar as from the smells that wafted up from the detritus in the darkened streets.

He had discarded the ill-fitting helm, and when he had seen the slight, shivering girl, who now rode on the same horse as Brinin, Coenred had given her the yellow cloak he had worn. She was a beautiful, fragile-looking child, and he had felt a strange mixture of emotions when Brinin had run into the stables holding her hand. Coenred was elated they had found her alive and, apart from a cut to her face, seemingly well. But his thoughts towards the men who had taken her and would have used her to satisfy their depraved desires, were far from the ideals of a monk. He hoped Beobrand made them suffer. He would seek penance later for his vicious thoughts, but for now, he was content to allow his hatred and disgust of Vulmar, Grimr and their ilk to wash over him as freely as the rain.

His horse stumbled, slipping on some unseen scrap of rubbish, and Coenred let out a small cry that was lost in the thundering of the rain and the hooves. The mount righted itself and galloped on. With an effort Coenred pulled himself back straight in the saddle. He was no rider, and to fall in this dash for the river would be disastrous. Not only would he surely be hurt badly, crashing into the pavings of Rodomo's streets at such speed, but even worse than that, the group would need to halt to see to him. They could not afford to waste any time. To tarry would surely doom them all. For it would not take Vulmar long to rally the men in his service to pursue them.

A furtive glance over his shoulder showed him that the glare in the sky from the distant fire had dimmed. The rain would help them get the blaze under control, and then, as soon as they could round up the horses, they would be after them.

Not for the first time, Coenred offered up his thanks to God. Without Halinard, they would never have been able to enter the palace. And without the Lord's protection, Coenred did not believe they would have succeeded in rescuing Ardith and escaping the enclosure with their lives. Beobrand was often said to be lucky, but Coenred did not believe in luck. For a long time he had believed Beobrand to be the instrument of God. A sharp and deadly instrument, that dealt death to God's enemies; even if Beobrand did not understand it, Coenred was sure that his friend was guided by the Lord and Christ protected him. He knew Oswald King had believed it too. Whenever Beobrand had heard anyone saying such things, be it his king or his friend the monk, he would grow sullen and angry. Coenred had long since ceased to speak of his thoughts on Beobrand's prowess and so-called luck to him, as he knew it would only lead to angry resentment.

And yet, how else was it possible to explain events like those of this rain-streaked night? Their plan had been simple, and it certainly had more chances of failure than success. But, against all the odds, it had worked. Beobrand and his gesithas had plucked Ardith from the palace, while Attor and Coenred had gone to the stables. As Halinard had said, there was but one young hostler sleeping in a stall. Attor had quickly bound him and dragged him out of the building, into the rain where the boy had squirmed and wriggled against his bonds. Attor had shown him the gleam of a seax blade then, holding the weapon's sharp tip close to the boy's eye. There was an eloquence to Attor's violence and he did not need to speak for the boy to understand. The hostler had grown still quickly enough.

Attor and Coenred had saddled and harnessed horses to add to those they already had so that they would all be able to ride. The remaining mounts that had been slumbering in the stables, they had driven from the palace grounds, through the gates they had already unbarred and swung open. Some of the animals had fought against them, snorting and stamping. The beasts did not recognise these two strangers who had disturbed their sleep and they did not wish to be sent into the cold and dark. Attor had pricked those horses with his knife, and soon they were speeding into the night, whinnying and frightened.

The line of riders skittered now around a corner and Coenred ducked low as they galloped close to a building's jutting gable. Ice-cold water streamed from the roof, dousing him and trickling down his back. They would soon be at the docks. At the head of the column, Beobrand slowed his steed and the others tugged on their reins, bringing their horses to a canter and then slowing to a trot as the wide river came into view. Coenred was still amazed that they had managed to ride away from Vulmar's palace. Beobrand's gesithas and Brinin and Ardith all trotted now through the rain, along the wharf, towards *Brimblæd*'s mooring. Halinard had veered off some time before into Rodomo's warren of streets, leading two riderless horses behind his own mount. He had gone in search of his family, but Beobrand had made it clear they would not wait for them. Halinard, understanding the urgency, had spurred his horse ever faster, careening away into the gloom. Coenred prayed he would return in time to join them. The man deserved a place in Beobrand's hall for what he had done. He may have had his own reasons for helping, but he had risked everything for a stranger's daughter. Such an act would be rewarded in heaven, Coenred was sure, but he also thought it should be rewarded on middle earth.

Nearest to Coenred rode Gadd, his anxiety clear on his pale features. Coenred thought he understood the man better than the others. Like Coenred, Gadd was no warrior. He did not wish to be here, in this night of fighting and headlong flight. He was terrified, but he was brave, facing the adversities that had been thrown at him without flinching. And the events of this night would change his life forever. Coenred thought back to the courtyard. Everything had happened so quickly. Fraomar and the other gesithas had followed soon after Brinin and Ardith. They had helped to chase the unwanted horses out of the palace enclosure and then, only moments later, Cynan and Beobrand had walked out of the curtains of driving rain.

"It is done," Beobrand said, grim faced and curt. "Now we ride for *Brimblæd*. But first, give Vulmar and his men something to keep them busy. Torch the stable."

The gesithas had rushed to collect coals from the braziers by the gate and set about putting the stable to the flame.

Gadd had stepped forward then and addressed the dour-faced lord of Bernicia. Coenred had seen the man swallow before he found his voice. Beobrand was not a man to approach easily, especially when he was still splattered with the blood of men he had slain moments before.

"Lord," Gadd had said, swallowing again.

Beobrand said nothing, but turned his frosty glare on him.

"Lord," Gadd repeated. "I cannot stay in Rodomo after this night. Will you take me with you?"

Beobrand had frowned.

"What of your family?"

"I have none."

"And Feologild? He is your master, I cannot steal you away from him."

Gadd squared his shoulders in what would have been a humorous gesture of defiance before the tall and hugely muscled warlord, had it not been for the indignant anger than came off him.

"I am no thrall," he snapped, for the first time showing outwardly some of his mettle. "I am a free man."

Beobrand had stared at him for a moment, as his gesithas had come out of the stable. Light flickered through the open doors of the building as the first fires caught and Beobrand had swung himself up into the saddle of one of the horses.

"Very well, Gadd. You have served me well this night. You can come with us to Bernicia. I will hear your oath and you will be my man."

Gadd had not seemed able to speak for a moment, perhaps not revelling at having to swear his allegiance to this brutal lord who had swept through Rodomo leaving death and destruction in his wake like a thunderstorm. But after a moment he mumbled his thanks and took the reins of a horse from Coenred.

Coenred had handed the reins of other steeds to the gesithas, and soon they were all mounted.

The rain had eased and the wind stilled for a moment and from across the courtyard they had heard a shout. Men were streaming out of the main doors of the hall. They bore torches and the light flickered red on blades and helms.

"Time to leave," said Cynan, and they had spurred their mounts out of the yard, through the gates and into the darkness beyond. Flames had reached the thatch of the stable by then, and despite the rain, thick smoke billowed and roiled from the building. A gust of wind blew life into the fire and the thatch caught with a flash of flames, throwing light across the puddle-strewn yard.

The last thing Coenred had witnessed as he rode out of the palace was a large man kneeling beside the corpses of the men Beobrand and his gesithas had killed by the side door. The man had one of the bodies in his grasp. He cradled it in his lap, hugging the limp form to his chest in grief. As Coenred had looked, the man had tilted his head up to the sky, bellowing in his sorrow and rage. Coenred shuddered at the memory of the man's grief-stricken face as the light from the burning stable had illuminated him. The man's face had been blotchy and smeared with blood. But it was the gaping dark hole where his left eye should have been that had seared into Coenred's memory. That face had been terrifying, scarcely that of a man, more fitting for a creature in a scop's tale.

Coenred tried to push away the fear he had felt at seeing that man's twisted, one-eyed face. Vulmar's men had the burning stable to contend with and they had no horses. Whereas Beobrand's band of riders was now at the river. Soon, they would be away and Coenred hoped he would never see the one-eyed man, or Rodomo, ever again.

The rain stopped falling, leaving the cobbled roads of Rodomo slick and glimmering in the dull light from the cloud-clad moon. The wooden walkways that lined the wharf were slippery and treacherous following the rain and Coenred still clutched his horse's reins desperately, white-knuckled and scared of falling. Off to their left the Secoana ran black and still.

There were torches burning on the docks before them. Figures were moving there. This was where *Brimblæd* was moored. Beobrand had mentioned that Ferenbald had returned to the ship that afternoon and was going to transfer the riches they had taken from Mantican's hall to Feologild's warehouse for safekeeping. It seemed the sailors were yet unloading the vessel. Coenred looked up at the glow of the moon. It would be dawn soon. Ferenbald and his men must have been toiling all night. They would be exhausted. Coenred smiled bitterly to himself. No different to the rest of them then. None of them had slept or rested. But they could not pause now. To remain in Rodomo would spell their deaths. It would be a long day ahead of them.

They neared *Brimblæd* now, and could make out the faces of the sailors and Ferenbald's shaggy mane of hair and beard as he shouted commands from the deck.

Before they could hail the ship, a group of men stepped from the darkness. Spears bristled and the torchlight gleamed on their simple iron helmets. These were Gozolon's men. In front of them, still wearing the too-small beaver pelt hat, wet and glistening now from the rain, stood the port reeve himself. The fat little man puffed out his chest and stepped forward.

"Lord Octa," he said, speaking in his reedy voice, "you should be," the briefest of hesitations, "abed. Now is no time to be abroad. We should all be asleep, and I would be too, if I did not have to supervise Ferenbald and those men of Feologild's. Could it not wait till morning?" He was yet full of the slimy self-confidence he had exuded when they had first seen him the previous morning, and yet there was something in his small, darting eyes. A nervousness that he almost managed to hide. Beobrand's arrival had clearly rattled him.

Beobrand and the others reined in their horses. The mounts snorted and blew hard, their breath filling the dock with clouds of steam. They had ridden them hard, recklessly, knowing they would not be taking the beasts with them. The horses trembled in the cold now, lathered in sweat and shaking.

Without a word, Beobrand slid down from his saddle. He walked, silent and menacing in the shadows, towards Gozolon. The port reeve took a step backward.

"Lord," he said, his squeaky voice cracking, "you must leave the port. Return in daylight."

Beobrand still said nothing. Without slowing his step he reached Gozolon in a heartbeat and grabbed the little man by the cloak. Gozolon whimpered. If he expected his guards to protect him, he was disappointed, for none of them moved. Beobrand ignored them as he dragged the chubby port ward to the edge of the wharf. When he reached the river's edge, Beobrand halted abruptly and shoved Gozolon over the side. The man's shriek was cut off as he splashed into the cold water and sank from view. There was a moment of absolute silence and then Gozolon's head broke the surface. He spluttered and coughed.

He screamed in Frankish, and Coenred could not understand the words.

Beobrand turned away from the water and faced the guards, all of whom looked unsure of what to do. There were ten of them, and they were armed. If it came to a fight, it would be a bloody affair. And it would cost them valuable time. Coenred shuddered. Would it end thus, cut down with the ship of their salvation in view?

"Gadd," Beobrand said, his voice strangely serene, not carrying its usual edge of violence, rather the softness Coenred had heard him employ when calming a frightened horse, "tell these men to let us pass. They can retrieve their master from the river or leave him to drown, I care not. But they are to leave him in the water until we are aboard and rowing away from here."

Gadd translated and one of the guards replied.

"He asks," said Gadd, his voice quavering, "what is to stop them from killing you and your men."

Beobrand placed his hand on Hrunting's fine hilt.

"Tell him that if he wishes to try, he is welcome, but he will feed the fish before sunrise."

Gadd again translated his words. The guard did not reply. From the water, Gozolon's splashing and cries for help were growing weaker. The guard stared at Beobrand for a long while. Beobrand seemed relaxed, as if he could stand there until dawn.

Coenred looked at him. His face was hard and scarred. Blood was splattered dark and stark against his cheeks. The light from the torches caught in his eyes and they seemed to burn. This was a man who had stared death in the face and known no fear. A warrior, for whom death was as an old friend; a fellow killer he understood intimately.

This was not a man anyone would stand against unless compelled to do so. Evidently the guards came to the same conclusion, for, without a further word, they parted, allowing Beobrand and the others to pass. Beobrand nodded at the grey-bearded leader and walked through their ranks, leaving his stolen horse where it stood.

The gesithas followed their lord's lead, dropping from their mounts and walking towards *Brimblæd* and the waiting sailors, who were now all staring in their direction.

With a sigh of relief, both at the lack of further bloodshed and finally being able to dismount, Coenred almost fell to the timber dock. His legs were weak and he felt light-headed, but he forced himself to stand tall as he walked behind Beobrand and the others.

Brinin dismounted and lifted Ardith's tiny form from the horse they had shared. The guards did not move or comment as they watched them pass.

The last to come were Attor and Bearn, who had waited to ensure the others were safely through the guards before they abandoned their mounts and walked slowly, almost casually, after Beobrand.

Gozolon was not splashing any longer. Coenred assumed he had clutched on to one of the quay's timber pilings. He knew the port reeve had not drowned or died of exposure, for he still gasped and moaned pathetically. His speech had an unusual, almost bird-like quality, as his teeth chattered so much that each word was drawn out and broken up in a staccato clatter.

"What tidings?" shouted Ferenbald from *Brimblæd*'s prow.

"We have her," Beobrand shouted back. "And we must sail now."

"These are good tidings indeed," said Ferenbald, "but we cannot sail now. It is too dark, the tide is wrong, and the men have been unloading the ship most of the night. We must rest."

As Beobrand and the others reached *Brimblæd* there came the distant echo of horses' hooves drumming through the streets of Rodomo.

"We are all tired, Ferenbald," said Beobrand, pulling himself up and onto the ship, "but if we tarry, we will all find the everlasting rest of death. We cannot remain here a moment longer."

The pounding of hooves grew louder. Down the quay, some of the guards had obviously found Gozolon's cries too pitiful to ignore. They were leaning over the edge, offering him a spear haft to drag him out of the numbing river water.

"We will lose all of the treasure, Beobrand," Ferenbald said, his voice hollow from tiredness and resignation of what he knew must pass.

"Would you rather we lost our lives?" Beobrand replied.

Ferenbald met his cool gaze and sighed.

"By all the gods!" he hissed bitterly. He spat over the side and then raised his voice for his crew to hear him. "Make ready for sail. We leave now!"

PART FOUR
WRECK AND RECKONING

Simle þreora sum
þinga gehwylce
ær his tiddege
to tweon weorþeð:
adl oþþe yldo
oþþe ecghete
fægum fromweardum
feorh oðþringeð.

Always and invariably,
one of three things
will turn to uncertainty
before his fated hour:
disease, or old age,
or the sword's hatred
will tear out the life
from those doomed to die.

"The Seafarer", author unknown – The Exeter Book

Chapter 56

Ardith shivered. She had not been able to stop shivering since she had fled from the palace. At first she had thought it natural. It was night, and the rain that sliced down from the heavens was so cold it was almost sleet. And she had been clothed in the thinnest of wisps of silk. But now, despite the cloaks and furs the gruff sailors and warriors had strewn over her, meaning that her body was no longer cold, her trembling would not abate.

The oarsmen grunted rhythmically with the effort of pulling the ship along the Secoana and out to sea. To begin with, the flow of the river had aided them, but after a time, as the river broadened, the incoming tide flowed against them and Ferenbald had cursed as their progress had slowed almost to a standstill. The lightening sky brought with it a breath of wind and Ferenbald had ordered the sail rigged, to help the beleaguered rowers. The wind picked up, and the ship, which she recognised as Hrothgar's *Brimblæd*, began to slide slowly toward the Narrow Sea. And Albion.

Home.

Ardith could still not believe what had transpired. That all of these men would have set sail in winter to bring her back home, made her mind spin. And those warriors, and the leader, Beobrand. She had often heard her mother speak of him, and knew she had met him once before, but she had been a small child then and could not remember. Whenever his name had been mentioned, her father would grow even more morose than usual, and at such times, he would often shout at them, before stalking out of the house and slamming the door behind him in a rage.

Ardith had watched the huge, fair-haired warlord at Vulmar's palace. The men, savage-looking killers by the look of them, turned to him for command without question. He spoke little, and despite having features that could make him a handsome man, his face was scarred and perpetually scowling. Beobrand frightened her. But her father disliked him, and her mother spoke of him in tones of grudging admiration. And he had led these men in search of her. He had even brought Brinin with him.

When she thought of the smith's son, and how he had embraced her, his strong arms lifting her into the saddle, her eyes filled with tears. He had come for her. Her love. And then she buried her face in the cloaks to stifle a sob. She was so ashamed. Her face throbbed from Draca's punch. Before they had mounted the horse that would lead them to the docks, Brinin had gingerly reached out to touch her cheek. She had recoiled from his touch and seen the hurt in his face. And yet it seemed she could no longer control her body. It trembled when not cold, and flinched away from the touch of the boy she loved. Somewhere in the bowels of Vulmar's hall, part of her had been lost. She sniffed away more tears, rubbing at her eyes and looked up.

Beside her, also huddled underneath layers of cloaks, furs and blankets against the cold, sat a girl. Maybe two or three years older than Ardith, her name was Joveta. Ardith knew that, because the girl's father, a man called Halinard, had told her his daughter's name when they had climbed aboard. Next to Joveta sat her mother. The woman had her arm about the girl and they had whispered in their Frankish tongue in the darkness. Neither of them had spoken to Ardith, and she assumed they could not speak Anglisc any more than she could understand Frankish. And so they sat in a heavy silence, the only sounds the creaking of the ship and the grunts of the oarsmen with each stroke of the long ash oars.

Joveta and her mother were both staring at her now, and she felt her shame more acutely than before. Mother and daughter had the same large green eyes, high cheeks and straight nose. Joveta was beautiful and Ardith thought her mother would have been too, not so many years before. All the men laboured now at the oars and the ropes, leaving the three womenfolk alone at the prow. Ardith did not really understand how it was Halinard had come to be with Beobrand, Brinin and the others, and there had been no time to ask questions, even if she had wanted to speak. All she knew was that as Ferenbald and his seamen had begun to manoeuvre *Brimblæd* out into the middle of the Secoana, Halinard and his family had come cantering down the quayside. The port reeve's guards had let them pass unhindered. For a moment, the three newcomers had sat astride their mounts and watched the ship leaving the port. Their faces had been pale, and Halinard's shoulders had slumped to see *Brimblæd* slipping away into the gloom.

But Beobrand had muttered to Ferenbald, and after a brief exchange, the skipper had cursed and ordered the men to take the ship back to the wharf. The sailors had groaned and complained, but even as they did so, they were turning the vessel and heaving it back to allow these last three passengers to board.

The sun rose, unseen through the low, dark clouds. With the sunrise, the horizon opened up before them, wide and grey as slate. Above Ardith the sail suddenly cracked and snapped in a freshening breeze. The ship heeled to one side and Ferenbald barked out orders. The crew adjusted the rigging to their master's liking and *Brimblæd* picked up its pace. As they left the mouth of the Secoana, the ship shuddered beneath her, rising on the swell of the waves. Ardith shivered again. The sound of the rushing water along the strakes reminded her instantly and vividly of her time aboard *Saeslaga*. Of Grimr. And Draca.

But this was not *Saeslaga*. She was surrounded by men of Hithe. She had seen pity and anger in their kindly faces as they had looked upon her. Shame welled within her at imagining what they must think of her. In their eyes, she was spoilt, sullied. She had not spoken out to tell of her ordeal, of how she had fought and escaped with her virtue yet intact. What would be the point? She could see in their pitying gazes that they each had decided what had befallen her since she had been taken from Hithe. No, not taken. Bought. Sold by her father. Tears rolled down her cheeks and this time she did not swipe them away. The wind chilled them on her face and she continued to tremble.

From the stern came a shout. Sad-faced Cargást was pointing back to the Secoana and the pale wake they left behind. Ardith pushed herself up to make out what he had seen. For a moment she scanned the distance, struggling to separate the dark smear of land from the iron grey of the broad mouth of the river. But then, though streaming tears blurred her sight, she saw it. A ragged sob caught in her throat and she sank back to the deck. Her shaking worsened and her face was wet with weeping.

A touch on her hand made her start. Looking down, she saw that Joveta had reached out her slender left hand. Ardith drew her hand away, cautious and tremulous. Joveta gazed at her. There was no pity in her eyes, just a deep sorrow. And understanding.

Joveta reached for her hand again and this time, Ardith allowed her to grasp it. At the warmth of the girl's touch, Ardith felt something deep within her give way. She clung to Joveta's hand for a moment and then the Frankish girl pulled her close. Ardith shifted her weight, leaning in to be embraced. She felt Joveta's mother's long arms wrap about the two of them, and through the wracked release of her weeping, Ardith was glad she would not face death alone.

And she was certain she would feel the cold hand of death soon. For on the distant horizon, where the dark clouds met the dull water of the Secoana, she had seen a ship's sail. It was a blood-red sheet and she knew well the sleek, high-prowed ship that rode the waves beneath it.

The wind gusted, slapping the sail and *Brimblæd* ploughed into a white-tipped wave with a splash of icy spray. The ship shuddered as if it too was frightened of the vessel that pursued it.

Ardith let her dismay overcome her and she sobbed into Joveta's hair. *Saeslaga* was following them and she knew that standing at its prow would be Draca, his one eye glaring out of his savage, scarred face. Draca, who had tried to violate her. Whom she had cut with Abrecand's knife. Draca, whose brother's corpse lay on a pile of his gut-rope on the cold cobbles of Vulmar's yard.

Saeslaga was surging through the sea behind them. Aboard its oaken deck came Draca. And Draca brought death.

Chapter 57

"That one-eyed whoreson is gaining on us," said Beobrand, raising his voice so that it would carry over the roar of the surf and the wind that whipped the sail and sang in *Brimblæd*'s taut ropes. Ferenbald did not turn to look at their wake. He merely nodded grimly and said, "The bastard can sail, that's as sure as eggs." He spat over the side of the ship, careful that the wad of phlegm would not blow back onto him or one of the crew.

Beobrand glanced behind them again. For a moment, he could not see *Saeslaga*, lost as it was in a trough between great waves. *Brimblæd* slid up a wall of water and in the moment, before it slipped into the valley beyond, Beobrand saw their pursuer. He remembered it well from when it had attacked *Háligsteorra*. It had the sleek lines of a bird of prey, a sea hawk, seeming to fly over the waves. *Brimblæd*'s deck heaved as they rushed down the waves and Beobrand grabbed onto the stern to prevent himself stumbling and falling. He could scarcely believe that this storm had come on so quickly. Dawn had lit a grey world with a dim, watery sun, but it had been calm enough. And yet the skies had quickly darkened and the wind had come in an angry rush from the south.

"It is as though the gods themselves have sent this storm to us," he had said to Ferenbald, "for it cannot be natural that the weather changes so speedily." He thought then of Woden and how the All-father liked chaos and wondered whether the god watched their passage and hoped to see them founder and sink.

But Ferenbald had looked up at the blackening sky and shrugged. His eyes were dark-rimmed, his cheeks drawn. They were all exhausted.

"It is winter, Beobrand," he'd said. "Storms happen." He had leaned into the steerboard, adjusting their heading slightly, though how he knew where they were going, Beobrand could not tell. The world ahead of them was just grey water and grey sky. "We will ride this wind, and with any luck, it will take us quickly to Albion."

Beobrand cared not for the mention of luck. In his experience, its use all too often presaged tragedy.

The wind grew stronger, but it blew towards the north-east and Ferenbald was right: it drove them quickly homeward. All the while Beobrand had stared behind them and watched the pirate ship draw ever closer. It was difficult to gauge, but after a time Beobrand was sure of it. *Saeslaga* was creeping nearer. The ferocious wind that aided them, also helped their enemy.

Beobrand grasped the timber wale of the ship and watched as *Saeslaga* crested a distant wave. His stomach turned over and his mouth filled with bile. Gods, he had thought he was done with the sickness, but now it returned to him in a rush. He leaned over the side and vomited into the fast-flowing sea. The gulls that followed the ship swooped into the surf, picking at the erstwhile contents of his stomach. The sight made him vomit again. Shakily, he pushed himself upright, hawking a final string of spittle into the ship's wake.

"You would do better not to watch behind so much," said Ferenbald. "That is a sure way for the sickness to get you."

Beobrand wished the man had said something sooner, but then he cast a glance towards the ship that was chasing them and knew he would have ignored the advice. In the belly of the ship, Bearn was wretchedly retching into the sea. The rest of his men were slumped amidships. Dreogan even slept. The others sprawled, with hooded eyes and open mouths, bodies spent from the previous night's exertions followed by the frantic rowing to escape the clutches of the currents and tides of Secoana's estuary.

Spray blew down the length of the ship and Beobrand saw how Ardith and Halinard's wife and daughter were doused by a breaking wave. Ardith and Joveta were huddled close, Halinard's wife held them both in her embrace. Beobrand frowned. He hoped he would see them all safe. He had hardly dared to believe it was possible, but now, so close to the shores of Albion he began to feel a sliver of hope. Once again he wondered whether this storm was Woden-sent, cruelly destined to destroy them just when they might believe they could find safety. He clenched his jaw tightly against the nausea. Still, there was nought he could do. *Brimblæd* was in the able hands of Ferenbald, who had already proved himself to be a sailor of great skill. Beobrand took a deep breath and looked back again, feeling his gorge rise as he did so. In the seascape of foam-tipped peaks, he was certain that their pursuer was even closer than it had been but moments earlier. However skilled Ferenbald, it appeared that the skipper of the pirate ship was either more so, or perhaps the gods wished to see *Saeslaga* catch its quarry.

"You think we can outrun him?" Beobrand asked, trying to keep his tone even, with no sign of the anxiety he felt. The idea of fighting aboard these ships, tossed like twigs on this storm-shredded sea, filled him with fear. But it would do nobody any good to know of his weakness.

This time, Ferenbald looked over his shoulder, judging the distance between the two ships. His hair and beard blew about his head as he shook it.

"No," he said, "I have never known a faster ship than that. It is a thing of beauty, is it not?"

Beobrand said nothing. He was aghast at the man's calm acknowledgement that they were to be caught. And he cared nothing for the quality of the pirate vessel.

He spat to free his mouth of the sour aftertaste of his bile.

"So, I should tell my men to ready themselves to fight."

"I think that would be wise," replied Ferenbald, looking intently forward, as if he expected to see something other than waves through the sleet that had started to fall. "But, if God smiles upon us and I know what I am about, I don't think they will need to fight on this unstable deck."

Beobrand was confused.

"You mean for us to board them?"

"No," said Ferenbald, grinning broadly, as he spotted something in the gloomy, drizzle-smeared distance. Beobrand peered into the storm, but he could see nothing beyond the endless mountains of water. The wind grew even stronger then, buffeting the ship in a chill blast, ripping the foam from the tops of the waves that surrounded them.

"Speak sense, man," Beobrand yelled over the scream of the storm. "Where are we to fight them?"

"Why, on land, of course," shouted Ferenbald. The man's smiling calm angered Beobrand. He could see no way they could avoid the pirate ship, and to fight in this weather would be treacherous indeed. "Tell your men to don their armour and to prepare for battle." Beobrand looked about him at the sea. All about them was chaos; a tumbling, churning confusion of surf and sleet. To fall overboard in this would be terrible, but to enter this chill water wearing a byrnie of iron would spell certain death.

"Are you moonstruck, man?"

"Perhaps," replied Ferenbald, with that annoying grin still playing on his face, "but do you trust me?"

Beobrand thought for only a moment. Ferenbald had proven himself over and again to be a man of great sea-skill and had never given Beobrand cause to doubt his sense, or his cunning.

"Yes," he said.

"Good," said Ferenbald, "then hurry to arm yourselves. I have a plan."

Beobrand gave him one last hard look, then nodded.

"I hope it's a good plan," he said, and staggered along the deck to his men. Their byrnies, shields and helmets were there, stored underneath sheets of greased leather, alongside their weapons and some of the items they had taken from Mantican, which had not been transferred to Feologild's warehouse.

"So do I," said Ferenbald to Beobrand's back. And then, as he saw the first plumes of spray thrown up by the waves pounding into the dark rocks that loomed before them, he bellowed to his crew. Unlike Beobrand, they did not question their captain for even a heartbeat. Ferenbald grinned with satisfaction as the sailors rushed to do his bidding.

Beobrand forced a look of determination onto his features as he reached Cynan, Bearn, Garr, Attor, Fraomar and sleeping Dreogan. He must not show them his fear, all they needed from him was self-belief and direction.

He glanced back at the skipper, standing resolute and firm-footed, commanding his crewmen with certainty. He still wore his broad grin and his eyes glimmered. Beobrand wondered at what portion of his demeanour came from certainty in his plan and his skills and how much stemmed from his need to show conviction to his men. He supposed it did not matter, as long as the results were the same.

"To arms, my brave gesithas," he roared, kicking Dreogan's uninjured leg to awaken him. The warriors all gazed up at him with questioning, pale faces. "Don your byrnies and heft your shields," he said and smiled when all of them leapt up to obey him.

And so, with the sea boiling around them and the wind howling through the rigging and snapping the sail tight, Beobrand and his gesithas shrugged into their heavy iron-knit shirts and prepared for battle.

And that was the moment when *Brimblæd*'s hull smashed into a rock that was hidden just beneath the sea's surface. The ship's timbers groaned and the deck pitched alarmingly. The jagged rock wrenched and ground along the keel, ripping and rending. The noise of the ship being torn apart was like the gods laughing, thought Beobrand, as he slid down the canted deck and was flung into the churning, freezing foam.

Chapter 58

Cold. So cold.

The freezing water gripped Beobrand in its icy fist as he sank under the churning surface. The current was strong and he could feel the waves tugging at him as he tumbled into the darkness. He would die now, drowned in the depths of the Narrow Sea. How the gods must be laughing.

His world was silent save for the rushing in his ears and the pounding of his heart.

Clearly, through the mists of memory, he thought he heard the shriek of the witch, Nelda, echoing in a cavern far to the north and many years before. This was to be the end she had prophesied then. Dying alone in the icy embrace of the sea.

Foam and bubbles swirled about him. His lungs began to burn. He had fallen into the water with no warning and so had not taken a deep breath before plunging over the side of *Brimblæd*. As his byrnie weighed him down, pulling him towards his death, he was suddenly filled with rage. Anger at this wasted death, at his failure to protect his men. Ire at what must surely befall the daughter he would never know. A chilling death or a lifetime of abuse at the hands of the pirates that pursued them awaited Ardith.

And then, just as he believed he would not be able to hold the scant air in his lungs any longer, his feet scraped on rock. He kicked against it, heaving himself upwards, or at least what he hoped was upwards. He strove towards the pale light of foam and surf. Towards the cold winter air.

Towards life.

His head broke the surface and his world was instantly filled with chaos and noise. He sucked in a great breath before a wave crashed over his head, tumbling him once more. The wave pushed him further ashore and moments later, he was able once again to get his feet under him, this time on pebbly sand. He pushed his head and shoulders into the air.

Another deep, shuddering breath and a second huge wave bore down on him. But Beobrand was ready now, and shoved himself upward to meet it, managing to keep his head above the surface as his feet momentarily left the ground and he floated, adrift like so much flotsam before the wave passed him by and he was once again standing, chest deep in the sea with a beach at his back.

Everything seemed to slow then, and Beobrand recognised the calm that settled on him in battle. Close to his position was *Brimblæd*. But the ship was no longer the proud vessel it had been, riding the waves like a watery stallion. The ship had capsized. The sail and rigging trailed in the surf like the entrails of a gutted beast. As he watched, a huge wave crashed into the hull, dislodging *Brimblæd* from the rocks and sending the ship rolling over to show the huge splintered gash in the keel. Figures leapt from the stricken vessel into the freezing maelstrom of the storm-swirled sea.

A third wave, white crested and bitterly cold, broke over Beobrand and he spluttered and cursed. He staggered backward, almost falling. Using the weight of his byrnie to help anchor him against the buffeting force of the sea, he waded towards the beach. It was hard going, but he slogged through the rolling waves and was soon in the shallows. The water sucked and tugged at his legs, but he was safe now.

Safe?

The storm was driving sleet into his face, but he could see clearly that they were far from safe. He realised now what Ferenbald's plan had been. He had surely meant to repeat the skilful manoeuvre that had seen them beach *Brimblæd* safely, gliding perilously close to jagged rocks before sliding onto the shingle. Ferenbald was skilled beyond doubt, for he had navigated through the storm to the same stretch of coast. The sea pummelled the black crags of rock that stood up from the waves like rotted, shattered teeth.

Undoubtedly, he had expected their hunter, not knowing this stretch of coastline, to career into the rocks and be lost. But it seemed there was a limit to Ferenbald's skills, or his luck had abandoned him. For it was his ship, and not their pursuer's, that had been wrecked.

Brimblæd caught another wave and was momentarily submerged beneath foam and spray. Beobrand could not see the ship's captain. Other figures dotted the waves, some swimming, some wading and flailing in shallower water. He hoped everyone aboard had survived. But watching the tumult of the stormy sea, he thought it unlikely the gods would be so kind. Ferenbald had been bold, and the gods liked brave endeavours. But the gods were also fickle and cruel, and they demanded sacrifice.

Beobrand looked beyond *Brimblæd*'s wreck and knew the gods would get their sacrifice this day. Those who did not drown, might die of the cold itself, he thought, his teeth beginning to clatter together despite his attempts to prevent them from doing so. And if the sea or the cold did not slay them, then Draca and his pirates would.

For on the wind-ravaged waves beyond *Brimblæd* came the sleek, menacing form of the wave-steed, *Saeslaga*. Her captain must be even more skilled than Ferenbald, or more reckless, for *Saeslaga* surged onward under a reefed sail, seemingly unconcerned with the spume-soaked rocks that lined the approach to the cove. The ship would pass *Brimblæd*'s wallowing hulk in moments. Beobrand dragged his gaze away from it with difficulty and scanned the beach for survivors. Someway down the beach Fraomar, Attor and Coenred were wading out of the surf. Nearer, a few of the crewmen were pulling themselves from the waves, coughing and spluttering. One of them had a deep cut on his forehead. It bled profusely, painting his face in a mask of crimson in the grey storm light.

Shivering against the cold that seemed to grip his very bones, Beobrand pulled his legs through the shallows, each step made difficult by the pull of the tide and the unsure footing as the gravel was sucked away from beneath his feet. Frantically, he looked along the beach for a sign of Halinard and his family. He did not see them.

His heart twisted, his anxiety gripping him. Where was Ardith? There was no sign of his daughter and he felt an emotion unfamiliar to him: panic. More men laboured out of the sea along the beach. Dreogan and Bearn. Cargást, looking more morose than ever, was half carrying another seaman. Oars and broken timbers washed onto the strand where they had spilled from *Brimblæd*'s belly. A sea chest tumbled end over end as the waves heaved it onto the sand. Its lid fell open spewing its contents. Another wave swamped the chest and whatever treasures it had held, washing over them and hiding them from view, burying them in the sand. Beobrand cared nothing for what was left of the hoard they had taken from Mantican. All he wanted now was to see Ardith, alive and out of the deadly clutches of the sea.

Glancing out to the wind-whipped waves, Beobrand saw that *Saeslaga*'s helmsman had expertly guided the ship past both the rocks and *Brimblæd*'s timber corpse. *Saeslaga* was coming on fast, and looked set to ride the waves up the beach, just as Ferenbald had delighted in doing. Tracking its path Beobrand saw it would come ashore quite a distance down the beach further eastward. As he marked where *Saeslaga* would run aground, Beobrand's heart swelled and a great relief flooded him.

There, climbing out of the churning breakers was Ardith, bedraggled and alone. But alive.

It was as though Beobrand had drunk from a cup of warm mead, such was the effect on him. The panic fled, replaced by an iron resolve. Draca would not take his daughter away again. By Woden and all the gods, Beobrand swore he would see Ardith safely home to her mother. Or his blood would be price enough to sate the All-father's greed for sacrifice.

His hand fell to his sword belt and with a shock he found that Hrunting still nestled in its scabbard. He cast about for a shield, but he saw none amongst the jetsam from the wreck.

Beyond Ardith, *Saeslaga* rose on a breaking wave, white foam boiling under its keel as it was carried onto the beach. It shuddered to a halt, but Beobrand could not hear the grinding rasp of the shingle beneath its hull. The air was full of the chaotic cacophony of sea and storm. Men were leaping from the pirate vessel even before it had ceased moving. They were closer to Ardith than Beobrand.

He broke into a lumbering run. It was difficult. The shallow water clung to his footfalls, his clothes were sodden, weighing him down. His byrnie was as ice, freezing him and slowing his progress with its heft. And still he pushed on.

From somewhere, Cynan was at his side, seeming to run more easily than his lord. In his hand, the Waelisc man held his own sword. In his left he held a black shield, though how he had managed to keep hold of one, Beobrand could not tell. Beobrand drew Hrunting from its scabbard. The sopping wool that lined it sucked against the blade, making him curse.

"Gesithas of Bernicia," Beobrand bellowed as he ran, wondering whether any would hear him. Even with his battle-voice, he could not be sure his words carried over the tumult of the tempest. "To me! To me!"

Cynan and he reached Attor and Fraomar. The two of them fell into stride beside them, splashing through the shallow surf, feet sinking into the sand and shingle as they pounded down the strand towards *Saeslaga* and the men it was disgorging. Attor pulled two seaxes from his belt, Fraomar seemed to have lost his sword and seax, but had found a short axe from somewhere, perhaps floating amongst *Brimblæd*'s debris.

Beobrand flicked a look over his shoulder. Dreogan and Bearn were some distance away, but they had seen their hlaford and were already chasing after them. He saw no sign of Garr.

Ahead of them, Ardith was out of the water. She looked so small and fragile standing there, surrounded by warriors and sailors and the crashing of huge waves. She gaped, staring about her as one in a dream, dazed and shocked to still be alive. Beobrand ran forward. But before he could reach her, the massive bulk of a man from the beached ship loomed up behind her. There was a dull gleam of steel in the grey, sleet-smeared air, as the man unsheathed his sword. He pulled Ardith to him roughly, holding her savagely, his meaty left hand encircling her tiny neck. He glowered at Beobrand and the approaching men, his one eye burning with fury and passion from between the great tusks of his brother's beast helm.

"You thought you could kill my brother and then flee?" Draca spat. "Thought you could steal this choice treat from me?" He shook Ardith. Her head lolled, her eyes wide with terror. "I will spill your guts, like you spilt Grimr's and then I will fuck the girl while you are dying. And then," he said with a leer, "I will let all my men have her until she is used up and begging for death."

With a roar of rage, Beobrand surged forward. He had to reach Draca before the rest of the pirates joined him and formed a shieldwall. If he could get to the man before that, he might be able to save Ardith. But as he sprinted forward, Draca shook her again like a child's toy and snarled.

"Halt, mighty Beobrand," he shouted, "or I will snap the pretty little thing's neck like a chicken bone."

The animal skull helm made Draca monstrous and Beobrand saw there was no give in his one glaring eye. Beobrand stopped running. His gesithas followed his lead and they all stood panting, sleet, rain and sea spray pelting them. Waves broke and crashed, sending sheets of foam sliding up the beach. The icy water washed around Beobrand's ankles.

"Let the girl go," Beobrand said in a voice as cold as the Narrow Sea and as jagged as the rocks that had wrecked *Brimblæd*.

"And why would I do that?" Draca laughed. He raised his sword and for an instant Beobrand believed the whoreson planned to slay Ardith there and then. Behind Draca, *Saeslaga*'s crew and warriors were amassing. There were many more of them than Beobrand's small warband.

Beobrand trembled with pent-up rage. Every sinew of his being screamed at him to leap forward, to hack and hew until all his enemies were bloody corpses. But Draca held Ardith and he would surely kill her if Beobrand attacked. Beobrand tried to think of some ruse, some clever retort that might throw Draca off his guard. But no inspiration came to him. The wind bit at their salt-rimed skin. The waves rolled in, crashing and shredding on the rocks. Spiteful sleet spattered them, adding to their cold misery. And still Beobrand stood, speechless and unsure.

Behind Draca, the pirates pulled themselves into something that resembled a shieldwall. Without paying them much heed, Beobrand could tell at once that the motley bunch of men were not trained warriors. They were strong, and eager enough to kill, but he recalled the attack on the North Sea and how he and Cynan had wreaked havoc on the pirates once they had clambered aboard their vessel. And yet, even without the years of experience and endless drills Beobrand and his gesithas were accustomed to, there were many pirates. Most had shields, and all had weapons.

And their leader, single eye agleam with loathing from within the shadows of the beast-skull, clutched Beobrand's daughter by the throat.

Beobrand noticed men joining his warriors. Turning, he saw Ferenbald, his shaggy hair and beard now plastered to his skull. *Brimblæd*'s captain had blood trickling from his nose, but he seemed well enough. Beside him came Cargást, his eyes sorrowful, but blazing with some inner fire. More seamen staggered along the beach and added their numbers to Beobrand's band.

"You are well come," said Beobrand. He spoke the words without humour, but Ferenbald let out a bark of laughter.

"It seems my plan did not go as I had expected," he said.

Despite himself, Beobrand felt a smile tugging at his lips.

"What plan ever does?"

Beobrand was surprised to see Sigulf pushing his stocky frame between Dreogan and Fraomar. The young sailor brandished a vicious-looking langseax.

"Glad you could join us," Beobrand said.

"Someone has to keep you alive, lord," said Sigulf. "Otherwise, how will you pay us the riches you promised?"

Beobrand grunted, but did not reply.

"You have run like a frightened fox before hounds," shouted Draca. "But the time has come for the hunter to take his prize. I will enjoy killing you, you Anglisc bastard, and then I will enjoy fucking this tight Anglisc cunny before your body is cold."

The blood seared in Beobrand's veins. His heart thundered and without knowing what he was doing, he took a step forward. This whoreson must die. But how?

The pirates were moving forward now, trudging through the surf. Soon they would join their leader and no doubt attack. Still, with Ardith in the one-eyed brute's grasp, Beobrand could see no way to enable him to press the battle to Draca.

A sudden movement caught his attention. One of the pirates shouted a warning, but their leader did not hear, or ignored them. Beobrand realised the man could not see the approaching danger, coming as it did from his blind side.

"I am not such an easy man to kill, Draca Grimr's brother," said Beobrand, pulling Draca's attention to him. "Killing your brother was as easy as eating pottage, and his belly as soft. It seems your mother only whelped fools and weaklings."

One of the pirates called another, desperate warning, but it was too late.

Out of the surging surf came Brinin. He bore a splintered stave of wood, some broken remnant of *Brimblæd*'s demise. Springing up from the waves in a shower of spray, he slammed the timber into Draca's helmeted head.

Chapter 59

Draca screamed in surprised pain and anger. His beast-skull helm tumbled from his head and was swallowed by the surf at his feet.

Relinquishing his grasp on Ardith, the pirate leader roared and swung his broad-bladed sword at his assailant. Brinin had pulled back his arm for another swing, but he was not fast enough. The smith's son was brave and strong, but he was no warrior and had not the skill nor the time to react. Draca's blade struck him in the face. Blood fountained, bright and horrifying in that grey day, and Brinin lurched backward, splashing into the shallow water and lying still.

But Brinin's bravery had broken the impasse.

Ardith had seized the opportunity to be free of her captor and had run someway up the beach. Even as Beobrand's heart was filled with sorrow over the loss of the brave boy, he was springing forward, Hrunting swinging.

There was no time to think. No time to mourn. Brinin's blood had sparked life into the fire of Beobrand's fury. Gone was thought. Now was the time for death.

Beobrand's gesithas and *Brimblæd*'s sailors came with him. They let out an animal roar that spoke of their wrath and determination. This one-eyed beast and his band of pirates had stolen one of their own, slain Brinin and caused their ship, their livelihood, to be shattered on the rocks of this cold cove. There would be no mercy shown on this beach now. No surrender would be accepted. Blood would soak the sand.

Draca, sword now smeared with Brinin's blood, recovered quickly, turning to meet his attackers. Just before Beobrand reached him, the rest of the pirates arrived to join their leader. A heartbeat later, the two lines clashed and chaos ruled.

Woden would have his mayhem.

Beobrand's band attacked with frenzy, pushing back the more numerous pirates. The salty, iron tang of slaughter mingled with the sea spray as axes, swords, knives and clubs battered and smashed in a welter of blows all along the line of fighting men.

Beobrand sensed that his gesithas were acquitting themselves well, but he could not look to see their progress. He needed all his concentration and wits to fend off Draca's blade. The man was fast, cunning and strong. Beobrand was sure he would be able to best him, in time. But he was unsure how much time he would have. It was clear to him now that one side would be totally victorious, the other slain to the last man.

He swayed to the left and parried a savage overarm swing from Draca. Hrunting quivered under the strength of the blow and Beobrand cursed. Whatever the outcome of the battle, he vowed he would see Draca dead.

Flicking a riposte at the one-eyed man's face, he drove him back a step. He stamped forward, his foot splashing into the frothing foam, already turned the colour of sunset by the blood of the fallen. Beobrand pressed his attack with a swing at Draca's unarmoured chest, but the brute was faster and more agile than he had any right to be and twisted his body, using his own blade to deflect the blow. The swords clanged and Draca aimed a punch at Beobrand. Seeing the blow, Beobrand avoided it easily.

All around them, the battle raged. Cynan screamed insults in his native tongue as he disembowelled a man. Dreogan hacked into another pirate's shoulder and blood bloomed, hot and scarlet. Ferenbald lay about him with abandon. He was flanked by Cargást and Sigulf, and the three of them seemed to be untouchable as they cut a swathe through the pirate ranks.

From further down the beach, Halinard came running into the fray. Gone was his yellow cloak, but atop his head was the simple helm of Vulmar's guards. Screaming Frankish oaths, he spitted an unfortunate pirate on the viciously sharp tip of a short spear.

Beobrand felt himself filling with a renewed vigour and energy. He moved in close and shoved Draca backward hard, pushing him off balance. This was it, he knew now that he would slay the bastard and then he would throw himself into the fight alongside his gesithas and *Brimblæd*'s crew and they would massacre the last of the pirates. All he had to do was batter down Draca's clumsy defence.

Draca staggered back, flailing and defenceless. Beobrand swung downward with all his skill and strength. He could almost see the blow already connecting, burying itself in his opponent's neck.

And yet the blade did not strike. Instead, it trembled and throbbed, sending a numbing pain up his arm. Somehow, Draca had managed to bring his own blade to bear, parrying what was to have been his death blow. Still, the force of it, delivered as he was stumbling, had driven Draca to one knee. From such a position, it would be easy to finish him.

Pulling his blade to the left in a feint, Beobrand watched as Draca's sword was drawn towards Hrunting. Then, in an example of the skill that had brought him such battle-fame, Beobrand shifted the direction of his sword, bringing it slicing down towards Draca's exposed head.

Once again, Beobrand's attack was thwarted. Draca flinched and allowed himself to almost fall into the bloody waves that lapped about them. At the same moment, with animal speed, he lifted his great blade to block Beobrand's blow. The two swords met, but this time, instead of the quivering clangour of previous collisions, Hrunting let out a sickening cracking and its once fine patterned blade snapped. Beobrand reeled, barely seeing his sword's blade spinning past Draca's face to disappear beneath the sea water that churned about them.

Draca recovered first and surged up, swinging his blade into Beobrand's stomach. It was a weak blow, delivered from a poor position, but nonetheless, it made Beobrand grunt and fall back. Beobrand stepped on something hard, hidden beneath the surf, a rock perhaps. He stumbled and fell. His belly throbbed where Draca's sword had connected, but his byrnie had saved him. As he splashed into the now knee-deep water, he knew that what had so recently seemed like victory, would become failure and defeat in a heartbeat. Stupidly, he looked down at Hrunting's hilt, there was barely three fingers' width of blade left. He flung the remains of his once proud sword at Draca. The man batted it away with a laugh.

He stepped towards Beobrand, a savage grin on his scarred face.

"I told you I would kill you," he sneered. "Not so mighty now, are you?"

He raised his sword. The blade was nicked and looked to Beobrand to be slightly warped. And yet, it would do its job, he knew. Beobrand scrabbled around in the water, seeking to be able to get to his feet before Draca ended his life. He knew it was pointless. The pirate leader was upon him. Beobrand was sprawled in the water, soft sucking sand and shingle beneath him. He had no blade. He could see the rest of the fight had moved on, his gesithas and the men from *Brimblæd*, driving the pirates towards their beached ship.

So much for my famous luck, he thought bitterly.

Draca was standing over him now, triumphant and gloating.

"Look at you," he spat. "Pathetic. Rolling in the sand like a child." Beobrand ignored him. Under the gelid water, his hand rested on something unyielding. The thing that had tripped him. He looked up at Draca and his fingers traced the object that was hidden beneath the waves.

"Speaking of children," snarled Draca, "where is yours? I would so like for her to see you die. If I am quick, you might be able to watch me pleasure myself with her before you choke on your blood."

"You will pleasure yourself with nobody, you one-eyed bastard!"

The scream came from Ardith, who sprang from behind Draca. He howled as she plunged a small knife into his back. It came away blood-smeared and she stabbed again. Her face was contorted into a mask of anger and despair. No longer the beautiful delicate girl that had attracted Vulmar's lust, she was transformed into a murderous creature, pale and shivering, hair lank, sodden clothes draped about her like seaweed. She seemed more like a monster from the deep than a human child.

Her knife came away bloody, but the blade was small and against a brute such as Draca, it would not kill. Certainly not quickly. Draca swung around, catching her tiny wrist as she sought to strike him again. Her eyes were full of madness and her whole body shook, such was the strength of her wrath.

Draca punched her full in the face and she went limp.

It seemed the Sisters of Wyrd had woven together many a weft and warp of destiny on this beach beneath a steel-grey sky that spat sleet and spite. And Beobrand grinned as his mind finally understood what it was that his hand rested upon beneath the water. He could think of no explanation for it being there in that moment, just when he had need for it, but he laughed to think of Woden and how he loved mayhem.

Beobrand leapt up from the water, raising the great sword he had taken from Mantican's hall in his right fist. The sword must have tumbled from the wreck of *Brimblæd* to await its master's hand. Water sprayed from the patterned blade. Sharp and sleek, the sword sang in his hand as it sliced into Draca's flesh. With a roar of such ferocity that it ripped his throat, Beobrand drove the blade deeper and deeper into the one-eyed pirate. Blood gushed over his hand, shockingly hot after the freezing water and wind. With his left, half-hand, he gripped Draca's sword arm, preventing a final blow, even as death claimed him.

"Go pleasure your fat whoreson of a brother," Beobrand spat into Draca's face.

He twisted the sword and Draca shuddered, letting out a sighing groan. Then, with a grunt, Beobrand stepped back, wrenching his newly found sword from Draca's flesh and shoving the pirate away. The light of life fled Draca's single eye and he splashed into the rising tide. Beobrand watched as the water washed over his staring face. Part of him expected the brute to spring up once more, to take a final swipe at him or Ardith before death claimed him.

But Draca did not move and Beobrand hurried over to the daughter he did not know. She was bloody-faced, bruised, bedraggled and trembling like a leaf in a storm. But she yet lived and she allowed him to wrap her in his massive arms as he surveyed the destruction on the beach.

PART FIVE
OATHS FULFILLED

Chapter 60

Scrydan stepped into the darkness outside the hut and cursed under his breath. God damn that son of a whore, Godstan. He must have been cheating, though how, Scrydan was unsure. He stumbled away from the building. A cold rain swirled in the wind, cooling his face after the clammy heat of the hut's interior. It was stuffy and overcrowded in there, but what had started out as a good night with the mead flowing, had degenerated into a misery of another succession of failures.

The stand of oak that overlooked the small house rocked and swayed in the wind that had come with the sunset. Scrydan shivered. He should have grabbed his cloak on the way out. He staggered over a branch that lay in his path and cursed. He should have stopped drinking too, he told himself angrily. He was never any good at knucklebones when he was drunk. He spat into the gloom. His head swam and he gazed about for a moment, wondering where his destination was.

"Follow your nose," Godstan had said, when Scrydan had said he was going for a piss. Damn the man and his cheery laugh and strong mead. If he wasn't cheating, surely he had plied Scrydan with drink in the hope of taking advantage of him. Bastard.

He fumbled at his belt, feeling absently for the pouch there. It was light. Much lighter than it had been earlier that evening.

Still, he had a couple more slivers of silver and a coin from Frankia – the last one he possessed. It would be enough for him to win back what that cheat Godstan had stolen from him. All he needed was to bide his time, stop drinking for a while and allow his head to clear. He grinned in the darkness. Yes, he'd show that friendly fool. But first he had to get rid of some of that mead he had already consumed.

Another gust of wind shook the trees, driving rain into his face. The cold water trickled down inside the collar of his kirtle. He shuddered. By Jesu's bones, it was colder than he thought it would be out here. Still, not half as cold as it had been in the winter. His mind threatened to take him back to those dark days when he had been forced to flee from Hithe. He had travelled from settlement to farmstead to hall until he had stopped here, in this small steading near Gernemwa. It was in the land of the East Angels, far enough from Hithe that nobody knew him. He had some silver and had soon fallen in with Godstan and his friends. Scrydan was no fool and knew that come the summer he would need to make himself valuable to them in some way. Especially if his silver had all gone by then. But that was in the future, and until then, he was happy to pay for his keep and to play knucklebones and tafl with the labourers, fishermen and, sometimes, the gesithas from the local lord's hall.

Once he'd even managed to get a fuck. In exchange for a few moments behind a cow shed, he'd given some fresh bread he'd bought to one of the goodwives. She was a scrawny young thing, with two grizzling children, but she was glad enough for the food and she did not fight him as he lifted her skirts and took his pleasure. He smiled at the memory of her.

"Don't you be spilling your seed in me, you brute," she'd said. Her husband had died of the pox that summer and he supposed that the idea of another mouth to feed was worse than anything else she could imagine. He'd gripped hold of her shoulders then as his knees had begun to tremble, thrusting into her, panting and groaning.

"Don't you do it inside!" she'd said, anguish in her voice. The sound of her fear had brought him to climax and he had not released her, instead pushing deep within her as she struggled and his manhood throbbed, pulsed and pumped.

When he had pulled away from her at last, she had slapped him. He had merely laughed.

He finally found the midden pit, its stench dampened by the rain and the wind that gusted its miasma away from his face from time to time. Tugging at his breeches, he was amused to find he had begun to stiffen at the memory of the skinny widow. He tried to think of something else, so that he could piss and be done with it.

It was cold out here and it stank. At last, after a few moments of trying to conjure up the face of Godstan in his mind and how he would look when Scrydan won all his silver back, a stream of piss spattered into the midden. By Christ, it smelt terrible here. He should just have pissed against the wall of the hut, not walked all this way. Again, he cursed how much he had drunk and how clouded were his wits.

He burped and spat, then pulled his breeches up.

The rain was falling more heavily now. In the distance there was a sudden flickering of light. For an instant, the trees where silhouetted, stark and black against the lightning-lit sky. Moments later, thunder rumbled over the land. By Jesu's cock, he would be soaked out here.

Turning, he hurried back towards the hut. The wind sloughed through the trees and the rain roared as it pelted down. The world about him seemed darker after the brilliance of the lightning and for a confused, drunken moment he was unsure on which direction he needed to go to get back to the hut.

Another flicker of lightning showed him the path.

And something else.

Was that a figure he had seen under the trees?

It couldn't be. Who would be out on a night like this? One of the other gamblers perhaps? Thunder grumbled, closer now. He must have imagined it. He quickened his pace, keen to be out of the rain and suddenly gripped with a great terror. There was someone out there, he was sure of it now. And they meant him harm.

Lightning filled the sky again. Scrydan looked back under the trees. Nothing. There was no figure. Nobody there. By Christ, he was drunk. Perhaps he shouldn't gamble again this night. He was imagining things in the darkness.

Just as the thunder followed the lightning with its distant crash, Scrydan turned to rush back to the hut. A fresh flash of light picked out the features of a man standing only paces away from him.

Scrydan let out a cry that was lost in the rumbling of Thunor's hammer in the dark heavens. He took a step back, hoping to flee. But to where? The man was too close. He was tall and looked broad of shoulder. He wore a hood and cloak that shadowed his face, but somewhere, dark and deep within him, Scrydan knew the man had come for him.

As that thought finally coalesced in his mind, Scrydan turned to run. But he had been right. The man was too close, and too strong. An iron grip grabbed onto his kirtle's collar, hauling him back. A heartbeat later, the deadly cold of a blade touched his throat and Scrydan yelped. Absently, with the strange detachment that came with drunkenness, he was glad he had just taken a piss, for if not, he was sure his bladder would have let go from fear.

Chapter 61

Beobrand stood in the shadow of the oaks. He pulled his cloak about him, stretching muscles that had grown stiff from inactivity. It was cold and his breath steamed in the cold spring night air. It had been uncomfortable waiting there, but their patience had been rewarded when at last, as the rain began to fall and the wind rustled the trees above them, they had seen the door of the hut open. Warm light from inside had momentarily lit the figure that had staggered out into the darkness.

Scrydan.

He had stumbled into the night, weaving and tripping. At times muttering to himself. Beobrand frowned to see the man he had once called a friend so lost to drink. But he felt no sadness or pity for him. That time had long passed. Now all he felt towards Scrydan was loathing and a simmering anger.

On seeing Scrydan, Beobrand realised with surprise that he had not truly been able to rest these last months. All through the long winter, since the battle in the land of the Dornsaete, he had been awaiting the moment when he could face Scrydan and fulfil his promise to him.

And to Udela.

He had been filled with something akin to joy when Ferenbald, now sailing *Saeslaga*, had come to Ubbanford not two weeks before. Beobrand had not seen the man since before Modraniht and had not expected him until much later in the year, perhaps at Thrimilci when the weather would have been more suitable for travel. But he had been pleased to see him and was glad to hear that his father was hale. Hrothgar had been dismayed at the destruction of his beloved *Brimblæd*, but Ferenbald had placated him, telling him how well both the ship and the men had performed. Ferenbald had spoken in tones of awed admiration for *Saeslaga* and how well she handled. Eventually, Hrothgar had gone down to the beach and walked around the new vessel, running his gnarled hands along *Saeslaga*'s sleek lines, nodding.

"She'll do nicely," he'd said at last before coming close to Beobrand and saying, "thank you."

"For what?" said Beobrand, embarrassed and saddened. He had lost the man's ship and returned with fewer men than when they had set out in pursuit of Ardith and her captors. Several men had died and more had been injured on the voyage and on that wave-tossed beach. Beobrand still felt a pang of sadness when he thought of Cargást's woeful eyes, staring up at the roiling clouds, the sleet settling icy and chill upon his blood-flecked cheeks. After the fight, Cynan had told him how the sailor had saved his life, leaping to take a blow that was destined for the Waelisc warrior's throat. As Cargást had lain on the beach, bleeding his lifeblood into the sand, Cynan had asked him why he had done such a thing. He was no warrior and Cynan wore a byrnie; it might have protected him from the blade that had surely dealt Cargást a killing blow. Cynan's eyes had filled with tears, his eyes looking as sad as Cargást's as he had told his hlaford of the man's words. "Remember, we are brothers now," the sailor had said, a rare smile playing on his lips before he died.

Back in Hithe, bringing the tidings of death and loss with them, Beobrand had not expected thanks from anyone, and felt awkward at Hrothgar's words of gratitude. But the old man had gripped his shoulder warmly and smiled.

"Why, you brought back my son to me, of course," he said, and his pleasure was real.

Beobrand could understand the man's emotion at having his son return to him; he recalled his own elation at having rescued Ardith. And yet he felt all too responsible for those who did not come back to Hithe. The sailors had followed him and many had died. They were brothers now, it was true. They had stood together and they had shed blood and given their lives for a common cause. Sigulf had survived and Beobrand had honoured his promise to the stocky seaman. They had lost most of the wealth they had taken from Mantican, and could not be sure that Feologild would not sell it all. Perhaps one day he would return to Frankia. If he did, he would visit the merchant and see what had become of the dragon's hoard of treasure that had been left in his warehouse. But for now, Rodomo would prove too dangerous. Vulmar yet lived and he was too powerful an enemy to face any time soon.

Beobrand had still been able to make rich men of the sailors who had travelled with him. He was a wealthy man and when he had found out that the contingent from Bernicia had already travelled northward from Cantware, he had needed someone with a seaworthy ship to carry him home. Ferenbald had eagerly offered and, after depositing Coenred on the isle of Lindisfarena, they had arrived at Ubbanford and Beobrand had ordered there to be a feast in Sunniva's hall. They had told the men and women of Ubbanford of their journey and there had been laughter, tales and tears.

Beobrand winced whenever he thought of the weeping that always seemed to colour a return home. There was joy for those that came back to their loved ones, but it was always a time when, as the hlaford of the people of Ubbanford, Beobrand needed to do that which he liked least of all in life: impart sad tidings.

Now, standing in the gloom beneath the oaks, his eyes prickled with tears and a lump came to his throat when he recalled finding Bearn on that beach. Around him were several pirate corpses, testament to Bearn's great battle prowess. And yet one of them had dealt him a vicious blow. A deep thrusting wound with a short spear had taken him under the arm and blood was already bubbling at his mouth when Beobrand had fallen to his knees beside his gesith.

All about the beach lay death. Every one of the pirates had been slain. Just as Beobrand had anticipated, there had been no mercy shown for these wolves of the sea and his gesithas, Halinard and the sailors from Hithe had fought like demons. The tide of the battle had turned when Beobrand had slain Draca. But it had still been an unsure thing until Garr, washed ashore far from the rest of *Brimblæd*'s crew, had found himself at the deserted *Saeslaga*. He had clambered aboard and found a sheaf of throwing spears stored near the prow. He had cut the cord that bound them and proceeded to launch the javelins at the rear of the fighting pirates. With his prodigious skill and strength Garr had killed or maimed many of them from his vantage point aboard their ship's canted deck.

Soon all of *Saeslaga*'s crew had lain dead, but not before they had taken several men with them to the afterlife.

Bearn had been the last to die. Beobrand had held him in his arms and allowed his tears to streak down his face. He could scarcely believe the man's bravery.

"Do not be sad for me, lord," Bearn had said, his voice already weakening as death approached, "there are good tidings to be found here."

Bearn had smiled. Beobrand had frowned.

"What good is there here, Bearn?" he'd asked. "I am losing one of my bravest and most loyal gesithas."

"Ah, yes, there is that." Bearn had chuckled before grimacing with the pain of his wound. "But at least I won't have to ride on that ship again. I'm done with that sea sickness for good."

Despite himself, Beobrand had smiled then, gripping Bearn's hand. He had looked about him at the death and misery along the beach. Already, some of the men had pulled timber from the waves and, using oil and tinder from *Saeslaga*, had managed to kindle a fire on the beach.

Bearn's hand was cold and Beobrand had looked down to tell him of the blaze where they could warm themselves. But Bearn had died, his eyes staring into Beobrand's gaze, with a look of pained amusement on his features.

Back in the gloom of winter, Beobrand had imparted the sorrowful tidings of Bearn's death to his widow. The statuesque woman had merely nodded slowly, as if she had known what she would hear before he had spoken, and left the hall. As ever, Beobrand had marvelled at the strength of womenfolk.

Beobrand had one of his great coffers brought out and he gave gifts to the men from Hithe and as their ring-giving lord, to his loyal gesithas. He had also given an arm ring to Halinard and a small, golden medallion to Gadd, who had somehow escaped both the raging sea and the battle on the beach. Halinard had accepted the golden band with a grave nod, but, with his wife and daughter at his side, his eyes sparkled. He stood straighter and several years seemed to have sloughed off him since leaving Rodomo. Despite the terror of the storm, the shipwreck and the savage slaughter on the strand, Halinard had done that which had been eluding him for so long: he had rescued his family from the shadow of Vulmar's perverse power.

After Beobrand had accepted the newcomers' solemn oaths, it had become a feast filled with joyous songs and tales of victories, for truly, despite their losses, they had succeeded against all the odds.

It had been months later when Ferenbald had returned to Ubbanford. Beobrand had been surprised at seeing *Saeslaga* rowing up to the pebble beach beneath the hill on which stood his great hall. He had hurried down the hill to meet the shaggy-haired skipper and the man's tidings had brought him his first stirrings of pleasure for many weeks. Ferenbald had heard from some Deiran traders where Scrydan had disappeared to. The man had travelled north and was now in the wic of Gernemwa in the land of East Angeln.

And so it was that a few days later, Beobrand stood in the rain, beneath these trees, watching the man, who had once been his friend, stumble into the night for a piss.

"Is that him?" whispered Cynan. He too was cloaked and hooded, almost invisible where he stood leaning against the gnarled trunk of an oak.

"That's him."

They watched as Scrydan paused for a time beside the midden pit. Beobrand wondered what he was doing, when at last he pulled down his breeches and took a prolonged piss. Chuckling to himself, Scrydan tied up his breeches and began to make his way back to the hut.

The rain began to fall more heavily and lightning flashed in the distance. Above them, the boughs of the oaks creaked and rattled in the wind.

"Shall we follow him?" Cynan asked.

"Aye, but let us keep our distance. We must only interfere if needed." He placed a hand upon the pommel of the sword at his side. Its form was not as familiar as Hrunting's had been, but it reassured him all the same. "I swore to Ardith I would stay close."

The rain hammered down now. They left the scant protection of the trees and followed Scrydan. It was easy to see the drunk man's path towards the hut by the flicker of lightning. The thunder that rumbled in the west echoed like the crash of boulders in a distant cave.

Seemingly from nowhere, a figure loomed out of the shadows before Scrydan. He staggered back. Beobrand and Cynan hurried forward. Beobrand would not intervene unless needed, but he had promised his daughter he would not be far from this confrontation.

Scrydan had his back to Beobrand and Cynan. As they drew near, lightning lit the land all about them and they heard him gasp.

"Brinin?" Scrydan said, his words slurred with drink. "Is that you?"

Beobrand could see Brinin as Scrydan saw him. Gone was the boy, replaced by a young man with hard eyes. His face was scarred from where Draca's blade had caught him. He had lain closer to death than life for many days after the battle at the beach. Fever had racked his body, but all the while Ardith had sat at his side and tended him. She had barely spoken and Beobrand had been terrified of what might happen to the girl should the boy die. But Brinin had pulled through and with his recovery, so Ardith had seemed to regain some of her youthful energy. Sometimes, though not often, Beobrand had even seen her laugh.

"Yes, you evil bastard," said Brinin. "It is me." His voice was harsh and deep, tense with his barely suppressed rage.

At seeing it was a boy whom he recognised standing before him, Scrydan seemed to grow in stature. He pulled himself up straight and hitched up his breeches.

"What are you doing here?" he asked, stepping towards Brinin, the threat clear in his movement and tone.

"He has come to watch you die, Scrydan," Beobrand said. He spoke loudly so that his voice would cut through the storm.

Scrydan spun around, terror on his face.

His gaze flitted about him, clearly seeking a way to flee. There was none. Cynan stepped forward beside Beobrand, his hand on the hilt of his sword menacingly, just in case Scrydan was not certain yet of what was going to happen here.

Scrydan's eyes were wide in the gloom. For a moment, Beobrand thought he would try to run again, but then his shoulders slumped, defeated.

"Brinin means to kill me?" Scrydan asked. His voice was dull, confused and dazed at the sudden change in his fortunes.

"Oh, he wanted to, Scrydan," said Beobrand, "but I said I had that right." Beobrand took a step forward and was pleased when Scrydan whimpered and flinched. "After all, it was I who swore an oath to slay you if you ever struck Udela or Ardith again."

Beobrand drew his new sword slowly from its scabbard. He had called it Nægling and its patterned blade glimmered and gleamed as lightning once more lit the sky with white fire.

"And it is a father's duty to protect his daughter," he said.

Scrydan's face was pale. He could see his death out here in the rain and wind.

"Ardith was my daughter," he stammered, panic in every word, "I could do with her as I pleased."

Without warning, he sprang away from the path, trying to dart between Cynan and Brinin. Cynan stepped quickly into his path and shoved him back. He followed up with a straight jab to Scrydan's face. Scrydan's head rocked back and he staggered for a moment before collapsing, moaning into the churned mud. He leaned over and spat blood from his split lips.

"She is my daughter, not yours, you nithing," said Beobrand, stepping forward and levelling Nægling at Scrydan's face. "I lay with Udela before you were hand-fasted. Ardith is mine." For a moment, it was all he could do not to ram Nægling into the bastard's throat. But he had made a promise, so he stayed his hand. "I only wish I had known sooner," he went on, "I could have spared them both the misery of living with you."

Scrydan spat again and then looked up defiantly, seeming to have found some bravery from deep within himself. Or perhaps he had decided he wished to inflict whatever pain he could on his foe; a dying man's final swing of a blunted blade. He would never best them with weapons and so he used words.

"Well," he sneered, "Ardith is gone. You will never find that bitch girl." He looked about him, making sure that Brinin too heard his spite-filled words. "She is the plaything of sailors," he was almost shrieking, "or she is dead."

Beobrand reached down and hauled him up. Then, tugging Scrydan forward by his sopping kirtle, Beobrand smashed his forehead into his nose. Scrydan slumped limply and Beobrand pulled him upright, not allowing him to fall. "You are wrong, you sack of piss," he said. "She is with me now. Safe in my hall. Along with Udela and Tatwine." Scrydan's eyes bulged at these tidings. "Do not fear for the boy," said Beobrand, "he cannot be blamed for the father who sired him. I will bring him up as well as my own kin. He will be treated well."

Blood and snot streamed down Scrydan's face. The rain fell hard, smearing his features crimson.

"You mean to kill me?" he said pitifully. He hawked and spat blood. Beobrand released him, leaving him to stand on his own. Scrydan swayed in the wind and rain.

"I did," said Beobrand, "but Brinin convinced me not to."

The faintest glimmer of hope came to Scrydan's eyes then as lightning again flickered, illuminating the darkness. Beobrand could not fathom how the man still believed he might survive this encounter.

Scrydan swallowed.

"So you will let me live?" His voice was the pathetic whine of a child.

Beobrand could not bear to be in the man's company any longer.

"Oh no," he said, taking pleasure at Scrydan's despair, "you will die this night and I hope you suffer before you depart middle earth."

"But... but... you said..." Scrydan babbled.

"I said it was a father's duty to take the blood-price for a crime against his daughter. Brinin convinced me that a husband's right was greater."

He smiled at Brinin then, proud of his daughter's husband. Glad that he had come to live with her at Ubbanford. Brinin tended the forge and had real skill. Beobrand remembered keenly his own lust for vengeance when he had discovered how Wybert had harmed Sunniva. He had been consumed with the thought of taking the blood-price from her attacker. He understood better than most how Brinin burnt for revenge.

"It didn't take long for me to see Brinin's way of thinking," he said. "Goodbye, Scrydan. Brinin, be careful not to make too much noise and attract the others from the house." Brinin nodded. His face was sombre in the gloom. Beobrand turned to leave. Scrydan whimpered. Beobrand ignored him. "And, Brinin," he said.

"Lord?"

"Don't make it quick."

Brinin stepped forward, drawing a wicked-looking seax from a sheath at his belt. Beobrand and Cynan walked away towards where they had tethered their horses beneath the canopy of the oaks.

Another flash of lightning and rumble of thunder. Beobrand hoped the storm would pass soon. He would return to Bernicia as quickly as possible.

"I think I will have Ferenbald leave us at Bebbanburg," he said to Cynan when they reached the horses. "I can see Octa and perhaps Oswiu will allow me to take him back to Ubbanford. The boy really should meet his half-sister and Tatwine too."

He remembered how he had heard tell of the king's fury at Beobrand heading off on a personal quest when he was ordered to bring back a royal bride from Cantware.

"That sounds like a good idea, lord," said Cynan, shaking his hand in the air and grimacing. Evidently he had hurt it on Scrydan's face.

"What are you smirking at?" asked Beobrand.

"Nothing, lord," said Cynan with a glint in his eye. "I was just thinking that it wouldn't be anything to do with seeing a certain princess there, would it?"

Beobrand frowned. This was not something to be talked about in jest. The ways of wyrd were unfathomable, but he knew that somehow, ever since he had first met her in the stable of Bebbanburg all those years before, his life's thread had been entwined with Eanflæd's.

"She is a princess no longer," Beobrand said. And it was true. As soon as Beobrand had left Cantwareburh, Utta and Fordraed had seen that Eanflæd was hurried north, to Bernicia. To Oswiu. To the king's marriage bed. The couple had been wed long before Beobrand had returned.

He sighed, sheathing Nægling and checking his mount's girth.

"No, she is our queen," said Cynan, and Beobrand could hear the smile in the Waelisc man's words. "Still, she is a good-looking lass."

"Enough," snapped Beobrand. "Do not speak thus of your queen." Beobrand tried to push thoughts of Eanflæd far from his mind, but he found visions of her coming to him in his dreams. And when waking his thoughts often wandered to moments they had spent together walking in the gardens of Eorcenberht's hall.

It was madness, he knew. He wondered at the twists and turns of his wyrd. How he had travelled south in search of a queen for his king and returned with a daughter... and a spark of some unthinkable emotion deep within him whenever he thought of Eanflæd. It was a spark he had never thought to kindle. Yet now that it had caught, no matter how much he told himself it was folly, the hidden flame refused to be extinguished.

In the distance, a thin wailing scream reached them. Beobrand stood still, breathing shallowly, open-mouthed and listening. Another scream, long and ululating. He let out a long breath, nodding to himself.

He needn't have worried about Brinin alerting the men in the hut. Whatever the smith was doing to the man who had believed himself to be Ardith's father, Scrydan's yells and cries were muffled. The sounds would be easily lost within the tumult of the storm.

Historical Note

As with all of the novels in *The Bernicia Chronicles*, this book is a work of fiction, but many of the events and people within the story are based on fact. The journey to Kent (Cantware) in search of a new queen for King Oswiu did take place sometime following the death of King Oswald at Maserfield (Maserfelth). Oswiu had hoped to retain the merged kingdom of Northumbria made up of Bernicia and Deira, but quickly found out that the Deirans were not keen on the idea. Instead, they installed Oswine, son of Osric, on the throne of Deira, leaving Oswiu not only grieving his brother's death, but also with a much depleted power base. Somehow, he brokered a deal to marry King Edwin's daughter, Eanflæd, hoping by doing so to strengthen his, and his children's, claim to Deira. This must have been traumatic for many of those involved, not least Oswiu's current queen, Rhieinmelth, who seems to have been cast aside in favour of this new political peace-weaver. It is not clear from the historical record what happened to Rhieinmelth, but it seems likely she would have been sent to a monastery to see out the rest of her days in prayer.

The Venerable Bede in his *History of the English Church and People* mentions that Utta, who was sent south to fetch Eanflæd, was given a flask of oil by Aidan, as the Abbot of Lindisfarena foretold that on the return journey to Bernicia by sea, they would encounter a great storm and contrary winds. He told Utta to pour the holy oil on the waves and the storm would immediately abate and they would have a pleasant and calm voyage. Bede says that this is exactly what happened, and that when Utta remembered to pour the oil onto the raging sea, it grew instantly calm. I have chosen to have the storm come upon them on their way south to the court of King Eorcenberht (a journey which, according to Bede, actually took place on land), and I have not had the oil work quite as miraculously. And certainly not instantly.

Much of this book takes place aboard ships and while a considerable amount is known about the vessels sailed by the Norsemen a few centuries later, less is known about the ships of the Anglo-Saxons. As no Anglo-Saxon ship has been found with evidence of a mast and sail, there is much debate about whether they actually had sails or were instead rowed everywhere. A book with insights into both sides of the argument is *Dark Age Naval Power* by John Haywood. As well as analysis of historical evidence and archaeology, great work has also been done by E. and J. Gifford, who reconstructed a half-scale replica of the ship from the Sutton Hoo burial. They named it the *Sae Wylfing* and rigged it with a mast and sail and carried out a series of practical tests proving it could be navigated very effectively under sail. Both of these works, and common sense leads me to believe it is almost certain that ships from the period had sails. The Romans, whom the Saxon tribes had interacted with for centuries, used wind power, as did the people from Scandinavia a couple of hundred years later, so, despite there being no firm evidence to prove it, I think it seems highly unlikely that the Angles, Saxons and Jutes had not worked out how to rig a mast and sail in their ships.

Beobrand's quest in search of Ardith is pure imagination, but as mentioned in previous books, slavery was commonplace and it was not unheard of for parents to sell their children into thralldom in times of dire need, to raise funds or simply to reduce the number of mouths to feed. According to a UNICEF report from 2005, about two million children are exploited every year in the global commercial sex trade. If that is the scale of the problem in the twenty-first century, when international law and the laws of 158 countries criminalise sex trafficking, it is plausible to imagine how easy it must have been for such practices to have gone on unchecked in the seventh century. It is abhorrent to decent, well-balanced adults to comprehend the sexual exploitation of adolescents or children, but sadly, such cases are all too frequent in the news today and I am sure that such repugnant acts have always been perpetrated by a certain type of individual. If said deviants were to have power and wealth, it would be a simple thing for them to acquire access to whatever perversion they craved.

The idea of Grimr and his motley crew comes from the fact that Saxons were notorious pirates. The Saxons (and the other northern tribes, such as the Angles and Jutes) could well be thought of as proto-Vikings, setting out in their sleek ships to plunder and pillage (and then settle) the coasts of northern Europe. The threat of Saxon piracy was so great that in the third and fourth centuries the Romans built forts along the coasts of Britain and Gaul in what would become known as the Saxon Shore to defend against the northern invaders.

Grimr himself is a purely fictional character. His name is taken from *The Færeyinga Saga* (The saga of the Faroe Islands). However, the Grimr Kamban in the saga is supposedly the leader of the first Vikings from Norway to settle on the islands in the ninth century and it is by no means certain that there were people living on the Faroes in the seventh century. But while researching for this book, I read Tim Severin's wonderful book *The Brendan Voyage*. In it he recounts his epic journey in a leather-skinned currach in which, along with a small crew, he travelled between

Ireland and North America, thus proving that the tale of St. Brendan's voyage could in fact be a fictionalised account of a real journey, using the different islands of the North Atlantic as stepping stones to the New World. Brendan could feasibly have made the journey in the sixth century and the islands he mentions as a paradise of sheep and birds could have been the Faroes. Of course, this means that people would have needed to have gone to the islands before then to take the sheep. Also, before the colonisation of the Faroe Islands by the Norwegian Vikings, Dicuil, an Irish monk and geographer of the eighth century, mentions monks living there. And so I decided to have Grimr hearken from the Faroe Islands. The other thing that sets him apart as different from the other men is the walrus skull helm he wears. I don't know of any such helmet existing, but I liked the idea of the tusks framing the face of the wearer. And if you are thinking that walruses are only found further north even than the Faroes, in 2018 a walrus was photographed as far south as the Orkneys.

As to the make-up of Grimr's crew, we know that there were extensive trade routes throughout Europe, the Middle East and Asia, so I think it likely that a particular kind of men from all countries and backgrounds would find themselves gravitating to a piratical crew and the promise of violence and lawless plunder.

The practice of wrecking, taking valuables from shipwrecks, was rife in the past and a way for some coastal areas to supplement their incomes. The premise behind Mantican's band of wreckers, luring ships onto rocks with false lights, to then pick up whatever can be salvaged from the shipwrecks, is based on the legendary accounts of such activity in the south-west of Britain, where the rocky coastline, with surge tides, hidden banks and exposed cliffs, has seen numerous wrecks over the centuries. It is uncertain that the use of false lights ever really took place in the way described here or indeed at all, but it is an enduring theme of folklore of the area and makes a great story!

Just as Britain in the seventh century was made up of many small kingdoms, what we now know as France was composed of smaller realms, each with their own people and monarchs. The kingdom that encompasses the city of Rouen (Rodomo) was Neustria. As in earlier books, where I have simplified all the tribes and kingdoms north of Bernicia, referring to them all as Picts, so here I have called all the people Beobrand encounters across the Narrow Sea as Franks. It may not be accurate, but it makes things a lot simpler.

Much of Rouen was destroyed in the ninth century during a Viking raid, but there has been a city there, on the Seine, since Roman times. The current Rouen Cathedral (Cathédrale primatiale Notre-Dame de l'Assomption de Rouen) is built on the location of an earlier church dating back to the fourth century. It almost certainly had a different name in the seventh century, but I couldn't find out what it was, so have chosen to use the name of today's cathedral – Our Lady of the Assumption. Bishop Audoen (later Saint Audoen, or Ouen) was a real person and very influential in the politics of the time. It is quite possible that he attended the Council of Chalon-sur-Saône (Cabilonen) along with thirty-seven other Frankish bishops. The Council was held sometime between 643 and 652 and during it, twenty canons were agreed, including one recommending private sacramental confession with imposed penances. This was a change from the public confession before that time. The practice of private confession and tariff penances was already common among the ecclesiastical houses of Britain and would have been the norm for Coenred on Lindisfarne.

The cheerful, gnome-like landlord, Amadeo, and his famous snails actually exist. However, they are not in Rouen, rather in Madrid, Spain, where, at the time of writing and the age of 91, Amadeo continues to run his bar, Los Caracoles, and serve up his delicious snails with a nice cold beer, or three!

Vulmar and his palace are inventions, but there is ample

evidence of Roman villas being used by later generations. Often these buildings were taken up by the church and converted into places of worship. For example, Stavelot Abbey in Belgium was founded around 650 on the domain of a former villa and the abbey of Vézelay in Burgundy had a similar genesis. Later in the century, in 698, an abbey was established at the site of a Roman villa at Echternach, in Luxembourg near Trier. I see no reason why at least some nobles wouldn't make use of well-preserved Roman buildings.

By the end of this book, Beobrand's horizons have broadened and his life has become more complicated than ever. He has acquired new family members and the population of Ubbanford continues to grow. It doesn't seem likely that his relationship with the ambitious King Oswiu will become any more settled, particularly in the light of the presence of the new, beautiful, intelligent and headstrong queen of Bernicia.

Oswiu's lust for power will continue to lead Bernicia into conflict and, as one of the most powerful thegns of the kingdom, you can be certain that Beobrand will again be called upon to wield his new sword in battle alongside his faithful Black Shields.

More intrigue, shieldwalls, betrayal and love await Beobrand as Oswiu seeks to expand his influence over the other kingdoms of Albion. But that is for another day, and other books.

Acknowledgements

A lot of people are needed to bring a book to publication, but there would be little point in writing at all without readers. So first and foremost, thank you, dear reader, for reading this book. I hope you have enjoyed it. If you'd like to know more about the novels and the history behind them, please connect with me on any of the usual social media platforms via www. matthewharffy.com. I love hearing from readers, so don't be shy. And if you could take a moment to leave a review online, I would be indebted to you, as it helps people decide to give a new author a chance. Of course, the best way of spreading the word is to tell your friends and family that you have enjoyed my books.

As always, I must thank my select group of test readers: Simon Blunsdon, Gareth Jones, Shane Smart, Emmett Carter, Alex Forbes and Graham Glendinning. Getting feedback on the first draft makes the finished product that much more polished and gives me some peace of mind when handing the manuscript over to my editor. I would have thought it would get easier with each book, but no such luck. It is wonderful having some people I can trust to give me an honest critique before letting the publishing professionals see my work.

Thanks to Caroline Ridding, Nicolas Cheetham and all the staff at Aria and Head of Zeus. Their passion for producing fabulous books is always evident, and the finished product you are holding in your hands owes much to the professional editors, designers, typesetters, and all the others involved in the publication process.

Thank you to Robin Wade, my ever patient and unflappable agent.

And I have to say a big thank you to all of the people I communicate with on a daily basis on social media. I am now "friends" with many, many readers and writers from all over the world, and it certainly makes the job of writing much less lonely than it would be without the Internet.

Extra special thanks to my great friend, Gareth Jones, for going above and beyond the role of test reader and accompanying me on a nautical research trip. We couldn't have asked for better weather, nothing like the storms endured by Beobrand and the crew of the *Brimblæd*, but Gareth still ended up a rather sickly shade of green at one point.

Thanks to Euan McNair, skipper of the *Sirius*, who explained the tides and prevailing winds and showed me suitable locations along the coast for some of the events in *Storm of Steel*. If you need to hire a small boat from Weymouth, look no further than Sirius Charters.

Finally, thank you to my wonderful daughters, Elora and Iona, and my ever-supportive wife, Maite, for putting up with the long hours of writing, and the frequent times when I am present in body only, as my mind is lost in the Dark Ages, trying to tease apart a particularly thorny plot point. I really couldn't do this without you.

About the Author

MATTHEW HARFFY grew up in Northumberland where the rugged terrain, ruined castles and rocky coastline had a huge impact on him. He now lives in Wiltshire with his wife and their two daughters.